Trickster Magic

Whitney Hill

BENU
MEDIA

This is a work of fiction. Any references to real events, people, or places are used fictitiously. Other names, characters, places, and events are products of the author's imagination. Any resemblance to actual persons, living or dead, or to actual events is purely coincidental.

TRICKSTER MAGIC

Benu Media

6409 Fayetteville Rd

Ste 120 #155

Durham, NC 27713

(984) 244-0250

benumedia.com

ISBN (ebook): 979-8-9873785-6-4

ISBN (pbook): 979-8-9873785-7-1

Library of Congress Control Number: 2023916234

Cover Designer: Pintado (99Designs)

Editor: Jeni Chappelle (Jeni Chappelle Editorial)

Content Warnings

This book contains strong physical violence and gore, on-page death, swearing, slurs (not toward any real racial or ethnic group/identity), alcohol use, knife violence, threat of sexual violence, mention of past abuse by a guardian, threats by law enforcement, blood-drinking, and consensual on-page sex scenes.

For those who are done playing other people's games and are ready to make their own rules.

Chapter 1

In a world without magic, Otherside was on the verge of collapse.

I sat at the dining table, numb as I stared at my inbox. More reports flooded in, the little number showing unread emails pinging upward every few seconds. The sun hadn't even set yet, but Othersiders up and down the East Coast were reporting in to their people, who traded information with mine, who passed what they heard along to me. And that was when people from outside my jurisdiction didn't contact me directly. Which was a thing they did now apparently.

It'd only been two days since Sutekh, the Ancient Egyptian god of chaos, confusion, and violence had preempted the other tricksters, gone rogue, and withdrawn the gift of magic from Otherside. A bare twenty-four hours since the celestial messenger Harqil had told me and Troy where to find it, right after I'd assured everyone in my local parliament that I had a plan.

I had no fucking plan.

I knew I needed to get to the Duat. I knew I needed a squad to succeed. I knew I needed to get magic back.

That was all.

And for all that Troy was an excellent king, general, and fiancé in the moral and strategic support arena, I found it hard to have the same faith in myself that he had in me.

There was no time for that imposter syndrome shit though. I had to take a leap of faith, and I had to take it now if I wanted to have any chance of staving off the growing disaster indicated by my inbox. It wasn't even just my inbox; I had the feds breathing down my neck as well. A subpoena I was expected to answer in the next five days, assuming Iago Luna couldn't stall them with legal tactics or get the subpoena withdrawn.

I shut the laptop with a snap. Freaking myself out with the damn notification badge wasn't going to get me anywhere. Just last night I'd been determined to rise to the challenge. I wanted to know what it felt like to finally be safe. To put down the obsessive need to take care of everything and push everyone forward for just a little while, so I could figure out what "family" meant besides dead parents, abusive guardians, and a collection of faction heads I cared about but who still made me take my role as Arbiter of the Carolinas and Dominion demesnes far too seriously.

People died when I had to get serious. I didn't like it.

Tough fucking shit.

I pushed away from the table and rose. Harqil would be here any minute for my answer on what I was going to do. I wanted Troy at my side when I gave it.

A peek in the bond said he'd finished whatever strategic planning he'd meant to do for the moment and was moving through combat forms in the backyard. That'd do as well as anything for my current mood, stretching too tight for comfort, like the air between clouds and earth in the moment before a lightning strike joined them together.

I changed my clothes quickly before joining him.

The gytrash, watching with something of a forlorn air, lifted their heads, but Troy pretended not to notice me.

Bullshit. He knew I was approaching. He could read the intent I allowed to slither through the bond: to attack him.

What I got back was the energetic sense of *I dare you.*

Ha. He wouldn't be holding back today. A bout, not a training session. Good. I had a lot of frustration I needed to work out.

I launched myself at his back, leaning fully into the increased speed I now had.

Troy, as an elf more powerful than any others, matched me. His spin kick would have caught me in the gut if I hadn't dropped to let it pass within a breath of my face.

While I was down, I reached for his ankle.

He danced back. "You'll have to be faster than that, my love."

The chill in his tone made me shiver. Challenge accepted.

Fists blurred. Feet scuffed. Grunts and snarls broke the suddenly silent clearing. Birds and squirrels tended to make themselves scarce when the primordial elemental fought her goldeneye elven lover. Even the trees seemed to hold their breath.

We fought each other to a standstill.

Bad luck in the form of a loose stone put Troy on his back under me.

I laid a thumb across his throat.

The fun thing about sparring with Troy was that he never took losses personally, except in the sense that my proving myself equal or stronger turned him on. Heat roared through the bond. Enough to distract me from the warp in reality that signaled a celestial incoming.

"It's amazing you two have time or focus to do anything other than fuck," Harqil's voice said off to the side. "The gods alone know the reason for giving elves that much hormonal attraction. I surely do not, unless it's a balance to check all the power. If I was hostile, you'd both be dead."

I scrambled off Troy, falling into a guard position without thinking about it even as I flushed with a combination of embarrassment and anger.

Troy just climbed to his feet with the slow satisfaction of a man who'd succeeded at something. "Harqil."

"Little king." The celestial crossed their arms and returned their attention to me. "So?"

I glanced at Troy. *Still on board?*

With ruling Otherside at your side? Don't threaten me with a good time and then not follow through, cariñamí.

"I don't know why you two bother with that when you know I can hear you," Harqil said.

"I like to think that you might learn manners one of these damn days," I snapped. "Stay out of our fucking heads."

"Stop projecting so loudly," they said. "All that aside, it sounds like you want to rule."

I couldn't help standing taller. "I want magic back for everyone." I hesitated then spoke the truth. The one that would let me feel safe. "And I want them to owe us."

Harqil studied me, their glance flicking to Troy before coming back to me. "Why? Gods know you've both suffered enough at the hands of various people. You could take your vengeance and just leave."

"We can't," Troy said firmly. "Or more accurately, I won't. I took up this responsibility. I won't leave my people."

"I won't either." I didn't bother pointing out that Harqil had already said vengeance was not an option for me. They were teasing or testing. Or both.

"You mean, you won't leave your bondmate." Harqil smirked when I lifted my chin and waved their comment away. "So. You want magic back, and you want to be owed. But I know that's not all you want."

"Anything else is our business," I said.

"If you want my help, it will be mine as well. I'm taking a big risk, picking sides like this."

I looked at Troy again. We were a team. I wouldn't unilaterally declare what we'd discussed last night.

He shrugged and tipped his head in a *might as well* gesture.

Turning back to Harqil, I said, "I want to feel safe."

"You're the strongest being on this plane, if we discount celestials and the Court of Nightmares. What could you possibly mean by— Oh. Ah. Of course. It's not just safety. You want to grow your House. With heirs."

I flushed. "Yes. At the very least, I need control of the Eastern Seaboard realm."

They stared at me, seeming to peer into my soul. "It won't stop there."

I knew the ring of prophecy when I heard it, having grown up around the djinn. "Of course it won't. Nobody has believed me when I've said it really can be easy. So they'll piss and moan and kick off, and I'll have to extend my control from the East Coast to half the country. Or all of it."

"You accept the responsibility that comes with that?"

"I accept that, if I don't, Otherside dies. People I care about will get hurt, and it'll happen because I instigated the Reveals." I shook my head. "It's my responsibility, and I won't be responsible for magic going out of the world. Not when I could do something about it."

Something about that idea broke my heart, even if Harqil was right about how I'd been treated generally. Everyone shouldn't have to suffer because a few people had been assholes to me and Troy. That wasn't fair, and it just wasn't how I did things.

Harqil turned to Troy. "And you, little king?"

"I want what she wants," he said.

"On the surface," Harqil agreed. "Deeper down, there's more."

Troy sighed and rubbed a hand across his forehead, smearing dirt and sweat in almost equal measure. "I want to solidify a new dynasty and reform elvendom." He glared. "Deep enough for you, celestial?"

"It'll do." They grinned. "In which case, I'm pleased to inform you about the first step in the process. You'll need to acquire a heart scarab."

I frowned. "A what?"

"Heart scarab. Mustn't go into the Duat without protecting your heart or securing your allies."

This was all gibberish to me, but I was already overwhelmed so all I said was, "Okay."

"And your squad, of course," they added. "Any thoughts there?"

"We've literally just—"

Harqil cut me off. "No. We need to be fast. Sutekh will be expecting some kind of movement, and I know for a fact he's already marshaling legions."

Fuck. Once again, I was already behind. Damn the gods.

Troy rested a hand on my arm. "We'll deal with it. Heart scarab first."

The celestial sighed so hard they seemed to ripple with it. "Fine. Fuck it. Luckily for you two, there's one nearby."

That seemed too fortunate.

"Where?" I asked suspiciously.

"A museum?" They shrugged and gestured vaguely southward. "That's the sort of place where mundanes tend to gather objects of power."

Troy caught on first. "You're telling us that before we get magic back, we need to put together a plan to steal an artifact from the North Carolina Museum of Art."

"That's the one," Harqil said, brightening. "And if we can do it tonight, so much the better."

I looked at Troy. "Please tell me the Darkwatch has schematics."

He smirked, answering the question.

"Do we have anyone who could help?"

"If you want to minimize human casualties, Dari would be ideal." Troy considered another moment. "Or maybe Thana. A good shadowmancer is usually trained in...material extractions."

Thieving. He meant Thana was a thief in addition to a bodyguard. And while Darius was apparently an excellent sniper, I'd personally benefited from his ability to steal fucking memories, the catch being that he wouldn't have Aether.

Unless we could figure out how to channel it through me.

"What did you just think about, Arden?" Troy's tone was carefully neutral, but I could hear the worry.

"You have magic because I do."

He went to the extreme end of that thought. "No. I won't share an Aetheric bond with someone else. I won't share *you* with anyone else. In any way."

I blinked a few times, both at the intensity of the statement—it was rare for him to declare something that strongly to me—and at the idea that I might even consider it.

"That's not where I was going," I reassured him as Harqil watched with sharp eyes. "I was thinking blood might work."

Even that got a snarl from Troy. My extremely powerful blood had been his and his alone since I'd claimed him as consort, with the exception of a few donations to Maria to shore up her power and secure the territory early in my rule as Arbiter.

I'd asked a lot of him. Especially lately. I needed to back off from this.

"Last resort," I offered.

His short nod told me that it was a good thing we'd been sparring or he would have been wound too tight to even give me that.

"We're not going to be able to manage all this here. Too many people and too much setup needed," he said, refocusing himself with a mental wrench. "Boathouse?"

I nodded. "Yeah. Good plan."

The large building I'd inherited when Troy and I killed first the Redcaps then a good chunk of the local elven conclave had always had bunks, bathrooms, a small kitchenette, and plenty of space, having originally been some kind of boat repair shop that'd gone under. The retrofit Troy had ordered for it had included camping amenities—a couple of covered outdoor showers, concrete slabs to pitch tents, latrines, firepits, and the like. We hadn't used it to host that many people yet, but it'd be perfect. A little basic, but I liked being outside and the elves would probably benefit from the fresh air as well.

I turned to the gytrash. "You two in? We could use security at the boathouse."

Both of the fae black dogs who'd become my personal house guards—and were now trapped in their black dog form, unable to shift to the humanoid form with the loss of magic—rose and shook themselves. Bás offered a yip, and Marú barked.

"Appreciated," I said. "So, there's us, Thana, Darius...who else?"

Troy toed the stone that'd taken him down, nudging it free of the dirt before picking it up and chucking it over the fence. Not with the furious strength that said he was still upset, fortunately. Just clearing the yard. "Etain and the Ebon Guard are still mostly on the Sons of Seth, but I want Haroun."

The grim note in his voice worried me, as did whatever we were doing with the Sons without magic to keep shifting their mindsets. "No disagreement, but why him in particular?"

"Because if one of us gets hurt, he or Dari are likely the only ones who'll be able to manage the other without being attacked."

I grimaced. Troy had a point. After the Wild Hunt, I'd nearly attacked Allegra when she'd gotten too close to an auratically drained Troy. Haroun had been the only one I allowed close, and Darius could apparently play a similar role as Troy's blood and my effective brother-in-law.

But that meant Troy was planning for one of us to get hurt. Bad. Like near-death bad.

I shivered.

Harqil was studying us with a harder expression than I'd ever seen on the usually amused-looking celestial. "I'm glad you lot are taking this seriously. Sutekh isn't one to be fucked with. You'll do best to avoid confronting him head-on."

"Even with the heart scarab?" I asked.

"Even so. He isn't the magician Iset is, or even Hor, but he's storm and desert personified. Blood and ash on the wind."

Well shit. I'd survived going head-to-head with the hunters. Barely. I was stronger now, but it sounded like I should expect Sutekh to be stronger still.

Harqil tilted their head. "Even if you don't leave, you could just rule, the two of you, with a magicless Otherside."

"No," Troy said before I could. "Unacceptable. The elves would die out."

"You mean faster than you already are?" Harqil sniped.

"Yes."

The flat admission deflated Harqil. "You're no fun."

"So I've heard." Troy turned to me. "Well, my love?"

"Make the arrangements for whoever needs to be at the boathouse and get the plans for the NCMA. I'll have another chat with Jo to keep her and the feds busy."

"Good thinking." Troy leaned to kiss my temple as he passed me to head into the house. "Watch yourself with her. She might be sympathetic, but she will try to dig for the truth."

"Yeah." I sighed, glad that I'd gotten some of my frustration out with Troy. Hopefully I could keep my temper and my wits as I used a mundane journalist to put the Bureau for Supernatural Investigation on the back foot.

Not only that but fired the opening shot in trying to turn public opinion against them. I hadn't openly claimed responsibility for turning Verve Health Solutions into a smoking slag pit of obsidian, but enough people were putting two and two together and getting elemental. Not that they knew what I was, but videos of the damage I'd done to Durham fighting the gods were filtering back in again and Omar's Darkwatch hackers couldn't catch all of it.

Shaking myself, I refocused on Harqil. "Sorry. Lots on my mind."

"I see," they said. "Am I welcome at this boathouse?"

"Of course. If you want meat and mead, I can offer some here though. It'll be a couple hours before we're ready to move on the NCMA. We'll shift to the boathouse after that rather than coming back here, if I know how Troy thinks."

Harqil smiled. "See, this is why I don't know why everyone hassles you, Arden. You are, by far, one of the more polite and sensible leaders in Otherside. One would think we'd try to cultivate that."

"Yeah. One would think," I muttered bitterly.

Too bad that, for the most part, Otherside ran on power and fear. And I needed to do a hell of a lot more to prove the former or instill the latter if I wanted to keep things together long enough for us to get magic back.

Chapter 2

Jo, bless her heart, was exceedingly skeptical about the timing of my call and my offer to provide evidence I'd previously been reluctant to share. Skeptical enough that I decided to share only one of the files—the one of my being taken in Durham, traffic camera footage hacked by the Darkwatch before it could be disappeared by the government.

Not the one where I blew up the van in Virginia and killed six humans, taken by one of the Ebon Guard.

The Darkwatch hadn't been able to turn up additional copies of that traffic cam footage, so we were hoping we had the only extant copy. Nothing for the feds to counter us with.

"And what about Verve?" Jo asked after confirming receipt of my file. "That has to have been Otherside."

"That was me."

The line hung silent before Jo said, "You? How? Why?"

"The Bureau for Supernatural Investigation was collecting werewolf blood and running experiments. On humans."

"*What?*" Rapid clattering said she was typing something. "You have proof of this too?"

"I have a witness statement. I will only allow them to speak anonymously and with every possible effort to conceal their identity. People died for this, Jo. I won't risk more of mine unnecessarily."

"So let me get this straight. You *melted* a *building*—"

"Without mundane—without *human* casualties," I interrupted, wanting to be sure that was very clear.

"Without casualties. Because, according to you and this unnamed source, the federal government is conducting experiments on both supernaturals and mundanes. And I'm assuming this is related to the docket number you gave me."

"That's it." I rubbed my forehead, glad that Harqil had gone back to report to Anansi after taking refreshment. They'd probably be amused at how much I was having to dance around my violent culpability to get the truth out.

"To be blunt, Ms. Finch, this is a little outrageous."

"Is it? The US federal government, various states, and wealthy individuals engaged in chattel slavery, forced sterilization, and genocide, ran syphilis trials, and opened internment camps, and that's just on US soil. Governments at multiple levels are currently dismantling themselves at a rapid pace to feed right-wing zealots. Law enforcement commits extrajudicial murder at the slightest provocation. They're talking about arming police robots in Los Angeles, for fuck's sake. You really think they wouldn't want to figure out how to get their hands on some loyal werewolf supersoldiers? With all this social unrest and protesting?"

"Jesus," she whispered after a few silent moments. "You're really serious."

"Deadly." I bit my tongue before I could add that I wouldn't have it. This had to be facts and agendas, not posturing. And with Troy busy making calls in the bedroom, I had to watch my own words.

More clattering in the background. "Okay. I will review what you've sent me. Oh, and I'm still waiting on the response to that FOIA request from your last tip, by the way."

"Fingers crossed," I said.

"Yeah. You know, Ms. Finch, if you're right about this...this could be big."

Again, I bit my tongue before I could say "Pulitzer big." I needed to lead her. But not that obviously.

Instead, I said, "I appreciate you hearing me out. My advisors weren't sure this was the best or safest path to follow, but I can't say I want productive relations with humans and then not offer action in good faith."

Jo snorted. "If you can call Verve good faith."

"Self-defense is all I'm claiming there. We tried going the legislative route, and I've tried working directly with federal representatives. Me and my people keep getting met with violence in response."

"Nobody is going to sit quiet and take it for long." She sighed. "I see where you're going with this angle. You take this action to avoid the backlash of a larger one from the supernatural community."

"No comment," I said blandly.

"Of course not. All right, Ms. Finch. I think I have enough to get started. Will you be reachable if I need to confirm details?"

"You can always try my cell," I said.

No way was I about to tell her that I'd be busy for a few days. Last thing I needed was a journalist trying to tail me.

"I'll do that. Thanks, Ms. Finch."

"Thank *you*, Jo."

I ended the call and went to find Troy in the bedroom. He was still talking to someone—Etain, from the quick response on the other end of the call—in elvish, so I wrapped myself around his back and hugged him.

He halted his pacing, settled a hand over my arms, and squeezed, taking a stance that would let me lean on him. I did, burrowing my nose between his shoulder blades. It wasn't just that we were still recovering, hormone-wise, from our extended separation with my solo trip to Asheville. He'd scared me with some of his prep suggestions, and the grim sense I was getting in the bond said he was getting ready for war, not just a thieving mission.

I couldn't lose him. I wouldn't.

Troy ended his call and tossed his phone to the bed. "You won't lose me. Because I won't let you go."

I swallowed fearful what ifs and loosened my grip enough to let him turn and hug me. The tightness of his embrace almost made me believe him. But he'd been the one to say he couldn't promise who would still be standing at the end of this.

"Arden." He leaned away and tipped my chin up. "This is the time to be cold. If you're worrying about me, you'll be distracted in a fight. Promise me that you'll put the mission first."

Staring into his eyes, I tried not to remember when he'd been laid out near death on this very floor. "I promise."

"You're lying." He smiled then kissed me. "But I'll allow it. Just remember the greater good, okay?"

"Yeah. Sure."

We'd already discussed that. The greater good, as far as I was concerned, was him. I might be trying to get magic back for all of Otherside, but at the root of everything was wanting them to owe me so I could carve out space to create a future with him.

For myself.

It was my fucking turn to know what it was like to live a normal life, with a happy family. I might not want it to come at the cost of the end of our civilization, but I wasn't gonna lie to myself in my own head about why I was doing any of this.

Troy sighed, like he could read the thoughts I hadn't sent him, and kissed my forehead. "Come on. Let's get this field trip figured out."

△▽△▽

The North Carolina Museum of Art was part museum, part outdoor gallery. Two buildings housing the exhibits were set at the northern end of a 164-acre park. The rolling hills were crisscrossed with paved trails and dotted with massive installation art. To my elemental senses, it was a blessedly peaceful spot bracketed by busy roads on the northwestern side of Raleigh.

I'd conjured up a storm well in advance of our arrival, doing my best to make it look like a feasible natural occurrence. Given that I'd dispelled a major storm not too long ago, we were pretty sure the wrong people would start asking questions about this one, but it was April in the Southeast during a time of climate change. What would have been a freak storm even five years ago was within the realm of plausibility now—if I gave it a few hours to build rather than wrenching a downpour from the sky.

The storm broke right as we hit Wade Avenue.

"Well done, cariñamí," Troy murmured as a massive crack of lightning split the sky and rain fell in buckets that forced traffic to slow to a crawl as other cars put their warning flashers on.

I squeezed his hand, still focusing on stalling the storm over Raleigh but glad he was in the back seat with me for once. Felip Luna was driving Troy's Acura MDX and Lachlan Sequoyah was driving Darius's Lexus ES hybrid. Good to have auratic and physical healers on hand, even if they wouldn't have magic. They knew first aid and CPR. That had to count for something.

We had them drop me, Troy, Thana, and Darius off in the neighborhood to the east and hurried through the woods to the museum property. Despite the soaking downpour turning everything to flood and mud, none of the elves complained.

Troy was straining with a pretty heavy "don't see us" casting and we were on a deadline, so I picked up the pace.

"You're up, ma'am," Thana said as we reached the last thin bunch of trees clustered around the open-air amphitheater.

I moved ahead of the three elves, reading the wind and the charge in the storm. As I waited for a lightning strike to build, I wove Air and Fire into a pulse that would knock out all electronic and magnetic systems around the museum.

Cameras watched every door, and a security system protected the works themselves. If this was some kind of heist movie, we would have had all kinds of sophisticated plans in place. Special tools and that.

But human thieves didn't have elemental powers that could drop a targeted EMP on an area without leaving a single piece of physical evidence.

"Here we go," I whispered as the storm and my electromagnetic pulse peaked.

Lightning ripped through the sky, directly over the museum.

In that same crack of time, I loosed my pulse and *pushed* with as much elemental force as I could muster, pressing my hands forward before spreading them wide for emphasis. I didn't need hand motions to do my magic, but it helped my mind shape what I wanted to do.

With a subsonic groan that I felt more than heard, all the lights in the park went dark, followed by all the external lights on both buildings, then all the internal lights, then the backup generators.

Troy gripped my arm. "Go," he barked. "We'll catch up."

Thana and Darius streaked forward, heading for the wing simply called West Building.

I shook myself, trying to pull my magic in enough that I wouldn't start an earthquake or something by accident.

"Good?" Troy asked.

Rather than answering, I lurched into a stumbling, mud-slicked run toward West Building.

Troy kept pace, catching me when I slid on the slick, polished floor of the entry. The other two had already picked the lock and were making their way toward the Ancient Egypt section. I followed more slowly, with Troy bringing up the rear in case we'd missed a security guard.

By the time we reached the section, Thana had picked the lock on the display case, and Darius was swiftly tucking what we'd come for into a black velvet bag.

Troy extended a hand. "Let me see it."

Darius handed it over.

"Doesn't seem like much," Troy said, passing it to me.

When I took it though, a tingle ran through me. "This is it."

He frowned. "You didn't even open it."

"I don't need to. It's making me tingle." That seemed weird, given magic was gone, but Cyrus had said that objects would keep their charge for a bit longer. "Here, take it back so I can clear out the water. Thana, Darius, lock up and go."

They did as I said. Nothing looked different in the case except the space where the heart scarab had been. Museum staff would find it missing in an inventory check, but we couldn't help that. We hadn't had time to make a copy.

Thana was giggling as she took off. Glad one of us was having fun.

As I had when I'd dropped the storm in my bedroom, I surrendered to Water and Earth and pulled every excess drop of moisture or mud from our footsteps, or what had dripped or splashed from us, into a ball in front of me. Troy guided me back toward the door with a hand on my shoulder. When we were back outside, I tossed the ball away and waited for him to pick the lock closed again.

We turned to run back to the meeting point—only for the beam of a flashlight to fall across us.

"Hey!" a masculine voice called. "Who are you? Stop!"

Troy struck with a lash of Aether. "You saw nothing. You don't know what happened to the power. The grounds were empty."

"Of course they are," the guard agreed. "It's a fucking thunderstorm, and I'm the only asshole out here."

I ran, not needing Troy's mental nudge to get my ass moving.

He maintained an Aetheric hold on the guard until we were out of sight up the curve of the hill to the Blue Ridge Road parking lot, then let go and ran hard.

Lachlan and Felip were pulled off to the side of the road, flashers going like they'd had one of the fender-benders that always seemed to be happening on the busier roads of the Triangle. Thana and Darius were already in Darius's car. Troy pulled open the back door of his and ushered me in before climbing in behind me.

"Go," he ordered.

Lachlan clicked off the hazards and slowly pulled away, turning down Reedy Creek Road at a crawl like we were just normal people trying to make it home in the rain and not fucking artifact thieves. Behind us, Felip kept driving on Blue Ridge Road. They'd meet us at the boathouse.

A giggle burst from me. All the tension that I'd kept compartmentalized up to this moment got to be too much. That, and the ridiculousness of what my life had become.

I'd been a Watcher before. I'd broken into places. Planted bugs. Gathered information.

But I'd never stolen a magical artifact from an art museum on the say-so of a celestial messenger with a double triad of elves as backup.

Ridiculous.

The other thing was that it had been so *easy* to use my magic like that. Not hiding who and what I was opened up options, but I'd been limiting myself to what everyone else could imagine. I kept laughing, this time because I was the one who kept telling people things could be easy and here I'd just had to prove it to myself in the most basic way possible: by using the gifts I was born with.

"She's fine," Troy said in response to Lachlan's concerned glance in the rearview mirror. He wrapped an arm around me to pull me close and said, "Congratulations. You've successfully completed a second Darkwatch mission."

That just made me laugh even harder. Me. Graduating from frightened elemental Watcher to badass elemental Darkwatch agent.

I'd become everything I used to fear, and the inversion of my life was too much for belief or rationality.

Chapter 3

I don't know what I'd expected to find at the boathouse, but an established operation was not it.

I stared at the orderly cars and tents as I got out of Troy's SUV. "How the hell did they get here and set up so fast?"

"We've been on war footing since magic disappeared," he said. "Everyone's been ready to mobilize. We just needed an objective and a location."

Shaking my head, I followed him across the damp ground to the boathouse. It hadn't stormed here, fortunately for whoever was staying in the tents, but it had at least drizzled. The air was chokingly thick with humidity, like the sky might change its mind about the precipitation at any moment, and the cooler bite to the air said we'd have fog by morning. Frogs called enthusiastically, and bats swooped to catch insects drawn by the lights shining from the roof.

Inside, the main room that had been largely bare during Leith's residence had been converted to neatly cubicled spaces. Elves sat on the edge of the overhead loft, legs swinging and arms slung over the lower rung of the railing, chatting quietly amongst themselves as they assessed the space. A long table filled the side of the room closest to the kitchenette, lined with metal folding chairs.

I rocked to a halt as a memory of a similar but smaller table intruded, Leith at its head as he watched me being dragged in. The bloodstains from where Javier Luna had been beaten almost to death had been cleaned up, and the eye ring the chain around my neck had been padlocked to had been removed, but—

Breathe. I needed to breathe.

I'd been back here before. Just not *inside* back here. Inside, where I'd been so terrified that Troy would discover the secret of what I was and hurt me with it that I'd exposed myself in a wild, failed effort to break free.

The silence in the room was what brought me back to myself. The air waves from speech and movement had stilled.

I blinked a few times. The layer of the past faded. Closing my eyes, I took a deep breath and unclenched fists now crackling with lightning. I might have been terrified almost into incapacity the first time I'd been in this room, but apparently my training had been such that I wouldn't let that happen a second time. I'd defend myself. Not wait to be snapped up.

Good.

On remembering that I wasn't who I'd been back then—and that Troy wasn't either—I let go of the elements completely and shook myself.

Troy searched my face with his gaze and the bond with his mind then gave me a small nod when he found me back to myself. *I'm sorry. I forgot you hadn't been inside yet.*

Not your fault. I offered a tight smile then spoke to the room at large. "Bad memories, y'all. I'll get over it. Nothing to do with any of you."

That got several understanding nods as the tension in the room eased and people got back to work.

I inhaled deeply and blew it out, relieved that my people seemed to accept it. There weren't many here, and most of them I recognized from actions in Virginia. Haroun waved from the corner that was apparently our IT setup before turning back to his conversation with Zadie and Etain. A quick pulse of elemental magic told me three more elves were outside, on guard probably. I was surprised to see Etain, but it made sense that she'd want to be wherever I was in case orders needed sending.

Darius, Thana, Lachlan, and Felip headed for the bunks where the Redcaps had once slept, black duffel bags in hand, while Troy steered me toward one of the bigger cubicles. It reminded me of the space I'd woken up in at the Virginia warehouse, small and square with two cots pushed together, only this one had a sort of canvas roof stretched over it to give more of an illusion of privacy.

Mostly it just made me feel claustrophobic.

I did my best to ignore it and dropped my own black duffel and my purse to the floor then followed them down as Troy tugged the canvas sheet across the doorway.

You sure you're okay? he sent.

Yeah. It was just a shock. I frowned. *This isn't your first time inside again, is it.*

The way he froze for a moment before smoothly settling onto the floor beside me told me there was something he didn't want to discuss. *No. It's not.*

I waited, but when nothing else came, I decided it was probably better to let it go. He wouldn't lie to me, but that didn't mean I necessarily wanted the answers.

"I should get showered and change," I said, even as I dropped my head to his shoulder. The adrenaline come-down from the mission had me exhausted. Adding the second dump from getting keyed up at entering the space and doing nothing with it physically hurt.

Troy passed me the small bag with the scarab. "What do you think we'll need this for?"

"Beats me. Harqil seems to forget that we're not all celestials and don't know what the fuck one of these is meant to do." I opened the bag and slid the scarab out onto my palm. It nearly filled it, a black stone heavier than it seemed like it should be. When I embraced Earth and reached for it, heat flickered.

Volcanic stone, then. The gently curved top was finely carved to resemble a scarab beetle. The flat bottom was inscribed with vertical rows of chiseled hieroglyphics. Magic leaked from the thing in waves.

"You really can't sense the magic?" I asked.

Shaking his head, Troy extended a hand. Aether flickered when I set it in his palm, then he shrugged.

"No," he said. "Nothing. Primordial?"

"Or godly. Or something of human magic that passed from the plane sometime between Ancient Egypt and now." I shivered as I put it back in the velvet bag. "We definitely need more details from Harqil before using it."

"Agreed." He stood and offered me a hand as a mischievous look flickered across his face. "Come on. Time to introduce you to camp life as a Darkwatch agent on a field mission."

Tired as I was, Troy kept me up until he was satisfied that I understood how things worked, what to do if we were attacked, everything from watch shifts to how to drive the damn motorboat now tied up at the dock. When I asked if the boat was the same one that'd been beached at the Sequoyah mansion two years ago, he just looked at me, asking with his expression if I really wanted the answer to that. Which meant yes, it was, but we could both pretend it wasn't.

Okay, so maybe I was still struggling with a few memories now that they were all being shoved in my face.

We were finally getting ready to go to bed when shouts rang out in the main room.

Troy burst out from our cubicle ahead of me in just his briefs, longknife bared and raised, drawing on Aether so hard it made my teeth hurt.

As I followed with lightning crackling, he muttered an elvish curse and lowered the blade.

"Harqil," he called to the figure encircled by grim-faced elves. "Don't tell me you're losing your touch."

The celestial grinned at the uproar they'd caused. "Come now, Solari. You know better."

"And *you* never learn." Troy made a hand signal, and the elves backed off reluctantly.

"Just a bit of fun." Harqil's grin took on a malicious edge. "You two are the only ones here with a chance at harming a hair on my pretty head."

Etain glanced at me. "Ma'am?"

"What he said." I nodded toward Troy; the gesture had been an order. "Harqil is an honored guest. A *celestial* guest. Although I would ask you not to tease my people, Harqil. We're up against enough, and they need their rest."

"Boring. But very well." The twinkle in Harqil's eyes said they might still take an opportunity if it presented itself, which didn't surprise me. The elves might have a cultural appreciation for guile but tended to be too orderly for practical jokes—aside from Troy, anyway, as much as that had surprised me the time he and Terrence had played one on me.

I waved Harqil to follow me and headed for the corner that'd been declared a briefing area. Troy, Etain, and Darius came as well.

Despite the novelty Harqil represented, there were wide eyes and pale faces as some of our people saw the extent of Keithia's cruelty in Troy's scars for the first time, but he—usually too ashamed of them to go shirtless or in shorts—ignored the reactions, completely focused on the celestial.

"Is this the part where you tell us why we had to take the risk of stealing an artifact from an art museum when the mundanes are already looking for any excuse to bring Othersiders up on charges?" Troy murmured. The gold flecks in his gaze snapped with the same intensity in his voice.

Harqil was almost unfazed. Almost. Whatever mocking quip their expression hinted at was held back. "Yes. As you know, you'll need a team. But therein lies a challenge: how do you get a party of people into a dream at the same time when only one of them is a Dreamwalker?"

I couldn't help my grimace. Cyrus had barely covered that, beyond telling me I'd failed at my one attempt when, apparently, I hadn't. Oh, and explaining how much danger I was putting Troy in by being bonded to him.

And by explaining, I meant guilt-tripping.

Harqil spread their hands. "Precisely. You can't bond all of them. Or rather, even if you could, the combined power you and your king wield magically would probably kill them eventually." They glanced between us, eyes narrowed. "Lucky thing, to have such an unusually powerful elf not inclined to kill an elemental on sight. Almost feels like the Fates' work."

"The scarab, Harqil," I said. I had enough trouble with the tricksters right now. I didn't need to add the Fates or the Nightmare Court or whoever else might wake up and take notice.

"Right," they said. "Your first trick—other than finding assholes reckless enough to join you—is to bind all of you to the scarab. With my help, of course, given the djinn are without magic. I'll need a few things though. Namely, a summoning bone, four scrying crystals, and the blood of all involved."

"I have the first two things at home," I said, slightly annoyed that they hadn't mentioned this sooner. Duke had given me the bone and the crystals as a teen, after my magic had started maturing, hoping that I might show more djinn talent than I did. "We can stop by tomorrow. Pick up the gytrash as well."

It would leave my house completely unguarded, but a house could be replaced—no matter how much it would hurt me to do so. The people here couldn't be.

"Good call, ma'am. We could use more guards on patrol," Etain said.

Troy, always attentive to my deeper mood, said, "Terrence and Ximena might be glad to have a bigger space for their people to seek refuge in. It can't be easy being unable to reach their cats."

A roundabout way of saying he thought he could negotiate an exchange with Terrence: safe territory for the werecats if they kept an eye on my land while they were there. I'd seen Darnell and how much he was pained by the halting, restrained transition from man to wereleopard. The born leopards might have been handling this time better, but we all knew the dangers of itchy weres.

I let my relief curl through the bond to him as I nodded. "Arrange it, please. Tell them they can use the house or camp on the land as needed."

I still didn't love having people in my house at all, but I couldn't send Troy to ask them to watch our land and expect them to shit in the woods and wash in the river. Of all my people, I trusted Terrence and Ximena to leave the place better than they found it.

"It can wait until you've rested, big brother." Darius glanced at me for confirmation as Troy turned for our cubicle and, presumably, his phone.

"Yeah." I scrubbed my hands over my face, my earlier exhaustion catching up with me again. "Which we should do now. Thank you, Harqil."

A grin flickered, like they were going to make a joke, but again they restrained their reaction to a nod. "Until tomorrow."

I was already heading for the cubicle when they shifted planes.

As Troy ducked back inside our space, Darius stopped me with a light touch to my arm and leaned close when I turned to him.

"How many of those scars are from the torture?" Darius whispered grimly, so low I could barely hear him.

I considered. "All but the line over his heart, the one on his hand, the claw marks on his left shoulder, and the bullet hole in his right shoulder. The Darkwatch gave him that last one when they took him from the bar. The claws were Callista."

"We can survive a lot, but that...Keithia wasn't going for a lesson, like with Uncle Cyrus. For him to be that badly scarred, he should have died."

"Technically, he did. I brought him back." I hadn't been done with him yet. Still wasn't. Never would be.

"Just Keithia did all that to him?"

"No. Some of it was Evangeline." I smiled, though not from pleasure. "I killed the former. You took care of the latter."

Darius's expression went through a few shifts: dismay, anger, resolution. "Then I can stop feeling guilty."

"Yes."

With another squeeze on my arm and a sharp nod, Darius left for the shared sleeping room.

Looked like I wasn't the only one coming into all this with ghosts clinging to me. I just hoped they weren't turned against us when we went into the Duat.

Chapter 4

We were up before noon and at home within the hour. I insisted on picking up breakfast on the way rather than eating at our camp. We were on multiple deadlines, and thinking about who I was going to ask to risk their lives, souls, and sanity coming to the Duat was making me snappish.

How the hell did one go about making a request like *that*?

"You just ask," Troy said as we walked up to the house, answering my thought.

I gave him a flat look. "Just like that."

"You're Arbiter and High Queen. So yes. Just like that."

"With no consideration of—"

"Arden." He halted my reach to open the front door, catching my hand and kissing the knuckles. "This is another part of asking for help."

"Asking people to possibly *die* on a mission that I'm supposed to lead with only the barest fucking idea of how to use the magic it requires?"

"Yes. That, and understanding that maybe, just maybe, people *want* to help. Has it occurred to you that everyone else is feeling helpless without magic? That they know their families and people are at risk without it? And that as a result, they are searching for something—anything—to do to fix it?"

"You make it sound like I'm supposed to be a savior."

"You are."

I froze, blinking. A chill went over me as my heart raced.

"I thought so." He took the keys from me and opened the door, taking care of the security while I stood there trying to figure out why that scared me so bad. Troy called from inside, "Where's the stuff Harqil wanted?"

Shaking myself, I came in and shut the door behind me then headed for my bookcase. My worn box, carved from black walnut, was nestled behind some books. I tucked the whole thing in my backpack.

"Get the stuff in the closet as well," Troy said gently. "We don't know when we'll be back next, and without wards or walls..."

"Yeah," I whispered. I should have thought of that before.

Now I was wrestling with the idea of being a savior or whatever. It was what I was doing, really, and had been doing for a while. But I was used to doing it as just me, or me and Troy, and having to wrangle everyone else into helping me. Then I could feel justified in getting their help because I'd earned it. I'd fought for it. I'd proven that our action was in their best interest and won them around to my way of thinking.

To just...ask? And have people want to help? Help me to help them? I didn't know what to do with that. I didn't know where the scales of obligation tipped then. If I didn't have to prove the need, what then?

"Stop overthinking," Troy said from unexpectedly close behind me. "Like you are so fond of saying, it really can be that easy."

I jumped, letting my breath out in a growl as I dropped the various dangerous treasures I'd collected in the last few years into my backpack. "You are entirely too good at sneaking."

"I'm an elf. It's what we do."

That might be so, but the smug note in his voice said he was especially proud of his ability to continually sneak up on me in particular.

Turning around, I looked up at him. "This is really the right call?"

"Of course it is. We need magic. You and I can get it back." He gave me the serious look he wore for politicking. "King to Arbiter? I'm asking for your aid. The elves cannot be without magic. Not with the Bureau for Supernatural Investigation moving to attack here. Not with our control of Richmond and Charleston so shaky."

Well. If he was making formal requests, I'd accept that as my comfort—I wasn't doing this for myself, for once.

"Okay," I said. "Let me get a few more things together." Definitely needed to take all the weapons and some clothes. It sounded like we were going to be at the boathouse for a while, and I hadn't realized Troy had intended us to camp there. It made sense. I just liked my own bed.

I reached for the land and river with my elemental senses as I packed a few sets of clothes and other things I'd need if we were planning to be away for a few days, wanting a last bit of comfort. As I did, I picked up an odd sense near the river.

Something that felt like a body.

Frowning, I closed my eyes and dropped my shields almost completely.

"Arden?" Troy said. "What's wrong?"

I ignored him, trying to focus.

A body. Moving stealthily. The way I would if I was moving from tree trunk to tree trunk, looking for traps. They crossed the river at one of the shallower points, drawing nearer, until they reached the bank on my side. The sense I got from the smaller plants was agitation. I'd fed blood to all of the earth bordering my land, but I'd nearly bled to death in the clearing by the river. When whoever this was stepped on that patch and knelt to touch the firepit, I gasped at the sense I got.

Someone who wished me harm was on my lands.

I sent a little nudge through the bond to Troy. *Intruder. Something our size, not a deer, maybe not human though, on the river side. They just knelt by the fire pit.*

A vicious thrill came back.

Troy was still quietly pissed about the Sons of Seth daring to attack our land and home, and he'd be sensitive to my general discomfort with leaving home. With the absence of magic, the survivors of the human attempt were currently drugged into a coma, according to the briefing Etain had given this morning. The Ebon Guard were being extremely thorough in reprogramming the bastards, although I might need to overrule them to keep missing person reports from being submitted and search parties directed our way.

Whoever was fixing to try us now was in for a bad time. Troy, ever-vigilant of my happiness and safety, was far more willing than I was to use deadly violence. We had our games, fake hunts that kept us both sharp, but he was a born predator and a trained commando. He enjoyed the real thing, and hunting deer didn't cut it.

He also liked it when I let him do his job. I stayed put, playing bait while he drew on shadows, suppressed every hint of his presence, and slipped into the trees.

While I continued to pack a last few things, I swept my elemental senses wider into the earth and sky. There was never just one attacker. Well. Other than the times Troy had turned up alone in the early days. While he hunted the one who'd come close enough to draw my attention, I sought their backup.

There. One more, slowly making their way in from the northern edge of my property. I couldn't find a third, and my range was big enough now that I knew that was all. Something was off about the second one. A vampire, maybe? Their undead signatures read strangely to my senses, which were more attuned to living things.

A crash and a startled, feminine-sounding yelp in the woods announced Troy springing his trap. I left my packed bags by the front door and went out the back to the deck to peer over the fence, putting up a quick wall of Air in case the other intruder had a rifle. It'd stop a bullet, and only another elemental could see it, although Troy would be able to sense it.

Minutes later, he emerged from the woods on the river side, pushing a woman ahead of him. She was between my height and Troy's, with the same leanly muscled build a lot of the elves had. Her tight, dark curls were shaved on both sides and highlighted with gold streaks. She was a few shades lighter-skinned than me, almost Troy's shade of brown, with a snake tattoo twining around her left arm. Her dark eyes held anger rather than fear—which made her either extremely confident or extremely stupid.

She'd put up a good fight, from the bloody nose and split lip she had. Troy only drew blood when pushed to it. Unless he was that pissed by the intrusion.

I reached out with another chord of Air and lifted her over the fence. Troy vaulted over after her, and I was glad Zanna wasn't around to see it. My kobold friend still maintained the house and hated when people did that. Bás followed Troy over the fence, her golden eyes baleful.

There's one more, I sent. *To the north.*

Troy scowled and sent a pulse of confirmation in the bond but didn't react otherwise, reading my intention.

"Who's this?" I asked aloud.

"Found her in the woods." Troy enjoyed the acting as much as the hunting, having been trained to subterfuge as a member of the Darkwatch. "When I tried to tell her she was trespassing, she drew this."

He tossed a knife in the dirt. I came down to the yard to look at it, going cold when I saw what it was made of.

This wasn't funny anymore.

"You're aware bronze weapons have been outlawed in this territory?" I asked coldly.

She gave me a cocky grin. "What of it?"

I frowned, as much for her attitude as for the accent I was unable to place. Something between French and British, maybe. "Nobody comes here. Nobody smart anyway."

Our captive shrugged. "Better lucky than good or clever."

"And you're obviously not any of the above," I snapped. "Who are you?"

"An assassin." She grinned at my consternation. "Hence the bronze."

"And your friend?" I nodded northward.

That sobered her. "What friend?"

"The vampire in my woods."

"Has the Mistress of Raleigh misplaced someone? How is Maria these days anyway?"

Nope. I was not playing these fucking games.

"Troy?" I said.

He took his cue from my mood more than anything else and kicked the back of the captive's knees to drop her. At her protest, he wrenched her neck to the side and tucked his longknife under her chin.

Not that it shut her up. Goddess but whoever this would-be assassin was, she had a mouth on her.

"Careful," Troy called after me as I walked to the edge of the yard.

I didn't answer him, seeking the sense of the undead now swiftly making their way closer. With a coil of Air, I snatched for them, lifting them over the fence like one of those claw machines and setting them in a shady patch of my yard.

Marú followed. Good thing the gytrash had had an eye on our intruders.

The vampire was a tall man, Troy's height maybe, and as lean as his counterpart. Very pale under a thick layer of sunscreen and a baseball cap, with hair almost brown enough to be black sticking out from under it and eyes about the same color. Attractive, even without glamour. He'd died about my age, maybe, late twenties, although I had no way to tell how old he was now.

"The vampire," I said, turning back to our first captive.

The vampire in question growled. "You hurt her."

Troy flashed a smile that looked calculated to hurt, proud and mean. "Only a little. I should have killed her."

"She's *mine*," he said. Like the woman, his accent was faintly foreign. British.

Great, now foreigners were after me.

Crossing my arms, I glared as I shook the vampire in my grip of Air. "And this land is *ours*. I know the No Trespassing signs are still up, but most importantly, nobody comes to this territory, on this land, with *that*"—I pointed at the bronze, elemental-killer of a knife still laying in the dirt— "unless they're looking for me. And not in a friendly way."

The woman grinned. "Told you this was the best way to get their attention."

The vampire who claimed her only scowled.

Troy shook her. "You named yourself assassin. Who sent you?"

"For me to tell you that, cousin," she said, "you'll need to unhand me and get your elemental queen to free my partner."

Partner. Interesting. Usually when a vampire claimed you, it was with them as master. Then my brain caught up. "Cousin?"

With a muttered curse, Troy wrenched her head back and frowned down at her. "I don't recognize her."

"You wouldn't," she said easily. "You were away the last time I was in town."

Troy sniffed then again, more deeply, and swore again in elvish. "Desmarais?"

"That's me." She grinned, probably going for cheeky, but the edge to it could cut steel.

I frowned. "Desmarais? As in, Lydia Desmarais?"

"The one and only. Although I prefer Lya."

I turned to the vampire. "Which makes you—"

"Cade," he snarled. "If you do any further harm to my solidaire—"

The gag of Air I shoved in his mouth cut him off, and I turned to the woman who was apparently the exiled half-elf Samarre had originally been sent to reclaim six years ago.

"Congratulations," I said. "You have my attention at a really shitty time. Talk, or I call Samarre and let her deal with you because today is truly not the fucking day."

That made Lya get serious real quick. "Samarre? She's here?"

"Sworn to my service," I said. "Along with Luc Lavigne, Jacinthe Proulx, and half a dozen other elves from Lyon."

Lya's lips tightened, and she darted a look at Cade.

I spun him around to face the woods. "Don't look at him. Look at me. And answer my Goddess-damned questions."

She stared at me, a level look with more maturity than I'd have guessed was in her up to that point. "Very well. We want to join you."

"You were hunting me on my land. With bronze," I said. "You were going to attack me. I sensed it."

"Which is what we were hired to do and needed to be seen attempting. If you know who I am, you know we're bounty hunters. Good ones. Even without magic."

I spun Cade back around and ungagged him. "And you?"

"As she says," the vampire snarled.

"Get to the point," Troy said flatly. "This was an elaborate plan to do what, exactly?"

"See if Rio Lestari was lying," Lya said with a sharp look at Troy.

Troy made no outward reaction, but internally, he shut down. In an icy voice, he asked, "And what does House Lestari want with the High Queen of the Chapel Hill Conclave?"

"Her head, of course. Rio claims the loss of magic is her doing and that killing her will bring it back. I called bullshit. Not to his face, obviously, since his conclave was paying big money, but he claimed to have intel suggesting that this particular elemental or her goldeneye king had something to do with magic going missing." She shrugged. "If nothing else, she's in charge and shit keeps happening here. Powerful people are nervous, and they might dislike like that even more than elementals."

"I didn't want to be in charge," I snapped. I thought the fucking elemental bounty hunts were done. I hadn't even heard of House fucking Lestari. But here we were, at the worst time for it. "I wanted to be left alone. But first I had to claim a prince. Then a conclave. Then a territory. Then a demesne and then another. Y'all better hope I don't have to claim the whole fucking world to get some peace and quiet."

Lya lifted her brows and glanced at Cade. "Right, not a megalomaniac at all."

The vampire hadn't taken his attention from me and caught the irate hardening of my expression.

"Not helping, love," he said.

She rolled her eyes but pressed her lips together.

Love, huh? These two just kept getting more interesting. I wondered if they were used to speaking telepathically, to be this loose with their tongues.

"What happened to Callista?" Cade kept his attention on me, although he clearly wanted to look at Lya—or threaten Troy.

Not the question I was expecting.

Exhaustion and the deadline we were on made me answer honestly. "Me and Troy fought her at her bar. I gave her to the goddess Artemis when she lost. Then I traveled to the gods' plane to get information from her that would stop the Wild Hunt and cut her throat in thanks."

Both Lya and Cade stared at me.

"That's the truth?" Cade said.

"Yes," I replied firmly.

The two bounty hunters looked at each other.

"We're in," Lya said.

I blinked at Cade's nod. "Excuse me?"

"Whatever you're doing. We're in."

I looked at Troy, confounded. *Were we being followed?*

No.

Then what—

I don't know.

"Well?" Lya said.

I studied her. "What exactly do you think you're 'in' for?"

Her wide smile was even cockier than the cockiest of Troy's shit-eating grins. "Getting magic back. What else?"

Chapter 5

I t was going to be a long damn day.

"You're coming with us. Right now," Troy said as I marched our two captives to the front yard with Air. "If you give us any trouble, I'll kill you myself. Prisoner or not."

Lya rolled her eyes. "You certainly don't disappoint on reputation, cousin."

I sighed. We couldn't leave them at Ebon Guard HQ, which was currently overfull with the Sons of Seth. These two had to come to the boathouse with us, which meant I had a short time only to figure out what the hell their deal was.

We took Troy's car because we wouldn't have gotten the two of us, our bags, two gytrash, and two bounty hunters into my Civic hatchback. The gytrash had to ride in the cargo area in the back, which nobody was happy about, but we couldn't afford to be pulled over for having humanoids back there without a seatbelt while apparent dogs rode in the backseat. That and Troy was precious about claws on his leather seats.

Our guests had wanted to be freed to get their own vehicle, but Troy flat-out refused before collecting their phones and weapons.

I twisted to look at them as Troy hit 751. "What—" The tight expression on Cade's face made me change what I was going to say. "What's going on with you?"

"I'm hungry," the vampire said roughly. "And this car smells like a buffet."

I glanced at Lya as Troy cracked the windows.

"No," Cade said, reading my next question in the look. "Without glamour...I could kill her. Painfully. With no magic to make it better." The look Cade gave his solidaire then felt real: deep regret, shame, pain. There was a past there, like maybe he'd nearly killed her once before. He shuttered it away. "So, it would be mundanes only but few and far between."

Lya looked tired and frustrated, all confidence gone. "We tried a little bite after magic went. It didn't go well."

Shit. Of course. Because without glamour, all of his feeds would hurt, plus if it was mundanes he'd have to take a big meal and then kill his prey.

"That's a problem?" Troy asked the question I was hesitating on, pointed and harsh. A test.

"Yes," Cade snapped. "I'm not who I used to be. I won't say I don't enjoy a good feed, but I'm not a savage." His voice dropped to a level almost too quiet to hear. "Not anymore."

I glanced at Troy and got the sense that neither of us knew who that was, which meant I'd be calling Maria when I had a quiet moment to figure out who exactly we had in the back seat of Troy's car.

Rings flashed as Lya laced her fingers between her vampire's. "I know we didn't have a great start to our acquaintance, Arbiter, but we couldn't think how else to ensure you'd notice us. And to be honest, Rio's queen offered up an elven prisoner as part of the down payment. Cade—he needed the blood."

Whoever this House Lestari was, they were firmly on my shitlist already.

Neither here nor there.

I studied the two of them. They were clearly a couple. They were hurting from the loss of magic, and whatever was between them was motivating them more than anything to do with me or Troy. They'd be perfect for the mission, if we could trust them. Capable, if what I remembered of Lya's dossier was at all accurate, but not *my* people. As cold as it was, it would hurt less if something happened to them than it would if something happened to Etain, Terrence, or even Darius.

We needed them.

I thumbed the ring Janae had given me and tried to let my mind blank, focusing only on the question of whether they were safe to add to the mission. The sense I got was more nuanced than it had been before: yes...but they were a package deal.

If I let anything happen to one of them, the other would become a deadly threat to me and Troy both.

Slumping in my seat, I mulled that over.

Troy nudged me in the bond. *Well?*

It's complicated. But I think they're okay.

I could run a Thread of Thorns.

It was all I could do not to grimace. I'd barely survived the interrogation procedure, and I'd nearly taken Troy with me.

No, I sent. *Look at them. If you hurt one, it would be like if someone hurt me. The other would come for you. We don't have time for a feud.*

I don't like the risk of just trusting them.

Neither do I. But I think they want magic back more than they worry about whatever elven House sent them. They're cocky as hell, or at least she is. They probably think they can help us and then fuck off without being caught.

It could be a double cross. Help us then try again for you.

Then which of our people would you rather risk on this?

Troy shut down again at that. I was tempted to push, but now—with Lya and Cade in the back—was not the time for anything less than a unified front.

We made the rest of the drive in silence.

When I opened the liftgate at the boathouse, the gytrash bounded out of the cargo hatch and scented the wind.

"Sorry about the ride over," I said. "Be welcome on my land."

Bás shook herself and yipped.

I had no idea what that meant, but they didn't seem too put out.

"We own the boathouse," I said, "the lakeside approach, and a good amount of the land surrounding it. The border is fenced. Roam and hunt as you need. Just please make sure any kills look natural or are buried. If there are intruders, especially humans, do your best to take them alive. But preserve your own lives first and foremost. Okay?"

That got the more enthusiastic head bobs and yips of agreement I'd learned to recognize.

"Great. Your support will be remembered, and King Rí will be told once we've got magic back."

Another more solemn pair of head bobs.

"Go on. I know you probably want to haunt the woods."

That got me a drop-jawed smile full of terribly sharp teeth from Marú before both fae bounded into the trees.

Lya was watching when I looked up. "How'd you get a pair of gytrash to answer to you?" she asked. "That wasn't in our briefing."

"Good to know House Lestari doesn't know everything about my defenses."

"Nah, just the wards, though not their nature. And your bodyguard, of course." She glanced at Troy, who was watching Cade watch Lya. "Although nobody quite seems to know what the hell he is to you."

"My king consort. Claimed and oathed," I said as neutrally as I could.

Her cheeky grin flashed again. "Of course."

I sighed. The woman was infuriating, and I couldn't even say why. "Etain!" I hollered.

My Captain of the Ebon Guard approached from where she'd been hovering closer to the door of the boathouse. "Ma'am?"

"Meet Lya Desmarais and Cade. He's a vamp. She's his solidaire."

Her expression hardened as she took them in. "What are a pair of bounty hunters doing with you, ma'am?"

"I don't know yet. They say they were hired by House Lestari and sent to kill me and that they only took the job to get an in with me and a feed for the vampire."

Etain frowned. "That's...strangely honest."

Lya shrugged. "We heard this new Arbiter likes honesty. And that she's fair. Even if you have to read between the lines to hear that last part."

Frowning harder, Etain studied Cade before bringing her attention back to Lya. "Could be a ploy to get us to trust you."

"Could be," Lya agreed. "But if you know who we are, you know I pissed on my mother's House to be with him. I could have been heir to a High House, and I chose to be a vampire vagabond's solidaire. Now there's no magic—no glamour—and he's suffering. I won't have it. You lot seem to be the only ones with any kind of plan or power to get magic back. So, here we are."

Cade bowed. "At your service."

"A word in private, ma'am?" Etain said after a few heartbeats eyeing them.

I nodded and followed her, waving for Troy to come with us when she ordered two triads of Ebon Guard to watch our guests.

"I don't like this," Etain said quietly. "I really, really don't like it. At the same time, we are up against the wall on numbers. If those two want to help, I don't know that we can turn them down. I just don't know where to put them."

"They come to the Duat with us," I said, equally as quietly.

Troy grimaced.

"I know, Troy. But I'll be in control there. If they fuck with me, they don't get home. If they fuck with you, they don't get home. I can literally change the shape of reality there, so even if they somehow pull a weapon on one of us, it only exists as long as I allow it to. They'll be asleep in the real, so we won't have to spare extra guards while you and I are in the Duat. The dossier I read on Lya after Samarre's arrival said she's been holding her own against full-blooded Othersiders for decades."

"I want to talk to Maria first," Troy said.

I shrugged. "Agreed. We keep them out of the boathouse for now to maintain operational security, just in case they're tempted to send info back to House Lestari for another check, but we set them up in a tent and send someone for their car."

Troy wore the distant look he got when he was trying to think through angles. "Fine. I'll go talk to Maria. You sort out whatever Harqil wants to do with this heart scarab."

I went on my toes to kiss his cheek. "This will work out. It has to."

He flashed a grim smile then headed toward the lake, fishing his phone out of his pocket.

"Desperate times," Etain muttered, seemingly more as a reminder to herself than to me.

"Yeah," I said. "I'll go give them the good news."

Their reaction wasn't what I thought it would be, but it did help convince me they were here for the right reasons. Lya slumped, eyes closed, cockiness fled, and leaned against Cade, who wrapped an arm around her to pull her in for a hug even as he inched them farther back under the shadow of the trees.

"I told you they'd listen if your plan to get their attention worked," he said quietly, for her ears only, even if he had to know we could all hear them.

She glared up at him. "You *know* what my history here is."

"I know. But Callista and Keithia are gone and the poison with them."

Lya pressed her lips together, like she wanted to argue but knew it would only be a shot to her own foot.

I cleared my throat. "We're on a tight deadline. We'll do a trial run tonight and then go tomorrow."

"Just like that," Lya said skeptically.

I shrugged.

"A trial run of what?" Cade asked.

"Dreamwalking," I said.

Before I could say more, a burst of power in the clearing made me spin. Harqil stepped through a portal from another plane and waved it shut behind them.

"Are these to be part of your team, then?" they asked.

Cade reached for the machete we'd disarmed him of, snarling when his hand brushed an empty sheath. Lya slapped at the similarly empty sheath on her arm.

"Who the fuck is this, and how did they do that?" Lya snapped.

Harqil grinned, pleased by the disquiet their arrival had brought. "You may call me Harqil. Celestial, messenger class. I'm supporting this little endeavor. And when I say supporting, I mean making it possible."

Lya's brows lifted. "Our briefing said nothing about celestials."

"You only see them because they want you to," I said.

"Just so," Harqil agreed. "Now. Where's your elf?"

I waved in the direction of the lake. "Making a phone call. He'll be done in a moment."

"Very well. We can sort out the scarab now, and I'll explain the first trial when he's done."

"Hang on," I said. "The *first* trial? You said we'd have to go to the Duat and get magic back."

"I did indeed." Harqil sobered. "But you didn't really think it was simply going to be walking into the underworld, did you? There are trials."

Tired and frustrated, I ground my teeth and breathed, trying not to show too much reaction in front of either our guests or the Ebon Guard still standing watch over them. "I see."

Troy rounded the boathouse, still on the phone, and I waved. He caught sight of Harqil and ended the call to hurry over.

"What now?" Troy asked.

"Apparently, this isn't a one-and-done deal," I said. "There are tests or some shit."

"Of course there are," Troy said. He looked at Lya and Cade. "Does that change your plans?"

Both shook their heads.

"Whatever it takes," Lya said.

Harqil clapped. "Lovely. Everyone is all in. Scarab first, then plan."

I dug in my bag for the heart scarab and held it out.

"You hold it, cupped in your hands," Harqil said.

I did so, trying to keep the anxiety causing my heart to race from my expression or stance. More elves had drifted outside to watch. People needed to see that I was in control of both the situation and myself.

"I'll need blood from both of you," Harqil said, looking at Lya and Cade.

Cade glanced at Troy. "Not him?"

With a dismissive wave, Harqil said, "They keep to the old covenants."

"Which means what?" Lya pushed.

"He's already five times bound to a trueborn primordial elemental—by Aether, oath, body, blood, and aura—and has walked Chaos spheres with her." They grinned maliciously. "I don't recommend that route. It would kill just about anyone else. It will probably kill him sooner rather than later, given he's going solo and not as one of a supporting triad."

Lya paled as she looked at Troy.

"Whatever it takes," he said grimly.

Her expression firmed, and she held out a hand.

Harqil turned to me. "Neith's gift?"

Grimacing, Troy dug in my bag for the lead-lined box containing the godblade and opened it for them. The bond both sharpened and roiled as Harqil took it; Troy hated the cursed thing for several very good reasons, mostly to do with how it tended to warp my mind if I used it for too long.

Lya's expression didn't change as Harqil glanced at the sun, muttered a short prayer, then made a quick, small cut over the heart line in her palm and guided her hand to the top of the scarab.

When Harqil enclosed our hands with both of theirs, magic sparked, making me hiss.

"Good, it's working," they said. Their next words were in an old, old language. Ancient Egyptian maybe.

"That's not ancient Greek or Latin," Cade murmured, confirming my thoughts.

Harqil ignored everyone as they chanted and magic built. I almost thought I could smell lotus and river water, dry desert air—the half-forgotten scents of the dream I'd had that'd made me dump a storm and desert sand into my bedroom.

Then with a last pulse of pressure, it was all gone.

Lya wavered, eyes wide, then dropped to her knees with a sharp inhale.

"Lya!" Cade knelt beside her, steadying her with a grip on her shoulder. "Are you—"

"I'm fine," she whispered. "That was just a load of heavy magic. Old magic." She looked up at Harqil, a new wariness in her eyes. "If you've fucked me—"

"Of course I've fucked you," the celestial said cheerfully. "Or to be fair, you fucked yourself in agreeing to this. Now you're bound to the holder of the heart scarab, which is, at the moment, the Eternal Huntress." They shrugged. "You said 'whatever it takes.'"

Her mouth tightened. "Yeah. I did. And I meant it, if it gets magic back."

"That is entirely up to your group efforts."

Cade growled and rose, extending a hand. "Then let's get this over with."

"Fair warning, I don't know how it will affect one of the undead. I *think* it will go easier on you, since you've already got one foot in the grave anyway."

He looked at Lya, and his gaze softened as he held out his hand over the bloody stone cupped in mine. "Whatever it takes."

Power slithered over my hands as Harqil repeated the ritual.

When the words were done and the magic faded, Cade squeezed his eyes shut. "That's distinctly uncomfortable."

"But you'll live. In a manner of speaking," Harqil said.

Cade nodded.

"Last part. It needs to be sealed." Harqil stood in front of me and clasped their hands around mine, murmuring once more as magic rose then fell, sending hot prickles over me. "There."

When I opened my hands, my jaw dropped to find them clean and the black stone now a deep red.

"Oh good, it worked completely." Harqil grinned. "It's been a while since I've had to use that particular spell. Iset must've turned our way."

Lya stiffened, looking ready to go off until Cade squeezed her shoulder and shook his head. Then she subsided, still looking pissed and more than a little suspicious.

I'd definitely have to keep the scarab safe. Binding these two to it might have added assurances for the mission, but if Lya decided this wouldn't work, the gods only knew what she'd do to free herself.

Chapter 6

"There are four tests," Harqil said. We'd moved to sit around the fire kettle once a sunshade had been set up for Cade, although Harqil was standing, hands behind their back and shifting restlessly. "The Lake of Fire. The Waters of the Drowned. The Caverns of the Damned. And the Primordial Darkness."

Lya grimaced. "That's all ominous as fuck."

"Of course it is." Harqil spread their hands. "It's the Duat. You're of this plane, not the celestial one, so you can't just make a hole in reality and go." They looked at me and tilted their head. "Yet."

My stomach clenched. This wasn't the first time they'd suggested I might become a celestial. "What's the nature of the tests?"

"Survival, mostly. Not just of body but also of mind and soul. Reach the House of Life in each stage. Get your prize. Make it back alive, sane, and intact."

Troy leaned back in his chair, scowling. "What's the nature of the threats?"

Harqil shrugged. "The usual ancient monsters. Akhu—hungry, angry ghosts—sha monsters, fire-spitting chaos serpents, the like. But there might also be physical manifestations of your worst nightmares, so be very careful what you think about while you're there." They pointed at me. "Especially you."

Lya frowned, looking me up and down. "How long you been doing this anyway?"

"Dreamwalking? Most of my life, informally. Controlled? A few weeks. With people? Only with him and one other." I tipped my head in Troy's direction and left off the part where I only walked with him by accident during separations.

"Weeks," she said flatly. The look on her face as she met Cade's gaze spoke volumes about her distrust.

"If you'd rather not help get magic back, you can stay here," I said coolly. It shouldn't have stung to be questioned like that. I didn't know them at all, and plenty of people had questioned me before. I had just let myself get optimistic at their statements of being all in.

Her lips thinned as she took my measure again. "I take my responsibilities as solidaire very fucking seriously. Taking my *undead vampire* into the *underworld* sounds pretty bloody serious."

"Lya, we—" Cade started, the first hint of a dominant bite in his tone.

Harqil clapped. "Which is why we'll do a trial run."

"When?" the vampire asked, ignoring Lya's glare.

"You're all technically nocturnal. No time like the present."

I wanted to ask what the rush was, but we all keenly felt the pressure to get magic back. I'd also lost a day on the subpoena, so yeah. We needed to get moving. I glanced at Troy.

"Let me call Terrence and get that arrangement sorted out first," he said. "And give Alli a heads-up."

Lya brightened. "How is Terrence?"

"Well enough, all things considered."

"Give him our regards."

Troy frowned but nodded and wandered a little ways off.

While he handled security for our land, I checked in with Etain. We moved out of earshot of the rest of the group before she sighed.

"How quickly can you get this done?" she asked.

"I don't know. Apparently, there are four trials. I'll know more after the first one. Why?"

She unlocked her phone and showed me a breaking news clip that looked like drone footage over a crowd of people in a city that the ticker said was Portland. "The mundanes are gathering in cities across the country. Just anti-Otherside slogans and counter-protesters for now, but our operatives say this time it could turn into a riot. My bet is on either a dark money super PAC or the Supernatural Bureau. Something to stir up a response, get you and King Troy to answer that subpoena."

I sneered. Then I went cold as I looked deeper. "There'll be bloodshed."

"Likely. If it's Otherside blood that's spilled, you'll be expected to respond by our side. If it's mundane, you'll probably take the fall for it."

"Fuck. I don't have time for this. And I don't have an alibi unless I want to burn this location and all of our people, or some of them at least."

"My thoughts exactly, ma'am." She offered a tight smile. "We'll do our best to keep tensions in check here but..."

"Yeah. The faster we get it done, the better."

"Exactly." She started walking backward, in the direction of the boathouse, and made a fist-to-heart salute. "I'll go get a tent set up for our guests."

I thanked her and returned to the small huddle that included Lya, Cade, and Harqil.

"Etain is getting your lodgings set up," I said to the half-elf and the vampire. "Harqil, anything I need to know about pulling them into a dream?"

"Technically, it will be a Chaos sphere. You'll do what you practiced with Cyrus. Can you sense them?"

I frowned. "No?"

"Focus on the scarab and look in your heart."

Giving up on decorum, I sat down on the ground and stared at the scarab, letting my vision unfocus.

"Close out your elf," Harqil suggested.

I disliked doing so completely, but now that I was paying attention, Troy was a constant undertone. I was aware of his heartbeat, his mood, the skim of his thoughts, the strength of his magic. I liked it like that; it made me feel like I wasn't alone in the world. But it also meant I couldn't really get a sense of the lesser bond created in the heart scarab.

With an effort, I closed Troy all the way out and was alone in my head for the first time in ages. I hated it immediately.

"Focus," Harqil chided. Then, "No, she's fine. She just needs to find the other two."

I missed Troy's annoyed response because I found the thread of Chaos linking the two bounty hunters to the scarab, and then the scarab, via touch and magic, to me. Carefully, tentatively, I extended a thin chord of my own Chaos to strum the two threads I'd found.

"Hey!" Lya snapped. "What the—"

"Shh!" Harqil knelt in front of me. "Good, Arden. Do it again."

I did.

"Now follow it to one of them."

It took me a minute, but once I thought of vines reaching for a new trellis, I got it.

"That's right. Can you see the shape of her mind?"

I could...sort of? I wasn't Troy, with his Aetheric talent for mental manipulation. But he'd worked his magic on me—and I'd reached back with Chaos— enough times that I could sort of see what Harqil was prompting me toward.

"Stop there," Harqil said. "Now—"

"It's missing something." I'm not sure the words came out clearly because the majority of my focus was on the magic. "An anchor. They're anchored into the stone. I hold the stone. But it would be stronger if…" I pushed myself to look deeper. "The tie should be reciprocal."

Harqil hesitated. "That would make it stronger, yes. But that creates a dangerous level of connection."

"In the real or in the dream?"

"Dream only."

"Dangerous how?"

"Your power would strengthen theirs. Their fears would have a greater chance of becoming real, in the dream at least. More variables."

I pondered that, hovering on a knife's edge of magic. "But it would make them better able to fend off Sutekh's magic?"

"It would."

Troy dropped down to kneel next to me. "Arden, what are you two talking about?"

Carefully, I withdrew the magic. Over Lya's sigh of relief, I said, "Blood." When he didn't answer, I glanced to the side to see him looking thunderous. Access to my blood was his special privilege these days. "I know. It's yours, and it's a risk."

"I would very much like to say no," he growled. After a few more heartbeats, he scrubbed his hands over his face. Choosing the greater good shouldn't feel like being kicked, but that was the sense I got from the bond when I peeked. "Fuck. I *really* want to say no. But the greater good is to strengthen the team so we can get this done." He glared up at a blank-faced Cade. "If either of you dare to abuse her gift, I'll kill you both. I don't care what's at stake."

Cade swallowed, more from the salivation of hunger than from fear of Troy. "I understand. I will honor this gift."

Lya just looked shocked.

"I'll get a cup or something. You are *not* biting her." Troy rose and stormed off.

"Shit," I muttered. I watched him go, unable to help my grimace. I would have to make this up to him somehow. This would have been a huge ask even if he wasn't still feeling off from my solo trip to Asheville. That he was fetching a cup rather than beheading a vampire only underscored my feeling that other elves thinking Troy was anywhere near feral was ridiculous.

Cade crouched. "He reacts like a master vampire who's been ordered to share his solidaire."

"Yeah. There's a reason for that," I said.

"Then the gift is even greater than I'd thought." He hesitated, and his next words sounded like they were being forced out of him. "I was ordered to share Lya once. Torsten wanted to humble me, after I'd promised Lya she was safe and mine."

This was a story I hadn't heard, and I appreciated the vulnerability in the sharing. "What happened?"

"I fought Aron and only won because Noah slipped Lya a knife and she had the courage to attack an eight-century moroi. I nearly lost her."

I glanced at Lya to find her scowling. Apparently, that was a very bad memory for them both. Despite that, she didn't stop him from telling the story.

She did say, "Is it strong? Your blood?"

"Maria got power drunk after a light feed. Before I grew into all four elements."

She paled. "Good to know."

Troy returned with a camp mug and the silver knife I usually kept in my nightstand and held them out with a grim look.

I rose and offered him my arm. "You decide how much."

"Not much at all," Cade said. "If she's that powerful, I don't want to be bound any more tightly than necessary to get this job done."

"Good," Troy muttered. He made a swift, shallow cut in the meat of my forearm, just deep enough to bleed, then applied pressure.

I hissed as blood started plinking into the cup. He wouldn't mean to hurt me, even if he was pissed, but usually he mixed an Aetheric pleasure sting in with bloodletting.

"Sorry, cariñamí." Shame flashed through the bond as he soothed the sting.

I nodded. *Pain for pain.*

He glanced at me but didn't deny that was fair.

When there were two swallows of blood in the cup and the wound was starting to close, he held the cup out to Cade and sealed his lips around the cut, taking his own swallow before pressing a cloth to it.

"Fuck," Cade said.

I looked up in time to see him drop to a knee and extend the cup to Lya with a shaking hand. She took it with trepidation and drank then dropped beside him, passing the cup back for him to finish.

"Fuuuck." This time Cade went all the way onto his ass and dropped his head between his knees as Lya dropped to her back, giggling uncontrollably. After a few shallow breaths, he looked up at Troy. "You drink this all the time?"

Troy licked his lips clean. "Often enough."

The unspoken, *And I'm still standing so don't try me*, was loud in his expression.

Shaking his head, Cade followed Lya. "Everything is spinning. No wonder Maria was able to jump to city master so early."

Harqil cleared their throat. "If you all are quite finished playing blood and power games, can we get on with the trial run?"

"Let's," Troy said grimly. "Etain!"

She jogged up. "Sir."

"Is their tent ready?"

"Yes, sir." She tilted her head in the direction of a double tent set apart from the cluster on one side of the boathouse, with three of the Ebon Guard stationed around it.

"Good. Get them into it. Don't let them out until Arden or I order it."

Etain saluted. "Yes, sir."

While that was being done, Troy looked down at me. I wasn't surprised in the least when he gripped my chin with one hand and kissed me firmly.

I allowed it. This had set him badly off-kilter. *I know that sucked for you. When this is all done, I'll submit to you or whatever will make it right. This might be for the good of the mission, but you come first.*

His severe expression cracked. *I want bites. And I will make you beg me for them.*

Deal. I swallowed, hard. A rush of heat swept through me. That was a particular game for him, if a rare one. One that usually went all night, taking me to the edge so many times that I'd forget my name and my pride, even when he didn't lean on Aether and used his considerable skill alone. *Whatever will make this right.*

He smiled darkly at the shift in my scent and the speeding of my heart. *Deal.*

Harqil was watching, bemusement on their features. "You two are the oddest pair I think I've ever seen. But whatever floats your boat or whatever the kids are saying these days. Are you putting the other two under, Troy?"

"Yes," he said. Something in the word made me think he was going to enjoy exerting his will over them, even if it was consenting. With a last kiss for me, he followed Cade and Lya, who were leaning on each other as they stumbled to their tent.

"I hope you know what you're doing," Harqil said, watching them.

"I never know what I'm doing, but it's worked out so far. What did you want to say for my ears only?"

They looked at me sharply. "Perceptive. I suppose you'll need that."

"Well?"

"You will need to make a choice. One that will pain you. I don't know when, and I don't know what. But when the time comes, it must be your choice alone."

"A choice," I said flatly.

"That dream you had was a warning."

I shuddered, recalling the dream of being surrounded by death and ruin, bones and dust, except where I stepped. "Of what happens if I choose wrong?"

Harqil nodded and sighed. "Sometimes I rather hate being the bearer of bad news."

"Only sometimes?"

They grinned. "Sometimes the recipient deserves it. But, I think, not you."

"That's actually comforting."

"It is?"

"Yeah." I wasn't about to explain how shitty I'd been feeling lately about the people I'd been forced to kill. Annoyingly, guilt kept trying to sneak in for killing Roman, even if he'd pushed me into it.

"Well then. Thank you for not shooting the messenger."

Troy was back before I could answer. "They're out. Let's get going."

He led the way inside the boathouse, to our cubicle.

As I laid back on my cot, anxiety roared to the fore. I'd never done this before. There was the one training session with Cyrus. Other than that, messing around with Troy in a Chaos sphere, sure. But he had the strength to match me and training of his own. Adding two more people was throwing me off. I'd never been responsible for so much as a Dreamwalker.

"You'll do fine." Troy's expression softened as he crouched next to my cot. "No matter what happens, I love you, and I have faith in you. Okay?"

"Okay," I whispered, relieved that he'd said it. I'd been dreading going to bed angry, so to speak. "I'm sorry about—"

"Don't be. I can't demand you act like a queen and then hold a grudge when that means I have to act like a king." He dropped a kiss on my forehead, and a tendril of Aether snaked through my mind as he did. "Sleep, my love."

I closed my eyes and rode Aether into unconsciousness, opening them to the windswept shore that'd become my default Chaos sphere. Cliffs rose in the distance, and a short, sandy beach edged into scrub ferns and then a mix of pine and cedar.

Harqil appeared beside me, feeling more real somehow than the rest of the dream. "Your king let the bond pull him under. You should be able to pull him in momentarily."

"It's that thread I'm looking for?" I didn't know how much of what Cyrus had taught me was correct. "Usually we only meet in a sphere when we sleep separately, and I just like, pull him in automatically."

"Can you sense the bond still?"

"Always."

That sent a sad smile flickering across Harqil's face before it twisted into something more amused. "Then you won't need to worry about finding the anchor thread. Just tug. Like the inverse of the feeling you get when a djinni is joining you."

I frowned, trying to conceptualize that.

"You're the anchor for all three of the souls you want to pull in here," Harqil said.

That helped, although I adapted it to be something more like the hand holding the string of a kite. Air metaphors always worked better for me.

I found Troy's "kite"—his soul, I guess?—and tugged.

Harqil grimaced. "Gently!"

With a pop, Troy was beside me.

He staggered before finding his footing. "That was...strange."

"Sorry," I said. "I don't think I've ever pulled you in intentionally before."

"No. But it's good we have this now." He inclined his head to Harqil, an acknowledgment.

"You two might be odd," they said, "but at least you're respectful. Bring the other two now, Arden."

That was harder than Troy. I searched but didn't find them. Maybe if I had the heart scarab as an anchor?

"Don't do that," Harqil said. "If something goes wrong, that's too much power in the hands of someone you do not want to give that power to. Focus."

With a frustrated sigh, I did as they said.

Searching...searching...there.

I found and tugged on another kite string, the same shadow-dark as Cade's eyes.

Cade popped in. "Fuck me sideways. Is this a dream?"

"It's a Chaos sphere," Troy said when I didn't answer, trying to stay focused on bringing Lya over.

She'd had less of my blood, but with Cade here, I had another thread to her. They were bound, like the sense I sometimes got of Maria and Noah but deeper somehow, despite Lya's relative youth.

And there. I tugged on a thread in a lighter, slightly luminous brown.

Lya arrived hollering. "What in the bloody hell— Oh. Oh, now this is truly bizarre. It feels like a dream but also not."

I shrugged. "Welcome to my Chaos sphere. A dream but not."

A sudden blast of heat washed over us, like an oven door opening in hell. Nothing of my making.

We whirled, and I caught Harqil's expression of utter dismay before the sky of my sphere was ripped open like tearing cloth.

"And welcome to the Duat," a deep, disembodied voice said. "A dream but not."

With an uncomfortable wrench, my Chaos sphere shattered.

Chapter 7

Everything went black before shifting to a desert of fine sand, although the heat remained, unlike any natural desert at night. I stood alone among tall pillars tortured by wind into the most unworldly shapes. The sky overhead was dark and scattered with stars under a new moon, and the air felt like it had never known moisture. A strange reddish hue tinged one horizon.

"Arden!" Troy shouted. Near-panic tinged the bond.

"Here! I'm here." I spun in the direction of his voice to see him emerge from behind one of the pillars. The bond settled—probably on both sides—when we laid eyes on each other. He was still in one piece. His gaze sweeping me head to toe said he was checking for the same.

"We're here too," Cade said from my right, coming around one pillar as Lya stalked from behind another to my left. "Wherever the hell 'here' is."

"The Duat?" I frowned, looking around. "But not what I was expecting. That's what the voice called it though."

"Voice?" Troy said. Alarm spiked again in the bond. "What voice?"

"Y'all didn't hear that? The one that said this was the Duat, a dream but not? Like it had been listening."

Everyone shook their heads.

I bit back a curse, then looked around. "Harqil?"

A fifth figure rose from the sand. Not Harqil. A dog of some kind, waist height and wiry, with red-streaked black fur, flat-topped squared ears, a thin tail with a split fork at the end, and far too many teeth. Saliva dripped from its jaws to hiss like acid when it hit the sand. When it threw back its head and howled like a jackal, I manifested Neith's gift out of reflex. The ivory hilt of the knife was solid against my palm as Troy fell into a ready position at my side. Cade and Lya moved to flank the dog, their empty hands up and fisted.

The dog made rasping grunts that almost sounded like chuckles, and a voice echoed in my head. *My lord Sutekh wishes a test, not a slaughter. At least for now. You will follow me.*

"Okay, please tell me y'all heard *that*, at least," I said.

They nodded and, as one, looked to me.

Right. Because I was in charge. It fell to me to figure out what in the nine hells to do about a telepathic dog-demon who rose out of the sand of a sphere or plane I'd had no hand in getting us to and had only the faintest idea how to get us home from. My head was spinning, as much from not having any idea what was going on as from being expected to lead this rodeo. We weren't supposed to be anywhere near the Duat yet; this was supposed to be our training session. The only conclusion I could reach was that something had gone terribly wrong.

I didn't dare ask where Harqil was. If Sutekh didn't know they were helping us, that would be giving up an advantage. They were a celestial, far more accustomed to these places and these power games than me. Which was why they were supposed to be here guiding us.

No. I stopped that thought in its tracks. There was no space for fear or imposter syndrome now. I had to step up. I had to be the guide.

"What are the terms?" I asked.

The creature growled, relenting when I stared it down. *The terms are simple. If you can make it past the Lake of Fire and into the House of Life, what you seek is yours. But this is your only opportunity. Fail, or leave before completing this test, and your prize is lost forever.*

My heart lifted but only for a moment. The prize in this House of Life wouldn't be magic. That would be too easy, and Harqil had said there would be four tests total. The gods' number of completion.

"And if we don't make it?" My tongue was drier than even the desert air could account for as fear stole the moisture in my mouth. My voice came out steady though.

The dog smiled, jaw dropping to show jagged teeth, and a red heat glowed within its black eyes. *Then your souls burn here, and your bodies burn in the real. You will be damned for eternity.* It tilted its head. *Both clever and foolish to bring so much of yourselves. Your strength is your weakness.*

Harqil hadn't said anything about that. About any of it. We were learning on the job, and I hated it.

"Those are the only terms?" I asked.

Would you like more?

I wanted to bargain. Safe passage or something. But from the hungry way the dog-creature looked at us, I had a feeling that would be a mistake. I tried leaning on the Sight, but it was a fickle talent, and nothing came. Here less than in the real, for sure.

Glancing at the others, I lifted my brows. "Last chance for someone to leave now."

"Staying," Troy said without taking his attention from the dog.

Lya and Cade exchanged a look then a small nod each.

"We'll stay," she said. "If we left and something happened, if we never got magic back..." She shook her head. "We'd be just as fucked."

Follow. The dog-demon turned and trotted off, heading for a high dune rising just past the end of the field of twisted stone pillars, in the direction of the red haze.

I wrestled my fear down and took the first step after it. Troy fell in behind my left shoulder—a bodyguard, not a king. In this strange place, I was the sole leader. Lya and Cade completed a diamond, with Lya behind my other shoulder and Cade taking the rear.

We followed the dog, stumbling in the powdery, sliding sand. When we reached the top of the dune, I saw why it remained so hot out despite it being night.

A literal fucking lake of lava stretched as far as the eye could see, burning with yellows and whites swirled in deeper, cooler reds. Smokeless fire danced atop it, and in the center rose a low island of stone. A stone building perched on the island, backlit by enormous braziers filled with yet more fire.

It looked like a moat surrounding a fortress of hell.

"Fuck," Troy muttered in elvish. "The Goddess is shitting on me." In the bond, he shut down almost entirely, disappearing to the place he went when he was being pushed to his limits and needed to retreat into the safety of emotional disconnection.

Harqil had said we'd have to face our worst nightmares. This much fire was definitely one of Troy's, and for him to betray a reaction, especially blasphemy, said he was already rattled.

Double fuck.

Behind me, Cade blew out a breath that sounded as shaky as Troy had felt in my head before he shut me out. Vampires were extremely flammable as a general rule, so that was two of our number effectively off their game, at least mentally.

The dog made the growling laugh again.

I would wish you good fortune, but I would rather eat you when you fail. A shame it's against the rules for me to curse you with ill fortune. With that, it faded into the sands again, one black or red grain at a time, dispersing until only the white grains of the desert remained.

Okay, so test one. A lake of fucking fire and two of my team shaky, if not out.

I twisted to glance at Lya.

Her slight nod surprised me. She was still with me, her earlier doubt buried under resolution. Even if it was just determination to protect Cade, that worked for me. I had a job to do.

Which started with figuring out how the hell to reach the island.

I didn't need to try making a round of the lake to know there would be no crossing. If it wasn't a lake, it was only a wider section of a river I couldn't see the end of. The more I focused on it, the more I was sure I could hear screams—especially when Troy's breathing through his nose became noticeable. When I made the mistake of listening, one of them sounded like him. He had to be able to hear them too. Or maybe something worse if Harqil was right about this place plucking ideas from our worst nightmares. This wasn't the Hell of the Christians, but it was *a* hell. Souls suffered here. Ours would join them if I didn't do this right.

And it had to be me. It hadn't escaped my notice that the first three trials Harqil had mentioned were explicitly elemental in nature: Fire, Water, and Earth. None of them elements I'd been born with. The challenge to the others was being here to begin with.

For me? There was another layer. I supposed I should be thankful it was Fire to start.

"Wait here," I said.

"Arden." Troy's voice was strained with a blend of different kinds of fear. Fear of this place and the fire below. Fear for me. But underneath it, dogged determination to keep me safe.

I turned to him, dropping the walls between us completely. "I will find us a safe way across. You stay here. Make sure nobody tries for me. Okay?"

"No." He stared down at me, the gold flecks in his gaze glowing with the backlight from the flames.

"Troy." I wrestled with what would get him to see I wasn't just trying to protect him this time. We didn't have time for his stubbornness or protectiveness right now. "It's me the gods want to test. You three are a bonus. They'll try for you if it will distract me, but the goal is to test *me*. Right?"

Another searching glance from him as Cade and Lya watched us with heavy gazes.

"Yes," Troy finally conceded.

"Weapons," Lya said. "You got a knife. Can you get us something?"

Good call. "What do you want?" I asked.

"A bloody big knife," she said. "Guns."

"Cutlass," Cade added.

I already knew what Troy would want—a copy of the enchanted meteoric steel longknife that had apparently once been my father's and was now his. Closing my eyes, I turned inward to focus. Conjuring things for other people was harder than just creating what I wanted for myself. Even changing things to be what I wanted them to be here was difficult, if I was thinking about it. Things happened of their own accord, if I felt strongly enough about it and didn't think too hard about how they happened.

I focused on the feeling of defense. Of strength. I wanted my people to be safe here, in this hostile, burning place. Safety. Defense. Protection. War.

Troy's grunt made me open my eyes. They all wore black body armor, like I'd seen on some of the Darkwatch. A cutlass stuck out of the sand in front of Cade. Lya had not only the fuck-off big knife she'd asked for but also a pair of pistols in holsters on each hip. Troy had a copy of his longknife from the real, as well as a copy of the other weapon I'd known him to carry regularly: his punchblade. I hadn't thought of all that specifically, so their own desires must have been in play.

I just prayed their fears weren't as well.

Troy sheathed the punchblade at its usual place at the small of his back but tightened his grip on the longknife.

"This is a start. But Arden..." His look said everything.

"I'll be careful."

Heedless of the other two, he threaded his fingers through my hair and tugged, forcing my head back and my gaze to his. "No unnecessary risks."

"I know."

Yeah, I knew. But I also knew I'd do what it took to get him home safely. Whatever had happened was not in any plan, and I was the only one who could do it.

I'd be damned, in every way possible, if I didn't.

Troy read that in my expression as much as the open bond. "Fuck. Go."

I reached up and pulled him down to kiss me. Foreboding washed over me, and what Harqil had said about making a choice hit me so hard tears prickled.

Oh no. Oh gods, please no. Not him.

I broke from Troy and hurriedly turned away to stalk down to the edge of the fiery lake, pulling up the wall, drawing the elements around me like armor, and praying he hadn't caught my flash of fear for him.

Heat blasted me, worse than it had when I brought the Verve building down. Winds—not natural, but whipped up by the fire—lashed me, tugging at my curls. I fisted my hands on my hips and glared at the flames and lava.

It would not take Troy from me. He'd die one day, as we all would. But I was determined that it wouldn't be by fire.

Not by one of his worst nightmares.

So how did I tame this?

I embraced Fire. It was eager to come to me. Almost too eager, dancing and leaping, twining through me almost as seductively as Troy's Aether could. I sent a tendril probing outward, exploring. The magic in Mixcoatl's arrow of lightning had been godly but still elemental in nature. Air and Fire, a hint of water.

This lake was...primordial, somehow. A blend of all four elements but with Fire topmost.

On impulse, I tried a poke of Chaos.

"Arden!"

Troy's shout pulled my eyes open. I turned to find the ridge of the dune we'd come over now lined with shapes dark against the starlit sky, some four-footed and vaguely canine, like the dog we'd met earlier, and others two-footed and still canine up top. All with the strange flat-topped ears. Interspersed among them were long, dark S-shapes. As I watched, some opened their mouths to release chilling screams and flame in equal measure.

Fuck.

I spun back to the lake. I didn't have time to think about this. If we didn't move *now*, we were going to be pushed into the burning lake by gods knew what celestial creatures with the high ground.

Passage. We needed passage. *Right now.*

Water wouldn't work. It would boil away to steam before it made a dent in cooling this lava. I needed Earth.

Drawing deep, I thrust my hands forward then lifted them. Resistance dragged at me like I was raising something physical rather than an ethereal bridge of obsidian. The smooth fireglass would be hard to walk across, but it was the easiest to conjure with all the sand around.

As soon as I was confident that it could be crossed, I took the first step, and found firm ground beneath my feet. "Troy!"

He didn't question me. Just came running, a vanguard of one charging across a battlefield.

Please don't take Troy, I prayed to whichever gods might be listening as Cade hustled past me next. *Please.*

"Let's go, Your Highness," Lya snapped.

I didn't even mind the little push she gave me to get me moving. Especially not when the obsidian bridge started melting into the fiery lake within moments of my leaving it.

"Go ahead of me," I said in a strangled whisper. "I'll hold it."

She hesitated then seemed to remember that Cade had already started the crossing and bolted.

As I backed away with increasing haste, some of the creatures launched themselves over the widening gap. I slashed at a half-man, half-dog with Neith's gift, catching it across the chest. It snagged my ankle as it fell, howling, and I went down.

The bridge wavered.

Arden!

Troy's shout in my head wrenched me back into focus. I couldn't lose him. I couldn't lose myself, lest he follow.

I stabbed at the nearest eye, and the creature fell away by reflex. Another used its burning body as a stepping stone, and I scrambled back, pulling the obsidian behind me as the glassy stone sliced my hand when I caught myself. The creature fell short, and then the gap was too wide for any more to cross.

Until the serpents slithered over the lava like copperheads moving over the dirt trails at Eno.

Fuck.

A slice of Water smothered the fireball the lead serpent spat at me in a burst of steam.

Pushing to my feet, I ran. At the other end, the other three waited—on a rocky ledge too thin for me to catch myself in my headlong sprint.

Before I could complete the thought that I was going to bounce off the wall and burn to death in a dream, Troy caught me, Cade anchoring him. Troy swung me against the wall and dragged me to him.

"I've got you," he growled.

Come hell or high water, he had me.

We'd crossed the Lake of Fire.

If only that was all we had to do.

Chapter 8

An arrow whistled past my ear and shattered against the rocky cliff face.

I pulled myself together and turned, just in time to see another arrow winging toward Lya. In the bare moment I had between thought and action, I threw a wall of Air between it and her.

She stared, not breathing, at the point a handbreadth from her left eye. "Good save. Thanks."

I spun the arrow around and threw it back. A barking cry in the distance said I'd hit something.

"Move!" Troy snarled.

Lya didn't argue. She scrambled up the narrow path leading to the gates to the House of Life. Cade followed her.

"Go!" I pushed Troy. There was no way I was going to squeeze past him on this ledge, and I didn't have time to widen it.

With a vicious elvish curse, he went. I followed, trying to shrug off the rotted-herb scent of terrified elf and the decayed ash scent of scared vampire. Trying to focus on shifting the shield of Air to cover us as more arrows flew and splitting my chord to throw serpents into the lake as they slithered up after us.

Somehow, we made it to the level ground at the top. I had a stitch in my side; even Darkwatch training hadn't prepared me for this.

"What now?" Cade asked as we stared up at the imposing stone pylons on either side of a yawning passage into the building.

"What we seek is inside," I said. "The dog said that if we make it into the House of Life, what we seek is ours. That has to be it."

"Sounds like a trap," Lya muttered.

A laugh echoed against the pillars of the courtyard, deep and booming. "That's because it is."

The being that materialized in front of us looked like the half-man, half-dog creatures we'd seen earlier but bigger. Where their gaze had been dead and black, this one had eyes like an eclipse: black pupils that were too big, with a thin, fiery ring of iris sparking on the outside. A memory flared and was gone as he whirled the same kind of *was* staff Neith used to carry and smiled with a vicious display of canid teeth.

My heart sank. "Sutekh."

At my side, Troy growled and tried to move between me and the god.

I thrust my arm out to block him, stiffening it when he tried to keep moving. "No. We reached the House of Life. We won."

"No?" The god mused over that then laughed. "No. The only 'no' is that you haven't reached the prize. You haven't won yet, and now it is you who shall be denied."

"Go!" I shouted as Sutekh raised his hands and all the creatures that'd attacked us before started rising from the sand in front of the temple. "Get inside!"

Lya and Cade bolted as I drew on Air and threw a gale to scatter the grains of sand trying to form into beings.

Sutekh laughed again, whirling his staff.

I had to trust that Lya and Cade would figure out what we needed to grab inside and get it. They were bounty hunters. I didn't know how old Cade was, but he was old enough to have learned a few tricks and Lya had survived both House Monteague under Keithia and the Raleigh coterie under Torsten. Screwing us here wouldn't help either of them get magic back.

Trust. I had to trust that our interests aligned, at least for now.

"Go with them," I snapped at Troy. Trust would come easier if the person I trusted most was overseeing them in whatever the fuck it was they needed to do in there.

"No." He spun the longknife and set himself at my back. "We'll buy them time together."

There was no time to argue because the dogs—the sha monsters?—on two legs and four, surged forward alongside fire-spitting serpents.

I struck with elemental force in a way that made every previous use of my magic trivial. Here, in this dream-but-not-a-dream, there was nothing I cared about destroying. There was nobody to censure or fear me. No politics to consider. I could unleash my full power.

So I did.

Tall columns crumbled and toppled. The sky split with the heat lightning I called to take down monstrous warriors swinging curved blades and seeking my throat with sharp teeth. The wind howled like a living beast, slicing through monsters and leaving them to disintegrate where they fell. Aether roared, and the scent of burnt marshmallow grew sickeningly thick as Troy cast spell after spell.

I should have been terrified, but all I felt was exhilaration at finally being able to exercise my magic to its fullest extent and having Troy doing the same at my back.

I had only just figured out that I should use the fucking power that came with being a Dreamwalker to try willing the creatures not to exist—and that I'd lost track of Troy—when the god outmaneuvered me.

"Little primordial," Sutekh's growling voice called.

I spun.

He had Troy by the throat, holding him up to dangle while Troy tried and failed to break the clasp. His longknife bit into the sand at an angle, out of both our reaches.

A jolt of fear hit me with a force that made my whole body hurt. "No! It's not him you want."

Sutekh smiled, all sharp teeth and wild discord. "You're right."

With a quick spin, his *was* staff became a spear. As I scrambled forward, he stabbed through Troy's body armor and into his stomach.

The bond closed down.

"No!" I pulled every element to me and crafted a ball of star-hot energy. But I couldn't throw it, or I'd hit Troy, who'd abandoned his efforts to break Sutekh's hold or get a breath and was trying to stop the spear from going farther through him.

"This was a good first round, primordial. Shame it'll cost you your mate." Sutekh dropped Troy to the hot sand and yanked the spear free.

I threw my primordial ball, but the god had already stepped through unreality to another plane. All around us, the attacking army blew away into motes of dust that stung my eyes.

It didn't matter.

"Troy!" I ran to him. Sand flew as I fell to my knees and put pressure on the wound.

I didn't hurt. Nothing hurt. I always hurt when he got hurt sparring, why didn't I—

He hadn't just shut down the bond. He was spending energy and focus to keep me out.

"Let me in," I insisted. My voice caught around the panic trying to wrestle its way out of me in a scream, and I forced it down. Swallowed hard and made myself take a breath.

"No." He squeezed his eyes shut, and his breathing shifted, becoming faster and shallower. "Get them home."

"But you—"

"Will die regardless. Nobody in real life...has magic."

I froze. This was a dream, but it was the kind of dream where things carried back to real life in physical form. His training regimen for me hadn't covered *what to do if he was dying* and I—

"Arden. Get them. Home."

Running footsteps forced me to shift around, one bloody hand raised, lightning crackling.

Cade and Lya skidded to a stop.

"Oh no," she whispered. "What—"

"Tell me you got it," I snapped.

"We got it. There was a key inside," Cade said. His expression was tight, both with bloodlust and like he was already seeing the end for Troy.

No. I wouldn't allow it.

But first I had to get these two home with the Goddess-damned prize Troy was dying for.

Closing my eyes, I focused hard on the boathouse and the tents outside it. My first attempt slipped, and I swore, dragging some of my attention away from the love of my life bleeding to death on the sands of some godsforsaken not-dream of an ancient underworld.

I found the space between the weft of the Duat and the weave of the dream, reached for the living Chaos in Lya and Cade and the bond of them and the heart scarab to me, and twisted, ejecting them, praying that Harqil had been right about me doing it correctly with Cyrus.

When I opened my eyes, they were gone.

Troy still lay under me, pale with all the blood staining the sand under the starlight. His eyes were closed.

"Wake up!" I slapped him.

He jerked and coughed blood. "Go home, Arden. Get out of here."

"Not without you!"

"Go. Home." A weak push of Aether accompanied it.

"You're trying to *compel* me? Fuck you." I'd save his fucking life if it killed me.

He was right that nobody on our plane could do it. Not without extensive surgery at a mundane hospital, a place we certainly could not go. Not in time. Not at all. This was a killing wound. A slow one. One that Troy had taught me, if I wanted to maximize pain, damage, and distress but didn't have to worry about noise or smell.

That fucking bastard Sutekh. I'd save Troy to spite him as well.

Cyrus had said that all things in a Dreamwalker's dreams were as real as the real. I'd once dispelled blood in a dream. Troy and I had fucked in a dream, and I'd woken up with traces of him in me and the pricks of bite marks on my neck. Just tonight, I'd summoned weapons and armor. I'd summoned an entire fucking obsidian bridge. Cut enemies to shreds and bits of dirt.

Which meant his body was probably dying in the real...but maybe I could fix him here. As a Dreamwalker.

If I was fast enough.

"Open the bond," I whispered.

"I won't—take you with me. Damn it, Arden—"

Fine. I pushed against the walls. I'd never done that before. Never tried to force him. But I would not. Fucking. Lose him.

Unable to resist me *and* keep his shit together, Troy let the walls keeping me out drop.

I hissed with the pain that hammered me and bent over him, dizzied by it. Fought to resist the reflex to grasp my own stomach and hold my insides together.

Follow the pain. I had to follow the pain. Pain was where it wasn't right. It needed to be *right* inside him. I plunged into my elemental senses, losing myself completely, and then fell past the bond, even deeper into him.

Nervous system. Blood. Bone. Breath. Fire, Water, Earth, and Air.

On my plane, they were just that. I was no healer. I never would be. Not there.

Here, I was a Dreamwalker. I could be whatever I needed to be if I had the courage and imagination to dream of it.

And right now, I needed to heal my bondmate.

Make this right, I told the elements. Troy's body knew what it needed to be. It was trying to be that; it just needed help. It needed power.

Like I had a long time ago, tracing the lattice of Earth and Fire in the lich lord's soul gem, I followed the paths of the elements within Troy. Drew on the surrounding landscape to feed more of whatever his system was calling for into him. Increased the oxygen carried by his blood cells. Knitted bone and flesh. Reconnected tissues. Eased the pain in screaming nerves.

I didn't manage all of it before I drained myself and dropped. But I did enough that he'd survive the shift back to the real.

I hoped. Prayed.

He didn't react when I pressed my bloody hand to his cheek to turn his head to face me. Just flopped like he was dead.

Shifting to press my forehead against his, I unraveled the dream of the Duat and focused on the boathouse.

My eyes flew open in the cubicle I'd laid down in. "Troy!"

Hands wrapped around my arms, dragging me to my feet. I groggily realized I'd fallen from my cot trying to get to him. Someone was pulling me away. I fought them, weakly, my hands sticky with Troy's blood. Then I opened myself to as much magic as I could hold, given the blood flowing from my nose.

I'd overdrawn myself. I didn't care. I had to know if Troy was alive.

"Arden. Stop!" Darius. It was Darius dragging me away.

I didn't care. "Let me go to him!"

"Stop. Haroun, get her other— Arden! Troy is alive, but you need to give Felip and Lachlan and Ophelia room to work if you want him to stay that way. Okay?"

Alive. Troy was alive. Not just in the dream of the Duat but here in the real.

I dropped so fast I took Haroun and Darius with me. We landed in a heap. The elves scrambled to get into crouched ready positions, hands out and ready to grab me again. But I stayed on my hands and knees, sick with pain and heartbreak and a power hangover as blood dripped from my nose to the concrete floor, staring at the canvas sheet making the door of the cubicle.

Darius looked at someone over my shoulder. "Get her some food. Whatever protein we have. And whatever booze is available." He refocused on me. "It's okay. Whatever happened on the mission, Troy will make it. I don't know how, but he started healing while Fi was triaging. Lya and Cade made it back in one piece with a key of some kind, which is in our custody. Everything is okay, my queen. Let's get you washed up, and then you can see him."

Modulated tones. The same ones Troy used.

Troy.

I staggered to my feet and lurched toward the cubicle.

"Goddess damn it." Darius's growl was no longer modulated. "Fi? How close are you to done with Troy?"

"Almost. Let her in. It might help both of them," the surgeon called back.

Darius caught me as I stumbled. As I had before, the same odd sense of safety trickled into me as I caught his scent.

"Brother-in-law," I mumbled. My brain wasn't quite working. Exhausted. I'd given everything in the fight against Sutekh's forces and then pushed to give even more to bring Troy back. I'd forgotten one of Troy's key lessons: to hold enough energy in reserve for the trip home. With the acknowledgment of how depleted I was, cuts and aches and windburn announced themselves all over my body, and my nose started bleeding even more from the magical overdraw, a steady pulsing throb rather than a few drops.

I swiped at it absently. It didn't matter. I had to get to Troy.

"Yeah," Darius was saying. "Brother-in-law. And Haroun is a cousin. Maybe don't make us regret it, my queen?"

I glanced at Haroun hovering on my other side, his expression pinched with worry. I couldn't make myself care. "Just let me see Troy."

With a sigh, Darius steadied me and got us back in the cubicle. Lachlan and Felip slipped out to make space for us, wiping their hands on red-stained towels. I dropped to my cot, Darius on one side, Haroun on the other.

Troy's cot and the floor underneath were drenched with blood. The scent of it hung heavy, chokingly thick with rosemary and sage under shit and iron and death.

Gut wound.

Killing wound.

His usually tawny skin was yellowed and pale. White bandages swathed his middle. But when I got past the memory and the smell to really look, he was breathing more deeply and evenly than he had been in the dream, despite the bruise staining his throat a blackened purple.

Fi glanced over her shoulder, like she was checking to make sure I'd stay put now that I could see Troy. "He'll live." Tension pinched every word. "I think. Somehow. I have no idea what happened, and without magic I'm only as good as a mundane."

"Sutekh stabbed him. The god. With a big fucking spear." My throat closed, and panic crept in at the edges. I paused and focused on breathing in time with Troy. "I healed him. As much as I could."

"*You* healed him?" Fi turned fully around this time. "An elemental with healing magic?"

"Only in a dream." I was shaking and couldn't stop, but I had to get this across before I crashed. They had to keep him alive if I went down. "I think. I—I read his systems. Nervous, cardiovascular, all that. Then fed his body my magic, fed it the elements. It was already trying to work. I just helped. I think." My head spun. "I hope."

What if I had made it worse?

"You fed him your magic. Raw elemental power. Goddess save us. I don't even know what the side effects of that are." She glanced at Darius. "Make sure Felip, Iago, and Allegra know that. I don't know what they can do without Aether to check, but who knows how this will play out."

Everything caught up with me, and I wavered and shifted to drop my head between my knees. "I feel like shit."

"Get her some water," Fi snapped.

A bottle appeared in the tunnel my vision had become, smelling of brandy rather than water.

I pushed it away, blinking fast to try clearing the nightmare of desert sands and flaming rivers of lava, of Troy pale in the shadow of a looming temple, from my memory. "Just put him next to me" was the last thing I managed to say aloud before passing out.

Chapter 9

S omeone was shaking me.

I was cold. Freezing. Like I had been in the brief flashes of memory I had right after Troy pulled me out of Jordan Lake.

"Arden!"

Troy? Was he okay? That was his voice. He must have been okay.

I tried to wake up. My mind managed it. Sort of. But my body was so, so cold, and whatever I was pressed against was as hot as the sun in the desert. My body tucked into a smaller ball without my say-so. I just wanted to be warm. And safe. And with my love. Even if he was dying. *Especially* if he was dying.

"What's wrong with her now?" Fi? Maybe? She sounded at wit's end.

"I'm draining her. She gave too much to heal me. Then when we came back, I must still have been too close to dead and needed more." A pause, followed by a frustrated sigh. "We don't just share vitality, Ophelia. We're bound all five ways. The connection might be obligatory symbiosis at this point. And if that leaves this room, I will personally kill whoever speaks of it."

That definitely sounded like Troy on a bad day.

"Goddess give me strength. I thought it was just sharing magic and energy, not your *lives*. None of us are trained for this, even if we had Aether. This is an entirely new branch of—"

"I know, Ophelia. Just help me—there."

A whimper built in my throat as I was separated from the warmth. That turned into a gasp as Aether flooded my nervous system along with a command: "Wake up."

I choked on my own breath and coughed as I finally came the rest of the way awake.

Troy's gaze met mine, sandstone and moss flecked with gold.

"Troy," I whispered. He was here, wherever here was, and he was alive. Or at least he seemed to be. That was good. That was real good.

He eased away when I reached for him with a shaking hand. "Not yet, cariñamí. I'm killing you slowly, touching you right now. You're hypothermic."

That didn't matter. What had happened? Oh. "Your stomach."

I watched, my vision hazy and wavering, as he first gingerly prodded his belly then frowned and unwrapped the bandages, grunting to find completely unmarked skin. Even the burns and scars of elvish writing that'd been over that part of his abdomen were gone, as well as whatever stitching the healers would have had to do when I couldn't finish the job.

Troy stared then brushed his fingers over smooth skin. "The fuck?"

Exhausted relief combined with the minor amusement of hearing him swear to pull a weak chuckle from me. "It worked."

"I thought I was— Arden, what did you *do?*"

I fixed him with as steady a look as I could manage, given I wasn't entirely sure I was really awake. "I decided I'm not living without you *or* dying with you. And fuck the gods for thinking they had a say in it."

A crinkling noise announced someone arriving with one of those silvery hypothermia blankets. I was sick of the damn things but, at Troy's stern look, allowed Darius to tuck it around me. In the process, I absently noticed someone had cleaned the blood from my hands, even getting under the fingernails. I must've been down hard to miss that.

Troy dropped all the way down to sit cross-legged on the floor and lean against the cot, his fingers coming within a hair's breadth of touching mine. "We got what we needed?"

"Thanks to you, and Lya and Cade, yes."

Darius and Troy went on alert, their attention snapping to the doorway where Cade now stood, hands up.

"And thanks to you," Cade said wryly, "we all made it back in one piece. Fuck me but I thought Callista was frightening. You're a whole new level of terrifying."

Everyone shivered as my power signature whipped through the room at the mention of my dead former guardian's name and lightning crackled over me.

"I'm not like her," I said.

"Oh, I know. That bitch would have taken the key and let me or Lya, or both of us, hang." The vampire tipped his head at Troy. "He would have been an acceptable loss. Instead, you nearly killed yourself and your mate defending our exit and getting us all back in one piece."

"What's your point?" I asked.

"I'm sorry we doubted you," he said, ignoring the glares the elves were giving him. "And I'm grateful for the continued gift of Lya's life. That arrow would have skewered her if you hadn't pulled your attention to a shield. It makes us both more inclined to trust you."

Mollified, I shifted deeper into the blankets. If Troy wasn't still dying and I didn't have to fight, I wanted to sleep.

With a last nod, practically a bow, Cade ghosted away almost as silently as an elf would have. The shadows of his escorts on the other side of the canvas door flap followed him.

Darius brought both hands around to his front, making me think he had weapons at his back. "I don't love having vampires here," he said in a low voice, "but that one might be okay."

"He loves his solidaire above all," Haroun murmured from the corner. "As long as she's preserved, his loyalty is too."

"He's a vagabond master vampire who's strong enough to have taken a royal-blooded half-elf as a solidaire and keep her sane," Darius replied. "Not to mention Maria's people saying he had a particularly nasty reputation a few hundred years ago. How—"

"Just trust me." Haroun's interruption and sharp tone were unusual, but he sounded as tired as I felt.

I wondered if he'd been on watch in the corner for however long it'd been since I'd passed out.

"Haroun, go get some sleep," I said. Every word slurred despite my effort to make my tongue work properly. "All of you get some rest."

"If our queen is well enough not to attack an elfess, I'm sending Thana to sit with you two," Darius said with a glance at Troy.

At Troy's nod, everyone got out of our cubicle. He shifted to his cot—a new one, apparently, given it and the floor were no longer soaked in blood—and dropped onto his side.

"I want to tell you not to do that again," he said.

I snorted and closed my eyes in a long blink before opening them again, wanting to see his face. "You like that someone cares about you that much."

"No. I *love* that someone cares about me that much." He flushed and looked away. "Even if I shouldn't. Arden, the mission—"

"Fuck that. You matter to me. You've laid your life down for me more times than anyone reasonable. And I don't get to find out what family means for me if you're dead."

That brought his gaze back to mine, hot and hopeful.

A knock on the outer wall of the cubicle announced Thana. "Am I interrupting?"

I let myself gauge my reaction to her before responding. "You're fine."

She ducked in, keeping her distance. "I'll just stay over here all the same, ma'am."

Tiredness rolled over me again. "'Kay."

I crashed looking at Troy's face, leaving the bond wide open so he'd know how much he was loved...and that he'd better not write himself off as dead again.

△▽△▽

I didn't think it was possible to feel worse than I had when I'd laid down, but the next time I opened my eyes, a bloody nose was by far the least of my worries. I might have used my magic at full strength in a dream, but dreams didn't have limits the way the real world did. For all I knew, I'd pushed well beyond what should have been possible. Sutekh's dog had said something about having more strength but also greater weakness.

From the extraordinary pain of my entire physical and auratic existence, I was discovering the fullness of that comment.

Troy startled awake before I could organize my brain to find the words to ask for help. He reached for me reflexively, only to jerk away when I flinched and groaned with pain when his aura crossed mine.

Everything. *Hurt.*

Not just the usual hurts either.

I hurt where Troy had been hurt. Like the cost of healing him so completely was to transfer the pain of dying to myself.

Even as I whimpered and writhed with the effort of swallowing curses, I accepted the price. I'd broken the laws of magic and nature by healing Troy. Better this than him dead. I'd do it again a hundred times.

The misery lapping against me in the bond said he didn't feel the same though.

"Arden, what can I do?" he asked. "What do you need?"

I couldn't answer despite the concern, almost fear, in his voice. Another wave of pain wracked me.

"Shit. Thana, can you get her up?"

"Gonna need help if she does what she did when you got back, my king."

Troy swore again and shouted for Darius.

My vision went white with pain, and shakes hit, making my teeth clatter. I didn't know how they got me up and outside, but it helped to be in clean, fresh air and under an open sky.

"Get the fire lit," Troy said as they laid me on the ground.

I forced my eyes open when my legs jerked. Darius had my shoes off and was rolling my pant legs up, a worried expression pinching his features. Troy stood over us, arms crossed like it was the only thing stopping him from touching me again.

"Put her feet in the lake," he said.

Darius gave him an odd look but did as he said.

"Anchor, Arden," Troy said. When I gritted my teeth and shook my head, already afraid of more pain, he said, "Try it. Please. You don't have to work magic, just open up."

Open up. I could do that.

I let go of the fingernail of control I was maintaining and dropped my shields completely, bringing him to a knee as my natural inclination to connect to the elements flooded free and overwhelmed him when it crashed through the walls in the bond. Thana and Darius wobbled at the force of my power signature, hissing in surprise.

But Troy was right. It helped.

I sank into it, grateful for the easing of pain. As the sun rose and tinted the sky, the earth under me, the lake at my feet, the breeze caressing my face, and the heat of the fire in the kettle behind us seeped into me, slowly healing my metaphysical overreach. Lachlan came and checked me over medically, frowning hard, then retreated.

Everyone retreated, except Troy. He sat cross-legged at my side, his longknife over his knees, glaring at something internal.

"Hey," I whispered when the last, smallest tremors finally stopped.

He blinked and looked down, expression easing somewhat. "You feel better in the bond."

"I feel better overall." I tilted my head back and glanced at the sun, now peeking over the trees. "That took a frighteningly long time though."

"I'm sorry. If I—"

"No. No ifs. We were up against a god. I made my choice. I won't lose you. End of story."

Troy looked like he wanted to argue but swallowed it down at my steady look. He lifted a hand then hesitated. I reached up and took it, towing it down to my chest and holding it over my heart. Both of us blew out heavy breaths of relief. It would have been unbearable if we couldn't touch each other anymore.

"Definitely good?" he asked.

In answer, I pushed myself slowly up to a seated position, feet still in the lake, and leaned into his hand.

Troy turned and hollered, "Get some food going," before shifting to rest the longknife beside us, sit at my back, and take my weight despite my damp clothes. His arms snaked around me, and he tucked his head over my shoulder.

That was better. That was much better.

I leaned just enough to give him a quick kiss before speaking to the dark thoughts I could sense trying to pull him under. "You are worth saving, Troy. You will always be my greater good."

"I want to argue."

"But?"

He sighed and pushed the thoughts away, a mental wrench in the bond. "But I would rather honor your action and the price you paid for it. Thank you. For my life and bringing me back. Again. I—"

He cut off and twisted as footsteps approached, one hand falling to his longknife.

"Just me." Darius sat beside us and glared out over the lake, uncharacteristically moody. "We need to talk."

"Talk then," Troy said.

His brother-cousin glanced at us sideways before returning his attention to the water. "We can't do that again. Everyone is shook. They're hiding it well, but..."

Troy sighed. "It's not good for morale or for operational efficiency to have both of us go down, and go down that hard, when we're the only two with magic."

"And with no children," Darius added bluntly. "Alli as heir might be enough to keep external Houses at bay, but she spends too much time in Raleigh. Dad's right on this one, as much as I hate to say it."

Troy bristled. "So you want me to send my queen into danger with two strangers at her back?"

"Send one of us in your place, brother. But you have to stay here on the next mission."

"Do I get a say?" I asked with forced lightness.

Darius grimaced and seemed to pull himself inward. "Apologies, my queen."

"It's fine," I said. "I'm guessing you drew the short straw out of you, Thana, Pascale, Etain, and Haroun to speak up." Those five and Allegra were the closest to me and Troy these days, and the most attuned to our moods and preferences.

Another, guiltier grimace. "Something like that."

I hooked my hand over Troy's arm and squeezed. *He's not wrong. I hate it but...*

I know, he sent back.

"Maybe the callstone would let you watch?" I said aloud.

"Worth a try." Troy squeezed me in a hug. "Would Harqil know?"

"They'd better." Now that I was feeling better, anger trickled to the fore. "Yesterday was supposed to have been a training session, not an ambush. I have a few damn questions."

Troy released me, reluctance clear in the slowness of his movements, although he stood quickly enough and caught me under the elbow when I wavered on my feet. "Take it easy."

"I should be telling you that." I slipped my arm around his waist, as much for comfort as for support, and hollered with a push of Chaos behind it. "Harqil!"

Nothing.

"Harqil, I know you can hear me. If you make me track you down, you will regret it."

The burst of magic to my left, on the other side of Troy, had us shifting to face that direction as the celestial manifested.

"After that showing, I actually believe it," they said.

The elves in the clearing spread out, expressions hard and hands on weapons like they weren't sure if there was going to be a fight. Even Lya and Cade stumbled out of their tent, looking haggard but ready to fight empty-handed.

I wasn't inclined to call any of them off. "What the fuck was that, and where in the nine hells were you?"

They halted just outside my reach and stood with arms crossed. "I...miscalculated."

"*Miscalculated?*" My voice was rough with the effort not to shout our business to all of Jordan Lake. "Miscalculating is what happens when you fuck up the tip on a meal out. Troy nearly *died.*"

"Yes," Harqil said, an odd expression on their face as they eyed Troy. "And yet you both survived your choice. Tyche had odds of a hundred thousand to one on that outcome, and Shai offered worse. You managed to win against Fortune and shift Fate, little primordial."

The usual mocking note was gone from their voice, but somehow that just pissed me off more.

I disentangled myself from Troy, letting fury drive my steps and keep me upright as I got in their face. "No more games. I want to speak to my patron."

"Bold of you to assume you have one."

"Don't fuck with me, Harqil. If the hunters assigned me a patron, the tricksters must have as well. They have two options. They can come here on their own. Or I can rip a hole in space and time and drag them here."

Harqil looked at me intensely. "You think to order the gods?"

"Y'all could have just minded your own thrice-damned business, but you had to come through and fuck up mine. So yes. Yes, I damn well do think to order the gods, and may the primordial darkness take all of you if you think this is gonna be just another trickster game."

They stared at me, their wide eyes and stiff expression my first clue that something had happened. The utter silence in the clearing was the second. Troy's carefully leashed blend of awe, fear, and protectiveness in the bond was the third.

Whatever it was, everyone could get with the fucking program because I still had shit to say. I lifted a finger to point in Harqil's face and froze.

I was glowing.

Sort of.

As had happened at the Wild Hunt, the primordial darkness I'd just invoked wreathed me, shot through with light. The physical manifestation of the two halves of Aether, trapped within me.

That kind of thing didn't just happen though, no matter how pissed I got. I should know; Troy knew exactly how to get under my skin, and I regularly got in his face when we sparred at home.

I rocked back, cocked a hip with more energy and attitude than I could really spare just now, crossed my arms, and lifted my chin. "Where are they?"

"Where is who?" Harqil asked.

I lifted a hand and waggled my fingers in their face. "Whichever god is present to draw out this little special effect. The last time this happened, I was giving the gods of the hunt a beating."

That was a slight exaggeration, but the tricksters enjoyed a little embellishment.

For a few tense heartbeats, Harqil stood as they were. Then, with a sigh, they reached into a pocket of their baggy trousers and extended their hand.

A tiny spider sat in it. One of those flamboyant-looking jumping spiders, in a rainbow of colors overlaid on black like an oil slick. It raised its two forelimbs, either in greeting or in threat. Harqil tipped their hand, and by the time the spider hit the ground, it was already the size of a golden retriever—and growing larger fast.

My stomach soured. This has to be Anansi, but all the tricksters were shapeshifters or at least not as defined in shape and form as the rest of us. For him to appear like this had to be either to scare me or remind me of the massive scorpion that'd accompanied Orion at the Wild Hunt.

Whichever it was, I didn't like it, and I could only hope I hadn't just let my temper lead me into a big mistake.

Chapter 10

"**Y**ou are one of the most delightfully chaotic people I've ever encountered." Anansi's voice was a deep, booming rumble. A stray thought had me wondering how the fuck a giant spider could talk, but his next words made me refocus. "That doesn't mean I will excuse insolence."

I bowed my head and kept my eyes down. "My lord."

Laughter like thunder burst forth. "Chaotic. Demanding my presence and then bowing your head."

"I could trap you here instead," I snapped.

That didn't get me the further laughter I was expecting, but instead, a considering *hmmm*.

What the hell did that mean? I would have expected a god to laugh at or belittle me. Not consider.

That was heavy.

On impulse, I pushed forward, leaning on the thread common to many trickster tales: rules that had to be outsmarted or leveraged with great skill. It wasn't about fairness but rather cleverness and daring. Some might have said the tricksters were cowards, given they weren't all warriors, but in a twist of insight, I saw that they fought in their own way—and wanted that recognized. "All games have rules, my lord. Either I was given the wrong rules, or I was lied to."

Another long pause, accompanied by the tapping of a spindly leg against the ground. "You were not lied to."

"Then Sutekh isn't playing by the rules," I said.

"He's playing by *his* rules."

That was clear as mud. I studied the spider, as though that would help me divine what the hell was going on. Eight unblinking eyes stared back, and I fought the reflexive shiver. Creepy as fuck.

"I suppose I should play by my own rules then," I said slowly.

"And what rules are those?"

I reached for all four elements, pushing past the headache that throbbed to the fore, and created a ball of primordial Chaos. "That the greater good is the only thing between me and a fresh start for this plane and every other one. Shall we see if the Duat can stand against a primordial elemental? Or the Old City? The Crossroads? The In-Between? Shall I unravel the gods' plane and force y'all here among mortals permanently? That worked for y'all before, when more of the world held faith equal to science, but will it work now?"

Harqil's sharp intake of breath was the only betrayal that I might have touched a nerve.

"You're not strong enough. If you could do it, you would have done it in this last trial," Anansi said.

"I'll be honest, on account of you being my patron." The words sprang from me before I could properly consider them, but I leaned into the flow of Chaos streaming through me and kept going. "I didn't realize I could. And I wouldn't be willing to risk the lives of my people being dissolved along with the plane." I let go of the primordial sphere before it could give me another nosebleed. "But if there's no other way to win? If I see a rampage on the other planes as the only way to defeat Sutekh, restore magic, and keep my people safe? Why wouldn't I try?"

"You wouldn't dare." Anansi leaned forward into my space, like he could will me away from that path. "The cost—"

"I don't need to care about the cost when I can preserve everyone and everything dear to me." I said that with far more confidence than I felt, but the weight of the spider's attention shifted to Troy before returning to me. I forced a smile. "My people happen to like things the way they are here—when they have magic. If y'all want to set us a test to recover it in order to restore balance in an agreement that nobody here remembers making, fine. It's horseshit, but I'll step up." I moved closer, overriding my desire to get the fuck away from the massive spider and its curved fangs. "But since I have stepped up, I expect *you*, all of you tricksters, to abide by the rules and terms you've set. And to force Sutekh to abide as well."

Anansi's spider mandibles quivered. Rage? A contained desire to eat me? Something else? Hard to tell on an arachnid. Finally, he said, "Very well. Not from fear but as a boon."

"Of course." I inclined my head respectfully, letting him have this out. I didn't want to know what a giant spider-shaped god would do if he felt like he had to save face, and like Darius had said, my people were already shook. Watching this was probably making it worse, regardless of whether they could see Anansi or if it looked like I was talking to thin air. "Thank you, lord patron."

More laughter. "I like her, Harqil. Serve her better than you have to date when you return."

Without warning, Anansi bounded into the air to block out the rising sun—and became tiny again, landing neatly in Harqil's extended palm.

They inclined their head. "I'll be back later today to discuss our next steps. For now, I recommend some planning around the Waters of the Drowned."

With a twist of magic, Harqil created a portal, stepped through, and closed it behind them.

I had no idea if Anansi really needed Harqil to carry him across the planes or if they just had business together elsewhere. Hopefully they were going to talk to the other gods.

With a shudder, I hugged myself, locking my knees so I wouldn't drop again out of exhaustion. Even without a clear explanation of what the Waters of the Drowned would entail, I had to assume it had to do with water, as the Lake of Fire had with fire. Water was, and always had been, my weakest element. Waters of the Drowned? All I could think about was drowning in the lake behind me—the moment when I'd opened my eyes and found a submerged boneyard of Leith Sequoyah's victims.

Troy's tentative touch at the small of my back brought my eyes open and my head up with a gasp.

He was looking at me like he'd never seen me before. "Are you well, cariñamí?"

I shuddered as I released the ghosts of the past and blinked back tears of relief that he'd still speak to me with terms of endearment. "I'm fine. Thank you. Another nap would probably do me good though."

"Okay." His hand rubbed along my spine, soothing me. "Outside still?"

"Yeah." I couldn't bear going back into the boathouse again so soon. Not when I was already this shaky.

Ignoring the stares of the thoroughly rattled elves still on defensive against a god that was no longer present—or maybe against me now—I dropped to sit cross-legged on the ground. Thoughts of the last evening and this encounter galloped through my head to the beat of the thundering headache.

Breathe. You've got this. Troy knelt beside me, resting a grounding hand on the back of my neck and sending a little tendril of Aether through me to ease the headache.

I couldn't formulate a response. My mind kept spinning on water. I thought Troy knew where I'd gone, but I didn't want to drag either of us deeper into that morass by confirming it.

Etain joined us. Not sitting, just standing and looking uncomfortable for the first time since she and Haroun got into my car to face the mundanes attacking Hope's shop downtown.

"What?" I asked when all she did was fidget.

She glanced at Troy and cleared his throat. "Um. Was all that meant to reassure everyone, ma'am?"

"How could it not be reassuring that I backtalk a god?" I snarled sarcastically.

Of course I had, once again, been *too much* for everyone around me. Except Troy. I reached for him in the bond, and he reached back with a soothing wave.

"Arden," he murmured. The bond brought his understanding of my mood, blended all the same with a push to remember that the gods might be normal for me but not for anyone else.

Even if they weren't normal for me. Not really. Not after just a couple of years.

"Sorry, Etain," I said. "But I'm going to need everyone to step up. This is what it will take not only to get magic back but to get it back before the mundanes can strike—or haul me in for questioning."

She hissed. "Iago briefed me on the subpoena. All right. I'll do what I can to settle everyone and swap out those who look too shaky."

"Rotate them to watching the remaining Sons," Troy said. "That's a clear and familiar mission and one that we do need to ensure stays on track. The Lyon elves can be rotated in here."

"You're counting on them wanting to protect Desmarais?" she asked.

"They did come into hostile territory to reclaim her before." He massaged my neck. "Worth a try."

"Yes, sir. Leave it with me." She was gone before I could add anything, which was a relief—both for not having to make more decisions right now and because she usually looked to me if both Troy and I were present. I needed to be sure she'd work directly with Troy if required, even if the Ebon Guard were technically mine.

"Chair?" Troy asked. "Food will be out in a minute."

I kind of wanted to stay sitting on the ground, but I pushed to my feet and dragged myself to sit in one of the chairs around the fire kettle, smothering the damn thing to put out the fire as I dropped again. We'd all had quite enough of that.

Relief swept through the bond as Troy joined me and tilted his head back to the sky.

Lya and Cade drifted over from their tent, hesitating until I flapped a hand at them to sit down. Their guards posted up nearby, keeping a wary eye on them but not interfering.

"Didn't think we'd see you alive again, cousin, let alone so damn perky," Lya said. The usual sharp edge was gone though, replaced by a little tiredness and a lot of wariness. She was a bounty hunter. She had to know what a death blow looked and smelled like.

"Not the first time Arden's stolen me back from death," Troy said in bland tones. "Probably won't—"

"Shut up," I snapped. "Don't jinx it."

He reached over to take my hand and squeeze it. "What can we do for you two?"

"That celestial—Harqil?—said something about the Waters of the Drowned." Cade traced a sinuous line in the dirt with a stick. "I don't know what exactly that means. But if we assume the next test is water, bringing someone who's naturally good with water could help."

I arched an eyebrow. "Let me guess. You just happen to have someone in mind?"

"Yes. We could try Mami Wata."

Lya grimaced, even as I gripped the arms of my chair. I knew that name. It belonged to the fae I needed to visit to secure the North Carolina coast and the last third of my home territory.

"How do you know Mami Wata?" I asked.

"She's an old friend, from back when I was a privateer," Cade said. "I don't know the full extent of her magic, but in some places, she's called the Mother of Waters."

A privateer. So, a pirate. I was super curious how a vampire survived with all the sun on the open ocean, but more pertinent to the current situation, a fae known as the Mother of Waters couldn't hurt if our guess was right and the next trial was around water, my weakest element.

"The fae don't do anything for free," Troy said. "Besides which, she won't have magic."

"On this plane," Cade agreed. "But the fae aren't of this plane. Who's to say she couldn't regain it elsewhere? I was able to sense Lya again in that dream place. Weakly, but she was with me again."

Lya nodded. "Same."

Good to know that they'd be more connected—and therefore more dangerous—in the Duat.

I forced myself to sit up as the scent of sausage and toast reached me. "That still leaves payment."

"I have thoughts on that, if you're open to hearing them," Cade said.

I waited until Troy, Lya, and I had taken camp plates piled with sausage links and toast from two of the Ebon Guard before saying, "Go on then."

"Callista never formally recognized Mami Wata's claim over the eastern shoreline. There was bad blood there."

Troy frowned and swallowed a mouthful of food. "Callista was a celestial. She could have destroyed a fae. No?"

Cade tipped his head side to side as he watched Lya inhale her food, looking grimly pleased that she was eating. "Some fae are stronger than others. Older than others. Even on this plane. I was, for better or worse, quite familiar with both parties. There was a reason Callista didn't push on Mami Wata, and it wasn't distance."

Lya spoke around a mouthful of food. "She keeps a low profile, but she's strong as fuck. That close to the water? I wouldn't want to try her as a bounty, and I've brought in a kelpie on my own." She cut a playful glance at Cade. "Tried for him too."

That sounded like an interesting story but not one for right now. A sea fae strong enough to give Callista pause could definitely be useful on a water mission. "So, she'll want what?" I asked. "Sovereign control of the coastline?"

"Likely. That and the return of magic would be a good start for bargaining," Cade said.

I glanced at Troy before putting my attention on getting food into me so it'd look like I was thinking it over. *Thoughts?*

I don't like sending you to another plane with an unknown water fae. He stabbed at his food and ate another mouthful. *That said, I don't know how many other options we have. I don't want to pull elves from defense if we can help it.*

Not to mention they were shaky enough as it was, without seeing what went on in the dreams. *Hard stops?*

I suppose you'll have to share blood with her as well. A disgruntled tinge flared and was smothered. *As long as she doesn't try to usurp you as Arbiter or take elven properties, I'll consider it not my business.*

Okay.

To my surprise, my plate was clean. Guess I'd been eating as quickly as Lya. "Can you contact her?"

"Sure, if you give me my cell phone back," Cade said. "It'll be faster if a flight can be arranged from Ocracoke as well."

"Done," I said.

"Excellent. Let me make sure she's amenable before you go to the trouble."

As I arranged second plates of breakfast for me, Troy, and Lya and the return of Cade's phone, Troy waved Darius over and wandered a short distance away to confer. We were in the grey area of managing demesne concerns with elven resources, so that fell to me.

Etain looked grim as she handed Cade's phone back. I didn't say anything as she hovered while Cade dialed.

"Hello, beautiful one," he said. "How are you? Minus the magical situation, of course."

I barely kept my brows from shooting off my face as I glanced at Lya, but she appeared unbothered. Not what I was expecting, given the jealous relationship one often found between master vampires and solidaires. She glanced at Troy then shifted over to take his seat, much to Etain's consternation.

"Like I said. I went toe-to-toe with her and count myself lucky to have left alive. She gave him blood, and I found him only a little less drunk than he was on yours," Lya said softly.

I blinked. "That strong?"

Lya's eyes narrowed. "You didn't know?"

Internally, I kicked myself. I hadn't meant to reveal that I was that ignorant of my own territory. At the same time, I kept saying I wasn't Callista. That couldn't just be when I didn't want to kill someone.

I hoped I wasn't digging a hole for myself as I said, "I've been locking down the Dominion demesne, the southern Carolinas, and the Blue Ridge Mountain territory."

"All that in a few months. Okay." Lya looked reasonably impressed, and I relaxed.

Cade had moved on from pleasantries when I refocused on him.

The vampire's brows lifted. "How fortuitous. A moment, my friend." He tapped, presumably to mute the call. "Arbiter, she's already on her way. The sirens are suffering."

Lya shuddered.

I barely managed to keep my reaction locked down, wondering what was going on there even as I was surprised to hear we had sirens in North Carolina. I didn't know much about that particular type of sea fae, but they were Mediterranean or Nilotic, if I knew anything. Not quite suited for the cold snaps we got in the Carolinas. Then again, what did I really know? If it was a bargaining chip, I could deal with being ignorant this once. "If Mami Wata consents to keeping the peace, she can join us here and make free use of the lake, if that will help anything."

Cade glanced at the body of water, taking in its size, then nodded. "I'm sure it will." He returned to the call and relayed what I'd said, adding, "I'll send the location momentarily. See you soon, dear one. Don't say I never gave you anything of value."

The call ended with a burst of feminine laughter that even I could hear.

The vampire looked guiltily at Lya. "You know how she—"

"I know." Lya rose and, rather than returning to her seat, dropped into Cade's lap. "I'm not the bloody idiot I was, and I'm not going to bollox up this shot at getting magic back. Do what you need to do."

He kissed her like he was trying to consume her as Troy resumed his seat. From the herby-earthy scent of blood, one of Cade's fangs had knicked Lya. Or maybe she'd done it on purpose. I could see myself doing that for Troy, giving him a taste to ground him in an uncertain situation.

Nice to know we're not the only ones who get lost in each other, I sent.

A little thrill came back to me through the bond, as we both accepted a second plate of food from the returning Ebon Guards. Not at what Cade and Lya were doing but at the idea of doing the same with me soon.

I just hoped we could wrap up this second trial quickly. Between the ongoing hormonal imbalance remaining from my separation from Troy and the added pressure of missing magic and the gods' interference, we didn't have time to waste.

And that was without the subpoena hanging over our heads.

Chapter 11

For all that I'd been expecting a political clusterfuck, Mami Wata was much less interested in me than she was in Jordan Lake when she arrived. I would have been insulted, but I knew what it was to need your element.

We'd barely completed the stiff formalities of meat and mead when she said, "Arbiter, I—"

"The lake is yours," I said, anticipating her request from her fixed gaze.

She murmured appreciatively as she passed, making a beeline for the water.

I shivered as she hit the shoreline and kept walking, her movement in her human form becoming sinuous, snake-like even, once the water grew deep enough. Her long braids streamed behind her as she cut through the water, rolling to make her loose clothes float around her, her dark skin flashing under the afternoon sun.

Cade watched from the shadows of the boathouse, Lya tucked under his arm. Mami Wata hadn't even acknowledged them. The drive from the Outer Banks was a good six hours, and from what Cade had said, Mami Wata hadn't left the coast since she'd washed up on, or been brought to, these shores some centuries ago. I tended to get cranky after twelve to eighteen hours away from land I'd claimed, but I was a primordial elemental. I had multiple elements I could draw on. A powerful water fae ripped away from a centuries-long anchor? I counted myself lucky that she was a fae and therefore prized courtesy and hospitality.

"I still don't like this," Troy muttered from behind me. His arms slipped around my waist and tugged me back against him. "I know you have to find allies. I know I can't go with you. But you, two bounty hunters, and their alpha fae friend?"

I stroked my fingers along his arm. He was right. This wasn't ideal.

The thought I had about Anansi, and about shape and form, came back to me. "What if I called on Mason?"

"The werewolf?"

"Yeah. The one I spared because he was honest."

Troy considered. "I don't like sending you with a werewolf either."

Anger simmered in the bond, swirled with something else I couldn't quite name. Something threatening.

I shivered, wondering how much longer the leftover ache from our extended separation was going to eat at him. "But?"

"But he might already be in town, given your invitation, and it's unlikely those three are connected with the wolves."

Personally, I had my doubts. Maria had mentioned receiving word about Evangeline's location via a vagabond right before the Wild Hunt. I didn't know how many vampire vagabonds there were, but here was one with an extensive history in my demesne already. The Sight and my ring weren't warning me off, so I decided to go with a leap of faith: if Cade was indeed that vagabond, he'd been on my side—or at least, not on Callista's—then, and he was here now. Bringing that to Troy's attention wouldn't fix anything, and I knew he had things he didn't raise with me. Fair was fair. Even if it made me feel a little twisty inside.

I pushed the feeling aside, telling myself this was for the greater good of myself, Troy, and Otherside. "Let me see if he's in town. There's something about 'shape and form' that keeps coming to mind. You saw Mami Wata's teeth, right?"

"Python," Troy said. "This isn't her only form. Just the one she's trapped in."

I hadn't known the species, but the way she was still cutting through the water, sinuously smooth, confirmed it. "Right."

When I didn't keep talking, Troy nipped my neck. "What?"

"The Darkwatch trials. The first one, the physical contest that I took, isn't the same as the second."

He hesitated.

"I know you can't tell me the details, but come on. Omar already said I'll never make full Darkwatch rank, whatever that looks like."

Troy's voice held reluctance as he confirmed it. "The second trial is very different from the first, yes. You're thinking this second trickster trial is also different."

"Yup. The first trial was physical. Could we hold off monsters and, gods damn him, Sutekh." I cut off as Troy's arms went dangerously tight around me and sent a dart of apology through the bond. He relaxed enough for me to continue. "So, if the first trial is physical, what's the second?"

Troy was silent for a minute. The subtle way he shifted against my back I'd call a squirm in anyone else, but he stilled quickly. "Darkwatch training tests physical, mental, and magical capability. In that order. That's why all half-elves wash out at the last stage. It's intended that they not make it, since they can't wield the full strength of Aether. But we still get well-trained, relatively disposable, soldiers for the Houses. Omar's words, not mine."

I went cold at that, remembering Etain and Haroun's prideful defiance as they insisted they could help. The Darkwatch sequence didn't mean the gods would follow the same pattern; the elves did things in threes, while the gods preferred four as their number of completion. The weres had a different sacred number entirely, something based off divisions of the moon's cycle. That being said, what if the pattern was similar? If I was thinking about Water, I was thinking yeah, literal water, but also blood and the other fluids of a body. When I'd killed the Sons of Seth, I'd corrupted the waters of their bodies. Filled their lungs with fluid, slowed their blood, unbalanced the salts in their veins.

But that didn't mean the gods would be thinking the same way. Water was also frequently associated with emotion. That wasn't on the Darkwatch training schedule—which, in my mind, only made it more likely that this next trial would draw on it. The trickster gods had been watching for months, I was certain. They'd have seen the preparations I made for the first Darkwatch trial. They'd be aware of the depth of my connection to the elves, despite my being an elemental.

No. Something about this would be emotional. Something the gods thought would drag me down.

Fuck that. I was stronger than that. I had to be.

Mami Wata cut toward shore, forcing my attention to the present.

As she pulled herself from the water, liquid streamed from her in rivulets, and the fae seemed to collect a measure of power. The loss of magic had impacted everyone except the elementals and Troy, but something had definitely shifted here.

She laid eyes on me and hissed. "When was the last time you cleansed yourself, girl?"

I stiffened. "Girl?"

"In learning and in age. To be as powerful as you are and ignorant of what you carry. Girl." When I didn't respond, she shook her head and spoke flatly. "You were Callista's weapon, weren't you."

This time, I was thrown. I squeezed Troy's arm to stop him from intervening as I said, "Weapon?"

Mami Wata pressed her lips together and shot Cade a dirty look. "You bring me to one of that bitch's children and expect me to do what?"

"She's good people," Cade said in a low voice, a tone for confiding and making deals. "Put herself and her bondmate on the line for all of us already. Real dead, Mami Wata. Not just reputation or wealth."

"Is that so?" The flat question was accompanied by an even flatter look. "You would vouch in blood?"

Cade studied me. Then Lya. Then said, "I would."

Mami Wata narrowed her eyes at him. "I've known you for half a millennia, Cade. If you fuck me now—"

"I wouldn't. Not when a blood oath would cost me Lya. You know what she means to me."

I barely managed to keep a straight face as the two of them stared at each other. Cade was five hundred years old? Maria's age? With Mami Wata being at least that much.

Troy whispered in my mind. *Didn't get a chance to fill you in on that. Maria says our...compatriot...wasn't just a privateer. He was once a city master known as the Butcher of the Bayou. Apparently, he has history with the New York coterie as well.*

Fantastic. Not only a vagabond master vampire but also one who'd made what sounded like a bloody reputation for himself.

Now do you see why I'm concerned? Troy sent. Then, grudgingly, *Even if Maria vouches for him.*

I squeezed his arm again to acknowledge that yes, he was right to worry. *I can handle them.*

I know. It's the only reason I'm accepting your choice here.

The staring match between Mami Wata and Cade ended with the water fae's sudden ruthless smile. It would have frightened me if I hadn't already been through so much, with so much more on the line.

"Good," she said, flashing recurved python teeth. "Swear it then."

Despite his declaration, Cade still looked to his solidaire first.

"We need magic back," she said. "Whatever the cost. Even me." She turned to glare at me. "But if you cost me Cade, I will hunt you to the ends of the earth, primordial elemental or not. Arbiter."

I wanted to snarl at them. I wasn't Callista.

But they didn't know that. I had to earn their trust if I wanted to be a protector and not a dictator.

"I understand. I welcome your input. All of you," I said. Even managed to make it sound at least a little civil. I had no idea what this cleansing Mami Wata had asked about was, but if we were dealing with the Duat and the undead, something told me I might want to pay attention.

Cade's lips thinned. Then he grabbed Lya's wrist and brought her arm to his mouth, his gaze locked on Mami Wata. "I swear on my blood and that of my solidaire that my trust in Arbiter Arden Finch Solari is genuine and in good faith, based on past actions."

Lya squeezed her eyes shut, pain tightening her features, as Cade bit deep into the meat of her forearm, then held it out to Mami Wata. For a bounty hunter of her experience to show that much reaction—especially given it seemed genuine—meant this was real and an even bigger deal than I'd thought, even with Mami Wata being possibly the strongest fae in the territory. She had to have some kind of elemental connection to magic, not just fae illusion.

Mami Wata looked at me after taking two swallows of blood from Lya. "And you? What do you risk forfeiting in this bargain?"

Before I could even consider, Troy circled in front of me, drawing and offering his longknife in a smooth motion. "My queen," he said. "I stand as forfeit."

What are you doing? I snapped in the bond.

What needs to be done for the greater good. I told you. Elves cannot be without magic.

Anger made my movements sharp as I clasped the wrist he offered and accepted his longknife. "My bondmate may offer himself in forfeit, but it's me who will pay," I snarled, unable to keep an even tone. I pressed the longknife against Troy's wrist, a symbolic gesture with no blood, then made a swift slice into my own forearm rather than offer his blood. "Take this as surety. If you dare, Mami Wata."

The fae's pupils blew to vampire black as the ozone and woodsmoke scent of my blood burst into the clearing, and her lips peeled away from bright white teeth. "I accept."

"Arden—"

I squeezed Troy's wrist and sent a heavy pulse through the bond to shut him up. He might be willing to sacrifice himself for me, but all of this was my doing, my path, my decision. Fuck the gods and every circle of hell if he thought he was going to take the fall.

Besides, it'd taken blood to tie the two bounty hunters to me. Offering Mami Wata my blood would tie her to all of us, just like it'd tied first Troy, then Lya and Cade, to me. She might think she was getting the better end of the deal, but she was only getting what I was willing to give. If I could make it look like I was making a sacrifice? So much the better.

A trick worthy of a trickster.

Mami Wata's mouth closed around the wound I'd opened. I'd expected her to bite down, like Troy did, but she respected the offering and her relative status and only took two swallows.

"Bloody nine hells," she muttered when she pulled away. She wavered, looking determined to stay upright.

Then she dropped to her knees, fingers digging into the earth.

Cade's expression said that he'd fully expected her to go all in on my blood and come out wanting. Lya's said that she'd expected as much and was pleased with the fae's reaction. Good to know the people around me already assumed I was the stronger power. That might nip some problems in the bud.

I spoke the words that came to me as Troy shifted to stand at my side, pushing past the simmering anger coming from his side of the bond. "By this blood, we are bound. Service for service, honor for honor, on this plane and all others."

"We are bound." Mami Wata acknowledged the obligation as she forced herself back to her feet with an obvious effort, but reluctance bit into each word. Magic snapped between us, like a rubber band against skin, and she jumped.

Whatever she'd expected in coming west to the Triangle, it wasn't this.

Suited me just fine. It was about time I got the upper hand in something, no matter how small.

"What's this about a cleansing?" I asked as I held my arm out to Troy. He gripped it and took a swallow of blood for himself as the wound closed.

The fae's lips thinned as she watched, waiting in vain for him to drop like she had. "Something not of this plane is clinging to you. If you've already crossed to the Duat once, it's likely that."

"How can you see it without your magic?" Troy asked suspiciously.

"It's less of a seeing and more of a feeling," Mami Wata replied. Reluctance and distrust made the words slow. "I have an affinity for both the dead and for Water. Elemental Water, not just fae illusion."

That made me think of the succubus who'd killed Torsten at the vampire Reveal. Dominique had been fae too—technically. She'd also had magic that went beyond run-of-the-mill fae glamour, leaning more toward something demonic.

Troy's face went dangerously blank. "How convenient."

She snorted. "Hardly. I'm one of less than a half dozen like me remaining." Her gaze hardened, and her tone flattened. "The elves didn't always care whether it was really an elemental they'd caught or something close enough. The other fae were jealous of our greater magic and rarely bothered to help."

I glanced between Troy and Cade. Troy's expression didn't change; he was clearly not going to take responsibility for the fae, at all and maybe especially because he was pissed that another person had been allowed to drink from me. Cade's features had sharpened, like this was news to him.

Mami Wata refocused on me. "Are we going to have a problem?"

"As long as everyone's blood stays in their own veins unless they're enthusiastically consenting otherwise, I don't see why we should." I forced a smile. "Besides, we are oathsworn now."

"We are," she said grimly. "And may the gods save us both."

△▽△▽

We ended up back at my house for the cleansing. The wereleopards and jaguars who'd taken up my offer of safe territory in exchange for guardianship stood watch outside. Troy, still cranky and resentful, posted up in the bathroom doorway, crowding the space. His reluctance to leave me alone with the fae further soured the bond, but neither of us had much choice.

Fortunately, I had everything she needed for whatever this ritual was. The smoke of frankincense and myrrh swirled, almost chokingly thick, filling my nose. Candles flickered on every surface. Mami Wata sprinkled salt and herbs into the bath, murmuring the whole time, then gestured sharply for me to get in.

I stripped, a little shy of doing so in front of a stranger even if she seemed completely unimpressed, then stepped in gingerly and gasped as I sank down. It wasn't like the baths I made for myself. Even with magic gone from the world, this one made me tingle.

"Good. Your elemental magic is enough to fuel the spell," Mami Wata said. Then she began chanting in a language I couldn't identify.

The words curled into my ears. Mesmerized me. I sank deeper into the water, drawn down.

Panic seized me, and I sat back up. I'd drowned once already.

Troy burst forward. "Arden!"

"You're fine, girl." The fae gave him a savagely mocking grin before turning back to me. "Tell him."

It took me a minute. Mami Wata just sat and watched though. Didn't push me or hurry me. Just sat with a knowledge as deep as the ocean and patience as inexorable as a tide.

I swallowed and settled myself. "I'm fine. Just surprised."

Troy's threatening growl made Mami Wata arch an eyebrow, but she said nothing as he settled back against the doorframe.

She turned back to me, rolling her eyes. "Under the water."

"And then?" I could read something of the spell here, kind of like I could sense the shape of djinn or elf magic even if I wouldn't work it. For all my and Troy's suspicions, it didn't seem malicious. I just wanted her to say it out loud.

"And then whatever you've brought back should slough off." She paused, looking like she wanted to hold something back, then sighed and continued. "It probably won't be comfortable. Like shedding a skin. Worse if it's been a while since you've cleansed yourself."

I looked over her shoulder at Troy.

If she fucks you, she's dead, he sent, gripping the hilt of his longknife where it hung at his hip. *I'd love the excuse.*

That, I had no doubt about.

Mami Wata seemed to think the same. "If our oath doesn't convince you, then know that I need magic back, quickly, or I will lose the sirens. I can't have that. I won't. That's why I broke centuries of precedence and custom, and risked your wrath, to drive so far to this gods-cursed inland territory."

Shivering, I took a breath and let myself slip under the surface.

My skin tightened abruptly, and I shot back upright. As my head cleared the surface, it felt like it was being peeled from me whole. I shrieked and froze.

"All the way up, girl," Mami Wata said. As Troy surged forward again, she added, "Don't touch her yet."

Troy froze, looking torn as I sat, panting, trying to gather the courage to stand the rest of the way. With a shudder and a heave of nausea, I made it slowly to my feet.

"Drain the water," she said.

Following Mami Wata's instruction meant I had to move. It hurt like a bitch to wrench my leg through water that seemed to burn and sting then nudge the plug out with a toe. As the water drained, I braced one hand on the wall and tangled the other in the shower curtain to stay upright, gritting my teeth to try locking in the groan of pain building deep in my throat as the feeling of having my skin and aura dragged from me worsened.

When the water was gone, the fae said, "Now shower. Ice cold."

I shot her a look.

"I'm not being sadistic, although I won't deny this is a spectacle."

Reluctantly, I flipped the cold water on, hissing as the prickles of magic intensified then shattered. The relief was so strong I dropped to a knee before pushing myself back upright. I would not show weakness in front of this fae. Not when I needed her respect and allegiance to get through this next trial.

"Still feel the magic?" she asked.

"Just cold," I said tightly, trying not to let my teeth chatter.

"Then you're done."

I switched the water off and stumbled out of the tub into the towel Troy held waiting. He wrapped it, and himself, tightly around me.

"That was a nasty one," Mami Wata said. When I shifted so that I could see her face, she wore an odd expression, equal parts amused by my pain but also mildly impressed. "Whose death did you swallow in the Duat, Arbiter?"

"Mine," Troy said. His voice betrayed an unusual amount of emotion, clearly shaken. His heart pounded against my ear as he rubbed my back. In the mirror backing the sink, his glare at the fae could have etched glass. "Sutekh dealt me a death blow in the Duat. She healed it there."

Mami Wata hissed. "No wonder. A disturbance that great to the natural order would carry a heavy price several times over. If you'd gone back to the Duat carrying that, it might well have damned you. As it is, I'm surprised you're still conscious."

The horrified expression that flickered over Troy's face was openly on mine. Sutekh hadn't just meant to deprive me of my bondmate. He'd meant to fuck my chances in the next trial as well.

"Trust me now?" Mami Wata asked.

"Getting there," I said.

"Good. Because I'll want payment for that."

Of course she would. "Magic back first. Then we'll talk."

"Agreed."

As Troy hugged me tighter, I prayed I hadn't just made a deal that'd cost more than I was willing to pay. Getting magic back and getting people to owe me for it, thus securing my safety, was the goal. Owing a debt to a powerful water fae was something I'd rather avoid.

But hey. This was turning out to be an all-or-nothing kind of mission. Maybe I should just pray me and mine made it through whole.

Chapter 12

B y the time we finished checking in with Terrence and Ximena and made it back to the boathouse, the Ebon Guard had located and brought Mason to join us. The werewolf was sitting on the end of the pier when I went looking for him, dangling his feet in the water despite the chill of spring.

He heard me coming and twisted, rising as he spotted me only to kneel and tilt his head to show his throat in a wolfish display of deference. "Arbiter."

"Rise and be welcome, Mason," I said. "No need for formalities, although I will need you to do a little blood magic."

"Blood magic." The werewolf blinked up at me, brown eyes big under an untidy fall of dark blond hair. Then he swallowed hard and nodded. "Yes, ma'am."

I hadn't realized I'd scared him that bad in Asheville. "You know I don't blame you for the Volkovs' maneuvering, right?"

"That's...good to hear, ma'am."

Biting back a sigh, I bounced the heart scarab in my palm. "Well. Come with me."

Harqil was waiting when I returned to the fire kettle and its cluster of chairs.

"Oh good," I said. "Glad you're taking Anansi's command seriously."

"Don't be a bitch," they said. Their surly expression matched their tone.

"Y'all could have mentioned the fucking auratic death magic trap or whatever the hell it was." Yeah, I was pretty pissed about that.

A wince flashed across Harqil's face before they gave me a flat look. "Not my area of expertise. But thank you for confirming that Sutekh has been spending more time with the death gods than we'd previously thought."

I stared, wanting to dig into that, but we had too much to do. That and I definitely didn't want the attention of the deaths. The hunters and the tricksters were bad enough.

After repeating the binding to the heart scarab with Mami Wata and Mason and giving Mason a single swallow of my blood that had him laid out flat on the ground giggling, I retreated to the woods. There were reports to catch up on, especially with the mundane protests, but I needed a damn minute to myself in the bare hour or so we had before we attempted the second trial. Troy was still a raging bundle of irritation and jealousy in the back of my head, made worse by the guilt underlying it, and as much as I wanted to comfort and reassure him, he wasn't the only one who rejected company when it was sorely needed.

I made my way to the edge of the bluff I'd launched myself off of during my Darkwatch trial a couple months ago, kicking my heels against the cliff face and slumping back against my palms as I dropped my shields and opened myself to the elements.

I didn't like any of this. I hated giving blood to people who weren't Troy. I was terrified of losing him or of being lost in the Duat myself. Of missing a slim chance to get another of the keys needed to bring back magic. But if I wasn't going to be Callista, it couldn't just be about the noble and easy things. It had to be for the gritty, damaging, hard things as well.

Didn't mean I had to like it.

A swirl of the air molecules behind me said someone was there, and the slight scuff of movement said they weren't a full elf.

"What?" I snapped, not turning around.

"Just keeping watch, ma'am," Haroun said quietly. From the shift of my sense of him, he dropped into a crouch. "King Troy didn't want you to be alone."

Shit. I started to rise. I wasn't the only one who needed care.

"He said to stay here. He's going for a run to the south."

Twisting, I found Haroun crouched, as I'd thought, his back to a tall, wide beech tree.

"You can sit with me, you know." I hadn't meant that to sound as grouchy as it did, but he didn't seem to take offense. When he had moved to lean against a tree beside me, I asked, "Is it true we're family?"

Haroun wrinkled his nose. "I suppose, although Darius was stretching it a bit. My father was a Monteague from the lesser branch, so Troy, Allegra, and Darius are technically cousins. Just distant ones I never saw before joining the Ebon Guard." He paused, glancing at me, then turned his attention back to the woods, scanning for trouble. "My mom was a human with latent psychic abilities. Had no idea what my father was, why she was so frighteningly attracted to him, or why he abandoned us. I only found out after one of Omar Monteague's sweeps found me at magical puberty."

That was more than I'd learned about him in the last year and some, and oddly, it settled me. "Thanks for sharing that."

He shrugged. "It's a little selfish, if I'm honest."

"Why's that?"

Another glance at me, gauging my mood maybe. "I never had much strength with Aether, ma'am. Not like a high-blood, at least. But now that it's gone..." He shuddered. "I really, *really* want it back. I guess maybe I'm hoping sharing some of my story will, I don't know, give you some kind of strength if you need it. I—" A wince accompanied a hesitation. "You take care of your people. Especially the people you know. It seems like it's because you know what it means to us that you do."

Emotions tripped through me, a bewildering swirl I couldn't begin to make sense of, although I had to smother a small spike of resentment. I'd help no matter what, but that didn't mean this was some kind of manipulation on Haroun's part. He was right. Having a concrete example of what I was fighting for, who I was protecting, had always spurred me on. Troy might be my greater good, but I couldn't lose sight of everyone else or I'd lose myself.

I took a deep breath. "You're not wrong."

A small smile curled his lips. "Good to know it's not just Mom's psychic ability that helps me read people then."

A snorted laugh burst from me before I could stop it. I didn't even know why it was funny. Maybe it was just nice to feel like Haroun was a friend. My friends among the faction leaders had been testing me lately, and I'd been starting to question the whole idea. Maybe Haroun couldn't be a friend, given the differences in our power and roles, but I could calm down and appreciate the courage it took to offer that much information about yourself to someone with the power to fuck your life up.

"I'll get magic back, Haroun."

"I know you will, ma'am. Never doubted it. Especially now that you've got scary water fae and master-level vampire vagabonds on your side."

I snorted another laugh then twisted in the opposite direction as the bond told me Troy was approaching.

Haroun scented the breeze blowing our way and straightened. "I'll be just over there."

He was out of sight but still nearby when Troy melted out of the trees, dropping his shadows as he approached. His expression tightened as he remembered what'd happened the last time we'd been at this spot, but he didn't comment on it.

I rose and went to him. We looked at each other for a few heartbeats, reading scent, posture, bond. He cracked first, opening his arms to me.

I folded myself into him, pressing up on my toes to take in the scent at the corner of his jaw. "I might have had to give them my blood, but you still have my heart and soul," I whispered. "You still have *me*. Always and forever."

"I know. And like I said, I can't say the elves can't be without magic and then be pissed that you're doing everything you can to secure the allies who can help ensure we get it back."

"That doesn't mean you're not allowed to have feelings about the method. Multiple things can be true, remember?"

Some of the tension still pulling him tight eased. "Thank you. I needed to hear that."

"Your feelings are valid. Mine are too. We're both gonna have to make tough choices to get through this, but like you said before, we work because we balance and we're going in the same direction. I have faith in us."

Troy squeezed me tighter. "I do too."

We stayed like that, grounding ourselves in each other, finding calm. I'd do whatever it took to see this through, and so would he.

The sun sank toward the lake, and reluctantly, I pulled away. "Wish we had time for a fuck."

Despite the heavy mood, he shut his eyes and shook his head, huffing a laugh. "Cariñamí, if we survive this, I promise we'll take a week off, during which I will tie you to the bed and ravish you for the entire period."

He might have been joking, but heat flared in me. "Really?"

That sobered him up quick. "You want that?"

I thought about being at his mercy for a full week. Prickles of desire raced over me, and my breath caught. Troy's skill and undivided attention, like that? When he was worked up about having to share my blood? He'd be merciless. "Yes. I told you I'd repay the blood sharing. I'll give myself to you, whatever you want, however you want."

The darkness of the predator slid into his gaze. "That's a dangerous promise to make."

"All the same." I leaned in to nip his throat. "It's not just you who needs to offer themself in this relationship."

He tilted his head back as the bond raged with hastily suppressed desire. "You're a gift, Arden. You don't even know how much." His gaze locked on mine as he brought his head back down. "Let's get this mission done. The sooner we're done, the sooner I can carry out every last desire I have. Or at least a few of them."

We both knew that wasn't his only motivation, but it was the one that fed both our feelings at the moment.

Nervous tension hovered over the camp when we returned, although a few people looked relieved to see us with our fingers interlaced. I made a note to myself that it made people anxious to see me and Troy at odds and resolved to be better about keeping our shit private, difficult as that might be in the current situation.

"Let's go," I hollered.

Everyone scrambled to whatever places they were supposed to be holding while we were gone. Cade, Lya, Mami Wata, and Mason stayed where they were around the fire kettle, their attention staying on me and Troy as we approached.

"Orders?" Mason asked.

"Troy will put all of you under, in your own tents," I said. "Then me. I'll pull all of you into a Chaos sphere, and we'll transfer into the Duat."

"And pray there's no fucking monsters this go-round," Lya muttered.

"That too," I said as lightly as I could. "Let's get to it."

△▽△▽

I managed to punch through to the Duat almost too easily this time.

The lowering sun painted everything a brilliant shade of orange. The bottle-green river stretched wide, far wider than the Eno, and from the cold, sluggish strength of the current I sensed, far deeper as well. On either bank, a thin, sandy beach gave way to a short spread of reeds and brush then a brief stand of palms before rising to sharp bluffs.

It was nowhere near as extreme as the Lake of Fire. It seemed peaceful, even. A place to smoke shisha, debate philosophy, and watch the sun race across the sky as boats cut up- and downriver.

This time, the temple—the House of Life—was on the opposite shore, perched on a high rise of rock and sand. It seemed simple enough. All we had to do was cross the river. The lava lake had been way more intimidating.

Something told me crossing a river was not all that we'd have to do.

"Let's go," I said when I'd taken in all I could from where we'd entered the Duat.

Without a word, everyone followed me down the dune and through the reeds to the riverbank.

A boat floated at the stone dock. And by "a boat," I meant some kind of historical-looking thing, shallow, with a high, curved line forward and aft. It was made of wood that smelled of werewolves, a bright cedar, with benches set along its length and oars laid across them. It was carved with lines of hieroglyphics and had two painted eyes on the front, one pupil black, the other white, both outlined in red. Even as I noticed them, the eyes shifted to look at me before returning their attention to the river and scanning this way and that, aimed down at the water more than anywhere else.

That wasn't freaky at all.

A shift in the breeze pulled my attention upward. Human-headed birds soared, their feathers shining in the last rays of the sun. When I reached with my primordial senses, I didn't encounter the expected composition of the elements.

I found metal. And Chaos. Then something else I couldn't identify, something far more ephemeral.

On instinct, I reached for my chest, where my father's pendant had hung my entire life. It was around Troy's neck as a callstone now in the real, but here in the dream, it sprang to life under my grasping fingers. My sense of Troy deepened with it.

"Are you okay, cariñamí?"

I jumped, not having expected to hear him in my head at all, let alone so clearly. Bless Harqil for this little gift.

"I'm fine," I answered via the callstone, like I would with one of the djinn. "We're fine. I just...can you see them?" I focused on the birds that weren't birds overhead and tried to push my sense of them to him.

Troy hissed. "They're souls."

"What? How can you—"

"I don't know. But the auratic magic my dad showed me? It was based on the ephemeral part of a being. A soul. It's the same feeling I'm getting from those...birds."

Fuck me sideways. It made sense, given we were in the Duat. An afterlife, a purgatory, a liminal space. But somehow, I hadn't really thought we'd see flying souls.

"Arbiter?" Lya called.

I pushed past my hesitation and clambered over the boat railing without looking back. The other four had no choice but to follow, given I was both the Arbiter and their ticket home.

Mami Water peered over the side once she was aboard and hissed. "There are souls below as well as above."

Startled, I crossed to stand at her side and looked where she was looking.

I needn't have bothered being so precise. Everything beneath us was water, and below that was a flashback to my nightmares: an endless, wavering field of the damned, both as they had appeared when I was drowning, and as they had been added to by my own actions.

I swallowed hard and controlled my breathing with an effort, drawing on Troy's Darkwatch lessons. Just as the Lake of Fire had been literal, so too were the Waters of the Drowned. Which meant they were both above and below. Or maybe it was only the damned below and another category above.

What did that have to do with the current trial?

A suspicion took root, based on the still-searching eyes of the boat: I'd manipulated the elements and fought off monsters before, but I didn't have the faintest idea how to work with souls. Was it even ethical to fight them? Could they be reborn again someday? My stomach clenched as I tried to square those ideas with my sense of right and wrong.

I didn't have time for it. If this trial was anything like the last, there'd be a deadline in the form of some kind of danger.

"I don't see anything," Mason said, interrupting my thoughts.

Lya peered over as well. "Me neither."

"Trust me. There's something down there," I said. "Cast off. Let's get this the fuck over with." All these souls were giving me the creeps.

Cade moved to obey without question, expertly handling the pole to get us away from the bank and instructing the rest of us on the use of the oars. Something about his mien shifted in the process, becoming even more confident and somehow more dangerous.

"He was a pirate, back in the day," Lya whispered from the bench opposite mine, probably in response to the frown pinching my brows.

Ah. Right, he'd mentioned being a privateer. That'd do it. Fate's hand at work again, to send me a pirate and a water fae for this.

The river seemed to stretch forever as we pulled at the oars, and forever again, never quite getting closer. Every time I thought of trying something to speed us across the river with the elements, the Sight kicked me in the opposite direction. The oars themselves caught and dragged as we pulled, until Mason's stuck hard.

"The fuck?" he muttered.

I got a real bad feeling as he stood and leaned over, plunging a hand in to wrench something off his oar.

"Mason, no!" I shouted.

Too late.

His oar bench was right in front of mine, and a full-body shudder wracked me as one of the dead souls in the water reached up and grabbed his wrist.

Chapter 13

I hauled on Air and caught Mason quicker than a thought.

Mami Wata snarled spells in a deeper, more guttural tone than she had in my bathroom. To my surprise, magic responded to her, flaring and pricking over me.

It wasn't enough. A second hand, pale brown and rotting, shot from the water and wrapped Mason's forearm. A third soul burst head and shoulders from the depths of the river, its scalp patchy and eyes white, to grab Mason's shirt and roar, showing broken teeth.

They kept pulling as Mason screamed, and the battle with my grip of Air threatened to tear the werewolf in half.

The godblade. I closed my eyes and fought to block out Mason's panicked shouts and prayers to summon it. Neith's gift settled in my grip, the cool, carved ivory hilt smooth and heavy. I lunged, stabbing the undead that'd risen fully from the water.

It screamed and fell away—but in leaning over the water, I'd exposed myself.

The water roiled as more souls erupted from the riverbed, tangled their fingers in my clothes and hair, and dragged me under.

I'd thought I was more or less over my drowning.

I'd been wrong.

Taking a little bath or dipping into the ocean was nothing compared to being hauled over the side of a boat and into cold water again by drowned souls.

Something wrapped around my ankles and pulled me deeper, like the concrete block Troy had tied around my ankles once upon a time.

All the power in the world couldn't save you if you didn't have the presence of mind to use it, and as water filled my lungs at my attempt to scream, I lost any sense or training I had. There was only colder than ice and darker than death...and the wrathful souls around me. Leith's graveyard come to life. Screaming without words. Reaching with rotting fingers and jagged nails to scratch and tear at my skin.

One of my worst nightmares personified.

Suddenly, they recoiled.

A monstrous snake lashed in their midst, snapping with wicked teeth. As it circled me, creating a barrier, more hands grabbed my clothes at the shoulders.

I fought them. The dead wouldn't get me. They couldn't have me. Even if that meant the river was going to get me first.

As strength and consciousness fled, I weakened.

With a heave from above, I broke the surface. The hull of the boat scraped against me, and with a thud, I landed on the deck.

The jostling triggered a coughing fit, which turned into vomiting up water. When I could breathe again, I rolled to my back—only to find the enormous snake slithering over the rail of the boat and coiling on the deck.

"Apep?" I gasped, trying and failing to scramble away. "I killed—"

The python became a beautiful Black woman in a ripple of transformation from head to toe, who slapped me the moment she had hands. "Wake up!"

That pissed me off, which helped me shake off the lingering terror. "I'm awake!"

Her little smile said she'd just wanted the excuse to slap me. "Good."

I pushed myself upright and let it go. If she'd been the snake, she'd saved my life. "Glad you're here," I said to acknowledge it without thanking her. I wasn't that addled or foolish. "Mason?"

"Here." His voice was roughened by fear, and he was shaking, eyes darting at the railings while Lya stood behind him.

Cade was at the front of the boat, scanning the water for more threats, pole in hand.

Forcing myself to my bench, I leaned over my knees and coughed, scrubbing my hands over my face, still trying to clear the images of the dead from Jordan Lake and those here from my mind. "This isn't working. Something's not right."

"What do you mean?" Lya asked. "We have to get to the House of Life again. Don't we?"

"Yes. But..." Carefully, I leaned to look at the water. It roiled with souls, and a low thump underfoot beat against the hull with an uneven rhythm that was slowly driving me out of my skull as it forced me to keep thinking about the dead below. Forced my memories of drowning to the surface rather than letting them sink and be suppressed again.

Focus. I needed to get my shit together, focus, and lead.

"The first trial was simple enough," I said. "Get across the Lake of Fire and fight some monsters. That was achievable with elemental power."

"Your point?" Mami Wata asked archly.

"Sutekh is both warrior *and* trickster. He showed us the warrior so we wouldn't look for a trick." I rose and scanned the horizon, looking for some hint or clue. "What do we know about the tricksters?"

"Are we really doing this now? On a boat that could get a hole busted in it at any bloody moment?" Lya snarled.

I closed my eyes and shut her out. I'd missed something. The boat had been a lure; it had to be. Or at least not the whole story. The pattern had been established in the first trial: cross the elemental hazard, steal the key. This first attempt to follow the pattern had sprung a trap—one that was testing me in more ways than one. I fisted my hand to stop the small tremor in it as the fear of drowning again clung to me like those dead souls' hands.

"Shape and form." It was what I'd thought when Anansi had shown himself. "They're shapeshifters. Water more than any of the other elements has that fluidity. It can be contained in any shape, in any phase of matter, but still be itself. One of you two"—I pointed at Mason and Mami Wata— "holds the key."

Lya frowned like she couldn't quite follow that leap of logic then threw her hands up. "I don't have a better idea. Just point at what you want me to hunt. Or better, kill."

From his spot in the bow, Cade hollered, "Arbiter, we're going to need to hurry this up. There's a disturbance in the water ahead. If we can't go forward, we need to decide real fucking quickly where we can go."

I turned to Mami Wata. "Did you see anything off when you were in the water?"

"Off? No. I—" She frowned, her gaze going distant. "Wait. The current was strange. I thought it was the boat and the souls, but I also don't know what else it could have been."

Turning to Mason, I said, "Could your wolf sense something?"

He frowned. "Smell, maybe. If I could reach him."

"Can you try?"

A minute stretched as Cade grew more antsy in the fore of the boat. Finally, Mason shook his head. "It's like the spark that ignites the change is gone."

"Well, how did you manage the shift?" I asked Mami Wata.

She shrugged. "I told you. I have talents with the dead and with Water. Liminal spaces are my domain, and this is one steeped in both death and Water. Magic isn't gone from here, only from our original plane. I simply shifted."

I pondered that. I was liminal, in that I was a being of the golden hour. Same with Lya. Cade as well, being between living and dead. Mason was too, in that he was between man and animal. But he needed a spark.

Hmm.

"Arbiter!" Cade barked in the tone of a ship's captain. "Whatever you're doing, do it now! Lya, keep an eye on our aft."

The half-elf obeyed, pausing next to me. "Any chance of weapons?"

I summoned some, finding it easier than last time. I had no idea what they'd do with them against souls, but they had to be better than nothing.

Much better than nothing would be getting the fuck out of here, away from the souls banging at the boat keeping us between life and death in this fucked-up dream of an underworld.

Mason jumped when I knelt in front of him and said, "I can try to give you a spark of Chaos. Maybe if you have fuel for the ignition, the magic of this plane can do the rest."

His gaze darted from me to the rest of the squad before settling back on me. "Worth a try, ma'am."

"Give me your hands."

When he did, I closed my eyes and opened my third eye, trying to read the shape of were magic, even if Duke had always told me it wasn't worth it to try reading magic that wasn't my own. Unfortunately, Duke had been right. I couldn't make heads or tails of the hot roil of energy raging in Mason's auratic points.

But his wolf could.

I fell back with a shout as a sense of something too wildly primal for me to comprehend lunged forth. Chaos burst from me to Mason—and he shifted. An enormous, brown-furred wolf loomed over me, lips drawn back in a snarl.

Drawing on Air, I readied a few coils to pull him away from me.

Mami Wata beat me to it and thumped him on the snout with a fist. "We don't have time for dominance games, boy. Use your Goddess-rotted nose."

The wolf showed her his teeth until she peeled her lips back to show her own and her eyes shifted to the flat black of a python.

"Work," she said, her voice a low, hissing growl. "Or you and your other spirit both die here."

With a last defiant snap, Mason padded to stand beside Cade and turned his nose to the wind.

I was just rising to my feet with a nod to Mami Wata when Mason howled and raced back to me. The wolf didn't quite know what to do to shift back though, so the spark of Chaos I'd used the first time around did nothing.

We needed more. Pushing hard with Chaos, I imagined him as a human. Fur smoothed out into skin under my hands, and when I opened my eyes, he was on all fours, panting.

"I smelled incense," he gasped. "And stone and metal, right in front of us. We have to stop the boat. Now, before we crash!"

Fuck.

As the others scrambled for the oars and tried back-rowing, I did the only thing I could think of: part the waters.

Or I tried. Surrender wasn't coming to me with the recent near-drowning, and I nearly panicked again. Then I flashed back to one of the earliest times I'd called Water.

Troy had been there, at my back, grounding me.

I reached for the callstone around my neck. "Troy!"

He answered in my head, like the djinn would, and his emotions swamped me enough that I had to lock my knees before we both walled up. "I'm here. Are you okay?"

"I need help," I whispered. "I need Water. You helped before. With Callista."

Mami Wata's attention snapped to me, and I forced myself to ignore her.

A pause. "Usually, it feels like this."

With the auratic and mental sensation of falling backward into a lake, he tipped me into Water.

I grabbed for the element, not bothering with any attempt at finesse, and threw my hands out to either side. A push of Water burst from me, down and out.

The river split.

The boat dropped amidst the screams of everyone else in it, hitting the mucky riverbed with a bone-jarring thud and a wet squelch. The dead stayed walled behind the edge of the water. I tied off the chord of Water and switched to Chaos, sending a reckless pulse outward and willing it to shatter illusions hiding the true shape and form of matter.

Just like Mason had said, stone appeared a few yards in front of the boat. Stone walls, the carved pylons I remembered from before. This House of Life was smaller than the first or the decoy across the river but tall enough that the tops would have ripped out the bottom of the boat and left us to drown among the damned.

I shuddered. I couldn't smell the incense, but the werewolf yelped.

"That! That's the smell. It's there."

"Go," I snapped at Cade.

He ran. Lya followed.

Mami Wata flicked her gaze over me. "What was that about Callista?"

"A story that will cost you," I said. "The beginning of her fall."

Again, the fae's eyes flickered to python black. "If I made it the price of the bath?"

I studied her, wondering why this meant so much and how I could get Mami Wata solidly on my side. Whatever happened with magic, I needed the eastern part of my territory secured. "Then I would accept. For the additional boon of a true partnership, I would offer the tale of her end as well."

"Partnership means a seat at the table. I wasn't sure if I wanted it before, but if you can do all this, maybe I do."

I'd set a limit of three members per faction in my parliament meetings, and Zanna was currently the only fae, given Ruprecht had more interest in fucking with police business than playing politics and the gytrash stayed on guard duty at my house. Before I could figure out how to agree without seeming too eager, my walls of Water buckled.

I cursed and squeezed my eyes shut, pushing harder. "Lya, Cade, hurry the fuck up!"

I had no idea if they could hear me, but if the length of this Nilotic purgatory was filled with dead souls, the pure weight of them might bust through my walls at any minute. I was powerful, but I was only one woman.

A scuff made me open my eyes.

Mason had risen from his bench. "I'll go see if I can help."

He vaulted over the side and hauled ass for the small temple before I could confirm, leaving me alone with Mami Wata.

She saw the angles as clearly as I did. "Interesting situation."

"Sure," I agreed, straining to focus on both Water and my words. "If you think you can get home without me."

Defiance flared in her expression—and then subsided. She smiled, looking genuinely amused. "I'd still like to kill you one day. Beings as powerful as you have proven to be bad for my health."

"I'm sure." I tried to keep my voice light, even as I wrestled a chord of Air to readiness. "That said, I'm sure you'll understand it's not just self-preservation when I say that'd be a really fucking stupid idea."

"Fortunately for you, Arbiter, I can read the chords of Water you're wielding right now. I've never seen anything like it, not in all the many centuries I've spent on the earthly plane." She paused, watching me sweat as I redoubled my effort to hold a whole fucking river and the death within it at bay. "You could turn a storm."

"Already have."

"Hmm."

Before our conversation could continue, one of the undead souls broke through the wall of water. It staggered toward us, gliding over the deep mud like it was solid ground. A sense of anger, of rage, even, emanated from it. It was wrath and hunger and hatred—and so were the ones who followed it through the hole it'd punched in the massive wall I was trying to hold.

I looked to either side, spotting more of them slipping through. I could hold the water away as we sat on the riverbed. But the effort that took meant the wall I created was thin. I had more power in a dream than I did in the real, but I was still just a dreamer in a world I hadn't created, trying to work against rules I hadn't made. This wasn't like trying to heal Troy. This was trying to manipulate the fabric of this reality, and as confident as I'd been with Anansi, this was only my second time at this. I was in over my head in more ways than one.

"Arbiter." The tension in Mami Wata's voice added to my own.

"I see them."

"And?"

I didn't answer immediately. Stopping them meant destroying them. It meant that these souls, angry as they were, would never have a chance to process whatever it was that was preventing them from moving on. They wouldn't be trapped with the possibility of freedom. They'd be gone.

Instead of protecting and building, I'd be destroying.

"Arbiter?"

How the fuck did I make that choice?

And then it came to me.

Troy.

If I didn't act, odds were good they'd reach the boat and kill me—or kill Cade, Lya, and Mason when they found the key.

I was not dying here. I was not leaving Troy to die without me in the real. And I had to protect both the chance of all of Otherside regaining magic and the lives of all the people I'd brought here with me.

Darkwatch training slammed through my consciousness. I had a mission. Whatever I might have worried about the souls, Troy above all was still my greater good.

I reached for Fire.

Asking Mami Wata for help would have been the wise thing to do in terms of preserving my energy but impossible in terms of the longer political game. My edge was a sliver greater than hers. I had to prove I was the stronger player.

With a silent, teeth-gritted snarl, I pushed a wave of Fire at the souls that'd broken through. They steamed first, waterlogged and slimy, before bursting like stinking balloons.

They were still bursting when Lya, Cade, and Mason hauled ass out of the temple.

"We got it," Lya hollered as she clambered back over the side of the boat. "Or at least the box. Arbiter?"

I was lost in creating a firebreak for us. Lost in the death I was dealing out, the finality of destroying souls.

It was Mason who pulled me out.

"Arbiter." He knelt in front of me. I hadn't even realized I was on my knees, hands still outstretched to either side. "Please. You take care of your people."

In that simple statement, I remembered Haroun's story.

With a soul-rending twist, I dropped Fire and Water. As the river crashed down over us all, I wrenched Chaos into the pinprick holes that were the weft of the Duat and the weave of reality, sending all of them home.

The river closed over me, and so did the dead.

Chapter 14

"It's okay. You're okay. You're alive. You're not drowning. You're okay."

The words rumbling against my ear anchored me in reality. I gasped, trying to free myself from the arms trapping me. The dead had come back with me, and they were trying to lure me with comforting words in a familiar voice even as their grip tried to drag me under.

"Arden! Shh. It's me. It's me, cariñamí. Shh, let go of the elements. You're safe." A burst of burnt marshmallow and Aether accompanied the words, but nothing attacked me. There was just a sense of ease. All was well.

I shuddered as I connected words with scent and sensation.

Troy. He had been left in the real. If he was here, I must be there. There was no more water. No more damned souls. Which meant I needed to get my shit together before I brought the building down. But adrenaline still seared through me, alongside the visceral memory of drowning myself, despite being drenched only by my own sweat.

"Help," I whispered. I didn't know what else to say. I just knew I could trust Troy to help me. He had before. Many times. It was safe to ask him.

With my acknowledgment—my permission—the weighty feeling of wellbeing and comfort increased.

"I've got you, Arden," he said in soothing, modulated tones. "I've got you. Ease down."

Drowning or not, dead souls or not, I knew down to my depths that Troy was my protector. He was here, wherever here was or would be. Heedless of my power signature, I dropped the walls and shields I reflexively tightened every time I woke and let him all the way in.

"Good. That's good," he murmured in a voice like satin that twined through my mind. His hands were warm where they held me close, nothing like the freezing river.

Languor replaced tension and fear as his passive power washed over me. I curled tighter against him, still shaking with remembered cold and anguish.

"T, if Dad finds out—" Darius's voice was close, low and urgent. Concerned. I hadn't even clocked that he was nearby.

"I know," Troy said. "I have it under control."

"Fuck."

Hearing the younger Monteague swear was almost enough to jolt me out of my newfound ease. Troy had what under control? Me?

"Go see if the others made it back. See if they brought anything with them, and make sure it's secured," Troy ordered in a low voice. His King voice, not his brother voice.

"Yes, sir," Darius replied.

Troy kept rocking me. The cot creaked alarmingly under our combined weight. Other scents filtered in: the stale herby scent of elves in close quarters; the vaguely stagnant smell of the lake outside; under it, a whiff of the underworld's Nile that made me shudder; more distantly, food. Voices came back into focus, going from a dull roar in the background to the chatter of at least a dozen people.

Beyond the immediate space, a storm raged. Something felt off about it.

"Did I make the storm?" I whispered.

"I think you did, my love. Can you calm it?"

Rather than answering, I reached for the elements—only to hunch into myself at the raging power hangover that hit me when I did.

All the same, a knock on the metal frame of the cubicle had me forcing my head up with a snarl, lightning dancing over me and my raised hand until Darius poked his head in.

"Whoa!" He ducked. "It's just me, my queen."

Troy kissed my temple despite the lightning. "Dari has a report, cariñamí. There's no threat."

Squeezing my eyes shut, I let go of Air and Fire with a magical heave as much as a physical one, barely managing to keep my stomach in check. Even as I released magic, the storm outside seemed to weaken.

Darius ducked in, eyes wide and darting over us as much as my lightning had. "Goddess. How are you not—"

"The bonds diffuse her magic. Status?"

"Cade, Lya, Mami Wata, and Mason all returned from the Duat safely, although the vampire is going to need to feed as soon as possible. They're recovering in their tents. Lya had this. Turned it over willingly but is demanding blood for her master." He stepped forward cautiously, his attention on me as he passed a small box to Troy.

He took one hand from its tight wrap around me to accept the box. "Is this what you were looking for, Arden? They brought back a key last time."

I made myself focus on it. Pushed again to embrace Earth and read what was inside. "Yeah. There's something key-shaped inside."

That last reach was too much. All of my muscles spasmed. Cramps dug vicious fingers into my stomach, tore through my guts as heat raced over me. I tried my damnedest to follow my training and swallow the pain, but I couldn't help a whimper.

Troy swore then shifted me off his lap to the cot and gently tugged me to lay on my side. His forehead was cool against mine, as was his hand on my cheek and his Aether skating across my aura as he whispered, "Breathe, Arden."

I tried, but I just tumbled down a rabbit hole of darkness faster than Alice ever had.

△▽△▽

I was only partly awake when I heard Harqil's voice.

"She didn't overdraw. She passed a threshold. Now she's recovering."

Troy's frustrated tones. "What in the nine hells does that mean?"

I was out again before I could hear more.

△▽△▽

There was always a price to magic. Especially, I supposed, when you were one of the only people with magic in a world without it.

I managed not to throw up when I woke, but it was a near thing. I still leaned over the edge of the cot and heaved then startled back at the unexpected trash can.

Troy was watching from his seat on the opposite cot when I looked up, and from the odd, almost fearful twist of his expression, he was thinking of my waking as his captive in his safehouse after the Jordan Lake incident as well.

Without a word, I extended a hand.

He took it, his movements quick and sharp, even as he slumped with his other elbow against his knee and looked at the floor. "When you started coughing up water that didn't smell like this lake, I was afraid I'd lose you. Either to the Duat or to the past."

I squeezed his fingers. "You were what got me through all of it. Duat and past."

Shock, pain, and gratitude shot through the bond in equal parts as he squeezed back. "Then I won't question it. How are you feeling?"

"Like ass," I grumbled, shifting to lay on my stomach.

"What can I do?"

"Hold me."

Troy's gaze flicked up to study the cot. "Not sure that'll hold both of us again."

"Outside then. On the ground." I squeezed again. "Please. I feel like I'm a million pieces that'll blow away if you don't—"

I couldn't finish. Even with Troy, it was too much vulnerability to say out loud.

He got it though, at least from what I understood in the bond. "I can do that."

Wearily, I pushed myself upright then to my feet. When I looked up, the low roof of our cubicle was too close for my comfort. I flinched then shuddered. I needed to get this whole bullshit test done fast because I didn't know how much longer I could stand to live in a little box, privacy and security be damned.

Everyone paused to salute, fist to heart, when we emerged.

With an effort, I pulled myself together and tried to be a queen. I was doing this to secure my reign and feel safe enough to give it a future that would outlive me and Troy. That meant securing my people's faith in me, no matter how shitty I felt.

"We've completed two of the tests," I announced, trying to make my voice stronger than I felt. "We have two more trials ahead. I promise, our king and I—and our new allies—are doing everything we can to ensure magic is stolen back for Otherside."

They hollered something in elvish and raised fists to sky. I nodded in acknowledgement and got my ass moving for the door. I needed outside. I needed the woods and trees, even the

Goddess-damned lake. I needed the cloud-laden sky that was lightening toward false dawn as we stepped out.

Mami Wata was studying the horizon, heedless of the rain that was already tapering off to a drizzle. She looked as exhausted as I felt. "I changed my mind about wanting to kill you," she said without looking at me. "Beings of our strength are so rare nowadays. I think I'd rather have your assistance in protecting my sirens and my coast."

I let her declaration of the coast as *hers* slide and squeezed Troy's wrist at his threatening growl. She could have it, just like the wolves could have the Blue Ridge Mountains, as long as they all answered to me.

"I told you my offer," I said.

"So you did." Her gaze danced over me. If I didn't know any better, I'd think she was surprised to see me standing. "I will think on it and speak to Rí when passage through the Veil becomes possible again. Until then, we may be at peace."

"At peace," I agreed before tugging Troy to follow me first to a sleeping Mason's tent then to Cade and Lya's.

She peered out at my quiet footsteps, held up a finger in a "one minute" gesture with a mouthed "please," then ducked back inside. The low sounds of an argument came from inside the tent before Lya said loudly and firmly, "I'm your fucking solidaire. It's my job to take care of you, and if you don't let me do it, I will bloody well kill you myself."

A threatening growl met her pronouncement, raising the small hairs on my arms and neck. If nothing else, it was good to know I still had survival instincts when it wasn't Troy's growl and teeth making the threat.

"Come at me then," Lya snarled back. "I'll break the pointy ones off and feed you those first, asshole."

I blinked at the thought of a half-elf a few years older than Troy taking on a half-century master vampire, but Cade must have believed her threat because the growl stopped and the tent flap opened. Lya came all the way out this time.

"Cade needs to eat. A full meal." Her glare and clenched fists said she expected to fight me over it.

"We'll get him one," I said as an idea struck.

"Arden—" Troy said sharply. The tarp he'd snagged on our way out of the boathouse crinkled as his fist clenched.

"Not elves, cariñomí." I turned to face him. "I'm asking too much of them already. But it occurs to me that we have half a dozen Sons of Seth, no magic to continue reprogramming them, and are sparing resources to keep them in custody."

He went very still. "You're clearing execution by vampire."

"Yes." My stomach churned. I wouldn't have had the strength to consider this even a few days ago, but I had to get. This. Job. Done. Cade and Lya had kept up their side of the bargain, whether I trusted them fully or not. Denying the vampire a feed wasn't just cruel; it was dangerous. However good his self-control was, he'd snap eventually, surrounded by a walking buffet of magicless elves like this. I didn't know if it was normal for him to growl at his solidaire like that, but the argument had been clear enough.

Troy eyed me. *You're sure?*

I answered aloud for Lya's benefit. I needed her to trust me or at least stop doubting me. Knowing how half-elves were treated in the Houses and her situation in particular, my hunch was that sharing information was the way to swing her—and through her, Cade—fully to my side. Having a pair of bounty hunters I could trust could come in handy, the way things were going.

"I know we were intending to release them to avoid a missing person's report, but if the feds erased the evidence of my kidnapping, they'll probably bury this too. Beyond that, the Sons attacked my home with intent to harm, if not kill, you, me, and the gytrash." Regardless of my intentions, it was hard not to sound defensive. "Have them brought here. Cade can have his fill. I'll get rid of the evidence."

Troy's pleased smile was a surprise. "As my queen commands."

When he stepped away to make the call, Lya huffed a sigh of relief. "Thank you. He was able to go a little longer than usual on your blood, but he hasn't fed properly in days."

"Sure. Thank you both for your help on this."

She offered a halting fist-to-heart salute then ducked back into the tent.

Good. She'd called me Arbiter or Highness, but there'd been a tinge of...not quite sarcasm. Maybe bitterness or resentment, like she'd learned the hard way that titles were just words you offered so someone wouldn't hurt you. The salute had been reluctant enough here that I might be winning her over, and I trusted Haroun's read of the situation: win Lya, and her vampire would come with her, as odd as that seemed, given what I'd observed of master vampires and their relationships with fledglings or solidaires in Maria's coterie.

That done, I headed for the woods, heartsore and tired, feeling like my knees were going to give out any minute. I made it a short distance in before I dropped—only to be caught and eased the rest of the way to a crouch by a silent Troy.

"The order is in," he said.

I closed my eyes and tried to find a peace I didn't feel. "Did I do the right thing?"

"Yes." The firm confidence in his voice should have reassured me.

But I still felt sick.

"You did, Arden. This solves multiple problems. It's not vengeance. It's making the most of the hand we've been dealt. I may not be keen on having a vampire here, but he's an oathsworn ally. Letting him suffer, or putting our people at risk by denying him, is wrong. Turning him loose to hunt and kill innocents in our territory would be as well. Not to mention stupid with

Sinclaire breathing down our necks." He spread the tarp then sat and squeezed my shoulder, coaxing me up and back. "I know that was a hard choice for you, and I'm proud of you. You're stepping up to be the leader we need right now."

When we were settled, him against a beech tree and me against him, I shuddered so hard I thought my bones would come free of my skin. Continuing to stress over something I'd already ordered done would help nothing, but I couldn't quite let go of the idea that I'd taken another roll down the slippery slope toward becoming Callista.

Troy sighed. Then a lassitude swept over me.

I was safe. I was home. I was on land I'd claimed, with my bondmate.

"Thanks," I said, shifting to tuck even closer against him and let his passive power in again. Funny how some of the things I used to fear about him were what gave me comfort now.

"It's the right thing," he insisted, nuzzling under my ear and breathing deep to take in my scent.

He'd called me out before, so I chose to trust he was telling me the truth now. I tipped my head to give him greater access to my neck and shoulder.

"Bite me," I whispered.

He stiffened, the hunger in the bond suggesting it was out of an effort to hold himself back. "But we're not—"

"I know. I just need something very much here and now." I waited as he hesitated then added, "Please, Troy. I know you need it too."

The quiet *snick* of his secondary teeth dropping was both arousing and grounding, as was the Aether he sent through me and the pinch in his shallow bite. I arched back and gasped, only for him to wrap one arm around my waist and grip my chin with the other hand to keep me close. He eased up quickly though, sensitive to my physical state as ever.

I relaxed, leaning fully into this moment with him.

I want you, he sent.

I can tell. I wiggled a little against the hard-on now pressing against my back. *As soon as we have some privacy again.*

Troy's attention sharpened—but not on me. He lifted his head and sniffed. "What, Dari?"

After a moment, a deeply embarrassed-looking Darius came out of the trees. His focus was on me as he asked, "All good, my queen?"

Troy sighed. "For the love of—"

He cut off at Darius's outstretched hand.

"He's not feral. I ordered this," I said, putting the pieces together quickly. "He's my anchor to this plane. Blood strengthens him and the tie both."

"Just needed to hear it from you," Darius said. "Sorry, brother. You know the Captain and Alli would beat my ass if I didn't check in." The odd abruptness with which he stopped suggested there was something he wasn't saying, and I fought to keep my expression neutral and pretend I didn't hear it. Whatever was going on with Omar in particular needed to wait.

Resentment simmered in the bond before Troy found neutrality. "What is it?"

"Three updates. First, the Ebon Guard and the Sons will be here in thirty. Second, the Darkwatch is getting reports that a queen has died in Detroit."

"Died?" The last thing we needed right now was instability in another elven conclave. "How?"

"Suicide. Apparently."

Troy went very still behind me. "Which queen?"

Darius grimaced. "Veisi."

Chapter 15

I started to get up, but Troy kept me in place. "Troy—"

"It wasn't a suicide. It was my father," he said grimly.

I didn't even bother to say we didn't know that. Cyrus had said he was out to destroy the matriarchy. He had a massive grudge against all queens. And as one of the only Othersiders with magic, now was the easiest time to strike.

Darius nodded and crouched. "T, she was influential. On the Grand Conclave. If Uncle Cyrus had a hand in this—"

"He'll be going after more queens. Fuck. I suppose I should be grateful he didn't try anything in territory we hold." His thoughts spun in the bond as he ran his tongue along the bite in my shoulder, cleaning up a few drops of blood before releasing me. "Thank you, Arden."

I rose, finding myself feeling steadier after this grounding with Troy, and offered him a hand up then a kiss on the cheek. "We'll figure this out."

"But not now." He grimaced, his gaze distant, before coming back to the present. "What was the third thing, Dari?"

"The action at Verve is inflaming sentiments, since there's no way that wasn't Otherside." Darius rose and scrubbed a hand over the top of his head, avoiding looking at me. "The mundane protests are ticking up and might be on the verge of rioting again. Anti-Othersiders are demanding new legislation. They want us rounded up and put into camps."

"Fuck that. They're gathering here?" I said.

"Washington, DC."

It was my turn to grimace. "That's too close to the Richmond Conclave. They're going to want assurances."

"My concern is with security here," Darius said, glancing at Troy. At his brother's nod, he added, "The storm you called was a big one, ma'am. The Guard and the Darkwatch are getting alerts of conspiracy theory videos already. It's adding fuel to the mundane protesters' grievances."

I sighed and leaned on Troy, looking through the forest at the distant lake. I needed sleep—I was finding that Dreamwalking rested neither the body nor the mind—but I had to secure us first.

The sun clearing the trees crawled into the space between treetop and clouds to sparkle on the lake, giving me an idea.

"I can handle some of the security," I said.

"How?" Troy asked.

"Kind of a shield. Blend Air and Water to create a mirror-like effect. If they find us, I can create something like a bug zapper to stop drones or whatever getting too close."

"Why not do it now?" Darius asked. "The zapper, I mean."

"Birds," Troy said, anticipating me.

"Yeah. I'd rather not have birds dropping from the sky." That'd break my heart. Probably wouldn't help with keeping the balance either. "Besides, if they did send a drone and happened to see a flock of geese or whatever crash into an unseen barrier, they'd investigate."

Darius frowned. "Okay, fair enough. We're running the electronics only as necessary, so hopefully they only do visual scans and not infrared."

"Might be able to help there too. Everyone on the ground would be affected by the cold though."

"Better they have to wear an extra layer than deal with a government assault team." Troy wrapped his arm around me and squeezed. "Sure you're up to this?"

"I have to be. We have two more trials. Unless you want to move us to the warehouse where we restored Iaret or the location in Virginia."

"Hmm. Not yet. This ground is ideal for the people we've assembled. There's no body of water at either of the other two locations," Troy said. "I have a feeling we'll need the lake to keep Mami Wata happy."

"Yeah. Okay. Let's get this done." I lurched into a walk, letting Troy support me under the guise of being possessive or whatever, his arm tight around me.

When we came out of the tree cover, the grounds were quiet. I had a feeling everyone was either resting or busy inside the boathouse. At the unlit fire kettle, I dropped into one of the chairs and leaned over my knees, trying to clear my head enough to focus. Something felt odd. Not like a power hangover but like a buzz in my skull.

When I cautiously reached for Air, my skin tingled.

That wasn't normal. But it didn't hurt and my nose wasn't bleeding, so I made the reach for Water. I was already so dead tired that it was easier to surrender this time, and I straightened then slumped back in my chair so I could see the sky.

I blew out a breath. "Okay. Let's see..."

"Get one of the drones," Troy murmured to Darius. "And a bottle of wine or brandy or something."

I stayed focused on my work. This was going to need to be massive, extending from the feeder road into the grounds, covering the grounds themselves, and then partially over the lake, both for our own boats and for Mami Wata to swim safely.

I'd never done something like this before, so it was all instinct and vibes.

Water surfaces were most reflective when they were still, so that had to be part of it. It needed to be permeable so birds and such could pass through. I needed to anchor and tie it off so

I wouldn't have to maintain it but be able to come back and strengthen it or add the lightning shield later if needed.

I fell into the work, soothed by the elements, despite the odd new sensations attached to it. Like an emergence of some sort, a kind of scraping or satisfying scratch of an itch. Or like the buzz of just enough alcohol to feel loose without tipping into intoxication. It was strange but nice.

Curl of Water there, woven through with Air. Pull tight. Weave matter and intention into overlapping chords to reflect and cool...like that.

When I finished, I exhaled and blinked to bring my attention back to myself and my immediate surroundings. I found Troy in the chair next to me, easing up on an iron grip on the arms with an exhale of his own. Darius, Pascale, and Haroun were on guard, and Mami Wata was watching both us and the sky.

You okay? I asked Troy.

Better now that you're done. That's a lot of magic, Arden.

Hopefully it's enough.

Darius stepped forward to offer a small bottle of brandy. "All good, ma'am?"

"Yeah. Should be." I took the bottle and cracked it open to take a swig. No power hangover now but better safe than sorry.

"I'll get the drone up," Haroun said.

I scarcely breathed as we watched the small screen on the controller, then whooped when it cleared the treetops and every trace of habitation disappeared, leaving only an illusion of trees and lake.

"Well done, my love." Troy reached for my hand and kissed it. "How long will it hold?"

I shrugged. "Should be until I pull it down, but I've left a thread for me to reinforce or reshape it if needed."

"Good. Now you need rest."

"I need to deal with these protests."

Troy looked at Darius.

"Captain's on it," Darius said. "We can't influence crowds the way we're used to without magic, but he's escalated the pro-Otherside infowar campaigns and activated smear campaigns against any identified anti-Otherside ringleaders."

The Captain might be on it, but this was my demesne. At the same time...

I sighed. I couldn't keep running things as a one-woman show. The bigger and further-reaching my ambitions and aims got, the more I needed to delegate to other people. Trying to do everything myself wasn't sustainable now, and it'd be worse going forward.

Before I could say anything about that, my phone rang. "Fuck. It's Sinclaire."

"Take it. I'll reach out to the parliament with an update," Troy said.

"Thank you." I stayed where I was as he moved off with Darius in tow. Haroun and Pascale stayed where they were, and I wove a small soundproofing barrier around myself before answering. "Finch."

"Ms. Finch. We're going to need your answer on the summons."

"We've been over this. I'm going to need you to go through my lawyer."

"The lawyers are playing their games. Well played, by the way, getting our murder investigation tied up in discovery. You've bought yourself at least a week. But I'm calling off the record to make you a direct offer because women like us don't have time for games."

Oh, I did not like the sound of this. "What's the offer?"

"Work for the Bureau, and I'll make sure the bills currently being debated in both chambers of Congress go away."

My gut clenched. We'd already tried legislation, and it'd been rolled back. "What bills would those be?"

"The ones that would satisfy the demands of the protesters currently marching in our nation's capital."

"I heard those were more like mobs."

She snorted. "You have no idea what they could become. Wouldn't you rather prevent loss of life?" When I didn't answer, she added slyly, "It'd be tragic for there to be a flashpoint."

Something about this was ringing all the alarm bells and waving all the red flags. Just like Senator Wright, Acting Director Lara Sinclaire only ever called to make demands, usually when she thought she had something she could use. She might couch them in thin courtesy, but they were still demands that I wasn't gonna bend to. I held my tongue, reaching for the Sight, but got nothing. I didn't know if magic could be tapped out, but I'd used so much of myself to Dreamwalk that the Sight was quiet, ring or no ring.

Shit. No free passes, even for me.

"Finch?"

"I'll be in touch." I ended the call and dropped my soundproof wall. "Where's Troy?"

"Inside," Pascale said. "Orders?"

"I need a private space to speak to the parliament."

"On it." She spoke into a wrist mic in elvish too quick for me to understand beyond catching the word for parliament. "King Troy is on with them now."

I followed her back into the boathouse, through to a small room that had been an office at some point. It was set up with a desk that Troy was currently behind with a laptop in front of him.

He looked up, cutting off mid-sentence when I burst in. "A moment." With two clicks, he turned to me. "Muted, camera off. I was just updating them on the mission to restore magic. What is it?"

"More threats. Sinclaire's trying to bypass the lawyers. Some kind of black ops offer, I think. Wants me to work for them in exchange for killing a couple of bills she says are under consideration, which would satisfy the demands being made by the rioters." I held up a hand at Troy's thunderous look. "That's not all. I can't get the Sight to confirm it, but I think she has some kind of ace up her sleeve. She said, 'It'd be a shame if there was a flashpoint.'"

"That sounds like a threat," he said.

"I thought so too. Troy, what if she has someone willing to be a scapegoat?"

He thought for a moment. "The fucking Ead royals. Has to be. No magic, no power. All they have left is vengeance. Maybe vengeance in exchange for power among the mundanes."

I'd been half afraid of that but somehow thought some shred of solidarity with the rest of Otherside would keep them from fucking everyone over. Apparently the rich and powerful would go to any lengths to preserve or restore themselves and themselves alone. If the rest of us were damned... well, fuck us.

"I need to share this with the parliament," I said. "They need to get the word out to their factions."

"Agreed. The elves alone can't handle this, not without magic."

I came around behind him as he turned the mic and camera back on, leaning down to see who was on the call. Noah and Doc Mike on one screen, looking like someone's home. Probably Noah's; I couldn't see Maria letting him go far these days, and I knew Doc Mike lived closer to the morgue. Maria, Allegra, Duke, and Giuliano were in another rectangle. Terrence and Ximena in a third that was clearly at my dining table. Zanna and Janae in my office at the bar. Vikki in a room with the mountains as a backdrop. Helia, Ninos, and Flint were in the last little rectangle.

"Good, you're all here," I said briskly." I've received a call from Acting Director Lara Sinclaire that gives me cause for concern. You're all aware of the protests in DC?"

Nods and affirmatives came as expressions hardened.

"I have reason to believe those are either an op or will become one. Sinclaire mentioned legislation against Othersiders being considered, potentially for a rushed vote, as well as hinting at a coming flashpoint."

"Flashpoint?" Maria asked. "What kind of flashpoint? We've got enough to handle in Raleigh."

"It might be something to do with the severed royals from House Ead," Troy said bluntly. "And I hope my directness in implicating another elven House underscores my sincerity and commitment to this group as a whole, not just elven interests."

The elementals looked especially grim and a little doubtful but nodded along with the rest.

I squeezed Troy's hand under the view of the camera. "I need everyone to do two things: remind your people to lay low and pass this along to your factional networks. It's possible this is bait of some kind, trying to get us to move for or against something. For the time being, we don't move—or allow ourselves to *be* moved." I looked at each little box on my screen then straight into the camera. "This has gone beyond the Triangle now. I want us to be not just a parliament for our demesnes but for the Eastern Seaboard and beyond."

Shocked or blank expressions met me before Giuliano leaned forward, dark eyes glittering in what might be anger. "You're empire building amidst a crisis, Arbiter?"

"I'm taking responsibility for the fact that the mundanes have focused on me as a leader in Otherside and my actions at Verve as a threat. I have no idea who else they might have reached out to or where, but I know our situation—our parliament—is unique. Callista was a tyrant, but she laid down four hundred years of precedence for mixed-faction relations that we can improve upon."

"You don't just want to improve. You're talking about expansion," Giuliano pushed. "The Eastern Seaboard realm includes New York City. Matthias will not be pleased."

"He can stand with me and the unified Carolinas and Dominion demesnes, or he can stand alone in whatever shitstorm the US federal government is cooking up," I said bluntly. "I am focusing on getting magic back for all of Otherside. The politics? That's up to y'all. And I am *inviting* you to share power with me. To have a working government, an Otherside government, in place that can work as a parallel to the mundane feds in leading and negotiating for all of Otherside, at least in the US. Surely you can find a way to frame it as a leadership opportunity to Matthias?"

Giuliano stared, unblinking, as a taut silence stretched. "You mean this."

"She means it," Maria muttered, looking at her nails. "She's as outrageous as ever, but the Arbiter has never been anything except brazenly earnest in her idealism."

I pressed my lips together at the backhanded compliment.

Ninos spoke up. "What does this mean for us djinn and the fae? Those whose homelands aren't on this plane."

"For the djinn, this is why I proposed we restore the old way of arranging Houses," I said. "You have representatives and ties here, which could now be extended via this demesne and the alliance in it. For the fae, they have always been welcome to come and go in my demesnes, so long as the terms of the Détente are upheld. Otherwise, I defer to Zanna as lead representative."

The kobold puffed up, her dark eyes fiery with the opportunity to do something as big as this. "I will draw up a proposal to share with King Rí as soon as the Veil can be crossed again."

"There you have it," I said. "The world is changing. We can take the lead in a once-in-a-lifetime shift. Or we can be dust and bone when all is taken and riven."

I cut off, and Troy's hand tightened on mine as the words from my dream poured out without my meaning to say them.

Fuck. Getting magic back wasn't all we had to do. This was also about order and disorder. Was this the real test? Not just stealing magic back, but how we would step up to restore balance once we had it? Would we lose it again if we didn't?

As my mind swirled on that, Troy finished filling everyone in on what we were doing to get magic back.

"There are two more tests," he said. "We're moving as quickly as we can, but this is incredibly dangerous on multiple levels. So, help us to help all of Otherside by doing as the Arbiter has asked and keeping your people under control. I know the protests add pressure to do something, but magic is the priority right now. That means order and calm are the priority."

From the expressions of several people on the screen, the question of *Even if someone dies?* was crossing more than one mind. To their credit though, nobody said it aloud. Just spoke closing words and signed off.

I didn't know whether I should be relieved that they were obeying or concerned that they might be losing hope and the will to fight.

Chapter 16

I wasn't sure how long I'd been asleep when shouting dragged me from the oblivion of slumber. I stirred, finding Troy passed out half on top of me, his nose buried against my neck and his hand heavy over my heart. We'd dragged the mattresses off our cots and removed the frames from the space so we could sleep together on the floor, and if this was how we'd ended up, that was probably for the best as far as his protective instincts went. It was a measure of how exhausted both of us were that the ruckus hadn't woken him. Or worse, how much my exhaustion might be draining him.

Damn it. I had to be better about remembering that. The more either or both of us pushed, the harder both of us went down when we did rest.

"Troy," I murmured, giving him a mental nudge in the bond.

He growled and curled closer.

I nudged again. "Hey. Something's happening."

With a sharp inhale, he found consciousness—then was on his feet, longknife in hand, as the sounds of arguing reached him. No matter how many times I watched him do that, I could not get over the speed with which he went from a dead sleep to fighting wakefulness.

"That sounds like Harqil." He glanced down at where I was just getting to a seated position and reaching in a stretch for my toes. Those mattresses were thin as hell, and the concrete floor was hard.

I took the hand he offered to pull me up, and we both put on clothes before stepping out.

"Enough," I said on finding Harqil again surrounded by angry elves, repeating it when nobody heard me.

Pascale nudged a red-faced Etain, and she and everyone else turned to face me and Troy.

"What's going on?" Troy asked.

Etain flushed even redder. "Apologies, majesties." She shot Harqil a dirty look. "We didn't want to wake you, but the celestial is insisting they have information that can't be shared with anyone but Queen Arden."

"Well, we're up now," I said. "Harqil? Let's take a walk."

To Troy, I sent, *Can you settle them and get an update?*

Will do.

I led Harqil out to the dock, barefoot despite the artificial chill created by my spell, and dropped down at the end of the dock to stick my feet in the water. "Well?"

"I've been looking around."

"Spying."

"Yes, if you want to be crass about it. Arden, the tricksters are split evenly on the matter of Sutekh."

"I'd thought they were agreed on letting me play this out? He's playing by his rules. If I don't get magic back fair and square, I'll play by mine. Isn't that what Anansi said?"

"Yes and no."

I twisted to glare up at them.

They held up their hands. "Look, I understood there to be an agreement. But that was before you scared them."

"*I* scared *them.*"

"You're not doing anything the way you're expected to."

"Okay, so that just makes me a proper trickster, right?"

"Exactly. That's the problem. They all thought that since you'd been claimed first by the hunters, that that meant you were definitively one of their children. Now you play the game as well as a trickster and worse—to them—gain from it." They paused, looking uncomfortable, then plowed forward. "Someone was supposed to die, Arden, and that was supposed to put you off this whole bloody quest because you're so damn tenderhearted. Then they could look the other way while Sutekh played his game without worrying about yours. It would upset a handful of gods within a single pantheon and be written off as just another iteration of the same old myths. Nothing to worry about or interfere with."

I tried to focus on the breeze coming off the lake rather than my growing anxiety. "What are you saying, Harqil?"

"The odds of you getting one key, let alone more, were heavily weighted toward death. Certainly for one of your squad, most likely your king. Yet now you're two for two, with all lives accounted for, despite bringing in fresh blood, and you weakened your own play to keep him safe. One more test to go and then the Box of Ages itself."

Anger flashed through me, but I was too tired to do more than grit my teeth and glare. "How is that not a good thing?"

"If you're not a piece, then you're a player. There hasn't been a new player in millennia. That risks shifting alliances and agreements between the various alignments, pantheons, foci, and agents." Harqil's gaze hardened. "That also makes you a candidate for the Court of Nightmares, when there hasn't been a new member in millennia. You're upsetting too much balance or, more honestly, resetting it. Even celestials can get comfortable, and you're making them decidedly *un*comfortable. First with reviving the old covenants between elementals and elves after more than four thousand years of war. Then growing into your potential as a primordial and surviving it. Then your dreams. Now this? You're a threat. Threats are dealt with. Except now they're wondering if you can be."

Great. I assumed the old covenants they mentioned were to do with the nature of the bond between me and Troy, and the rest was just me living my life. So, it wasn't enough that I had to play politics with the mundanes and the Othersiders, but now apparently, I had to play against the gods as well. "I just want to keep my people safe and explore what family means with Troy. That's literally it."

"You've got to be fucking kidding me."

I blinked, taken aback by the vehemence of Harqil's response as much as the cussing.

"You say that, and then you instruct your people to effectively begin building you a political empire spanning the entire eastern realm of one of the most powerful regions on the modern map."

"So that I can secure our safety! If everyone had just let me the fuck alone—"

"That's not going to fly anymore," Harqil said, so sharply that their words seemed to flay me. "Enough with this poor-little-you bullshit you've been telling yourself and everyone around you for the last two years. Give. It. Up. You could have chosen to abdicate, and then everyone would have left you alone with your king safely in control of both the territory and you. You would have had *exactly* what you claim you want. Peace and quiet and space to fuck your elf until you were permanently bow-legged with a dozen heirs. You're deceiving yourself if you think the path you've chosen *for yourself* is going to lead anywhere but power, and self-deception is the worst trick anyone can play."

The anger in me smoldered like searing hot embers, practically suffocating me with indignation. I hadn't asked for any of this. I hadn't asked to be born or be born to a six-millennia djinni and an elven prince with an agenda. I hadn't asked to be drawn in by first the hunters then the tricksters. I hadn't asked to be hunted or pushed into deposing Callista and killing the queens of the Chapel Hill Conclave to save Troy and myself.

"No," Harqil said more gently as they settled next to me on the edge of the pier, an air of tiredness making them less graceful than usual. "You didn't ask for any of it. But is it worth it, to have your sovereignty and your mate? To make the changes you both want to see in the world? Not just for yourself but for those like you both."

A dagger plunged into my heart at the idea of not having a say in what I wanted and deeper at the idea of not having Troy. "He's worth everything. He's the main reason why I bother to do any of this now. I want him to have something good in his life. For his life itself to be good."

"Then be very careful about trains of thought like the one you were just having, or you may well find out what the alternative is."

I snapped around to look at them.

"I'm not threatening Troy. Nobody is, to my knowledge. Their focus is on you now that you've preserved him from Sutekh."

Which meant that, once again, I was the greatest threat to Troy's safety. Every time I thought I was used to that idea, I found that I wasn't.

I shook it off. Even if I told Troy he could leave me to save himself, he wouldn't. I believed that to my bones. And if I was selfishly honest with myself, I was glad of it. I'd wanted someone to put me first my whole life. Now that I had him, all I could do was honor his choice. I sure as shit wasn't going to give him up if I didn't have to.

"What's the bottom line here, Harqil?" I asked.

"Your next moves, both on this plane and in the Duat, will carry more weight than anyone had anticipated at first. Expect the next trial to be more aggressive and the last to be deadly—but not in a way that you'll anticipate."

"I mean, that was all kind of a given, based on how things have been going."

Harqil sighed. "You're missing part of it. Your dream, Arden. The apocalyptic one. Speaking as myself, as a friend...that will come into play. Part of it already has."

Shaken, I thought fast, dredging the words from my memory in Troy's voice and mapping them to what'd happened since that dream. "Comes and goes is Dreamwalking? The balance is what was taken and riven, and the fire going out is losing magic?"

They nodded, opening their mouth to speak before pausing then grimacing and going on. "Cyrus is the crow."

A chill raced over me. The queen of House Veisi—Cyrus's birth House—had been the first to die. Ishtar slay me, I'd spoken my own future, and there was one more part of it.

"All that's left is dust and bone." I shuddered. "That's why the tricksters are so upset. The Nightmares sent me a threat or a test, and I'm facing it?"

Harqil shrugged, looking sick.

"I won't let that happen, the dust and bone. I'll relight the fire and bring the crow back, if I have to."

"But what price are you willing to pay?"

Anything but Troy. I kept that answer locked in my heart, already wary of losing him.

"You're learning," they said. "Good."

"Are you going to join us on any of these trials? Or just play commentator?"

"Ouch. I think that one actually hurt." They kicked at the water with a suddenly bare foot. "Despite appearances, I'm meant to be a neutral party."

"Meant to be."

Harqil's snort made me glance to the side in time to see a wry smile. "None of us tricksters like playing by other people's rules."

Before I could comment further, reality twisted, and they vanished.

I stayed where I was, pondering that. Was that a declaration that they'd help if it really came down to it or simply a comment that they wouldn't like not helping? Or was it about the sudden flood of secrets they'd just unraveled for me?

No way of knowing.

I sifted through the conversation, still rocked by what I'd learned, looking for anything that'd help me avoid the dust-and-bone part of the dream.

Troy's presence drew closer in the bond, and I twisted to find him coming out the back door. When I waved, he jogged over and took Harqil's place next to me, although he sat with knees up and arms wrapped around them rather than dropping his feet in. Not surprising. He didn't have my cold tolerance, and he absolutely hated being cold.

"So?" he asked.

"Trying to sort that out. A few things. First, something I've done has unsettled some of the celestials. The Nightmare Court came into it. And my dream. The fucked-up one." I chewed my lip. "It's already coming to pass, Troy. The Dreamwalking, the loss of magic, even your dad going home to House Veisi."

"Harqil said all that?"

"Sort of." I filled him in on the disturbing conversation about the dream he'd recounted to me.

He grunted, looking grim. "Lovely."

"Yeah. Second, my choosing to claim power means there's no turning back. For either of us."

"How so?"

"My decision not to abdicate means that, even if all I wanted was to secure our safety, I can't step back again like I did last year. Not and keep both of us safe." I glanced sideways at him. "They're not threatening you directly."

"Collateral damage."

Grimacing, I shuddered at his casual tone. "Something like that."

"I accepted that when I accepted the offer to be your consort. What else?"

I frowned, still not comfortable with the casual way he accepted threats to his life. "We beat the odds on the first two trials, so—reading between the lines—the last two will be harder than they would have been if I'd let someone die." He didn't tell me about all the threats against me, which meant I was not going to share that he was supposed to have had the best odds to die.

"They didn't get their blood sport, so they're upping the difficulty level."

I nodded.

"That doesn't seem in keeping with the rules."

"There's three sets of rules in play," I reminded him. "Theirs, Sutekh's, and mine. I didn't see it before just now, but mine only really kick in if we fail to restore magic. But the chaos that'd cause..."

"You think they'll try to push that outcome just to see what happens."

"Fuck around and find out is the definition of tricksters, so yeah. I mean, aside from this threat that I apparently represent."

Troy stayed silent, looking out over the water. Then he shrugged. "I don't like any of it. But I don't see a way around it, only through. The plan's the same. We get magic back. We secure the Eastern Seaboard. We get control of the federal government." He glanced at me, a devilish look with a dash of hope in it. "And then we explore what family means."

A shiver ran over me, a mix of his hope and a new feeling of anticipation despite the magnitude of the plan and all it entailed. "Yeah. Sounds about right."

At my confirmation, he leaned over to kiss my temple. "We'll get it done, cariñamí. I won't have it any other way."

"Neither will I." I rested my head on his shoulder, glad all over again to have him at my side and trying to let his confidence settle me. "What updates from the Guard and the Darkwatch?"

"The protests are spreading to major cities nationwide, and confrontations with law enforcement may be next. We're going to have a serious problem on our hands soon. I know you're tired, but the sooner we can get to the next trial, the better."

Exhaustion rolled over me at the idea of doing more today. The sun was overhead, which meant we'd only gotten a few hours of sleep.

"I need to rest a little more before I try another Dreamwalk. Especially if Harqil's hinting that the next one will be worse somehow." I didn't quite know what could be worse than the drowning, but the gods had been around for far longer than me and had far too much practice with being inventive. They'd think of something. I needed to be in good enough condition that I could survive it.

"Glad to hear you say that. First, though, you need to eat."

Right. Food was a thing. I couldn't remember my last meal—breakfast yesterday, maybe?—which meant it was past time to eat something. Especially if I was dragging Troy as deeply into sleep as I had earlier.

"Let's sort that out then," I said.

△▽△▽

The dream started with me running along a path in the woods. On either side, tall trees rose. Pines, from the smell and the feel of them. The ground was carpeted with leaves and pine needles. It seemed so much more peaceful in the trees, where there were clear paths for those who had the eyes to see them and clever feet to find them.

I made a conscious decision: I would run on one of these other paths.

There was more challenge in that choice. Rock to turn ankles underfoot, muddy puddles to catch shoes, fallen logs to trip over.

And yet, it was good. I felt better. More alive.

In an eyeblink or an eternity, I came to a clearing. Or almost a clearing. A tall stand of trees occupied the middle. My path went straight between them, illuminated in gold as the sun set. The goal. *My* goal.

It seemed too easy.

I looked around. To my right, the forest ended abruptly, dropping away to a cliff. A stone viewing point projected far out over the waves I could hear crashing below, and beyond the cliff, eternity stretched. Endless darkness and sparkling stars.

So, it was too easy. There was another choice: the golden grove or the eternity of stars.

I climbed a deadfall to balance on another log and study the path through the trees then the overlook. The log rolled away as I tried to find a higher vantage, and I almost fell. But I recovered and climbed up toward the highest point of the log I was on. There was definitely an ocean below the cliff. I could see it now. As I reached with the elements, I sensed interminable depths. Something bigger and grander and vaster than I could ever imagine lay in that direction, if I had the courage to look.

The golden woods seemed quaint in comparison. Small. Limited. And yet...there was a warmth there. A comfort the grandiose vision of the other path lacked.

"Both paths will offer security," a deep voice said from behind me.

I nearly fell from the log, not having sensed anyone present. Nobody was behind me, or above or below or anywhere, when I managed to get my balance and look.

"What will you choose, I wonder?" the voice boomed again, louder this time, from all sides.

Something wasn't right.

There was a presence here. Something as real as it was ephemeral.

"Who are you?" I shouted.

"Who are *you*?" it shot back.

True names were dangerous, especially in dreams. Being raised by djinn had taught me that. I steeled myself and answered. "I am huntress and trickster. Queen and exile. Lover and beloved. Maker and unmaker."

"Four times named, in duality." A sense of menace grew, reminding me of the rabisu. "You're claiming godhood, then?"

I froze. I hadn't meant to claim anything at all. I didn't even know where those words had come from. "I claim only myself."

"*Only* yourself?"

More words came from me. "Myself, which includes those bound unto myself in any of the five ways. By oath and Air, by body and Earth, by blood and Water, by aura and Fire, or by magic and Chaos."

A sense of anger flickered, heating against my metaphysical senses. "Too clever."

I bit my tongue this time. Something was very wrong. This might be my dream, but this entity—whatever or whoever it was—was not something of me. This was something that bore me ill will. Again, like the rabisu, but with deadly intelligence rather than mindless hunger.

I had to wake up. I had to get out of here.

But I couldn't reach for Troy, lest whoever it was trace the link back and find him.

Light flashed, pulling my gaze. Despite the looming sense of danger, I stared in shock. I had no idea what my mom looked like—I'd never seen any photos of either of my parents, given the only ones available were those the coroner had taken, and I hadn't had the courage to look at them. But this woman looked enough like me that I couldn't imagine who else she could be. Darker eyes and skin, with an elf's sharp, white secondary teeth as she snarled at the point in space where the presence was strongest. But she carried a djinni's bright lemon-zest scent.

"Mom?" I whispered.

"Meddler," the presence raged.

"The Court has no business with her. Not yet," the woman said.

"The Court has business with whoever we choose. Especially those who claim making and unmaking but embody order and disorder."

"Not this time. You sent your warning. This is just intimidation." Her voice became darkly teasing, almost a threat. "Are you that afraid of a mortal?"

The presence rose, deeper and darker. Angrier. "We shall evaluate. And then we shall act."

The woman who might be my mother turned and pushed in my direction with both hands. "Wake, Arden."

I sat up, gasping for breath, tears running down my face.

"Arden?" Troy bolted upright. "What happened? What's wrong?"

"A dream." I couldn't say the rest out loud. *I had to make a choice. And then there was some kind of presence, asking who I was. It didn't like how I named myself, and something was wrong. But then there was a light and—oh Goddess, my mother.*

Your mother? You dreamed of her?

No, she was there, *in my dream. It had to be her.*

Troy stewed on that. *Real? Alive?*

Not like it feels when we're Dreamwalking. I don't know. I think maybe it was her ghost or her spirit or something. Tears fell hot and fast down my cheeks, and I had to push the elements away lest I summon another storm. *She was there, Troy. She protected me.*

Okay, my love. I believe you.

With his faith, I calmed down a little bit. I might feel like I was losing my mind, but if Troy could take my ramblings on faith, so could I. Slowly and haltingly, I laid back down, heart still pounding. *They're coming for me, Troy. Just like Harqil said. My other dream was a threat, and we're running out of time.*

He laid down beside me and gently tugged at me until I was on my side then wrapped himself around me and kissed the back of my neck. *Whoever threatened you, I'll kill if they try for you.*

What if it was the Nightmare Court?

Troy didn't hesitate. *Anyone. Even them.*

Chapter 17

My sleep was restless after that, with echoes of the words "order and disorder" loud in the back of my mind. I couldn't help but think it was a clue to the next trial, like "shape and form" had been before the last one.

When I gave up on sleep and dragged myself outside, everyone caught my shitty mood and gave me a wide berth. With a dull resignation, I first destroyed the corpses of the two humans Cade had fed on sometime in the last twelve hours. Then I showered, ate, and sorted out all the necessities to keep my body in good order.

Or almost all of them. I could use a good fuck, but between the lack of privacy, the deadline, and our overall tiredness, Troy and I settled for my perching on his lap at the fire kettle, much to the consternation and confusion of everyone except him. Yeah, it was highly inappropriate, completely unprofessional, and was probably undermining my own authority, but the effects of my trip to Asheville lingered for both of us. I needed the closeness, doubly so with my inner agitation.

Troy was delighted at the clear mark of my favor, probably especially with all the people who'd received my blood recently. He lounged in the chair with a king's satisfied arrogance, even as he played furniture, one hand loose on my hip, the other swiping out a text message to Allegra as I nibbled on a toaster waffle and stared out over the lake, considering the small box in my other hand.

Both our hearing was good enough to catch the sounds of Cade vigorously fucking Lya in their tent a few yards away, even if they were trying to be quiet about it, but I wouldn't begrudge them the moment.

Troy finished his message and shifted us to shove his phone in his pocket. "We need to figure out next steps."

"Mmm." I took another bite of my waffle. The blueberry in it tasted fake, which was kind of grossing me out after getting used to Troy's homemade food, but it would give me a little carb boost. One I badly needed, given I was running on fumes. "The first trial was Fire. The second was Water. I think the third will be Earth."

"And the fourth Air?"

"No. They won't give me Air. That would be too much of an advantage on my part. Chaos, maybe."

"I'm coming with you this time."

My heart squeezed as the mental image of him bleeding out on firelit sand intruded. "No. I need you to anchor me here."

"If the trial is to do with Earth—"

"I know. You carried me out of the lich's lair. That's why I need you here." I leaned to kiss him, hoping to take the sting out of my order and the tight tone I delivered it in. "I keep thinking about the last trial. The water crashing down. Troy, I think I only woke up because I was trying to get back to you."

He cupped my cheek and pulled me forward, resting his forehead against mine. "Thanks, I hate it."

I snorted, amused at hearing one of my phrases from him despite the seriousness of the situation. "I know. But something is shifting. My magic feels different somehow. If I made a storm coming back the last time, what might happen this time? Would I bring the building down and kill everyone in it?"

"I suppose it's best we don't find out the hard way. Or try not to."

Light footsteps pulled our attention to Mami Wata, who circled and dropped into the chair opposite ours. "I'd forgotten the stamina a vampire his age has with a good feed. Goddess preserve me. We'll be here all day."

"We were just talking about the next trial," I said, deciding not to comment on other people's sex lives, given I'd be after Troy like that the first chance I got, exhausted or not. "Are you amenable to another trip?"

Her dark eyes glittered with amusement. "You do show better sense and respect than the half-elf did when I first met her, and it's good to touch magic again. Besides, my sisters need this. I suppose I could join you."

"Glad to hear it. I think we can take the rest as well, if they're up to it."

She glanced over my shoulder. "And your king?"

"Holding your exit," Troy said.

The fae considered that. "You must be even stronger than you let on, to anchor a primordial elemental alone."

Troy's grip on me tightened for a moment before loosening again. "She keeps me around for more than my pretty face."

Hmm. Did Mami Wata know about that legend Harqil had mentioned—Adhara?

Did Troy?

I felt like I was missing something here, and not just here. There were a few other half-remembered comments that I'd thought were dreams but maybe weren't. Now wasn't the time to ask though.

I pinched his chin, scratchy with the beard he was letting grow in, and shook his head lightly. "I certainly do, although a pretty face doesn't hurt."

Mami Wata snorted. "You might think differently if you met my sisters."

The sound of a tent opening behind us said Mason would be joining us momentarily. I finished my waffle in two undignified bites and hefted the box we'd stolen on our last trip as he settled carefully in a chair between Mami Wata and me and Troy.

"Arbiter. King Troy. Lady fae," he greeted us politely.

"Sleep okay?" I asked.

He grimaced. "Bad dreams. But if that box has the second key, worth it."

Cade and Lya made their way to the fire kettle while we finished up with pleasantries. The vampire was moving more fluidly than I'd seen up to now, with an air of menace hanging over him. Not directed at us, just the honed confidence of a five-hundred-year-old apex predator, even without his glamour. He took the chair deepest in the shadows of the sunshades that'd been set up to accommodate him.

Lya looked smug as hell as she settled on his lap and snuggled into him, making me and Troy look demure.

"Feeling better?" Mami Wata sniped.

"Much, thank you, darling. A good solidaire is a blessing from Hekate, especially in difficult times." Cade practically purred the words, completely unbothered, one hand caressing Lya's unbitten throat in what seemed like absentminded possessiveness.

The bounty hunter didn't seem to mind at all, so I ignored it.

"Now that we're all here," I said, "I need to understand why we got a key the first time and a box this time."

Cade answered. "Key was in an unlocked box in the first trial. We just had to figure out which of the four inside was the one we needed."

Blood drained from my face. "There were four keys? How do you know we got the right one?"

"That's the only one that tingled," Lya said. "I didn't get Aether back over there, per se, but I got a sense of... I dunno. Like the one we brought back had power. The others felt like nothing. The only thing in the second temple was that box—surrounded by traps, by the way, like some kind of

Goddess-damned adventure film. We grabbed it as quick as we could and ran like hell."

I did my best to keep my expression neutral. There was no going back now, and I had to trust that everyone here needed magic restored badly enough that they would try their damnedest not to fuck it up. The sharp edge to the bond said Troy was reining his reaction in as well.

Shifting on his lap, I fished for the first key in my pocket.

"Is that the most secure place for it?" Lya asked.

"*You* might want to try a primordial elemental, cousin. Most people have more sense," Troy said.

The lightness of his tone and his acknowledgment of their family tie made the half-elf purse her lips as though she was looking for an insult then grin. "Touché."

I bounced the key on my palm, unfocusing my gaze and falling into it with Chaos. The spark I got from it made me hiss. "It's definitely got some kind of charge."

Passing the key to Troy, I perched the box on my fingers and peered at it. At first glance, it was a solid cube of stone, squat with small feet on each corner. Hieroglyphics marched in straight lines along the top edge, all the way around. The more I stared at them, the more I fell into the box.

Lya's distant voice: "Is she okay?"

"She's fine," Troy said. "Shh."

There. A crack, finer than a hair, all the way around. So, it was definitely a box. Drawing on Earth and a little Fire, I delicately traced the crack, rotating the thing as I did. On the third side, there was a divot.

I halted before I could lose it and shifted my grip to hold it in one hand. "Key."

Troy placed it back in my hand.

A resonance started.

"Why is she rocking?" Lya asked.

"Shut. Up," Troy responded as Cade shushed her.

Their chatter was a little distracting, and I closed my eyes completely, letting my third eye and my elemental senses tell me what was going on.

Ah. It was Earth and Fire, blended with Chaos as an illusion. What looked like a slip of the chisel was a keyhole, off-center and obscured.

I started to put the key to it—then froze as the Sight screamed. No. Not there.

I turned my wrist to show the fourth side, where there was no divot, only smooth stone under my fingers, but where my senses said there was another keyhole.

"Show me," I whispered with a push of blended Chaos, Earth, and Fire.

The spot under my thumb roughened with the outline of another keyhole, and I grinned. This time when I lifted the first key, nothing stopped me.

Carefully, so carefully, I inserted it. Held my breath. Turned it.

With a small click and a puff of frankincense, the lid loosened. I exhaled and held out the key again, waiting for Troy's hand to engulf mine and take it before letting it go. Then I gently pried the lid off.

The inside was filled with sand.

Something was wrong about it though. Another trap. Legends of the fae Sandman came to mind, and it suddenly seemed like it'd be a very bad idea to reach in there.

After a brief hesitation, I used a tendril of Air to fish the key out, staying focused on not scattering sand as it emerged. I cleaned it off with a burst of Air and hovered it over my hand, unwilling to risk Troy directly if I'd missed some sand.

It fell into my palm without incident.

I sighed with relief. "Don't touch the sand in this box. I don't know what will happen, but something's not right about it."

"Delicate bit of work," Mami Wata said as Troy carefully pressed the lid back on the box.

I didn't answer, too busy studying the key I'd fished out. There was something wrong with it, like if I held it too tightly and shifted my fingers...

It split in two down its full length.

I stared at it.

"Was it...supposed to do that?" Mason asked cautiously.

"I hope so," Lya muttered. "I'm not going back into the river to look for another one."

After reading it with Earth, I pinched my fingers and snapped it back together, then split it again, then made it whole. "Order and disorder. We have two keys, and we also have three." I looked at Lya. "Guess you grabbed the right key. Thank you."

She grinned. "Glad somebody sees my talents."

Cade nipped her neck, making her yelp.

"Somebody *else*," she amended.

"That's more like it," he murmured, sounding amused more than anything else.

"So, what now?" Mason asked as he studiously ignored the pair. "We've got two keys. Or three. What else do we need?"

As I started to answer, Lya looked at her phone and swore.

"You wanna share with the class?" I asked when her expression blanked.

Cade leaned to look at it over her shoulder. "Complication with our handler. He wants to meet."

"Handler?" Mason asked.

Lya smiled brightly. "We were hired to kill the Arbiter."

The werewolf paled as Mami Wata burst out laughing.

"Of course you were," she said. "Especially *you*."

When Lya rolled her eyes, I assumed that last was aimed at her, but I didn't have time for whatever history was between those two and Cade.

"What's your handler want?" I asked.

"An update," Lya said. "Face-to-face. Or rather, face-to-video. He wants to know what's taking so long, as though just anybody could walk up to you and take your head."

"Can you get out of it?" Troy asked.

The tight note was back in his voice again, but I got the feeling it was for more than the threat to my life. There was something between him and whoever had sent the bounty hunters. House Lestari? I didn't even know where they were based.

Lya twisted to look at Cade, who grimaced and shook his head.

"The terms were pretty ironclad," he said. "Check-ins every week, on video, were one of the conditions."

"You're only just now mentioning this?" I snapped. I had thought we were making progress on trust but apparently not.

He shrugged. "They're early. We weren't supposed to be contacted for another three days, and from your plan, it sounded like we were going to be done by then. Magic would have been returned, and we could have played it off like we'd succeeded long enough to disappear again."

I rose from Troy's lap, too agitated now to sit. "What happens if you don't check in?"

"They wait six hours, try again, then another six. If we don't respond, they send another team."

Troy rose as well, looming with arms crossed. "Standard Darkwatch protocol. The other team will already be here. Probably have the place you were supposed to be staying staked out. Your extended absence spooked them. Damn it." He started for the boathouse, calling back over his shoulder, "I'll update Etain and get Omar on counter-espionage."

Which left me to sort out what to do about the mess now.

Mami Wata stood and stretched. "Always dragging trouble after you, girl."

Lya started to snarl back, pressing her lips together when Cade squeezed her shoulder.

"Why not go for a swim?" he suggested. "We'll need a short while to sort this."

"Not a bad idea," she said. "Arbiter?"

"Yeah, give us half an hour to figure this out, please."

With a flash of python teeth that seemed mockingly threatening, she headed for the lake. Mason also excused himself to his tent, leaving me with the bounty hunters.

"Good thing we're not tempted to take that bounty," Lya quipped lightly as she drafted, erased, and redrafted a text reply. "I'm surprised Troy would leave you alone like this."

"He knows I can handle myself," I said. Personally, I suspected this was a loyalty test for these two. That, and I could sense the Ebon Guards camouflaged in blinds in the woods, and the metal of the rifles they had aimed at the other two. I wasn't sure when those blinds had gone in, but I was glad of them now.

"I'm telling them that we're at a critical juncture," Lya said. "No time to call."

We waited for the message to go through, and for the reply.

"Bugger." She glanced at Cade, who shrugged and turned to me.

"They want video," he said. "Your call, Arbiter."

I crossed my arms to stop myself from indulging in a zephyr to calm myself while I thought. "Where's House Lestari based?"

"Seattle," Cade said.

Not too long ago, Troy had mentioned being in Seattle. Offhand, like it hadn't been much of anything, but now I was wondering if it was something more—and if it was tied to this assassination attempt. That seemed like too much of a coincidence, my former-assassin fiancé being in the city that was now the source of an assassination threat.

Something was off here, as it had been for pretty much everything in the last few days. I was getting tired of it.

I didn't push Troy on his past as a general rule. Too much of it was brutal and ugly and sent him to a bad headspace when he dug too deep or looked too close before he was ready. He was slowly working through it, sharing pieces with me as he felt able. I definitely couldn't and wouldn't push him on it now, not when I needed him to be my anchor so that we could get through these bullshit trials.

But as soon as we had magic back, it was gonna be time for me to ask the man I loved some questions I wasn't sure I wanted the answer to.

Chapter 18

After a short argument, we ended up taking Cade and Lya back to my place for their video call. I didn't like it, given this new wrinkle in our trust situation. But everyone knew by now that I lived near Eno River State Park, and if the call was traced, it'd look legit. They could just say that they were doing recon, having nearly been caught by the gytrash on their first attempt.

While they handled that under Thana, Vern, and Pascale's observation, I checked in with Terrence and Ximena. Those of their cats who'd been trapped in leopard or jaguar form were doing just fine roaming my grounds. Darnell was struggling with his leopard but hanging on with Lola's help. My fenced backyard had tents pitched in it—the pride might be using my land, but even the alphas thought using my bedroom was a step too far.

Privately, I was grateful for it. My bedroom had always been my inner sanctum, the one space I didn't let people into unless there was a real damn good reason. I'd told myself the loss of magic was a good reason when I'd offered the pride the use of my house and grounds, but in my heart of hearts, I was pleased they were only using the bathroom and kitchen. Better still, most of them weren't staying at my place permanently but hiking in or out as needed to be with those of the pride trapped in cat form or to run in the safety of my woods. That kept the number of people down and didn't make any obvious traffic up and down my driveway.

Formalities complete, I headed down the river trail to my practice area with Troy a silent presence at my side. Despite the chill, I stripped off my shoes and socks and walked straight into the river, dropping onto one of the bigger rocks in the middle with a sigh of relief. I'd claimed the land at Jordan Lake, but no land would ever be as much mine as this.

Troy stayed on shore, looking unusually fidgety. I gave him space, figuring he was working himself up to something and trying to have the patience to wait it out even if he was giving me fits of paranoia like he had in the early days.

"I should tell you something," he finally said.

I kept my attention on the river. "Should isn't must, or want for that matter."

"Are you giving me an out?"

"Do you want one?"

He hesitated as guilt filtered through the bond. "Yes."

"Then you have one." I turned to give him a serious look. "I know House Lestari is out in Seattle. I know you were in Seattle. I'm clever enough to see those facts are probably connected somehow and connected again with our bounty hunter friends. But unless it has a direct bearing on getting magic back, I don't need to know the details right this second, okay? I trust you, even if I'm curious as fuck."

That cut the tension in the bond a little. "Thank you."

"What'd Omar say?" I asked to change the subject after a minute of silence, in which he seemed to be putting dark thoughts into mental boxes to deal with later.

"We have a serious problem."

I closed my eyes with a sigh and leaned over to trail my fingers in the river, soothed by it as I hadn't been by the Nile full of damned souls in the Duat and grateful for that. I don't know what I would have done if that last experience with water had screwed me out of enjoying the Eno.

When I was calm enough not to snap at him, I asked, "What kind of problem?"

"More dead queens."

This time I couldn't help the sharpness of my attention on him. "Excuse me?"

"All either apparent suicides or coups."

"When you say 'all,' how many are we talking?"

"Half a dozen now." His tone flattened out even further. "Nobody's saying it, but I think we both know it's my father. Either directly or via incitement of local actors."

My whole body tightened as my guts clenched. I couldn't tell if it was outrage or fear, but I was *not* happy. "Are you shitting me? Troy, I just told the parliament to keep their people under control and—"

"I know, Arden. I know." The bond roiled with his agitation. "I ordered Omar to look into it. Dad's striking places outside our claimed territory though. Detroit, Niagara Falls, Knoxville."

I dug my fingers into my temples, trying to stave off a headache. "Treading the line between not making it my problem because it's literally not in my territory, as ordered, but making it my problem because I'm directly responsible for his freedom and repatriation."

"Yes." Troy sighed and crouched at the river's edge, dipping his fingers in as though he was seeking the same calm I was. "And honestly? I don't think he'll stop until we get magic back. You heard the things he was saying."

Cyrus had made his pitch to end the elven queens at a family lunch before I, backed up by Troy, had shut him down. I hadn't wanted more death. But Cyrus was on a goddamn mission, and thanks to his trickster patron, he still had the magic to back it up. Even if my mom had wanted to destroy the matriarchy for reasons only she knew, this ran the risk of becoming the kind of hard reset neither she nor I had been able to achieve.

For my part, I hadn't wanted it like this, elemental bounties or not. I suspected part of the reason the elves were so damn reluctant to actively support elementals was out of a fear we'd do to them what they'd spent the last few millennia doing to us: hunting us out of existence. But from what I'd seen, elementals—including me—would be happy with being left alone to thrive in peace.

We couldn't change the past. We could only build better futures.

I really did not want it to come to hunting down Troy's father. But as it stood now, I might have to. I couldn't give an order to maintain control to the parliament alongside a statement that I was going to get control of the entire Eastern Seaboard and then have Cyrus fucking Veisi going vigilante on the queens.

I didn't even know how he was picking targets. And all of a sudden, I was too tired to care. "I can't make this my problem. I might have brought him back, but I have bigger shit to deal with. We brought him back under specific conditions. He broke them. He's responsible."

"That will only fly if we get magic back."

Frustrated, I stood and splashed my way back to shore. "Then let's get going. Between him and the mundane protests, things are about to go to the ninth circle of hell on the express handcart."

Cade and Lya were leaning against their Ford Escape when we made our way back up to the house. One of the Ebon Guard must have fetched it over for them because last I knew it'd been at HQ for processing.

The vampire straightened. "We were thinking we should go back to our lodgings temporarily. Be seen—"

"Restock," Lya interrupted, patting her curls. "I need a few things if we're going to be living in the woods another few days."

I glanced at Troy. *Send the triad?*

Definitely.

"Fine," I said to the pair. "But the Ebon Guard stays with you."

"Sure," Lya agreed easily.

I didn't know her well enough to know whether it was real or fake. I wanted it to be real. They'd proven themselves capable and we needed more Watchers in the territory. But I didn't know them outside of a few missions into the Duat, which ultimately served their interests—getting magic back and fucking off.

"Okay," I said. "Good hunting."

That brought a grin to her face. "Always is."

Once they were gone and the unhappy triad of Ebon Guard with them, Troy and I hit the road for Jordan Lake. I found myself dreading it slightly and tried to distract myself. "How far do you think we can trust them?"

"Helping us gets magic back, which helps them," Troy said, echoing my earlier thoughts. "We can trust them not to stab us in the back until then at least. But I reread Lya's dossier. She'll look to herself first, her vampire second. Maybe him first in certain circumstances. But outside the two of them? Nobody. Not without a good reason."

"So, you think they still have trust to earn."

He grunted a yes, and we fell into silence.

It should have been an easy and peaceful one, but I...itched. There was no other way to describe it. I was alone with Troy, really alone, for the first time in days and still agitated by my extended absence. Agitated as in, increasingly horny as hell the longer I was alone with him in a confined space that already smelled deliciously of him.

We were on a deadline. We were stressed out and tired and frustrated by everything we couldn't control. But just now, I needed a little damn quality time with my mate, or I was going to have a problem.

I decided to choose me—or rather, us—before the feedback loop building in the bond made one of us do something we'd regret at camp.

As we turned down the road to the boathouse, I said, "Was it you who found my car?"

From the sudden tension and uneasy sideways look, he knew what I was talking about. "Yes."

"You remember the turnoff where it was?"

"Yes. Arden, what—"

"Pull in there."

That got me a full-on frown. "Why?"

"Because it's a good hiding spot."

Mild confusion filtered through the bond, but he did as I asked, slowing to find the small gap in the trees where I'd parked my car on my first mission to stake out Leith's Redcap base. It was more overgrown now, but the higher carriage of Troy's SUV managed the terrain fine.

"Okay, now what?" he asked.

I leaned over to nibble his ear, smiling at his sharp inhale. "Turn off the car and get in the back seat."

Heat burned through the bond as he finally figured out my plan. "You seriously want to fuck in the back seat like teenagers?"

"I never did it before, so yes."

A slow grin curled his lips. "You know what? Neither did I." He opened the windows a crack.

"What's that for?"

"I don't need my windows blown out when you come." He turned off the car and stepped out, leaving the bright scent of fresh herbs behind him.

The casual statement of assurance in my impending pleasure made my whole body hot, and my skin prickled with desire. I hurried to follow, shrugging out of my coat and sliding into the back seat, glad for the tinted windows on top of the secluded location. There were too many people around and had been for too many days on the back of my return from Asheville. While I didn't mind public displays of affection and couldn't help if our lovemaking could be scented by any Othersider, I still found it awkward for people to hear us having sex sometimes. Or at least I did until Troy made me forget myself, but I wanted to serve him without worrying about that. Remind him that I knew he had needs, both physical and emotional, and even with the world falling apart, he was still a priority to me.

He held himself in check as he slid in beside me and closed his door.

A pleased, aroused growl rumbled in his chest as I straddled his lap then slowly pulled my shirt over my head.

"I like where this is going." He gripped my hips tight, thrusting up once. The gold flecks in his gaze sparked, and hunger tightened his expression.

Grinding down onto him, I unhooked my bra without breaking eye contact and tossed it aside then gathered my breasts, pinching and rolling my nipples as I presented them to him. "Good. Take what's yours...my king."

Where there was heat in the bond before, it flared into an inferno now. If Troy loved anything in bed, it was the taboo of being served by a queen and, on top of that, being verbally acknowledged as not only a king but an equal—or in this case, more.

With a dangerously intense look, he lowered his mouth to one breast, suckled, then shifted to the other.

I arched back in pleasure and encouragement, continuing to grind on his lap. When he added teeth to the mix, I gasped as my core tightened, even if it was just the blunt ones.

He lifted a hand from my hip to my hair, forcing me to arch back further and stretching my entire body in a long line until the front seat stopped us. A single finger dragged down my front from chin to navel before he leaned forward and kissed my neck then nibbled it.

"Get out of those jeans," he ordered in the lazy, arrogant tones he used when playing the king. Not the clipped and direct way he spoke when giving orders as king in public. Just when he was stepping into his role as *my* king. The sexually dominant one. The side of himself he had only ever shared with me and even then only occasionally.

I flushed, as always equal parts embarrassed by how much I enjoyed this side of him and utterly aroused by it, and hesitated.

Troy arched an eyebrow and lifted his chin. "If I have to tell you again..."

"Yes, my king." I scrambled off his lap and worked my jeans off.

He tugged off his jacket and dragged his shirt over his head to reveal toned muscle. "That's more like it."

The newly smooth skin on his belly surprised me for a moment before I remembered it'd healed after what I'd done in the Duat.

"Traitor no more," he said when he caught me looking.

I froze. "That's what that word was? It said traitor?"

"In elvish. Evangeline's work."

Horrified by his family all over again, I stared.

Slowly, he reached out and clasped my throat. "I wasn't finished with you."

I went on autopilot, letting him lead as he pulled me back onto his lap. Then I flipped from shock to outrage, renewing my determination to show him he was important and needed and *mine.* I couldn't do the same tricks he could with Aether, but his body was so painfully attuned to mine, the hormonal connection so intense, that my touch and the hunger of my kisses on every part of him I could reach with my mouth had him tilting his head back and panting in an effort to control himself and let me serve him.

"Fuck it," he snarled. With rough movements, he opened his jeans. "Up."

I lifted my hips long enough for him to work his jeans down. Then he grabbed me again and, slowing only long enough to fist himself and align with my entrance, pulled me down onto his length.

I cried out as he held me down and ground up, as much from the pleasure as from the intensity pouring through the bond. The animal part of my brain took over, and I let go, riding him with hurried rolls of my hips.

"I love you. I'm yours," I gasped, kissing his neck and running my hands over him, desperate to stay close, to reconnect even days after my return. "Always."

Troy's phone buzzed, and he snarled but ignored it, shifting his jaw to drop his sharp teeth.

I tilted my head and stretched my neck on the opposite side of that he'd bitten earlier, knowing what he wanted and offering it before he had to say anything.

He bit deeper this time. Not a little nibble to humor me but a claiming as he thrust up into me with a chest-deep growl that sent a thrill of excited fear through me. Whatever that did to my scent made him climax hard.

Mine followed as I rode his pleasure in the bond to my finish, clenching around his cock almost painfully. It was a good thing he'd cracked those windows because I did slip on my grasp of Air.

His grip tightened around me as he withdrew his teeth but kept sucking, pulling hard at the meat of my shoulder to both take blood and leave a hickey. I was distantly aware that I'd neglected him too long if he was doing all that, but it felt too good for me to worry.

We stayed joined, both of us panting and shaking from the ferocity of what'd passed between us, until Troy's phone buzzed again.

"Fuck," he muttered.

With an arm tight around my waist to keep me pinned against him, he leaned and reached blindly for his jacket and the phone in its pocket.

Tingling with contentment, I collapsed against him and nuzzled into his neck, satisfying us both with a long, slow inhale of the scent patch at the corner of his jaw. "Who's it?"

"One from Iago. He thinks they've managed to stall the subpoena. Another from Dari. Worried that we're late."

A dial tone said Troy was calling.

"It's me. We're fine," he said when the call was picked up.

The tinny, distant phone-voice of Darius said, "Where the hell are you?"

"We took a detour."

"A detour. An *unscheduled* detour, alone, when you're the only two with magic and we're on a deadline. What if there are more bounty hunters?"

"I needed to attend to my queen."

A long pause. Then, in a lower, exasperated tone Darius said, "Please don't tell me you have half the camp ready to go on a rescue mission because you wanted a quickie."

"Duty called," Troy said smugly.

"My fault," I said in a slightly slurred voice.

"Just following orders," Troy agreed. Both of us snickered at the irony of it—him unwillingly being trained to serve a queen, only to enjoy it this much because said queen served him as well.

"Goddess save us all. Just get back here," Darius snapped.

The call ended.

"I need a minute," I said. The social hormones underlying the bond were running at a peak, and all I wanted was to stay pressed against him.

"You can have it, but I might fuck you again," he said.

I almost called bullshit, but he was already getting hard again inside me.

"Don't threaten me with a good time," I said, throwing one of his phrases at him.

With a low chuckle and a kiss, he did more than tease.

Chapter 19

Darius was standing with fists on hips, wearing a glare I wouldn't have thought he could summon when Troy pulled up to the boathouse.

"You two have got to be kidding me," he snarled in the low voice of Darius the Knight of Monteague—not Dari the younger brother—when we got out. Then his nostrils flared, and he looked straight at my bitten shoulder, like he could see the mark through my T-shirt and jacket. His expression shifted to one so much like Omar's look of disapproval that it stung. *"Seriously?"*

"Mind your business," I snapped. "Spoiler alert: this isn't it."

Troy sent an Aetheric nudge to calm down. "Wait and see what happens if you bond," he said in quiet tones. "Even without the bond, trust me when I say Arden's more effective when she's satisfied and calm."

My flush probably matched Darius's. Troy wouldn't have intended to embarrass either of us, but we had just been responsible for a massive security concern and I supposed the reason had to match the impact or both of us would look weak—lost to our hormones.

Darius gave Troy a hard, thin-lipped look. "Fine. But, T? You *tell me* next time. I can't protect you if I don't know where you are."

Troy stiffened, looking like he wanted to argue before loosening his posture to his usual combat-ready ease. "I'll keep that in mind."

Rolling his eyes, Darius shook his head, like this wasn't the first time he'd dealt with Troy's stubbornness in the face of a request. "We're just waiting on the bounty hunters."

I glanced at the fire kettle to find Mami Wata conversing with Mason. The werewolf's expression was somewhere between fascination and horror, and I really hoped she wasn't scaring him off somehow. I was starting to think he was a bit of a softie, for a wolf, or at least not as driven by all the political ambition as the rest of Blood Moon had been, for all that he'd made it to fourth rank in the clan.

"They might be a little longer," Troy said.

"Shaking the other team?"

"Trying to." Troy checked his phone. "Nothing from the Captain on House Lestari yet. Nothing from anybody on the mundanes. Just media hysteria."

Darius studied him. "You don't like the idea of going in without knowing more."

"No, I don't." He lowered his voice. "Arden's vulnerable when she's Dreamwalking. It's hard for me to wake her. That makes me vulnerable."

I frowned. "Even with the callstone?"

"Yes. That just lets me talk to you." Troy leaned to kiss my head. "Don't get me wrong—I'm glad to have it. I'd rather not give you a pain sting if it's not needed. But if the others can't reassure the Lestaris, or worse, bring them back here..."

"Yeah," I said. "You're stuck with half your attention on me in a dream while trying to protect me and give orders."

"Do we need more people?" Darius asked.

"Can't risk it. I wouldn't mind having Alli back up here, but good luck getting her away from Maria right now with anything less than a direct order and a fight over it."

"She can do her Goddess-damned duty and report in."

I blinked at the unexpected annoyance in Darius's voice.

"Apologies, ma'am. I just... Nothing. Never mind."

Troy was looking at him strangely as well, which made me wonder if this was about the as-yet unanswered marriage offer from Sonia Bedoe. As far as I knew, Darius was still considering what to do about it. This reaction suggested he wasn't too keen. Combine that with me and Troy disappearing to fuck in a love-addled fog for a good hour, and the normally even-natured Darius was apparently feeling the pinch of what he felt duty called for. And maybe what he really wanted.

I squeezed his arm briefly. "When this is over, we can talk about options for you, okay?"

He froze. "I didn't— Really, it's fine."

"It's not. Nobody's asked you what you wanted," I said, remembering my thought that he might well have been something other than Darkwatch, had it been left up to him. We'd just kind of rolled him into my security detail because, as Troy's brother-cousin, he registered as safe to both of us. But that wasn't really fair. Troy wasn't the only traumatized Monteague who'd never been given a choice.

The conflicted expression that flickered across his face before he could hide it said I was right. "I..." He looked at the ground and rubbed a hand over his head, looking like he was gathering his courage. "Okay, yeah. I'd appreciate that."

As Troy pulled him into a sideways hug, reality twisted.

Mason leaped up with a growled curse, but Mami Wata was completely unimpressed by Harqil's arrival.

The celestial made a beeline for me and Troy and leaned close to speak for our ears only—quite the feat in present company. "We're about to have trouble with the elves."

I barely stopped myself from saying, "Again?" and instead asked, "What kind?"

"The kind that involves Cyrus."

Troy closed his eyes, breathed deep, and shook his head. "We know."

"You know he's behind the deaths of queens, I'm sure. But you don't know—"

Troy's phone rang.

"Get that," Harqil said.

With a glance at the caller ID and a sharp look at Harqil, Troy answered. "Hi, Dad. What kind of trouble are you up to these days?"

I shifted closer to Troy and leaned on his back, which made it easy to hear the elder man's response.

"Oh, you know. Vengeance and chaos." A low, almost savage chuckle. "The good stuff."

"You need to stop," Troy said harshly. "You've made your point."

"Have I? Hmm. I'm surprised at you, boy. After how Keithia treated you? And the things I've heard about that Vina and her mother."

Troy went rock solid under my hands. The bond plunged into the nasty, dark depths where his assassin mindset lived, before he walled himself off from me, and his next words were devoid of any tone or emotion. "Think very carefully about what you say next."

"All right. In that case, you need to stop pushing so hard on getting magic back."

"And why is that?"

"For my part, because I still have work to do. Protecting Ninlil's daughter long enough to shepherd her into Dreamwalking was only half the oath I swore, and Ninlil isn't the only one I swore to."

"That sounds like a you problem."

Cyrus sighed. "I was afraid you'd say that. Let's try this, then. If you don't get your queen to back off from getting magic back, you will both regret it."

Outrage flared in me. *I thought he swore an oath?*

"What happened to your oath to protect Arden?" Troy said.

"It had a completion condition, or I wouldn't have sworn it. That condition has been met."

Goddess damn the man. I hadn't even thought about a loophole like that.

"So you're threatening my queen," Troy snarled. "My *bondmate*."

"You know I'd free you from her if I could."

Darius's eyes went big and round, like he couldn't believe what his uncle was saying.

"I don't want to be free of her." Troy turned and pulled me tight against him. "I want to marry her."

Another heavy sigh from Cyrus. "Then as grateful as I am to Omar for keeping you alive, Goddess damn him for indoctrinating you. And damn *you* for settling. You're a goldeneye king, Troy! You could have the entire continent on your own. But you settle for being the toy of another queen."

Somehow, those words hit me like a hammer blow. I'd found Cyrus difficult to deal with, but I thought I'd treated him fairly. Had that just been me patting myself on the back and seeing myself as his savior? Or was this nothing to do with me and everything to do with hurts two or three times my lifetime in the making?

Rather than continuing to argue, Troy gathered himself.

"Make your threats," he said calmly.

"Delay your queen. I don't care how. Advise her to go handle the mundane riots. Fuck the ever-loving daylights out of her for a few days, if it pleases you. But if she tries for the third key before the coming eclipse, we'll bury her."

I stiffened. Not just at the threat but also at the timeline. He wanted us to do nothing for a full nine days? While mundane protests made a magicless Otherside extra vulnerable? He had to be insane. Or was something worse planned at the eclipse? Cyrus had said that things like artifacts and mindmazes would stick temporarily. Maybe that was when they'd fail? I tried to remember if this was a surge eclipse or a draining one, but that was more the witches' purview. Either way, eclipses always impacted magic somehow.

Troy's grip tightened around me. "We?"

"My Patron. Or me." There was a long pause during which neither man spoke. Then Cyrus said, "I don't want to lose you, Troy. Not again. But I'm beginning to fear that I already have. In that case, what have I got left to lose?"

The call ended.

With sharp, deliberate movements, Troy tucked his phone back into his pocket and wrapped both arms around me.

"Orders?" Darius asked softly from behind Troy.

Well? Troy sent.

"I won't run scared," I said aloud. "Not of Cyrus, not of whoever his patron is, and not of Sutekh or anyone else. That never works out for me."

Harqil circled to stand in front of Troy, waiting until I turned in his arms to speak. "He could do it, Arden. Bury you."

I tried to sound casual, despite the pounding of my heart and the small tremor adrenaline was sending through me. "I already figured Earth would be part of the next trial."

The haunted look on Harqil's expression made my heart skip a beat. "That's putting it lightly."

"What do you mean?" Troy asked. A low growl underscored his words.

"I mean, you might want to take some shabti this time." At my confused look, they said, "You know. Alternates? Made of clay or whatever you have to hand."

I still didn't get it. "Alternate what?"

"Yous. Or thems." They waved in the general direction of first me then the fire kettle. "Literal effigies of earth, hand-sized. Traditionally, a shabti took on any unwanted labor in Aaru, the true afterlife. Who wants to work in the paradise that is the Field of Reeds?"

Troy held me even tighter, enough that I had to wiggle to get him to lighten up as he said, "The only labor in this trial is fighting or dying."

"Always did say you were cleverer than you looked," Harqil said. The quip landed flat though, like the topic was too close and too real for even a trickster celestial to make light of it.

"Fuck," I whispered.

"You seem more attached to this squad you put together than I was expecting, and Anansi did say to serve you well," Harqil said, looking at their fingernails rather than at me. "I suppose I'm assuming you'd be aggrieved if something *untoward* were to happen to your people."

"Yes. Fuck yes. I'm responsible for them, Harqil. They go in because they trust me."

"They're desperate," the celestial said.

"We all are. But they're risking themselves specifically, rather than waiting for someone else to do something, because they have faith in *me.*"

I waited for someone, anyone, to contradict me, but nobody did.

Fantastic. Sometimes I hated being right.

"How do we make shabti?" I asked.

"Your djinn can help. I'll just fetch them over here." Reality twisted again, and Harqil disappeared, leaving only the scent of hot stone.

I gave myself a few more seconds of the comfort of Troy's arms before pulling away.

He let me go. "Arden, the lives or deaths of people here aren't all on you."

I just looked at him. We both knew that, as High Queen and Arbiter, they ultimately were, at least for the people I was directly responsible for taking into the Duat and bringing back out again. Oh, and the people of House Solari and the Chapel Hill Conclave, the Triangle territory, and two demesnes. Even beyond that, I was responsible for a growing slice of Otherside. Was it fair that lives and deaths beyond that were on me? I didn't think so. But both of us knew by now that life wasn't fair and never would be. We could do our best to level things out for people and lead by example, but it had to be a collective effort. I could claim the whole Eastern Seaboard, or even the entire continent, but I still couldn't allow myself to take responsibility for the actions and beliefs of each individual in it.

That was the catch with claiming a leadership role though. Collective failure on any point—whether it was caring for neighbors, securing those of our community most in need, or redistributing resources—would be placed at my door. I could enact all the right policies, be as beguiling as Orpheus, lead from the front, all of it. But if people didn't pick up their share with the opportunities I created using my political power, it'd just be me—or me and Troy—pissing into the wind.

Closing my eyes, I inhaled and exhaled silently. Indulged in swirling a zephyr. And accepted the responsibility. The buck stopped with me. But I also had to have the trust, hope, and faith in both me and those around me that setting the example, rewarding the good, and correcting the wrong would get us all on the right track.

Light footsteps made me open my eyes to find Mami Wata approaching.

"Harqil always seems to bring difficult news. Quite the burden, leadership." She looked me up and down and, for once, didn't seem to find me wanting. "I wanted you to be more like Callista. Then I could hate you. Betray you, even." She made a strange expression, lips pulled back and tongue out as she inhaled, which I belatedly realized was an approximation of a snake tasting the air. "You've made a choice that pains you."

"I'll explain when Lya and Cade get here. Until then, I'm taking a nap."

Because sometimes, the only good part of a day was laying down and letting it be over for at least a little while. If I was going to be defying Cyrus Veisi and his godly patron now on top of everything else, I had a feeling I was going to need my rest to keep myself and the people I'd adopted as my squad alive.

Chapter 20

I woke to the bickering of djinn.

"I told you that's not the right character to anchor this spell," Iaret said in the teasing sing-song that indicated she was delighted with someone's failure.

Duke swore. "You said to use—"

"*This* one, not that."

Harqil's voice. "Would you two *please* just pick one so I can try it again? Gods but I wish I'd learned Egyptian magic."

My bones hurt as my body caught up to my mind. I shifted, eyes still closed, and my cheek rubbed against something broad and solid, overlaid by fabric. That was odd. I'd fallen asleep on a blanket on the ground under one of the few oaks this close to the lake, unable to bring myself to go back into the little cubicle that was my room with Troy before I absolutely had to. It was small and enclosed, and Troy had nearly died in it. Then I had woken up from a dream of drowning in it. I was starting to hate the stupidly limited space.

I opened my eyes to find what had to be Troy's knee in my immediate field of vision. Rolling to my back had me looking up at him, still asleep, his long, dark lashes kissing his cheeks, even as he slumped chin to chest against the oak I'd laid down under. He must have been exhausted to fall asleep in the open like this, especially with me already out. His hand had shifted from my hip to my lower belly with my movement, but he still didn't wake.

The heavy warmth of his palm there made my breath catch as I remembered the deep-down personal reason why I was doing all this rather than trying to rule Otherside as a lone elemental queen.

I wanted to give family a try.

A family Troy and I made together, flesh and blood and magic bound with love.

I reached up to caress his jaw, heavy with surprisingly soft stubble now. Between the unusual facial hair and the shagginess of that on his head as it grew out of its usually careful cut, he was beginning to look less tidily royal and more than a little roguish.

It worked for me, even with the djinn still bantering with Harqil in the background.

Troy came awake suddenly, his gaze locking on mine. My hunger for him reverberated through the bond, and his secondary teeth flickered as his jaw dropped and shifted under my hand. Slowly, he turned his head to kiss my palm.

"Later," he murmured, knowing exactly what'd been on my mind.

I rolled my hips.

His gaze darted to where his hand rested on my belly before coming back to mine. "Trust me. I will be figuring out how to make you feel safe the minute we get magic back."

Reluctantly, I pushed myself upright and propped my elbows on my knees as I leaned against him. "We need to get going on that."

"Sounds like the djinn are still making shabtis."

"Then it's time for me to light a fire under some asses."

With a smirk, he rose and helped me to my feet. Usually, it exasperated him to watch me jump into the bickering alongside the djinn, but sometimes he was just glad to see someone call Duke in particular on his bullshit.

We made our way over to where Duke, Iaret, and Harqil sat as three points of a triangle, with Mami Wata, Mason, and a few of the Ebon Guard watching from various distances. My elemental senses told me a couple of people left posts in the woods when Troy and I moved, but I didn't draw attention to them.

"How's it coming?" I asked. I had serious questions about how Harqil had managed to convince Duke, in particular, to come and help with Dreamwalking given he'd been so against it before. Losing magic was probably the one thing that'd get him to change his mind though, and now wasn't the time to poke at him.

Iaret looked up and grinned, sharp black teeth and fire opal eyes dancing in a dark-skinned face. She'd been trapped in mostly human form just like Duke then, probably while spying on the Bureau for Supernatural Investigation. The djinn features worried me, but at least she was here now.

"Look who's up!" she said. "Silly sleepyhead. Did you let the stars fall on you again?"

Not quite in her right mind at this particular moment then, which was probably good for working on magical artifacts. I was definitely glad to have her here and not trapped in DC and gave Harqil a tiny nod to thank them for bringing her here, to relative safety. Maybe they were responsible for her not being discovered in her current state as well.

They nodded back. "Iaret, dear, I think our deadline approaches."

"Bollocks. The deadline is today *and* yesterday."

Definitely not quite in her right mind. Being trapped mostly in human form probably wasn't helping. I exchanged a quick look with Duke, who offered a sad smile that spoke volumes. She might not be the person she was when he'd fallen in love with her, but he was going to stay at her side and love the person she was becoming. That might weigh more than the loss of magic in getting Duke to help with Dreamwalking.

I knelt and fingered one of the five unmarked clay figures laying in the middle of the triangle the three of them made. "Can we go in an hour?"

Duke grimaced. "That's all we have?"

"How quickly do you want magic back?" I asked.

He glanced at Iaret. "Fair point, for once."

Harqil just watched me with a solemn expression, knowing better than all of us that something terrible awaited if we pushed, even if they couldn't tell us what exactly would happen.

In the end, they got the shabti done in forty-five minutes. The sun had just set, and the moon hadn't yet risen, leaving us in the uncertain illumination of twilight as we finished preparations.

I gritted my teeth as I went into the cubicle assigned to me and Troy in the boathouse. Part of me imagined that I could still smell Troy's opened belly and near death. The concrete floor looked clean but felt bloodstained. I stood there shaking for a good minute, bond closed, before I could get my shit together and lay down on the mattress. Even then I kept trembling.

I was not okay.

I could pretend I was while I was up and doing things or resting outside. But here, this space? I didn't know how much longer I could do this.

There were security concerns though. I couldn't put Troy and the Ebon Guard at risk just because I couldn't get my head in the game.

"Come on, Arden," I whispered.

"What's that?" Troy asked as he ducked in.

"Nothing."

Tilting his head, he scented the air and prodded the closed bond. "Really."

"Yeah. Let's just get this done."

He waited another few moments. It was clear he wanted to argue with me and equally as clear that he didn't think he'd win. "If you're sure."

"I'm sure." I bit my tongue before I could add that this was bigger than me, that it was more than my memories of near-death in a dream. "Everyone else is under?"

"Mm hmm. Just you now."

"Great." I shifted again, trying to get comfortable.

After another short evaluation, Troy settled against one of the poles near my head, pulling me and my pillow partway into his lap. "Comfortable?"

"Yeah." Physical contact with him made this much better. "I love you."

"I love you too." Sadness flashed through his gaze before he shuttered it away as he caressed my jaw. Aether slithered through me. "Sleep now, my love."

The scent of burnt marshmallow flared, and I rode it into a Chaos sphere. Pulled the others through as I had twice before now. The tug and tear into the Duat didn't happen this time though.

"Motherfucker," I muttered as I stalked along the shoreline of my Chaos sphere. I'd washed Roman's blood off in this spot, but that was neither here nor there. I needed to find a way through to the Duat, and it wasn't opening.

"What's wrong?" Cade asked.

"The first time, we were attacked and dragged through. The second time, there was a pull that I followed through. This time, it feels like we're walled in."

A sixth presence flashed into my sphere. "There you are," Harqil said. "It seems your little squad has become a true threat, Arden. Sutekh is barring the passage into the Duat."

"Can he do that?" I asked.

Harqil tilted their head side to side. "Not really. Usir!"

I jumped at the strange resonance in their shout and the way magic seemed to crawl over my skin as it echoed then stared as a green-skinned being wrapped in tattered linen and missing an arm faded halfway into my awareness.

The god whirled a flail banded in gold in the general direction of Harqil's throat. "I warned you about Summoning me, Messenger. I am not yours to command."

"Acknowledged and noted, my lord. But your brother isn't keeping to the Agreements again."

Pressure grew as the god glared, and an unseen, unfelt breeze shifted the plumes in his tall crown. "I am not one of the tricksters."

"No, my lord. But your brother straddles his domains and yours with his recent actions in the Duat. I mean, using a death curse on this primordial?" Harqil bowed their head, looking almost demure. "And all this with taking magic from those of the earthly plane and keeping it for himself? One might fear he was making another play for Iset."

"He dares!"

"It seems he does, my lord Usir."

Another pause seemed to last an eternity as Usir—Osiris?—looked all of us over. When his gaze came back to me and stayed there, I lifted my chin and met the dead white of his gaze, despite my shudder.

"The primordial Dreamwalker," Usir said. "How interesting."

I swallowed hard, trying to work spit back into my mouth. I didn't want to be interesting to a god associated with the deaths. The hunters and the tricksters were bad enough. "My lord, I ask safe passage for me and mine to the Duat, that Otherside might be reborn on the earthly plane with a new appreciation for the magic the gods were so great as to gift us."

Usir didn't do anything I expected. No preening. No sneering. No attacks. Just a simple look like I was being weighed on the scales of judgment.

"I'll allow it," he said. "This once."

With an enormous ripping sensation, my Chaos sphere flipped ass over tits and became the Duat. Everyone cried out and staggered like there'd been an earthquake.

Night hung heavy, and stars shone like diamonds without the presence of the moon. It was cold enough for my skin to prickle in goosebumps as a wind skirled across jagged cliffs in a light stone, rising high overhead. The sand underfoot was as fine and pale as it had been when Troy lay dying on it, and I shuddered more from that than the temperature.

This version of the Duat put us at the entrance to what looked like a tomb, hewn into the rock face and angling steeply downward. I did my best not to swear aloud, although the fresh threat from Cyrus was at the forefront of my mind. What better place to bury someone?

"So, which one?" Lya asked.

I turned to find three more entrances scattered nearby, one at each compass point. Each yawned dark and empty, with no marks to suggest which one we should choose. Maybe Earth would tell me something. I reached for it, more cautiously than usual, but nothing odd happened. Relieved, I sent a pulse into the ground, frowning to find passages branching from each reaching irregularly into the rock. Some followed natural seams; others had been carved with unnatural straightness.

That seemed odd, but I chalked it up to order and disorder needing to be in balance. As I continued reaching, I found a river coursing deep underground.

"That's strange," I muttered. "I would have thought the Nile was the only river here."

"What river?" Mason whispered, sounding confused as he sniffed.

I ignored him, surrendering to Water even more carefully than I'd reached for Earth and closing my eyes to focus. There was definitely a smaller river down there and then...a large platform? With metal on it. When I opened my eyes again, I'd drifted closer to the entrance on my right, the one that felt like west, where Mason stood.

"This way." I strode forward, my boots crunching on the gravel-strewn sand, trying to look confident when I felt anything but.

I *hated* being underground. Even visiting Maria in her nest under Claret was enough to send me into a fit of anxiety. It was just so enclosed, with so much weight overhead and so much darkness surrounding me no matter how many lamps and fires she lit.

This? This was going to be so much worse. I could already feel it. Worse than the lich's lair, even.

"Arbiter?"

I jumped at Mami Wata's voice, not having realized that I'd stopped out of pure reluctance to go down there. "Just double-checking," I said, hoping nobody noticed how much rougher my voice was. "I imagine Usir punching us through set off some alarm bells somewhere, so I don't want us to have to try a second tomb."

She hummed, a noise that could have been agreement or derision.

After taking a moment to summon weapons, armor, and torches for everyone—it seemed more appropriate than a flashlight, and the fire could burn something if we needed it to—I floated a ball of Fire over my hand and started down. The first few feet were bare stone, which gave way to brilliantly painted walls. The ceiling was a dark blue with white, five-pointed stars. Every inch of the walls on either side was carved with hieroglyphics in neat columns, interspersed with richly detailed scenes of war and victory, hunting and wealth.

The ramp deeper into the tomb was very nearly a slide. Fortunately, the stone was rough enough to give our boots something to grip, but I wasn't the only one with an arm extended for balance. We were moving at a crawl though, and I wanted to get this last key and get the hell out.

"Hang on," I said.

Nobody said anything as I focused harder, exerting my will over the dream that was the Duat until, with a rumble, the ramp became stairs. I started down again before my claustrophobia could take advantage of the stop and get me to turn right the fuck around. The rest of the group must have caught my mood because, after an initial exclamation, everyone was quiet. Only the sound of our breathing reverberated off the walls.

Where the air up above had been dry and parched as the desert sand, this air was getting more humid. It wasn't just our breath. It had to be the river I'd sensed.

Down and down we went, passing rooms carved off to the sides. Some of those rooms had hissing snakes. Others had haggard souls that watched us malevolently until I willed the doorways to close into firm walls. If the descent hadn't been so steep, I probably would have been running. The others could probably smell my fear, but as long as I kept going, kept lighting the way, kept the dangers trying to flank us from reaching us, they'd say nothing.

Besides, they stank of fear as well.

We reached the river.

I halted so fast someone nearly careened into me before scrambling to the side. There was a swear at that, and then I dropped one myself as I became aware of the creature laying on the platform I'd sensed on the far side, next to a boat similar to that we'd taken onto the river in the last trial.

The creature looked massive in a low crouch, but then it rose and shook itself.

Lions were big enough when they were just lions, their shoulders easily reaching the height of my chest and their paws as big as dinner plates. Same with crocodiles—a big one might have a head the length of my arm. And hippos could be my height at the shoulder, two or three of me long.

This creature was a hodgepodge of all three that would have dwarfed any of those. A crocodile's head, a lion's mane and forequarters, and a hippo's rear, done in godly proportions.

When it spoke, the rasping roar of its voice echoed in the chamber. "I was sorry to have missed you at the Lake of Fire, primordial. But I suppose it is more fitting that I meet you here, in the Caverns of the Damned."

My heart hammered and my vision seemed to sharpen. "Who do we have the honor of addressing?"

The crocodile jaw dropped in what I took to be a smile, full of dagger-teeth the length of my hand. "I am Ammut, She Who Is Great of Death and Devourer of Hearts."

Great. Fan-fucking-tastic.

I sent a little prayer of thanks Harqil's way for telling me not to summon the heart scarab into the Duat. That would probably be disastrous.

"Greetings to you, Ammut." I didn't know what flattery to offer someone who called herself "great of death" so I just kept it moving. "What price to cross?"

"Joining the damned only has a price when you seek to be free of them," she said. "The knowledge of it is gained when you reach the threshold, just as the living learn of death as they broach the boundary."

I ground my teeth at that. It seemed straightforward enough: we could cross the river that way, but coming back would have a price. Probably a bad and bloody one.

The question now wasn't whether we could afford to pay it.

It was whether we could afford not to.

Chapter 21

I gave the rest of the squad a say in whether we crossed. They all looked grim, but they all agreed to come along. I could have made us an elemental crossing, but Ammut sent the boat. Part of me wondered if that was going to add on to the final price, but the part that was worried about defending against a demon-goddess won out.

We took the boat.

I got out closest to Ammut, putting myself between her and my people. Her vertically slitted green gaze was amused as she stared down at me, but other than a shift of her paws that made long claws click against stone as she flexed, she made no move.

Probably for the best for both of us. With the stone weighing heavier than ever overhead and the lights of our torches seeming more trivial than before in the renewed darkness on this side of the river, I didn't know how forceful my reaction would be. Likely very, given how jumpy I was getting at every echo and shift in the air molecules as everyone moved.

Goddess, I hated being underground.

With a quick, respectful incline of my head to Ammut, I turned to lead the way deeper into what she'd dubbed the Caverns of the Damned.

My sense of control lessened, and my chest tightened as we pushed deeper. The space grew narrower and darker, seeming to eat the light from our fires. There was no air stirring down here except for our own breaths. There was no light except for our torches. The ceiling kept getting lower. Nothing moved except for us, so even the air molecules seemed abnormally still.

In spite of that, whispers slashed through the darkness, pleas and prayers, threats and warnings. An endless assault of sound with no air movement attached that confused my inborn sense and experience of how air and sound should behave, even as some of the things the voices said horrified me. Disembodied arms clawed from the walls, reminding me viscerally of the zombies in the lich's lair. If I didn't stay exactly in the center of the tunnel, they snagged my clothes, tearing them, or scratched me with ragged fingernails.

All of my attention zeroed down into not. Freaking. Out.

I summoned the callstone between me and Troy, clutching it as I reached for him and spoke mind-to-mind for only the two of us to hear. "Troy?"

"I'm here, my love. You're okay. Breathe."

"It's—" I couldn't bring myself to describe it.

"I can see through your eyes," he said after a moment. "Do you need me to wake you?"

"No!" I nearly panicked all over again. There was no way I could bring myself to do this a second time, and that assumed we were allowed a second time. I didn't know if the terms of the first trial—succeed or die—also extended here. "I just need air. I can't *breathe* down here, and it's tight and it's small and it's dark and there's *no air.*"

A mental distance accompanied a pause.

Long enough that I sent, "Troy!"

"I'm still here. We're getting fans."

Fans. I hadn't even thought of that. Maybe if my body in the real felt air movement, it'd help here. I swallowed the lump in my throat.

"Thank you." Hot tears burst into my eyes, and I blinked fast, glad that I was in the lead and nobody could turn around and see me. "I need to focus."

"You've got this, Arden. You're tough and strong, and I'll be here when you wake up."

"Okay." With an effort, I released my hold on the stone and dissipated it, not wanting anything to happen to Troy if something happened here and one of the damned followed the link back to him. If a heart scarab was bad, that callstone had to be worse.

Guilt assailed me at the risk I'd taken. But the ceiling was sloping enough to force first Cade, then Mason, then Mami Wata, Lya, and me to crouch. The way forward was only getting worse, and I was starting to wonder if the challenge of this trial was simply me retaining my sanity.

Of course it wasn't that easy.

As we reached a pinch point that forced us into a crawl, an unearthly howl ahead made me freeze.

"Arbiter?" Mason asked from behind me.

"Hang on." I pushed through the gut-wrenching fear with a pulse of elemental magic then, when all I found was an open space ahead, with Chaos. The magic bounced off of souls, like the ones that'd been in the river but somehow more corporeal.

Not just them either. Beings of various sizes, all oozing ill will.

"We've got trouble ahead," I said, explaining what I'd sensed before scanning again. "I'll hold them off. The rest of you go for the key. There's a side cave or room. It feels carved or shaped or something, and there's metal off in that direction. Forward and to our right."

"Got it. We're right behind you," Lya said, sounding more focused and businesslike than usual.

Taking that as a sign that I needed to get my shit together and lead, I took a deep breath and pushed forward. Right as I did, a sense of a breeze caressing my face and arms brought goosebumps. Nothing was moving here and my sweat stuck hot on my face, so I had to assume that was the fans Troy said he was having brought in.

Thank. Fuck.

It steadied me enough that I pushed through the smallest part of the pinch, dropping to my belly to drag myself through over rough stone—only to find a yawning cavern on the other side.

Stalactites sharper than Troy's teeth threatened us from the ceiling as blunted stalagmites reached for them from the floor. When I sent my ball of fire sweeping to either side, I found a narrow trail leading to the next part. The ledge was barely wide enough for feet and broken by gaps.

Shaking my head, I closed my eyes and gathered myself. I had to do this. We had to get this fucking key. There was no way out but through.

"Here we go," I whispered.

I started along the trail, sending my ball of fire upward and making it bigger to illuminate our path in the utter darkness. Somehow, I sank into Troy's training and moved on autopilot.

Cross the gap by using the pillar of stone as a pole to swing around and then steady myself against the wall at a sharp dogleg in the trail. Clamber over sliding, loose stone where an underground rockslide had washed over our path. And definitely—*definitely*—don't look over the edge, into the endless depths where there was no bottom save for the fingertips of reaching souls.

We made it to a downward-curving ramp that ended in a vertical cliff. My fireball glinted on crystals above, sending spears of white light and bolts of rainbow dancing on the walls.

"Holy bleeding fuck," Lya muttered.

"What she said." Mason drifted ahead of me, jaw dropped, eyes on the space.

"Where now?" Mami Wata's voice came in an unexpected sibilance.

I turned at and jumped to find her a massive python again.

"Up there." I pointed at the cliff wall then walked to it.

It stretched overhead, a good fifteen feet of crystal-laced rock straight up. As I studied the wall, I found both divots and nubs that could make hand- and toe-holds.

"Anything you can do about that?" Mason asked.

Frowning, I tried to exert my will on it like I had the ramp near the surface. It resisted me though, as though we'd come so deep into the heart of this dream of the Duat that I was powerless as a Dreamwalker.

That really could not be good.

All I said was, "Not this time. I could lift y'all with Air—"

Gathering himself, Cade leaped, caught the ledge, and hauled himself up. After a moment, he leaned back over. "We're clear up here."

Mason shook his head and looked at me. "Maybe in a few hundred years."

A roar behind us pulled me around.

The shambling dead were coming, breaking free of the walls. They were flanked by cobras who spat fire as their scales drank in the light, more sha creatures with their flat-topped ears, and swirling clouds leaking a sense of evil that reminded me of the rabisu.

"I think the key is up there!" I lifted Mason up, then Lya, then Mami Wata in her python form as creatures approached.

For myself, I had to climb the first ten feet, picking my way up the face bit by bit with fingertips and toes until Mami Wata could extend down long enough to coil her tail around me. She lifted me over the ledge just as a cobra struck and broke a fang on the wall where my leg had been a moment before.

I stared at the glittering crystals that surrounded us, awed for a bare heartbeat before a scream of rage from below pulled me back.

The carved side chamber was to the right.

"There," I said. "Go. I'll hold these off."

Nobody asked how we were going to get back out. They just hauled ass. Of course. They trusted me to push them out of the dream when they had the key. But based on my struggle to reshape the Duat just now, could I even manage it? And how would we get out if I couldn't?

No time to think about that.

I tried the thought I'd had at the Lake of Fire, to simply dispel all of these beings and shape this reality as my own. But just as the wall below had resisted me, so did the rest of this dream. Switching to Fire, I sent a wave down. It rolled over the undead, bursting them like the ones at the river. The snakes and sha creatures were untouched though.

Fine.

Air was harder than it'd ever been to reach down here, but I closed my eyes and focused on the phantom sensation of moving air from the fans in the real. Drew it in and made it manifest here. Pushed with all I had to send some of the creatures screaming into the darkness on either side of the trail that'd led here.

Earth came easily enough. Almost too easily, just like it had when I'd gained the element in the lich's lair. I set the ground to shaking, willing a crevice to open. It sliced through the ranks of monsters, consuming them before closing again.

Sweat was rolling down my face again by the time a hand landed on my shoulder.

I spun with a snarl, a ball of Fire at the ready.

"Whoa!" Lya jumped back. "Just me. We got the key, but Mason's hurt bad."

My attention darted over her shoulder where Mami Wata was supporting the injured werewolf. Or rather, nearly carrying him, given his left leg dragged. It looked like it'd almost been ripped from the socket.

A human would have been dead.

"Fuck." I turned back to look over the battlefield below. The creatures were still regrouping.

Dashing to Mason, I dropped to a knee and reached for the elements in the same way I had with Troy.

"Torn ligaments, damaged nerves," I muttered. There was no time to ask what'd happened.

Latticing the elements was harder this time. Something here was still resisting me. I pushed through and healed him enough that the leg would be salvageable when he woke, not trying to heal him all the way. I'd barely survived it with Troy, and I still had to get the rest of them out.

Stable. I grabbed the shabti from his pocket, just in case Harqil's hint that the little figure could stand in for a body still mattered. With a twist of Chaos, I sent Mason home.

"Lya next." Cade said. "She has the key."

"Shabti." I held out a hand. "All of you, leave them here."

Lya's thumped into my hand. The other two set the carved clay figures at my feet. Another twist of Chaos. Another squad member home.

Scraping behind us.

"Now Mami Wata."

If that was the order Cade wanted, fine. The twist of Chaos was harder this time, the warp and weft of Chaos and the dream tighter. She popped through with a wrench.

My first attempt to send Cade home failed. My upper lip itched as a nosebleed started. I swiped at it out of reflex then ignored it as it continued.

I had. To get. My people. Home.

"Reach for Lya, in whatever bond you two have," I said hoarsely.

He nodded and closed his eyes.

This time, he went. Leaving me alone in the glittering dark with sha creatures and damned souls just making it over the lip of the cliff we'd scaled.

I tried to step out of the dream.

Nothing happened.

Nor on my next attempt or the one after that.

Damned souls reached me. My magic sputtered as my overdraw reached its limits, and they clawed at me. Bit. Scratched. Stabbed, even, with jagged knives. I fought them off as best I could, but there were too many. They backed me against the wall, even as I kept fighting with all the skills I'd learned and sheer wildness to keep me going.

I'd never been unable to step out of a dream. If being trapped underground had scared me, this was a whole new level of terror.

I was trapped underground.

In a dream that might not ever end.

Even if I died here at the hands of these monsters.

My worst. Fucking. Nightmare.

Just as my mind was spiraling on that idea, reptilian laughter broke out.

"I thought that might trap you." Ammut's crocodile snout poked over the ledge as she dragged herself the rest of the way up, hippo's ass or not. "And how unfortunate for you that you've dodged the price. That means you're the only one remaining to pay it. Assuming you want to go home, that is, and not stay here to play with me."

The toothy drop of her jaw said she knew good and damn well what a taunt that was.

The monsters attacking me fell back.

"I'm going home," I snarled. My blood dripped to the stone floor in slow plinks, every wound on fire. Defiance might not do more than save face, but I'd be one of the damned here before I just gave up.

"Not until you pay me for the four damned souls that have already escaped. Plus your own, of course."

Damned souls. Including mine.

I'd known I'd slid a ways down the slope as I gained power, even if I hadn't intended to become Callista and actively tried to choose other ways. I hadn't realized I'd slid all the way into damned.

My fist tightened, and I remembered Mason's shabti in it. "I have payment for four here."

"I don't believe you."

I tossed the shabti toward her, flinching as she snapped at it. It crunched in her jaws.

"Mmm. Powerful. Especially with that delicious smear of your blood. Maybe you do have payment. The rest?"

Forcing myself forward, I pushed through the crowd of the damned to find the other clay figures, scattered by shuffling feet but mercifully unbroken. One by one, I pitched the shabti in her direction, my hand shaking with pain, fatigue, and frustration.

"That covers your awoken undead, your dusk walker, your beast-souled, and your lady of the waters." Ammut tilted her scaled head as more of the damned climbed over the lip of the wall. "The remainder?"

I fished in my pocket for the last shabti, feeling a spike of relief and triumph as I tossed it to her.

"And that covers you, Dreamwalker. But what of the fallen shadow whose soul is bound to yours and far more damned?"

Blood drained from my face.

"Fallen shadow" had been how Duke described Troy in the first vision the Sight had ever granted him. We hadn't made Troy a shabti. He was holding our exit, not coming in. None of us had thought there was a need.

"He's not here," I whispered.

"Your life or his, it makes no difference to me. Sutekh promised me a banquet of souls for this trick, and I will have my full due." She stepped closer, giving me a whiff of rotten-meat breath. "This last is a feast of violence and broken faith. I want him."

This was too much. Outrage flared, burning hot in me. "He's *mine*, and you can't have him."

"Then you can't leave. My friends and I will enjoy the games we'll play together."

Something in me snapped.

That Sutekh wasn't playing by the rules was bad enough. To have him think he could take *Troy*, by proxy? After all I'd done and sacrificed to keep him alive and with me? To help him find his way through his healing processes, physical, mental, and otherwise?

Un-fucking-acceptable.

"You should have made a better bargain." My snarl had my whole chest behind it, raw and angry.

If my soul was damned, then let me be damned. Troy had done as much for me, to be with me and stay with me. He'd put himself on the block beside and ahead of me time and again. If anyone thought I'd trade his life for mine, they were fucking delusional. I let go of the idea that I somehow had to be better, to play by the rules, to meet the expectations of others and preserve the peace. I was the only living primordial elemental, and I would carry through on my threat to Anansi.

There was no overdraw here. That was my new rule. Maybe there was in the real. Maybe I'd pay for this when I woke.

But for now? Now, it was my rules that mattered.

And here, in the dream, there was no such thing as *too much*.

Blood dried on my lip and flaked away as I tapped into a reserve of power I'd never known existed.

"What are you doing?" Ammut roared.

The undead, the sha creatures, even the fire-spitting cobras roared with her as I pushed beyond anything I ever had and reached out with Chaos to slice the web that was the reality of the Duat.

If there were no rules, then there was no reality. There was only what I willed into being.

And I would not be here. Even if I had to destroy everything here was.

"No! Stop that!" Ammut lunged at me, trampling smaller monsters underfoot.

"Then free me." I sliced again.

Crocodile jaws snapped in my face.

I threw myself backward—and the dream of the Duat shattered.

Chapter 22

I didn't quite manage to wake up all the way.

Instead, the weightless dark and bright stars of the In-Between held me.

Sutekh manifested in front of me. "I should kill you for what you just did. That will have unimaginable consequences."

"As if you could kill me," I spat back, too furious to have any sense. "May you be damned in a thousand eternities, Sutekh. There are *rules* to games."

"There were," he agreed easily. "And don't you sound like an elf now?"

Whatever else he said next, I didn't hear. A shimmer caught my attention when he said elf. Something that reminded me of the aura I'd seen around Cyrus during one of our Dreamwalking sessions.

What had he called it?

A buffer. But why would a god need a buffer? Was that really what it was?

Didn't matter. It had seemed important to Cyrus to hide it, so it might be important to Sutekh to keep it.

Without warning, I struck with an edged lash of Chaos.

Sutekh roared and struck back.

I barely turned the edge aside then honed my Chaos into a point sheathed in primordial order and disorder, a making and unmaking of the blended elements.

And sheared the whatever-it-was from around the god.

The backlash crushed me, worse than the cave-in at the lich's lair, because here in the unending liminal space, there was no Troy to shield me.

It was just me and the god and the magic. Endless, burning, searing, freezing, stabbing magic.

My gut wrenched as pain wracked me, internal to match the external.

"Arden, wake up!"

I followed Troy's call, his Aether and the pain of the cramps he was shooting through me, back into my body.

Breathing hurt. *Everything* hurt.

"Lachlan! She's back."

I stiffened and drew the elements to me.

"Wait! Stop." Troy's voice again, harsh with worry.

"She's—"

"If you touch her now, she might kill you without realizing it."

The low warning growl under Troy's words comforted me. He'd protect me. I was safe. But safe or not, I was afraid and depleted and couldn't see through the white-out of pain, and *oh my god everything hurt.*

"I've got you, Arden," Troy said. "You're home. Let go of the lightning."

Lightning?

Pain.

"It'll stop hurting if you let go of the elements, my love. It's okay now. Everyone's out. Your team is safely back on this plane. Mason is being tended. Let go."

If I let go, I didn't think I'd be able to control the elements again any time soon. Ammut might come for Troy. Sutekh might come for him.

But I'd blasted Ammut. I'd hurt Sutekh.

Troy should be safe.

"Troy?" My voice quavered.

"I'm here."

"You're alive? Safe?"

"Yes, cariñamí." He kept murmuring to me in elvish, words I didn't have the presence of mind to follow, even if I knew more than a few of the phrases I heard most often.

With an effort that twisted my insides, I forced myself to drop the elements.

If I'd thought everything hurt before, it was worse without the buffer of magic. Gritting my teeth, I curled tightly into Troy, his broad chest and reassuring scent, the security of his hand cupped against the back of my skull to hold me close as his other arm stayed tight around my waist. His touch seared my over-sensitized skin and pulled at open wounds, but I'd rather feel that than anything else right now.

"Now," Troy barked in a low voice. "I've got her."

Cold wetness skated over my arms. Pulling and pinching.

Troy explained what was going on, a running commentary of cleaning, closing, and bandaging wounds as I was shifted about like a doll in his arms, eyes closed, trying my damnedest not to push through the burn of overdraw and lash out. I should have started healing, but I hadn't. God-inflicted injuries tended to have that effect.

I held it together until Lachlan or whoever else finished and Troy said, "Thank you. Make sure we're not disturbed."

Then, in the silence, the memory of the crushing darkness, the lack of air, the tight and enclosed spaces crashed over me. It was all I could do to bury the sob in my throat as I shook violently. Desperate for grounding, I sought the scent patch at the corner of Troy's jaw.

Aether flared as he muttered under his breath in elvish.

"There's a soundproofing spell up," he murmured as the kiss of magic faded. "Let it out. Let everything out."

I was too lost to do anything other than what he said, breaking down as he rocked me. The physical hurts, the terror of being buried alive, of losing him, and the further risk of standing up to gods...it was more than a mortal should have to bear. A wild thought of, *Is this what makes a celestial?* pushed to the fore and was lost as I spiraled.

I couldn't get enough breath, no matter how much I tried. My bones rattled in my skin. My heart tried to break free of me. My head was going to explode.

Until a cool wash of Aether wrapped me.

After all the constriction and constraint and pressure, it should have been terrifying. But this magic had the flavor of icy midnight woods, accompanied by the scent of rosemary and sage chased with burnt marshmallow.

Troy.

Gratefully, I let him in. My shoulders dropped as I caught my breath. I kept trembling, but slowly, I got control of myself. The fans blowing helped, but it was artificial. I needed the real thing.

"Outside," I rasped.

"Can you walk? Or should I carry you?"

Truthfully, I wanted him to carry me. But given whatever the hell people were thinking, considering the blood I could smell in this cubicle and the soundproofing spell Troy had cast, I had to walk out of here on my own power.

"I'll make it."

Bless the man for not arguing because if he had, I might have folded. Troy made sure I was stable then disentangled himself, stood, and drew me up.

I spread my feet when I wobbled on a leg that felt like someone had tried to tear it off at the hip—like Mason's—dropping my head and squeezing my eyes shut as I wished I was on my own land at the Eno. I'd claimed this place though, so it would have to do. I brought my head up and accepted the arm Troy offered, telling myself it could be seen as a courtly gesture and not one that screamed weakness.

I had to believe that. Because I wasn't getting out of this cubicle without it, and I could not stay here.

As we emerged, the thump of a dozen foot stomps and chest thumps made me jump. All the Ebon Guard on duty were lined up, saluting me.

What—?

You were gone an extra day beyond the others, Troy sent back. *Wounds kept appearing, and we couldn't wake you. They told us what happened. Or the part they were there for, anyway.*

A day.

I'd lost a whole day to Ammut and Sutekh.

Before I could spiral into what we didn't have time for, Troy nudged me.

Salute back.

I did, forcing a smile that felt fake as hell but probably said something for the effort if nothing else, given the reassured expressions.

Another nudge from Troy as he got us moving again. *Give yourself the same credit they do.*

Then we were outside.

I stopped dead at the relief of feeling real air, no matter how cold, caressing my face.

A little farther, Troy prompted.

I made it to halfway between the fire kettle and the lake shore, splitting the difference between Fire and Water as I dropped to my back and let go of my shields. Stars sparkled overhead in a blessedly clear sky that made the night even cooler than my illusory shield overhead, but counting stars had always soothed me. I needed the wide-open sky more than ever now as I fought to bury flashbacks of the Caverns of the Damned.

Troy dropped to sit next to me, the unusual heaviness of the movement screaming his exhaustion. If I'd been gone more than twenty-four hours, he'd have been awake the whole time, trying to run triage at the same time that he was keeping tabs on my mental and auratic state. He was spent.

When I could breathe normally again and my heart felt like it might stay a while, I shifted closer and reached up to cup his cheek, running my thumb along the edge of the dark circle under his eye. I'd only seen one that was exhaustion rather than a bruise on him once, maybe twice. I hated seeing him hit the limits of even his impressive stamina like this. Telling myself it was his choice didn't help because I didn't think he had much of a choice at all with the bond, even if he'd say that too had been a choice.

"I'm sorry." I couldn't help the tear that slipped free. I was just so exhausted and so frustrated, and seeing it physically drain Troy as well broke my heart into jagged little pieces and made me miserable as hell.

"I'm not. We're doing what needs to be done." A grim half-smile tugged one side of his mouth up. "Besides. It's not like I was expecting to see forty anyway."

Horror chilled me. I wanted us to see two hundred or more together. That was the whole point of doing all this. "That's not funny."

He shrugged. "My life is better than it was. I'm happy with my choices. If I do die in this, at least it's for more than Keithia's petty greed and ambition. Let it go, Arden."

Closing my eyes, I wrestled with my fierce urge to keep him alive and whole, reminded myself that he had his own reasons for wanting magic back on top of mine, and did as he asked. "I love you. Thank you for pulling me out."

"What happened at the end? There was this weight all of a sudden."

I explained what had happened after I'd sent the others home. More tears slid free.

Troy's expression grew increasingly stony. "And you don't know what you sliced from around Sutekh?"

"No." I switched to telepathy. *Only that I saw something similar around your dad.*

Maybe Harqil knows what it is.

I'm too tired to ask.

"You need to eat," Troy said, accepting what I'd said without comment and refocusing us both on the here and now.

I opened my mouth to say I wasn't in the mood then shut it and nodded. If I didn't eat, my body would draw what it needed from Troy, at least in terms of vitality. I'd still be starving myself, even if I was temporarily functional.

He shot off a text message then caught me up on what had happened while I was out. Iago had confirmed the subpoena was delayed, but the mundane riots had intensified. Property damage and threats of bodily harm from mundanes, mostly, but other than another elven queen dead of a suicide we both knew wasn't one, Otherside was cutting me a break and behaving for once.

"Probably because I allowed the Guard to leak a staged photo of the box," Troy said when I commented on it. "Matthias called, making demands and threatening to let his vampires loose in New York City if magic wasn't returned so he could keep everyone in line."

I just sighed, too tired even to swear, and counted the stars one more time to slow my heart back down. I could not allow myself to be sidetracked with worrying about vampires rampaging in major cities—because almost every major city had at least a small nest or a powerful lone vagabond. If one kicked off, the rest would follow suit.

No. Not something for me to worry about. I needed to keep my focus on the biggest picture and, simultaneously, the smallest one: getting magic back and not killing myself or Troy in the process.

After a few more minutes, Lachlan approached with two plates of what smelled like sausage and toast. Hesitation made his normally smooth grace jerky, and Felip hovered, worry clear on his face.

"What's wrong?" I asked quietly as I sat up.

These two had been on my side since I'd learned what the Ebon Guard was, and I didn't want to scare them off.

Lachlan hesitated then glanced back at Felip as though for reassurance before kneeling and handing us the food. "My queen, we checked your biometrics against the baseline on file. You're in bad shape." He hesitated and glanced again at Felip, who nodded forcefully. Then, in a rush, he said, "You might not survive another trip. Your heart could give out. Or a blood vessel could burst in your brain. Or you might fall into a coma." He paused, swallowed hard, and pushed on. "As one of your healers, I have to insist you don't do this again."

All of which was incredibly unusual for me, who'd never been sick and normally healed with nearly the speed of an elf. I wasn't usually being attacked by celestials while Dreamwalking though. I didn't know what was normal here. Only that I had a job to do.

I took a deep, settling breath and looked at Troy. Read the despair alongside the resolve in the bond.

"The greater good," we said together.

I nodded then forced myself to start eating. I'd need the food to keep going. Or, more important to me, not kill Troy.

He turned to holler over his shoulder. "Alli, get over here."

I frowned, not having realized that she was on-site. That extra day I'd been trapped must have been bad if it'd been enough to pull her from Raleigh. I didn't even want to know what I'd looked like when I'd awakened.

"What? What's wrong?" she asked in a terse whisper.

"The succession plan is ready?" Troy asked.

"Yes, but— Oh no." Allegra stared at me, a hard, evaluating look that I had to fight not to squirm under. "What's wrong with her?"

I shook my head and spoke what'd just occurred to me around a mouthful of food. "I'm fine, except for the part where I think I'm trying to handle celestial powers. I might be a primordial elemental, but the shit I have to do right now is above my pay grade."

Allegra stared at us, gaze darting from Troy to me and back. "But there's one more test."

"I know." I tried to find calm. It wouldn't help anything if I melted my brain or my heart without even starting the last journey.

"You're going to let her do this?" she snapped. "T, we could lose—"

"I know," he said, starting on his own food, his massive bites betraying his physical state as much as his heavy drop to the ground had. "But unless we find a celestial who is able and willing to do what Arden is doing, we're out of options for getting magic back."

An idea hit, based on the passive grounding I'd done to recover before.

"I'm gonna try to draw some elemental energy from the surrounding area. Maybe it'll give me enough of a buffer or a top-up to survive the last round." I finished my plate, chewing mechanically but quickly until it was gone, then set it aside, laid back down, and nudged Troy. "You'll wanna close off for this."

"No." He lay down beside me, shifted close, and took my hand. "I could use some rest too."

"But—"

He spoke over me, facing his sister-cousin. "Alli, get a tent pitched and get me up in six hours if we don't wake up first. Use the defibrillator if you have to."

"Troy—" both Allegra and I started.

"Do it. The both of you." He turned his head to rest his forehead against mine.

I was too tired to argue further. While Allegra cussed a blue streak, I opened fully to the elements and to Troy.

Then nothing else mattered because I—we—existed on earth time.

Chapter 23

A tent was over us when I woke. I waited for the sense of panic to set in at being enclosed, but my back was on bare ground still and small currents of natural air slipped through cracks in the window flaps. There was no need to panic when I was simply outdoors and sheltered from the more uncomfortable effects of the elements, rather than enclosed inside a tiny canvas space within a small, concrete space.

Troy slept on, so either it hadn't been six hours or Allegra had ignored his order.

I sat up, rolled my neck, and stretched, feeling strangely good.

At least, until I poked my head out of the tent.

Not only was it late afternoon, from the position of the sun—far more than six hours later—but the vegetation nearest the tent was also dying, yellowed and brittle. The earth was cracked and parched, spider-webbed with deep, irregular lines. My sense of the lake seemed okay, like it was big enough to handle the relatively distant impact, but the air had chilled dramatically. Fine in the tent, where my passive power had buffered the small space and kept the temperature comfortable, but outside had dropped a good ten to fifteen degrees.

What had I done?

Oh Goddess. Troy.

A shout indicated someone had seen me, but I scrambled back inside and reached for the pulse in Troy's throat, laying two fingers along the side that usually jumped with the liveliness of his carotid artery.

Still there. Fainter than usual, but he was still alive.

I hadn't killed my mate.

As I slumped in relief, he inhaled deeply and swatted at my hand before catching it and holding it tight, his voice rumbling as he said, "Arden? What's wrong?"

"Open your eyes." I had a sudden, nightmare-fueled fear that they'd be as white as the damned undead or the fire-rimmed black of Sutekh's. But when he sleepily blinked them open, they were the usual gold-flecked hazel.

Still, I peered at them, tugging his eyelids open farther, then checked his pulse again. It was weird that he wasn't doing his usual thing of coming immediately awake, combat-ready and snarling.

"Hey." He twisted away then kissed my knuckles. "I feel fine. Better than in weeks, even. What's wrong?"

"I think I— I killed all the plants. And maybe drained the soil of nutrients. To feed us. Troy, we've been out for almost the whole day."

"What?" He sat up.

Before I could explain, Darius's voice called from outside. "You two all right in there?"

"Fine," I said, my gaze still searching Troy's face for any sign that he was unwell. The words were an outright lie. I wasn't fine. In trying to regain enough energy to undertake the last trial, I had dramatically unbalanced the immediate environment. Exactly the opposite of what I was supposed to be doing. A stab of fear ripped through me as I remembered my nightmare, the prophetic one, and I would've sworn I heard the ethereal laughter again.

Was it *me* who had caused the destruction in my dream? Was that why it all came back to life when I passed?

Troy must have guessed the path of my racing thoughts or read them directly, given how open the bond was. *We'll figure it out. If you can destroy a dream, you can create a reality.*

That simple faith brought me back to earth. *I hope you're right. Right or not, what's done is done.*

There was that as well.

"T?" Allegra's voice was farther than Darius's had been but getting closer by the syllable. "I'ma need you to explain what—"

He surged upright and pushed past me to burst from the tent. "I told you to wake me after six hours." The low growl under his words held a threat even I could hear.

Allegra hesitated then answered in a lower voice than she'd used previously. "I— That was my call. I talked to the team here and checked in with Etain. Everyone said neither of you had been sleeping or eating enough. People are concerned."

"If we don't get this done, they're going to be more than concerned," Troy replied. "We're doing what needs to be done."

Etain was aggressively assertive as she said, "Getting magic back isn't the endgame. If we lose the two of you in the process and have to figure out how to fight off multiple demesnes' worth of enemies simultaneously, all of whom have been waiting for the opportunity to get magic back and flex? We'd lose the Chapel Hill territory at best, the demesne at worst. And that's assuming that pushing this hard doesn't burn out our queen. Or worse. Too many people are relying on us to allow that to happen." She seemed to realize what she was saying and who she was saying it to because she added, "Um, sir," in a fainter voice.

I had to rein myself back from joining Troy outside by reminding myself that he needed to be responsible for the Ebon Guard and his sister. Just like I couldn't handle the vampires in New York right now, I couldn't be responsible for keeping everyone here in line when I needed to focus on my mission. Besides, if Etain was standing up to Troy when she usually deferred to me to have the hard conversations with him, things were worse than I'd thought in our camp. This conversation was probably long overdue.

And then there was the odd feeling like things weren't being said. What did Etain mean by something worse than my burning out? Was it to do with the storms I kept calling?

"Fine," Troy said after what I assumed was a culturally defined length of time spent glaring at each of them according to their stations and his personal grievance with each individual. "I'll talk to her. But if I find out you were too busy paying attention to Arden to focus on external threats—"

"We get it, T," Allegra interrupted. "Punishment fitting whatever befalls your queen."

"That's right," Troy said with the dangerous softness that always worried me. That was his assassin voice, and the bond said he was edging that way fast. "And if you do it to yourself, I won't save you. Arden is all I have time and energy for right now. Her success means we all succeed. So, get back to work and make sure all of our allies have what they need to keep business running." His voice hardened even further. "The next person I find loitering around this tent will get a not-so-gentle reminder about boundaries. Now, was there anything else? No? Good. Dismissed." When he ducked back inside the tent, he sighed at whatever expression I was wearing. "I imagine you have questions."

"Yeah." I had several, but the one that I blurted out was, "Are people afraid of me?"

His face blanked, telling me the answer. "They're concerned. Some are afraid *for* you, others..." He trailed off, looking like he was trying to choose his words extremely carefully. "Some people will always be afraid of those standing in their own power."

I tried to read between the lines. "My magic intimidates them. The storms, the Dreamwalking, all that."

"Yes."

I studied him. There was more here. "What aren't you telling me? Was there a threat while I was in the Duat?"

"Just the usual ones."

"What are you trying to protect me from?" These short answers weren't telling me anything, and he'd been sharper than I'd expected with Allegra, Darius, and Etain just now.

The muscle in his cheek jumped. Something about this conversation was definitely pushing buttons. "Arden, there are a lot of people who would want to take a shot at a primordial elemental, even if just for the bragging rights. Some will have other reasons." His gaze searched mine, like he was imagining all the threats he never showed me and trying to remind himself that I was still here in front of him. "I'm doing what I can to keep you safe."

"Never doubted it." I took his hand, turning it over to trace the lines in his palm and caress the callouses from long hours of practice with his longknife. "If it's the storms and such that are scaring people, or the dead plants and that outside, maybe a day off would help. I hate it, but you're right about my lack of control when I'm exhausted. The longer rest did me good, but if I killed that much vegetation, I can't be eating enough."

Troy's shoulders dropped. Subtly but enough for me to catch it as a blend of relief and guilt swirled through the bond. "I don't want to delay the mission any longer than we have to, but I'm also not willing to lose you over it. If what Lachlan said was right, you—we—are pushing way too hard. Etain was right about that, even if it's irritating."

"Okay. Another twenty-four hours."

"Of *rest*, Arden. Not running around fixing problems."

I winced. "Do video calls count as running around?"

"Yes."

"Are you going to rest too then?"

He started to answer with a no then realized I'd trapped him. "Maybe a few calls. *After* we eat." His stomach rumbled, like it agreed with that decision, and he grimaced. "I could probably finish a deer."

"I could eat you," I said playfully.

Troy's attention homed in on me, hot and sharp. "As much as I want more of the other day, sex is *not* rest." He leaned close for a quick kiss. "Your enthusiasm is noted and appreciated though."

"Fiiine." After peeling off the bandages to find all of my wounds fully healed, I let him lead me out of the tent, feeling like shit all over again at how badly I'd trashed what had been a beautiful piece of property yesterday. Maybe I could—

"Do not even think about trying to restore it until we're done," Troy said firmly, looking down at me.

I barely reined in the reflex to stick my tongue out at him. That wasn't very queenly, and there were enough people around that someone would see.

Over the next few hours, I stuffed myself with protein and vegetables until I thought I'd explode, delegated the obscene number of missed calls, texts, and emails that had accumulated in two days, made an inspection round as much to make sure everyone saw I was okay as to see what was going on, and told Duke and Iaret what had befallen their shabti. Iaret was delighted, at least until she tried to summon a notebook from beyond the Veil. When nothing came, she cussed a blue streak in some ancient language, something that made even Duke's expression blank in surprise. When she presumably tried to teleport out only to be reminded that she was in a mostly mundane form, Duke had to take her for a walk before she stirred up the elves worse than they already were.

I checked on my squad as well, ensuring that I gathered the key from Lya and checked on Mason in particular. He would heal, but he was out for the next mission. I was starting to get an antsy feeling about bringing any of them at all. They were all as exhausted and stretched as thin as I was, without the support I had in the land and Troy. We'd all been having nightmares, so the sleep we did get wasn't good sleep. Even Mami Wata was beginning to look rough, losing her ageless look as dark circles formed under her eyes and her skin dried too quickly, despite multiple swims.

I had just disposed of the remains of another of the Sons of Seth Cade had finished off in the woods, far enough away from camp that nobody except Troy and the guards haunting the trees might see what that did to a body, when my phone rang.

It's your dad, I sent to Troy.

He snarled, probably because the last call had been a threat. *Answer it.*

"Cyrus," I said on doing so. "You are not the person I expected to hear from today."

"Arden. Aren't you just the little troublemaker." His tone was jovial, like he hadn't threatened me directly the last time he'd called. "It seems my boy didn't pass on a message I'd given him for you."

"Oh, I got it." I couldn't help the hardness of my own voice or the bitterness as I asked, "What the hell did I ever do to you?"

The light tone slipped into a growl. "You won't let my son go. He has a destiny to fulfill. On his own."

"I told you—"

"All queens lie, and you've got him so tangled up in you that my truthread says he thinks this auratic bullshit is the truth. That he'll die if he leaves you or fails to protect you."

I almost asked what reason I'd have to lie but didn't bother. We both knew that any queen who could look past the oyëoro would find a prize in Troy. That my reasons were different from another queen's would have been—that I genuinely loved and cared for him and that Cyrus had seen that himself—didn't matter. If Cyrus thought I'd somehow managed to bespell Troy, it was a short jump to thinking I'd bespelled him too. Besides, what mattered was the outcome: Troy refused to leave me or choose his father's mission over mine regardless of the hurts and wrongs he'd suffered.

Fine. Sometimes people were gonna think ill of you no matter what you said or did to the contrary. Trying to convince them otherwise was a waste of energy, time, and peace, and I was already running short on all three these days. I'd tried with Cyrus. I really had. But he'd had twenty years to stew in solitude on his vengeance and his plans. Oaths to my mother or not, I clearly hadn't been a factor in them, or if I had, not as a queen and bondmate to the son he was dead set on rescuing, whether the grown man wanted to be rescued or not.

I looked at Troy.

Do what you need to do, he sent.

Which, to me, meant "step up."

Subtlety wasn't my strong suit, but I'd had plenty of practice acting as a private investigator. I dug deep and found a memory of Callista's sugary sweet venom, letting a sneer curl my lips and pulling on as much attitude as I could muster. "Well. I can see there's no fooling you. But it's a good ploy, isn't it? Troy's dropping some of his aura into me at the Wild Hunt was just the cherry on top. I own him, Cyrus. More than Keithia ever did, in ways she never dreamed were possible. You might as well stop trying to take him from me. When I get magic back and secure the territory, I think I'll feel safe enough to cycle. And if I got pregnant? You know he'd never leave his wife and child." I paused just long enough to make the next words hurt. "Like you did."

Troy froze, like I'd been so believable that *he* believed what I was saying. Or like he heard a twisted version of the truth in my words, one that pained him. Then he closed his eyes and shook his head, nudging me to let the wall down between us.

I did, needing him to sense the churn of my stomach under the honeyed poison of my words. *I'm sorry.*

No need. I just heard my own demons, and they got a little too real.

Cyrus was rattling off what were probably threats or curses in elvish when I refocused.

"Now, that's not friendly at all," I said, speaking over him. "Especially with me treating your son so well. Come on, Cyrus, you've seen us together. He's happy enough. More than he ever was with Keithia, that's for sure. He *wants* to be with me."

"I've seen what you wanted me to see," he snarled. "And he wants what you want. Goddess *damn* your mother for convincing me to help them. It might be too late to kill her myself, but I will deal with you."

"You can try," I drawled, as though my heart wasn't shredding at Troy's hopes of a happy reunion with his father being further destroyed.

"Back off of restoring magic. I have work to do. You're making it harder, and that makes you a problem."

"If I decide I like being a problem?"

"Then my next trip will be to Richmond. If the gods didn't bury you in the Caverns of the Damned, then I'll destroy this little empire you've started building. When it's nothing but ash, I'll bury you in the rubble. Believe me, little queen, when I say that with a god as my patron and two decades of fury and madness to fuel me, I can do it."

The call ended, leaving me staring at Troy with all the heartsickness I felt painted on my face and his buried behind a painfully blank expression.

Chapter 24

We found Etain in the boathouse's small office, glaring at the computer screen.

She took one look at our faces when Troy and I slipped in then shut the door and grimaced. "What happened?"

"My father," Troy said.

"We haven't managed to locate him." Etain typed something, her fingers flying almost as quickly as Zadie's did. "Last known location was outside Knoxville."

"He'll be going to Richmond next," I said.

Etain typed again. "No evidence of that here. We've accessed his credit card account and—"

"He threatened Arden," Troy said. "Said he'd pull down her empire and then come for her. Starting with Richmond."

My captain looked up from the computer screen. The tightness of her expression said she desperately did not want to have this conversation but was going to do her duty anyway. "Target?"

"Unconfirmed," Troy said. "Given that we severed the Ead royals, either the next in line for the throne there or House Hilith would be my guess. Bedoe...they've always played a quieter game. Less ostentatiously awful in how they treat elven males, at least, which I think is his motive."

Etain nodded, her gaze going distant as she ran the possibilities. "Well. Without magic, we're short on options."

"I know. Permission granted to engage with lethal force."

She blinked.

I flinched. "Troy—"

"No, Arden," he said. "This is my call. For more reasons than you know."

The haunted note in his voice both piqued my investigator's instincts and wrenched my heart at the same time. There was something extremely strange going on here. Even if I didn't trust my own instincts, the Sight and my ring were buzzing in a way I was learning meant secrets rather than threats.

From the way Etain went a little green around the proverbial gills, glanced at me, then looked down at the desk, she might know part of it.

Damn it. I knew Troy still had secrets—lots of them, some of them real bad and real ugly—but I'd hoped the worst or at least the most recent had all come out by now. It'd been more than two years since I'd met him.

Maybe it was unreasonable to think that you could know everything about someone in two years though. Maybe it was just our connection in the bond that made me think that, since I knew so much about every facet of his current daily existence.

Was now the time to push? Maybe not in front of Etain but—

"I will explain, cariñamí," he said, softly but still aloud for Etain's benefit. "Just not here and not now."

Which meant it was one of the extra bad, extra ugly secrets then. One of the ones that involved him doing something that hurt him as much as someone else.

"Okay," I said. *I will trust you until you show me I can't.*

He just nodded. The muscle in his cheek jumped, and the shape of the thought that flitted across his mind before he brought the walls between us up a notch made me wonder if this was him showing me now that I couldn't.

No. I couldn't go there.

I couldn't make assumptions based on the bond, both because I knew how tangled up he got in his past sometimes and because we'd promised brutal honesty to each other. That kind of talk had a time and place, and it wasn't now. Him wanting to hold it back was fair.

Etain blew her breath out and shook herself. "All right then. I'll coordinate with Omar. We both had people in Richmond when all this kicked off. Do we alert the Conclave or..."

"No," Troy and I said together.

He waved for me to answer further.

"I was...playing a role when he called," I said. "Part of that role is the arrogance to think I'm untouchable. If we warn them, they'll act differently. That will change what Cyrus does."

"Exactly," Troy said when I finished.

"Wait though. Hang on." A thought skittered across my mind, prompted by the mention of the Eads. "Our working theory is that the severed Eads might be Sinclaire's pocket ace, right?"

"Yes." Troy's gaze unfocused as he tried to figure out where I was going with this. The Bureau for Supernatural Investigation, and Acting Director Sinclaire's insistence that I work for them off the books, had slipped both our minds with the greater urgency of getting magic back.

"Are any of the Richmond Conclave in government?" I asked.

"Several of them," Etain said. "Both publicly and clandestinely."

I thought furiously, rocking on my toes since the office was too small to pace, especially with three people in it. "What if I got in touch with Sinclaire and told her the Eads were working under Cyrus's direction to threaten government agents? Like a double agent kind of thing."

"That will give her the flashpoint she wants," Troy said. "And it assumes the Eads are actually working for her. It's just conjecture at this point."

"Can we confirm it? Quickly?"

Etain tilted her head from side to side. "It would mean re-tasking the teams in Richmond. They're the closest ones, and

I don't dare reassign anyone from your property or this one, ma'am. Or anyone currently on infowar ops."

I pushed down the reflex to grab Air and make a zephyr. "Okay, so the options are: confirm the Eads are working with Sinclaire and leave Richmond unwatched and unprotected, confirm and tip off Richmond, or not confirm and make Richmond and Cyrus our direct priority."

I looked up at Troy.

"Your call, my queen," he said. His formality said this was an even bigger decision than I thought.

Closing my eyes, I crossed my arms and bowed my head. How did I want to run my territory and my demesnes? Was it more important to play a role or embody a principle?

"Tip off Richmond," I said. "And re-task the team there. We need physical surveillance in Washington to get ahead of this, rather than just relying on our hackers to find things." Thoughts raced. Mine, since Troy was walled off protecting his own. "Wait. Tip off *Sonia* and only her. I want to solidify that relationship and reward House Bedoe for collaborating from the beginning. That was Sonia's choice, not her mother's. This way, we find out something about her objectives, we secure our strongest ally, and once I call Sinclaire back, we start our own game with the Sinners instead of constantly reacting to them."

I didn't need to explain myself, but in this case, I needed to say it aloud to make it make sense. This wasn't the way I usually did things, and I could trust these two to check my thought process.

The thrill that jolted through the bond startled me enough that I twitched and looked at Troy. Delight shone in his gaze, and when I glanced at Etain, she was hiding a smile.

"I agree," Troy said. He turned to Etain. "Get it done."

"As you will, majesties," she said. "Was there anything else?"

"Any updates from the parliament?" I asked.

Etain clicked a few times. "Nothing that hasn't already been forwarded to you, although we're watching a situation in

New York. The protests are getting more agitated, despite the progressive lean of the territory. Property damage only so far, but when shit's on fire, bodies tend to hit the street sooner or later. Matthias might be preparing to make a move, either to ensure or prevent that. We aren't sure yet what he thinks will keep his people safest."

"Okay. Keep me posted. Thanks, Etain." On impulse, I added, "You're doing great. I know none of this is what you signed up for, but I have no doubt that the reason people are still here despite all the elemental shit is because of your leadership and your demonstration of loyalty to me. I appreciate that, and it won't be forgotten."

She blushed, her pale skin going a deep red as she dropped her eyes. "Thank you, ma'am. It means a lot to hear that."

With a last respectful nod, I led Troy out.

That was well handled, Troy sent as we left. *She's one of your most loyal, and she was passed over multiple times for key positions in House Sequoyah after washing out of the Darkwatch.*

I couldn't help the little spike of satisfaction at that. *What made you so happy earlier?*

You're thinking like a queen. Moving like one. Without sacrificing yourself. You're finding options for us instead of raging against brick walls or letting yourself be pushed. And you're not trying to do everything yourself. I'm so proud of you, my love.

Thank you. I couldn't help my flush at that. I didn't have Troy's political training, and I left a lot of the Ebon Guard and Darkwatch decisions to him. But I had to stop thinking he could just run the demesnes for me while I fought the gods. We had to do this as a team, or I had to get out of my own way and his.

He threw an arm over my shoulder and tugged me against him, kissing my forehead when I wrapped an arm around his waist and curved toward him, secrets or not. We got strange looks from the elves keeping the camp and all our ops running, but fewer than before. Some looked relieved. This public display of affection thing was unusual for elves, but Troy and I were known for it by now. If we were falling into our usual patterns rather than me sprawling out on the ground or unintentionally calling storms, they'd be reassured.

I hoped they would be anyway. I was feeling recovered after stealing from the earth—physically, at least—and buoyed by Troy and Etain's reaction to my decisions, but this had been an exceedingly weird, high-pressure few days. As I let my attention drift from person to person, I could see the cracks. The tension. The lack of sleep, the pain of being magicless, the weight of what we were doing.

It was hard to feel like my taking twenty-four hours to rest and sort out what needed doing to keep my demesnes running and safe wasn't a selfish indulgence.

Troy squeezed me briefly. *Doing what you need to do to keep yourself going isn't selfish. Or rather, it is, but not in the negative sense.*

I knew he was right, but guilt still nagged at me. *I need to call Sinclaire.*

You need to eat again first.

Tempted as I was to argue with him, I also knew that'd been the point of not going straight back into the Duat.

That, and the feeling that I needed to go alone was getting stronger. I couldn't even say what it was. Just a sense that, with all the threats on the people with me, all the hints that one of them should have died by now combined with Troy nearly dying, someone actually would die at the next trial if I took them.

I wasn't sure I could bear it. Lya and Cade were, well, who they were. Fiercely loyal to each other and nobody else, unapologetically enamored with each other, and only allied with us because it benefited them directly. But that could just as easily describe me and Troy, and I had to be careful of projecting my resentment that he and I couldn't just walk away from everything like they were planning to. Mami Wata had her own little fiefdom in the east that could eventually become a problem, but again, I was letting my fear make me think that, especially given she'd never moved against Callista to my knowledge. Mason was just Mason—almost sweet in his lack of ambition, even as he joined us to make the kind of plays that would secure his reputation for life.

I didn't want to lose any of them.

You won't lose them, Troy sent as he spooned a double serving of scrambled eggs with peppers from the hotel buffet-style warmers onto his plate, then a third, followed by a spoon of a bean-based dish I'd only heard called ful and three sausage links.

I know. The decision firmed in me as I added a single serving of the eggs. *Because I won't be taking them.*

That set him off badly enough that he stopped and turned to glare at me, completely ignoring the fact that people could see us reacting but not speaking. *Excuse me?*

I'm not taking anyone. There've been too many threats. And the Sight is practically screaming.

It does that when you *are in danger. Not others.*

I shrugged. *Maybe taking them would put me in danger. Even if it didn't, Mason won't be able to walk for at least a week, let alone fight. Mami Wata is deteriorating fast, even with shifts in the dream. Cade might be feeding, but he's been bonded to Lya long enough and tightly enough that they're both increasingly distracted by the missing bond. We pushed them too hard, Troy.*

He thought that over as he finished filling his plate. *Your read is that they've become more liability than support.*

I grimaced at his putting it that way but...

Yes. I was firm in it, knowing I was right, even if I felt like a terrible team leader. If I'd been better at pacing us, we might not be in such dire physical and mental straits. At the same time, each trial had been difficult in ways I couldn't have anticipated, and waiting until everyone was fully recovered would stretch this mission out to weeks or months. Time we didn't have.

Troy didn't answer me as we took our food outside to eat sitting at the end of the dock. He cleared his plate, waiting until I finished mine to speak. "If you think going alone is the best choice, then okay. I don't like it. But I know you don't like having to trust me with what I'm not telling you. Fair is fair."

I couldn't help a flinch at his admitting outright that there were things he was still keeping from me, feeling the heat of shame as I wondered if that made me a fool.

"How bad is it?" I blurted.

He turned away from me, looking out over the lake. "Bad."

"People died?"

He nodded, a single jerk of his head.

I didn't bother to ask if it was his fault. Whether it was or not, he thought it was. Not only that but he was ashamed of it. There wasn't much that shamed him these days, so this was gonna be a messy one to untangle.

I finished my plate, set it aside, and leaned against him, tipping my head to rest on his shoulder. There was no point in saying anything. The mood I was getting from him in the bond was dark and brooding, remembering things he'd rather not.

"Let's drop these plates off and see about getting a little more rest," I said.

That gave him an action and permission to take care of me, in a way, so he was up and pulling me to my feet within moments. After we dropped our camp plates in the tub for washing—one chore I was glad wasn't assigned to me as queen—I nudged Troy away from the cubicle still set up for us inside and toward the doors. I couldn't be in here longer than I had to. Security considerations said we had to be there for the last mission, but I would not be going inside that space until it was the last second before I needed to go.

We'd barely stepped outside when reality tore and Usir stepped through, still green-skinned and dressed in tattered rags.

I pulled up short as shadowfire wreathed me as it had with Anansi's presence.

Troy looked around to see what had caused it, failing to find anything until he dipped into my mind and saw the god through my eyes. Usir wasn't fully present here, likely only visible to me and maybe other celestials, which meant that both me and Troy stopping to talk—or in Troy's case, snarl—at empty air ran the very strong risk of making us look like absolute lunatics who had pushed far too hard in the last few days.

"You made such grand threats to Anansi about making and unmaking." The god's flail rattled then thumped against my chest as he tucked the end of it under my chin and tilted my head up.

I threw out a hand to stop Troy's reflex to pounce. Not only did I not want him hurt, but it wasn't like he could catch a god that was half-corporeal or less. He would look silly or dangerous trying though.

Troy restrained himself physically, but fury raged in the bond and a growl slipped from his chest.

Easy, I sent. *Don't let them call you feral.*

Troy cut off his growl but hovered in a ready stance, prepared to throw himself at a god to save me.

"Does your Hunter think he can take a god?" Usir asked dismissively.

"He serves his queen," I gritted between my teeth, keeping my response as noncommittal as possible in the hope of hiding both Troy's value to me and his power.

The god stared at me with eyes the unseeing white of death. Somehow, I was certain he could see not only my physical form but my aura, soul, and the bonds with Troy and, via the heart scarab, the rest of my squad. He definitely saw the blended shadow and sunlight wreathing me.

"You hold old magic," he said. "But you also *are* old magic. Existence and nonexistence in a fragile shell, held together with threads of brightest sun and endless night."

I didn't know what to make of that, but it made me shiver. Something in it called to me. Stirred a memory in my heart. Not one I'd lived, I didn't think, or if it was, then it was something from when I was a baby. It felt more...ancestral.

"You will suffice," Usir said after a long stare. "My brother is using the magic stolen from this plane to craft a spell to trap and compel Iset. I won't have it. You will go on your final mission. And you will go now."

There was a push against my mind then, like when Troy used Aether to put me to sleep, only magnitudes stronger.

It infuriated me.

I was no toy for the gods. Not anymore. I refused.

"No," I growled, using Chaos to slice at the magic trying to drown me. "I will go on *my* time."

The snap of Usir's spell breaking rocked him back a step. Rather than the outrage I was expecting, he laughed. "So Harqil spoke truth."

"What do they have to do with this?"

"Any good messenger is also a good psychopomp." Pressure from the end of Usir's flail forced my head higher. "Anansi may have claimed you for now, but he will not always."

I clenched my fists to keep the fire now wreathing them from searing the entire area. I might have attacked Sutekh, but I'd had reason. Nobody—none of the celestials, at least—would consider any of this reasonable. Not for the hierarchy of god to mortal.

"Good," the god said. "You do have control. That is important, even if the Court of Nightmares is all you attain." He tilted his head. "If you go by sunset, I will grant you a boon."

It was all I could do to control my expression. A god, bargaining? This definitely outweighed Cyrus's threats to slow down. Whatever was going on with this fight between Sutekh, Usir, and Iset, it must be big.

"What kind of boon?" I asked suspiciously.

"One of my choosing."

With a suddenness that left me gasping, Usir disappeared.

"What. The. Fuck," I whispered.

The Nightmare Court? As something I could attain?

And what the hell was that about being existence and nonexistence in a body?

Chapter 25

A few people had gathered, standing awkwardly a short distance away.

"We're fine, y'all," I said. "Just one of the gods checking in."

"*Just* one of the gods," Troy muttered as he followed me back to the tent set up for us near the lake. "You know that's not normal for most people, right?"

"It's not normal for me either."

"Isn't it? Arden, you didn't miss a beat."

I shrugged. Maybe he was right. Maybe I was just too tired to make a big deal out of yet another god making their business mine. What was it about me that was so damn special, anyway?

You know what, Troy sent.

Sighing, I ducked into the tent. There had to be another primordial elemental somewhere, right? Or maybe that was just wishful thinking. I'd made enough of a stir without wanting to that we probably would have heard of another. Loneliness washed over me at that, and I threw myself down to lay with my head in Troy's lap as soon as he'd come in and sat down.

He threaded his fingers through my curls and started massaging my scalp, careful with his movements to avoid tangling them. "Did I hear something about the Nightmare Court?"

"You can't hear the gods?"

"Not fully, not when they're appearing like this one was. I only get a shimmer and kind of a roaring of ideas when I tap into your senses of them."

"Oh." I repeated what Usir had said. "I want to know what Harqil has been saying and what the hell it means to join the Nightmare Court."

A pull on my awareness of the area made me sit bolt upright a moment before the celestial messenger stuck their head in.

"About all that," Harqil said.

Troy leaped up, snarling with the sharp teeth down, and barely checked himself from an attack. "I warned you about sneaking up on me again, Harqil."

They grinned. "But it's so much fun. Can I come in?"

"Now they ask," Troy grumbled, dropping to sit again and waving a hand at me.

"You might as well." I sat close to Troy, as much for comfort as to make space for Harqil. "I have questions."

"I thought you might, after our last conversation. Especially given what I've just seen outside. Are you trying to make that dream come true faster?" they asked. When I just gritted my teeth and glared, Harqil came all the way in and dropped fluidly to sit, knees up and arms wrapped around their shins. "You remember I told you the tricksters are split on the matter of Sutekh? I've been...pulling some strings, let's say."

"Anansi?" I asked. "Or is this you not liking to play by someone else's rules?"

They shrugged, not committing to an answer. "There are loopholes in the celestial existence, so to speak."

"The celestial existence." I leaned heavily against Troy. "I'm not a celestial." Their glance at Troy had me sitting up again and looking between the two of them. "Right?"

The hint of a grimace tugged Troy's mouth. "Sort of."

"Hang on, when the fuck were you going to say something?" I hissed, trying to keep my voice down, both to avoid attracting attention from outside and so that Troy wouldn't feel like I was attacking him. I was surprised and annoyed, but he'd also been managing a million things while I was in the Duat, including the physical state and safety of my sleeping body.

Harqil waved a hand. "That's not important. What's important is that you, my lady Dreamwalker, have definitely started punching above your weight class. It's making people—and by people, I mean some of the gods—nervous. That can have some, shall we say, mortal consequences."

I pressed my lips together and glared at them both. "I'm assuming that means death."

"Among other things." Harqil rocked back, balancing perfectly on their ass with their bare feet in the air. "What's *important* is that if you continue to be this interesting, the Court of Nightmares might just reveal themselves to you."

"Shit." My stomach sank. "I think they already have."

"Oh?" They rocked back onto their feet. "Do tell."

"I had a dream. There was a presence. It accused me of naming myself four times, in duality. Then I think my mom might have stepped in? But she couldn't have. She's been dead for twenty-eight years. I just— Whoever it was, she said that the Court has no business with me yet and that they were just trying to intimidate me after already sending a warning."

"Ah." Harqil grinned. "Good to have confirmation that it *was* the Court that was behind that dreadful dream of yours, which makes it half prophecy and half roadmap. Not so good is that this offers opportunity and threat all in one."

"Explain," Troy said.

"If they opened the channel for a prophetic dream to come through, Arden was already on their radar. It was a test, so to speak, which she unfortunately passed with flying colors." They raised a hand, anticipating my question. "Unfortunate, because the Court is only ever comprised of four: Despair, Rage, Terror, and Shame. For you to join, another must step down—or be ejected by other means."

"But what even are they?" I asked, exasperated and too tired to dig into the grim names. Once again, a position or role that I hadn't asked for or intended to occupy was being thrust upon me. And yet people kept accusing me of power grabbing. "*Who* are they? And why did you want me to look into them before?"

"For the why, to poke the hornets' nest and see what flew out. As to who, they're beings who straddle the lines between the worlds. Dreamwalkers all." Harqil grinned. "You see why the djinn hate and fear Dreamwalkers so much."

I sighed. "And why Duke started avoiding me. If Dreamwalkers cross between planes or whatever and can do what I've done outside, that puts the Old City at risk. Which they won't tolerate."

"Unless you're constrained by the agreement their inner council has with the Court, yes. Hence my pulling strings and rubbing elbows with various entities. Smoothing the way, so to speak. There hasn't been new blood on the Court in millennia. Either the djinn kill off prospects when djinn-blooded Dreamwalkers are born, or the elves hunt them down."

Troy grunted as surprise flashed in the bond. "Another reason for the elemental bounties."

"Precisely," Harqil said. "Atlantis was just the biggest excuse."

"What about the rest of the factions?" I asked. "Do they know? Care?"

"They're exponentially less likely to produce a Dreamwalker than the djinn or djinn-blooded. The occasional elf with auratic inclinations and the oyëoro might manage it." Troy stiffened as Harqil gave him a darkly teasing grin before refocusing on me and continuing. "Which I suspect eases your pulling him into Chaos spheres. The witches might, but more often they produce astral travelers or prophetic dreamers. Different sciences entirely."

My head was spinning at all this new information. "Okay. Why tell me now? What does this have to do with getting magic back? And what's in it for me?"

"As for what's in it for you, power, protection, and influence beyond this plane. You wanted to feel safe enough to start a family? This draws in agreements and laws going back past Atlantis. Neither the elves nor the djinn could touch you without serious consequences. Apocalyptic consequences, even."

I shivered. Power for me, fine, if only to protect myself and Troy. But that level of it? To be untouchable in Otherside? Yeah. That'd go a long way toward making me feel safe enough to cycle into fertility. Of course, there'd always be somebody who wanted to fuck around and find out. Or somebody who had no idea the Court of Nightmares existed or simply didn't care. But if those who were powerful enough to know were constrained? That'd give me a lot of breathing room.

At my side, Troy was practically vibrating with the force of the strategic considerations flying through his head.

"What's the catch?" he asked.

"She has to go beyond being a primordial and prove herself to be a Nightmare. A being capable of cataclysmic destruction, borderline-celestial power, and unquestionable potential, in addition to being a Dreamwalker. That and demonstrate a willingness to use the power." They gave Troy a significant look. "Your people will have a problem with that."

"I'll deal with them." The heat and depth of Troy's commitment deepened his voice to a growl. "Arden, if you want this, we will get it done."

I wanted it. Maybe. "What are the responsibilities?"

Harqil grinned. "Already proving yourself worthy of the role with that question, rather than simply powerful enough to take it. That'll be a change. Responsibilities are similar to what you already carry and are working toward, just on a bigger scale.

Arbitration, law-giving, the like. But beyond the territory you hold or are planning to hold."

"How often?" I asked.

They shrugged. "There hasn't been a case in three generations. Long enough that many have forgotten the Court exists."

Something told me the rapid changes instigated by my Reveals would change that, but I still couldn't help but be intrigued. "Let's see how getting magic back goes."

"Fair enough," Harqil said. "If you pass this last trial alone, it'll be another test passed in terms of your fitness to join the Court."

I shook my head. "I knew there had to be a reason why I felt like I had to go by myself."

Troy tensed but kept quiet. I'd already said I had to go alone, and now it was confirmed for reasons he personally wanted.

"So clever. Well. I'll just be on about my business then." They sobered suddenly. "Arden, this last trial is one of existence and nonexistence. I'm not permitted to tell you what that means, lest it disqualify you from the Court, but understand that of everyone you've gathered here, you're the only one who could navigate it. And that only if you're prepared to be more than you've ever been."

More than I'd ever been. My stomach twisted. I already felt like I was too much. How could I be *more* than that?

"Okay," I whispered.

I'd figure it out. If this was the path to safety and family, I had to.

With an apologetic smile and a nod, reality twisted, and Harqil was gone.

"Harqil popped in after the second mission," Troy said while I was still trying to wrap my head around that. "While you were recovering. Said you'd passed a threshold. They warned me that I might not be enough to anchor you on my own."

The shame and frustration in both his voice and the bond went a little ways to explaining why he hadn't mentioned it earlier and why he was so touchy lately.

"I don't want to be shared," I said.

"Good," he snarled before I could continue. "Because I—I *hate* the idea of adding two more to make a triad around you. I know it'd probably help both of us, but I was solo for so long and then you've been mine alone and—"

Holy shit, my strong-and-silent mate was rambling.

I rested my fingers on his lips. "Hey, it's okay. I should feel guilty for making you shoulder this alone, but the idea of letting anyone be as close to me as you are in any way makes my insides twist too much to feel anything other than deeply uncomfortable."

Rather than responding verbally, he shifted his seat, snagged me, and pulled me between his now-upraised knees, wrapping his arms tight around me as he pressed his face against my neck.

That conversation really had set him off. He'd probably been trying to force himself to get used to the idea that I might want, need, or demand more support or telling himself that he should insist on it for my good. I wasn't having it either way. We'd get through this together, the two of us, just like we'd gotten through the Wild Hunt together.

"Let's get some more rest," I said when some of the tension had eased from him.

"Sinclaire," he growled.

Goddess damn it, with all the supernatural business, I'd forgotten about that bitch. I took a deep breath and let it out slowly, trying to calm myself and organize my thoughts.

After a few breaths, I dug my phone out of my pocket and dialed.

"Sinclaire," I said when she answered. "It's Finch. This a good time for a quick chat?"

"It's always a good time if you're calling to let me know you're ready to work with the Bureau," she said.

"I'll be honest, I'm not quite there yet. But I wanted to offer an indication of my goodwill." I tried to inject a little uncertainty into my voice. False confidence, even if I was deeply confident that I was on the right track now.

She pounced on it. "I'm listening."

I paused to give the impression of hesitating. "You wanted information."

"I still do."

Another pause.

"Finch?"

Good. I had her hooked. I cleared my throat like I was trying to push myself into this. "I don't want to do this."

"I understand. But you're a good leader, Finch. You know you have to protect your people. The Bureau for Supernatural Investigation is the best way to achieve that."

Furious disbelief slashed through Troy's thoughts, forcing me into another pause as I tried to separate his feelings out and refocus on my task.

"I have reason to believe there's a threat on federal employees," I said quietly. "But I want your promise that my people will be safe before I say more."

"I can't promise that," Sinclaire said. "We have to investigate everything."

"*My* people are safe from investigation," I said. "If I hear the Bureau is hassling them, I'll have a problem. I'll stay out of the way otherwise. And I want the subpoena withdrawn completely."

"You're asking quite a lot for someone who claims to be innocent and above-board."

That made my lip twist in an involuntary sneer. Of course someone with all the political and social power in the situation would think I was asking too much. Asking anything at all was too much, and putting any timeframe on it would make it too soon. It was always ask less and wait a while longer. For truth, for justice, for representation, for compensation.

Anger got the better of me. "I guess now wasn't a good time after all."

Behind me, Troy tensed. *My love...*

Trust me. I've played hard-to-get until now. Rolling over too easy would be suspicious.

A swirl of uneasy assent spun through the bond. Troy might be solid on Otherside politics, but Darius had said he'd spent more time on missions against other elves than usual on account of the oyëoro. I had to trust myself on navigating human politics. I'd spent most of my life pretending to be one, pretending to assimilate and get them to trust me, and I'd been damn good at it.

"Finch, if you know something and are withholding information, I'll have that added to the list of charges already standing against you." When I didn't answer, she added, "Not because I want to. I have to play the hand I'm dealt. For me to get my deal through on your behalf, I have to be able to demonstrate that you're willing to play nice with us."

Bullshit, I sing-songed mentally to myself and Troy.

Aloud, I said, "I guess we'll both do what we have to do then."

"I guess we will. Oh, in case you hadn't heard, there's new legislation making its way through both houses of Congress. Othersiders would be declared enemies of the state and required to register themselves or be lawfully detained. You wouldn't want to give my friends on the Hill more of a reason to pass that, would you?"

"Like I said, Acting Director Sinclaire, we'll both do what we have to do." I ended the call with a sick feeling, praying that my playing chicken with the Sinners wasn't the final straw that damned us all.

At the same time, nothing I did with Sinclaire was going to sway politicians dead set on gaining re-election. The left had been bending over barrels to prove themselves to the moderates for years. The right kept dragging everyone further that way, shifting the middle along with them. The Reveals had only hastened the shift and worsened the rhetoric.

I couldn't own this. Not alone. I could act, and I would. But owning the bullshit that would be perpetrated against me and mine regardless of how far I bent myself over said barrel would be what damned me.

I just had to get magic back and ensure that Otherside was prepared to face what was coming. Being surrounded by hostile mundanes, with my people unable to help me fight back, was not how I was going to start feeling safe.

If those mundanes went beyond protesting and tried to hunt us down? Yeah. I'd be too busy fighting them off to do anything else because there was no way I was leaving my people to burn.

Chapter 26

F inding rest was hard after that call, despite my insistence to myself that I couldn't own what Sinclaire or the elected officials here or anywhere else did. I wanted to go out and run, but I'd already been so drained that I'd destroyed the campground, so I forced myself to lay down.

With a wall up between me and Troy in the bond, he fell asleep with a soldier's practice at catching rest where he could. He had to be having nightmares about the Lake of Fire, but he was always better about listening to his body. I lay in his arms, fretting. Replaying what I'd said and done. Praying I was right in my assessment that giving anything up too easily after being so insistent that I wouldn't snitch on Otherside would be suspicious and therefore to be avoided was the right call. Worrying about what my people here were thinking, with dead vegetation around them, four drained squadmates, their king almost killed, and seeing me speak to the air and claim it was the gods.

How much could people take before they lost faith?

How much could *I* take before I collapsed?

Had I become too much this time, in truth?

Was I going to kill Troy with this insistence or indulgence or whatever it was in us being determined to stay a pair rather than bonding two more elves in to support us? Harqil had said something about that ancient primordial elemental, Adhara, having three elves to back her. Troy was strong, and I was stronger, but we were still just two against the world.

My throat was tight, as was my chest. My stomach kept wanting to heave. I was too hot and too cold at the same time.

"Relax, Arden," Troy murmured at my back.

I jumped, not having realized he'd been pulled awake. "Sorry."

"I know there's a lot at stake. But you need to rest for the best outcome. Do you want me to pull you under?"

I hesitated. Allowing him to do that felt like taking the easy route.

"You're the one who keeps saying life doesn't have to be so difficult," he pointed out. "Use the resources available to you and let both of us get a couple hours of sleep."

"Fine. Do it, please."

The scent of burnt marshmallow spiked. Aether washed over me with soothing tendrils twining through first my nerves then my mind. I shuddered, reflexively fighting him.

"Shh. I've got you," Troy said. His hand rested heavy on my hip, grounding but not constraining me, thumb stroking along my skin where my shirt had ridden up and sending chills over me.

I tucked myself closer against him and dropped my shields. As my power signature spilled out, he slipped in and pulled me under.

△▽△▽

I woke just before sunset feeling unsettled and tried to tell myself I was ready.

Troy and I showered. Dressed. Ate. Had final briefings with the squad we'd built, with the parliament, and with Etain, Darius, and Allegra.

Then it was time.

One more challenge.

One more. We'd succeed. We had to. For all of Otherside.

Except when I walked into the cubicle I'd woken up in three times already, I froze.

My heart raced. I couldn't breathe. Couldn't *see* because I was dizzy and sick and oh my Goddess I was going to die if I did this again.

The first time I'd gone into the Duat, I'd nearly lost Troy. *I'd watched him bleed out on the sand.* I'd held him together, made up magic to heal him. Smelled his death in the space I had to enter now, seen him pale and lifeless and *gone.*

The second time, I'd been drowned again. Dragged under. Held down. Water crashing over me with a heavy inevitability that would wash me away as it stole my breath and my warmth and the movement of air around me.

The third time, I'd been practically buried alive while being scratched and clawed by the vengeful undead. I'd been *alone* and in the dark. There was nobody there to stand with me. Nobody to help. Nobody. Nobody. Nobody. Just Ammut and my own screams of fearful rage as the earth closed in and the dead surged and fed on my flesh.

All of my worst nightmares, brought to life.

If I died, Troy died with me. I'd drag him down into the depths when he was just coming into his power. When he was finally healing.

If I died, I'd go to the lowest circle of the nine hells for all I'd done to get here.

And I'd be alone again.

If these dreams of the Duat were the path to an alternate version of the afterlife, how much worse would it be to die for real?

No waking.

Only endless darkness and pain and misery and loneliness and—

Arms caught me from behind.

A hand shifted to cover my mouth and catch my scream as Troy murmured, "Shh, shh, it's just me. You're okay. You're safe."

I couldn't move, even to nod. All I could do was stand there, shaking like a sapling in a hurricane as I stared at the mattresses still laid side-by-side on the floor.

Was it just my imagination, or did Troy's blood still stain his? Was mine still pooled where I'd huddled in his arms after the last trial? Could I still smell a bad death in the close confines of the low-ceilinged space?

"It's okay, Arden. Easy. I'm here. We're both safe."

The hint of strain in his voice was what finally pulled me out of my tunnel-vision focus on the cubicle.

The ground was vibrating, a tremor that had everything clattering. Sharp voices called out in elvish as things crashed to the floor or toppled over. In the bond, Troy was scrambling to find the balance between soothing me and not adding to my terror with the wrong Aetheric working.

I couldn't make it stop.

"Breathe with me," he said.

I tried. Choked on the air, chest heaving uselessly.

"One more try."

This time I gasped.

"Good. Now with me."

I let Troy's voice wind its way through my brain. Squeezed my eyes shut like a scared kid in the dark.

"That's right. Don't look. Let me guide you." He took a deep breath in.

I matched him, teeth gritted, as he held it before letting it out.

Again.

A third time.

On the sixth breath, I finally stopped shaking. From the silence, so did everything else.

"Good," Troy said again. "That's very well done, Arden. Keep breathing, okay? I'm going to back us out."

Panic tried to ratchet up again. "No! I have to—"

"Listen. Just listen." He waited to make sure I'd do that before continuing. "What you have to do now is not trigger another quake. That's all."

Oh no. Oh shit. "Quakes have epicenters," I whispered. "Troy—"

"I know. We've already got the Darkwatch doing what they can to hack systems and shore up defenses here."

That was too much for our overstretched forces to manage. But we didn't have time to get somewhere else for this last stage. We had to go now, or Sinclaire would move on Otherside. The US House and Senate would pass their bills and start rounding us up. The people I'd claimed as mine would be in danger because *I was falling apart* when I was needed most.

I had to pull myself together. Now.

"Let them do their jobs," Troy said in a low voice. "Let everyone else do their jobs. Focus on you."

"This is... It's my fault. I can't—"

"Do you really think you're the first or only queen to make a misstep that required a cover-up? Do you think any of the old queens would have stepped up the way you have, torturing yourself for the good of everyone else when you'd be just fine, or better off, doing nothing?"

Immediately, my mind tried to make this about me being an elemental queen. The usual need for perfection. To set an example. To prove myself.

But right this second, I was far too much of a wreck to worry about perfect anything. I could barely *breathe* with the tightness in my chest and the way my head spun around a white tunnel of narrow vision fixated on the damn mattresses.

"Take another breath, Arden. You're here with me now. I won't let anything happen to you or to our people." Troy let me find a measure of control again before squeezing me in a hug then turning me in his arms to face him. His gaze was shadowed labradorite, the gold flecks shining brighter than ever, and his expression was serious. "What do you need, my love?"

I started to glance around him. My face flamed as I realized what a public mess I'd made. Nothing remained on a surface. Some of the boathouse's windows were shattered. A few cubicles had fallen. It'd been a proper earthquake.

"Oh no," I said. "Troy—"

"No." He caught my jaw in one big, firm hand and forced me to look at him only. "You. What do *you* need?"

"I can't do this in here." I choked down the lump in my throat, my tongue tacky in my dry mouth as I thought about laying down again in this little space. "Outside. I need to be outside."

To my surprise, Troy didn't argue with me. Didn't say anything about security or risk. Just said, "I'll have someone bring more supplies out to the tent we used before. We'll get a guard set up. Come on. And chin up. You're still a queen."

The gentleness of the last part made it encouragement in the face of my embarrassment, not an order. I nodded tightly and put my hand in the crooked arm he offered, like we were walking into a dance rather than out to the woods.

Allegra and Darius fell in on either side of us.

"Orders?" Allegra asked from my right in the same gentle tone Troy had been using.

"Get the tent restocked and make security arrangements," Troy replied as we exited. "Have Ophelia, Lachlan, and Felip on standby. Prep for emergency evac, land and water. Prep anti-air defenses as well, in case the reflective layer Arden put up already isn't enough."

"Okay." Allegra slipped an arm over my shoulders to give me a quick hug, letting me go when I stiffened at the scent of another strong female. Rather than being offended though, she spun to walk backward in the direction of the shed that'd been my cell under Leith. "You've got this, Arden. It's okay. We're all rooting for you."

I nodded weakly, trying to accept the reassurance for what it was rather than feeling more pressure even as my head spun. She wasn't mad or doubtful. Just oddly calm and reassuring. Like having the shit hit the fan made her more sure of what needed doing rather than less.

Darius handed Troy my comb when we drew to a halt near the fire kettle. The two men exchanged a look, and Darius said, "It worked for Alli and Evie." A smile flickered. "And me."

I frowned, distracted from my worries by the strange comment and the mention of Evangeline. "What worked?"

Troy sighed and righted the nearest chair before gesturing for me to sit in it. "Being the eldest child comes with responsibilities with regard to the younger children in the family."

"When I or my sisters woke up scared, it was Troy's job to get us back to sleep," Darius said. "At first, he tried reminding us that we were the ones that went bump in the night, like he was supposed to. But that only goes so far when you're five years old and have had a nightmare inspired by the adults in your life. Who also went bump in the night. Sometimes violently."

"I used to braid their hair for them," Troy muttered, seeming almost embarrassed as he slapped the comb against his palm. "In secret. I was supposed to be toughening them up. Pushing them to be harder and stronger. But they were practically babies. They needed care, not more threats."

"So, he'd come in and shush us and tell us whatever he thought any passing adult would need to hear him saying, all while carefully braiding our hair or even just brushing it. And when he was done and we were calm again, he'd undo all his work and hide the brush and comb for next time." Darius gave Troy a sad look. "You were probably the only one who ever offered us any affection as children, brother."

I stared at the two of them, distracted from my attack and the earthquake it'd caused by equal parts horror and heartbreak, wondering if this was part of Troy's drive to have kids—so he could raise a new generation differently than he had been raised. Not just *be* the change but raise it. I also wondered if this was why the twins were so devoted to Troy, despite the tension of recent days. Yeah, they were his sibling-cousins, as well as his knights. But the relationship had always gone deeper than that, on both sides.

I studied Troy, reading his aching need to do something that would help chase away the nightmares and anxiety attacks delaying this next mission. Not for the sake of the mission. For me.

"Okay," I said, settling in the chair. "I really would appreciate not waking up with my hair a tangled mess again." I'd forgotten any kind of bonnet or even a spare hair tie in the hurry to get over here and get started.

Darius nodded approvingly, seeing that I was supporting Troy as much as he was me. "I'll go help Alli with the prep."

Despite my initial skepticism and the swiftness with which Troy put my hair into a French braid, it did soothe and center me. Gave me space to gather myself, while being attended to. Like we were prepping for battle together but with a tenderness that helped me remember that part of battle was what drove me to fight to begin with and what would be waiting when—not if —I made it back.

"There," Troy murmured, switching back to English.

I had no idea what he'd been saying in elvish. But Allegra had given him a solemn, sad look when she drifted past with supplies for the tent and handed him the hair tie from her wrist, so I was pretty sure it was his habit of working through his deepest thoughts aloud and to me, just outside my full comprehension. I suspected that was why he'd quit pushing me to learn elvish.

He kissed the top of my head. "You can do this. And when you get back, I will be here. Ready for whatever you need to be okay."

I leaned back and tilted my head so he could kiss me, upside down though I was. "Thank you. For this and for earlier. For stopping me from bringing the building down. Or hurting someone."

"I told you. I don't need a complete triad to support you. We've got this. The two of us. Together." His lips met mine, settling me.

When I sat up, I was prepared to see a crowd of worried people surrounding us. But nobody was standing around. Everyone, including Cade, Lya, Mami Wata, and the djinn, were moving with purpose to get things packed and ready for a quick exit. Even Mason sat in a chair near the road, a semi-automatic rifle on his lap as he faced outward.

"See?" Troy said. "Everyone knows they have to do their part so you can do yours. We're all in this together. You're not alone."

Not alone. That was a concept I could barely encompass, even if I'd had Troy and the Ebon Guard and a parliament to work with for just under two years now.

If they could do their part despite seeing their leader have a panic attack, I could damn well pull myself together and do mine.

It was time for Sutekh to be taken into account, for Cyrus to see he couldn't get away with threatening me, and for the Court of Nightmares to see that I could pick up anything they threw down and survive it.

It was time to get magic back.

Chapter 27

This time when I stepped into the Chaos sphere that was my jumping-off point, something had shifted. The usual friendly clouds painted purple by the setting sun had become stormy. Lightning crackled in the distance, and an ominous silence hung over the woods behind me. The trees themselves had grown dry and brittle, and the ferns were dead.

I didn't like it. I didn't like it at all. This was supposed to be *my* place. Mine and Troy's, since it'd first manifested when our bond had deepened enough that we'd started affecting each other.

"Sutekh isn't happy."

I whirled at the sound of Harqil's voice, not having sensed them crossing in. "Is that the storms? The dead plants?"

They nodded.

When they didn't say anything more, I asked, "Are you coming with me?"

"No. Just seeing you off." Harqil shoved their hands in the deep pockets of their voluminous trousers, all done in shimmering patches this time and set off by their sherbet-orange T-shirt, and stared out over the stormy ocean. "A reminder: this is the big one. There will be some kind of trick, a battle, something. You have to stay the course and keep moving forward. If you go off track, you die. If you take a box that isn't the Box of Ages, you die. If Sutekh finds you, probably worse than death."

Something was shifting about them. I'd never been so able to see them or their clothes so clearly, like it wasn't important before or it just happened to slip my mind every time.

I'd ask when I survived this. "What about Usir's boon?"

Harqil's head snapped around so quick I thought they'd break their neck. "You made a deal with Usir?"

"Not really? They offered a boon if I came by sunset."

Stars danced in the depths of their gaze as they stared at me. "I don't know if that was exceptionally clever or outlandishly stupid of you to accept. I suppose that depends on whether you succeed."

Goosebumps rose on my arms. "Why?"

"You've just given the psychopomps a hook into you. One they likely didn't have before." They sighed and shook their head. "Nothing for it. You're the new curiosity. Anansi's been crowing about— Well. Never mind. Survive this, Arden. Keep moving forward."

Under the firmness of their tone, I heard something else: fear. Again, I stopped myself from probing. They had a personal stake; that much was clear. But nothing mattered other than getting through this next trial.

"I will."

They moved toward me so fast I jumped, even as their arms closed around me, squeezing briefly in a quick hug before letting me go.

I stared, not sure what that was.

"It's good luck to hug an angel." They grinned then lunged again.

This time, their hands struck me square in the chest, propelling me backward—and out of my Chaos sphere.

At first, I thought I was in the In-Between. It was that dark and that cold. But there were no big stars here. Just curling fog and mucky ground underneath. A sense of light without a source made the darkness shimmer as I took a step forward then another one, before I stopped.

I swallowed hard. There was nothing to see and, as far as I could tell, nowhere to go. I sent out a pulse of Chaos. It sped into the darkness in all directions and tripped nothing. No spell, no trap, no item or artifact. I tried each element in turn after that. Air, then Fire, then Earth, then Water.

Nothing.

Where had Harqil sent me?

A sense of dread settled over me. Had it been a trap? Or had Sutekh intercepted me?

Keep moving forward.

Harqil's words seemed to echo in my head, alongside a ringing like bells. I shook my head to clear it then figured I should do that—move forward.

As I did, the sense of dread grew. Behind it came fear, the prickling sensation that I was being followed. I stopped in my tracks and spun, finding nothing behind me but more darkness.

Shit. How far had I spun? Which direction was I facing now?

What the hell was I doing here?

My breath quickened until I was almost panting. Was I really lost in a godsforsaken corner of the Duat? In the final test?

The earth started shaking again, and I swore. If that had translated to real life, everyone I loved was in even more danger.

Wait.

Earth.

The ground underfoot was muck, but I still got a sense of my footprints. That and the feeling that they were fading fast. Not just sinking into the mud but like something was coming up behind me.

Shit. Was that why Harqil had said keep moving forward?

I spun back around until I was oriented on the line my footprints had come from and pushed myself into a run. My heart pounded in my throat as my feet squished, and I barely kept my footing on the slick ground. I quickly lost track of how far I'd run or how long it'd been. There were no landmarks. No sense of time passing. Just the sensation of the world ending behind me. Like if I didn't keep moving, it would catch up with me and I'd fall off the earth.

Fear slid into doubt and then into despair. I'd been tricked. Whether it was Harqil or Sutekh or someone else entirely, I'd failed. I wasn't going to make it.

I crossed into the grounds of the boathouse at Jordan Lake so quickly I lost my breath as Troy threw me against the wooden wall of the shed he'd trapped me against with a hand around my neck.

"Easy, Finch. Damn. I'd really hoped it wouldn't come to this."

My mouth moved of its own accord. "Fu—"

Just like before, his hand tightened to stop me.

Unlike before, Callum stabbed Troy in the back and me in the heart.

"No more loose ends," he said as he watched us die.

I woke up in my bedroom, moments before the rabisu crawled over the lintel of my door. There was no Troy this time, and I gasped as the demon reached down to tear me to shreds—

Only to find myself facing Callista at the bar. I threw a bolt of lightning at her, hitting the desk as she dodged out the door. She and Troy fought...until she tore open his shoulder with bear claws and swayed him with honeyed venom. I watched the decision filter through him. That we couldn't win. That I was the wrong one to back. That the greater good was too high a cost and to preserve what remained of his life, he had to strike a deal with Callista so she'd smooth things over with Keithia, even if that meant submitting to her will and being used as a stud.

"Troy, no!" I shouted—only for a dart of Aether to sting through my shields as he shouted, "Be still!"

I dropped, landing on one knee in the small guest apartment on Keithia's property. Even as I looked up, Troy breathed his last, his body going utterly slack in the chains suspending him. I was too late, and Keithia's laughter twined with Evangeline's as they turned to me.

"No!" I screamed—only to forget why as I came to myself, sitting on the edge of the bed in a small bedroom that reeked of elven blood and weighed on me with the residue of old, old power. Dismembered bodies littered the space. I rose to break the window and escape...but then a box on the nightstand caught my eye. Ornately carved rosewood, gilded, even heavier with power than the hint of the goddess who'd been here just before.

Box.

I needed a box.

That thought slammed me back into my own mind, and the scene around me faded away until all that remained was me, the nightstand, the box...and the memories of might-have-beens. Forks in the road of Fate and Fortune.

Hand shaking, I reached for the box.

A cramp clawed my fingers as the Sight screamed.

No. Not this box. I could have this box, if I wanted it. There would be a gift inside. Something glorious and special. Something just for me, a reward for all I'd been through. But it wasn't one that contained the sparks that'd been stolen from Otherside. There was no magic here—or rather, there was, but it wasn't the magic I sought.

I dropped to my knees as I tried to process what this meant.

Keep moving forward.

I gathered the tattered shreds of my courage. Rose. And walked around the box, running forward into the mist until I crashed through to another vision of a past that might have been.

Over.

And over.

And over.

More forks and dead ends. In some, Troy had been there but turned against me. In others, he just hadn't been there. There were more where I'd lost him. In a bare few, I chose someone else over him—Roman or Maria or half a dozen other people I had no waking memory of. All of those ended in disaster.

I fought the gods of the hunt and lost. I fought Sutekh and lost. I fought and lost and fell, only to open my eyes on a new fork in the road.

Existence and nonexistence. What was and how it could have been.

No mortal should have to bear that. Although maybe it would be worse to be immortal.

I'd never know.

I arrived at box after box until the Sight stopped howling. This one was simpler than some, more ornate than others.

Mouth dry, heart pounding, I reached for it, afraid to hope and on my last shred of faith.

My hand didn't cramp this time.

I froze, scarcely daring to breathe as I trembled with the weight of the moment.

What happened if I was wrong?

Warmth at my back.

"You're not wrong."

I twisted at the woman's voice. The same woman from the dream of the grove, the one I thought might be my mother.

She was behind me, in the same form as before. Elfess, with sharp, white teeth in her smile. Dark-skinned. An abundance of curly, black hair, longer than mine, and black eyes that flickered to the old-blood red of garnets as she gazed at me with something that might have been affection.

Not an elfess. A djinni.

"Mom?" I whispered.

Was this another test? It had to be. Another fork, this one if they'd never died.

My heart broke. Of all the possible futures I could never have, this one hurt the worst. I bent over my knees and tried to breathe.

I had no more tears. Not after what I'd seen in my own personal purgatory.

"Aww, my baby girl." The man's voice pulled me upright almost against my will, but there was only shadow.

"We hated leaving you, but this isn't another test, Arden." My mother looked over her shoulder and smiled sadly. "I was never fated to see you grow up. I knew that as soon as I knew I was carrying you. And Quinlan was always going to follow me, except for the one time it was his turn to lead. But I knew, somehow, we'd see you again."

My heart stopped. I knew what she was talking about.

My father had died first.

The shadows cloaking him fled as he stepped to her shoulder and rested a hand on it. He was lighter than Troy, more tan than tawny with wavy hair in a dark brown rather than Troy's raven black, but he and my mom looked so much like the image I saw of Troy and me in the mirror that I choked on another sob.

"Hello, little bird," he said.

That broke me. Tears slid down my face. "You know? That I'm a sylph?"

Quinlan—Dad?—gave a lopsided smile that was almost roguish, especially with the scar through his left eyebrow. His amber eyes sparkled. "You're more than that. You think we haven't been watching? Arden, we're so proud."

I couldn't answer. The idea that they'd seen, that they knew, that maybe I hadn't always been so alone...

Rather than telling me not to cry, both my parents pulled me upright and folded me into a hug. Their arms came around me, lacking the warmth of life but still full of intent.

"We're glad you found Troy," my father murmured. "All those futures you saw where you failed without him? Those are your fears, not your truths." He cupped my chin and swiped a tear away with his thumb. "You'll need him. Not because you can't do this on your own but because you shouldn't have to."

"Told you," Ninlil muttered. The smokeless fire of her nature heated us as her temper—my temper?—flared.

"Yes, that one I'll give you," Quinlan said easily. "Although I still wish you'd have let me tell Cyrus more. That old bastard is going to make trouble for everyone, even if he thinks he's helping."

"It's his nature and his purpose." My mother pulled away enough to tilt my head up in her cupped hands. "And yours, my heart, is not mine to tell but yours to decide."

I struggled to catch my breath, distracted from the idea that Cyrus might be helping by my mother's statement that she couldn't tell me my purpose. "But Duke said—"

She smiled sadly, shaking her head. "I saw more than most. But you? Arden, you were always destined and fated to be beyond what even I could see. But remember this: it is all still your choice in how destiny and fate trap you."

My breath caught. "Being trapped is being free."

Ninlil beamed. "You understand."

I wasn't sure I did, but Anansi had given me more than he realized.

Everything shook, and I jumped.

My father looked up and growled. "Give us a moment more, Usir."

The shaking grew worse.

"You know better by now. Even this was more than we had a right to." Ninlil kissed me gently on each eyelid and then in the middle of my forehead, where my sense of my third eye lived. "Go with vision and strength." She pressed a hand to my heart. "Know we're with you. And tell my asshole baby cousin that I consider his debt paid."

While I was still processing that, my father wrapped his arms around me and squeezed me so tightly he almost felt real. "I love you. Trust that Troy does too. The longknife will obey him, and only him, as long as that's true. Your mother cursed it so that it can't be used otherwise, or at least not its full power."

Ninlil pressed the small box into my hands. It was heavier than it had a right to be, rough against my fingers.

Before I could get clarity from either of them, everything shattered into countless jagged pieces.

I sat up with a gasp, the box clutched in one hand. The tang of blood scented the air from where my own fingernails bit into my chest over my heart as I wrenched breath into my lungs and let it out in a sob.

The sky opened up in a downpour that hit the tent overhead with enormous raindrops as Troy dragged me into his lap and wrapped his arms around me. The earth shook as I did. All I could do was curl around the box I'd paid for with shards of my soul, drowning in the misery of every secret fear I'd ever carried in my heart being laid bare and faced in the purgatory of the dream.

Eventually, I became aware of Troy speaking urgently. "Arden, please talk to me. Please."

"They were there."

His breath hissed in, a relieved inhale spiked with fear. "Who?"

"My parents. They said this was the right box. They said they were proud of me."

"Oh, my love. Okay." An internal struggle wrenched in the bond. "We need to move. It's not safe here anymore. Can you get up?"

I tried. I really did.

"No."

As the word left my mouth, I slumped in his arms.

△▽△▽

I woke at Troy's deep growl, at my back but inside the tent. "Back off, Omar. Now."

"We're exposed, and she's losing control."

"No. She's been pushed to her limits by Goddess knows what celestial torture. But she's still in control of herself and her magic."

"I'm within my rights to take control of this operation."

"You want to try a coup?" Troy's voice was deadly soft. "Are you sure about that?"

A taut silence stretched. I tried to pretend I was still sleeping so Omar would keep talking. What was the sudden concern with my losing control? Why was Troy so upset? Why would Omar suggest a coup?

The Captain growled back, quieter, smaller somehow than Troy. A protest in the face of a stronger sovereign. "You know what she is. What that means."

"I knew earlier than anyone. Including her. And I know better than anyone what that means."

"Then you'd better be prepared for when she becomes too much because—"

"Stop."

"My king—"

"I said stop." The ice in Troy's tone was colder and harder than I'd ever heard it before. "She will never be too much."

"That kind of arrogance—"

"It's not arrogance. It's faith. We keep trying to make her small enough for us to comprehend. To handle. That stops now. She was always more than we will ever be. I won't allow anyone to cut her down and make her less. Not at all. Certainly not out of fear."

A longer silence than before stretched before Omar said, "You'd risk damning us all."

"No. I choose to have faith that she will prove the old stories to be just that: old stories, spun into propaganda." Troy's attention turned toward me in the bond, and he mentally flinched when he realized I was awake. "Get out. Continue evac preparations and stage for the return of magic. And Omar? Do not let me catch you alone with her."

The rustle of fabric said the Captain had left as a closer, softer one said Troy had seated himself behind me.

"I'm sorry," he said.

I turned over. "What did he mean about me becoming too much?"

Another mental flinch from Troy. He knew that was one of my fears, especially after what he'd said about some people being afraid of me.

"Arden..." He sighed. "I promise I will explain everything. This and everything else you have stopped yourself from asking me over the last few days. But right now, we have to go. We've picked up two threats incoming, one mundane, one that might be my father. A helicopter has already buzzed us. We think your reflective layer hid us, but we have to go *now*."

My hand ached from where it was still clutched tight around the box, and the pain as I flexed it refocused me. "Okay. Let's get out of here."

Chapter 28

Outside the tent, it was pandemonium.

"We're not going to have time to pack all this up," I said.

Troy's expression was hard as he surveyed the progress that had been made—or hadn't—in the faint light of the rising sun. "We can't leave anything that can be gathered for intel."

"Then get the most sensitive stuff and leave the rest. You and I can set a ward."

"Are you up to it?"

"I'm damn well gonna have to be." Truthfully, I was still woozy as fuck. Lost. Unsettled. Scared. But I couldn't let my upset or my weather and geological disturbances be the reason my people got rounded up and imprisoned.

As Troy snapped orders into his wrist mic in rapid-fire elvish, I crouched in the mud and grounded myself. A pulse of Chaos scared away any animals that would need to leave the area, not that there were many remaining in the dead zone.

Shit. That'd be a giveaway that something wasn't right here to anyone coming in on foot.

I sank deeper into myself. Sought out the pain, fear, doubt, and disbelief that was poisoning me and poured it into my magic. I'd taken from the land, and now I'd give back. Yeah, the place might be haunted as hell for a bit, but the witches could help with that when we managed to open this fucking box.

I focused on my memory of what the place had looked and felt like when we'd arrived a few days ago and *pushed* with the blended elements.

The space fell silent.

"Keep moving!" Troy roared.

My sense of the people in the area redoubled in energy. I ignored it and continued working until it felt right again.

When I opened my eyes, I was trembling and gasping for breath, but the land was as I'd willed it to be: thriving trees, new grass, nourished earth. All of our waste completely decomposed and distributed, the plastic gathered in a neat heap for disposal. Maybe better than we'd found it but not so much better that anyone would notice.

Troy leaned over and hauled me to my feet with a grip around my bicep. "Move."

Part of me wanted to snap and protest at his tone, but he was in military mode with one objective: protect his queen.

I stumbled along with him as he yanked the door of his car open and handed me up to the passenger seat.

"Ward," I gasped before he could shut the door. "Fear barrier. Get everyone out and then cast it."

He glared at the necessity of us being last out for that but gave the order.

The grounds emptied with alacrity. The elves left as soon as a car or a boat was full of people and supplies. Cade and Lya sped off, followed by Mami Wata with Mason in the passenger seat and the djinn in the back.

Sirens rose in the distance. Lots of them amplifying each other.

"Go!" Troy barked at Darius and Allegra, the only two who hadn't gotten in their car and left yet, aside from the gytrash in the back of Allegra's.

"'Til death," Allegra said.

Darius just nodded.

"Fuck." Troy closed his eyes and, in the bond, plunged into his magic as his power signature roared. My head spun as he chanted something ominous. The monarch-level dread spell that, I hoped, would turn people away from here without realizing it. Combined with the haunting I'd just poured into the area, it'd be a hell of a deterrent.

Allegra and Darius were pale and sweating when he finished, eyes darting as though looking for something they could sense but not see. The gytrash were glaring out the window, teeth bared, apparently more affected by elven magic without the protection of their own.

The sirens had gotten closer. Too close.

I shuddered. "We're not going to make it."

"Like hell." Troy shut my door and ran around to the driver's side as Darius and Allegra scrambled for their cars. As Troy got us in gear and on the one small road in or out, the scent of burnt marshmallow filled the car, and his power signature slashed with icy claws. He muttered more spells, all in elvish, glaring at the road ahead like he was daring someone to turn down it.

We hit 751 and turned onto it so fast we would have spun out if I hadn't tapped the tail end of Troy's SUV with Air to keep it stable.

As we did, a convoy of black vehicles with flashing red-and-blue lights turned onto 751 up the road—and sped past as Troy pulled off onto the shoulder, his smile a dangerous snarl of victory and sharp teeth.

When the last car had passed, Allegra's silver MDX pulled out of the service road leading to the boathouse, followed by Darius's Lexus.

"Can you erase the tracks?" Troy asked.

I pushed through my exhaustion to smooth all trace of traffic onto that road then, with a small prayer of apology, toppled a tree a short way in to block it.

Troy studied my work. "Good. That's all we can do."

He pulled onto the road and headed north at a normal speed. Allegra sped up to overtake as Darius hung back to cover our rear, as much Troy's knights as they'd ever been.

I stared at the box I had clutched to my chest. The Box of Ages, Harqil had called it. Now that it was back on this plane, it practically screamed with magic, despite its relatively unremarkable appearance. Was that how I'd pushed through? How Troy had convinced an entire convoy of mundanes that there was nothing to see?

"We'd be so powerful if we just...kept it," I whispered, mesmerized.

After a long silence, Troy asked, "Is that what you want?"

The dead tone pulled my head up. His eyes were on the road, but his attention was almost fully on me in the bond.

"You have no idea what I went through for this," I said when I couldn't figure out how to answer.

"That's right. I don't. I only know that you woke up crying, made another storm and a small earthquake, said something about your parents, and passed out for an hour. That's why I'm asking what you want."

The magic in the box called to me, utterly beguiling.

"Arden. Is that what you want?"

I gasped, pulling myself out of it. "No. That's not the greater good."

A subtle, silent exhale left Troy. "I'm glad to hear it."

My chest tightened as tears I refused to cry heated my eyes. "I saw every hell where you weren't with me." The whisper was guttural this time. Dragged from me. "I saw every choice, yours and mine, that meant we faced everything alone. And failed and lost and *died.*"

Troy flinched. "I won't leave you."

"I know. Quinlan said those were just my fears, not my truths."

"Quinlan?" Troy frowned. "Your father? I thought that was just an illusion or a dream or something."

"No. Apparently Usir's boon was to let them visit me, just this once. That was the sign that I'd found the right box."

The bond swirled with Troy's effort to find the right response.

"It's okay." I slumped in my seat and reached to settle a hand on his thigh. "I'll deal with it when this is over. Where are we going?"

He took a hand from the wheel to lace his fingers through mine. "Chapel Hill."

"Your old safehouse?"

"Yeah. Alli and Dari have their own units in the same building. Different floors. They're going to check on your place first though, to drop off the gytrash and make sure the weres haven't been disturbed. And so it's harder to track us all coming and going together."

That was a relief. I missed my land and my home. Part of me wanted to get this damn box open and get all of this over with as quickly as possible. The rational side of me knew that we needed a plan though. People needed to be warned. My people first, starting with the weres watching my house, then the rest of the Eastern Seaboard and out from there. We'd been moving so quickly that I hadn't even thought of how we'd go about doing all of this.

"Stop," Troy said. "You need to sleep before we do anything."

"But—"

"No."

"Troy—"

"*No*, Arden. You're exhausted. *I'm* exhausted. We cannot lead effectively if we can barely think. We need sleep. We need food. And then we can open the Goddess-burned box and restore magic."

"I have a feeling it's not going to be that easy."

"It won't. Cyrus diverted from Richmond when he realized they'd been warned. We're expecting him soon."

"Which could mean his patron is in play as well. And Sutekh. And whichever of the trickster gods think it's unfair that a death god and a celestial messenger meddled in their game. Fuck."

Troy looked at me for long enough that I almost told him to put his eyes back on the road. "Please don't tell me the death gods are going to want a turn."

"I don't think so? Usir just wanted Sutekh prevented from using whatever this spell is to steal Iset."

"Great. So, all we have to worry about is a vengeful trickster-warrior god, my homicidally delusional father, and the inevitable bloody drama that will ensue when Otherside gets magic back. I love this for us."

I stared at Troy. The deadpan tone could have been serious, but the words weren't. I busted out laughing, completely thrown.

"I love you so much," I gasped as I tried to catch my breath.

"You'd better." His tone softened. "Because I love you too."

"We're getting married," I said. "This year."

"Don't play with me, Arden." The same flat voice, only this time there was a thread of hope in it.

"I'm not. Let's just do it." I leaned against him for a moment before sitting back upright so he could drive. "It's going to piss someone off no matter when we do it or how we do it or why. I know we still have shit to talk through. I know you still have secrets. But, Troy, like I said, I saw every fork in the road that got us here. None of the ones without you were good. The ones with someone else were worse."

"That could have been a trick," he said.

"So what if it was? I choose to believe that as fucked up as all of this is, the best possible road is the one I walk with you."

Leather creaked as his hands tightened on the wheel, and the muscles in his jaw bunched as he gritted his teeth against the emotions raging in the bond—what felt like an effort to suppress elation to avoid the risk of disappointment, blended with deep desire, soaring hope, and gripping fear.

"I want this so much it scares me," he finally said, his voice rough. "And I'm scared that you'll change your mind when I've told you everything."

"Then we'll figure it out later. But the door is open. Okay?"

"Yeah. Okay."

We passed the rest of the drive in silence. A companionable one, even if I had to put the walls up in the bond because Troy's mind was ricocheting wildly between what I'd said and what he still had to tell me while trying to ignore all of it to stay focused on the security needs of our current situation and plan ahead for what came next.

When we got to his Chapel Hill apartment, I froze. More than one of the might-have-beens had ended here.

Troy gave me a concerned look but opened the door and stepped aside to let me see.

It was completely different.

My breath shuddered out. "You redecorated."

"I had one of Terrence's people do it, but yes."

Cautiously, I stepped inside, still shaking from the adrenaline of expecting to face a nightmare. The layout had been rearranged. It was cozy now, with the dark grey sofa that used to randomly face the front door—or not randomly, since Troy slept on it to watch the door—now backed against the wall nearest the window. That wall was now painted a rich blue, adding a pop of color. The other walls had been repainted a light blue-grey that actually worked and brightened the space. Two silvery grey armchairs faced the couch, a low coffee table in dark wood between them. Soft-looking blankets in the same blue as the wall were thrown over all the arms. The kitchen table had been replaced to match the coffee table.

"All the way in, please, my love."

Troy's low voice got me moving away from the door so he could shut and lock it. There were, of course, two more brand new locks in place and a new security system. My step in let me see the bedroom, which had also been redone to match the living room and kitchen. An incense burner rested on the dresser.

It was still relatively bare and functional compared to home, but there were touches that said he'd expected to have to come here with me.

"It's nice," I said.

"Good." His gaze darted over my face as he searched the bond, trying to gauge my mood. "I figured you had enough bad memories of it as it used to be. If we needed to come here again, it would probably not be for the best reason, so I hoped a fresh look would help somewhat."

I smiled. "It does."

Troy pulled me to him and dropped a tender kiss on my lips. Not sexual. We were both too tired for that. But care, tenderness...we both needed it.

I melted against him. Ran my hands up his back, under his shirt. Slow and idle.

On seeing that I understood, Troy relaxed. Cupped my jaw and tilted my head back, sweeping his thumbs over my cheekbones. "I will always, always love you," he whispered. "No matter what happens. A piece of my heart and a piece of my soul live in you now. And you'll keep them as long as you live."

I don't know why that made me cry. Maybe because it felt like he was cursing himself. Damning himself. "Troy—"

"Accept it, Arden."

Accept me was the wish underneath. *Keep me. Stay with me.* He didn't say it in words or whisper it in a thought. But it was in the way he looked at me. Something in his touch, in the faint pinch of his expression.

I went up on my toes to kiss him again, even more gently than before. "I do. And I offer the same."

Troy rested his forehead against mine. "Then we'll make it through this. Whatever comes. Me and you."

"Holding hands while the world burns."

"Yes."

We stayed like that a few moments more, just breathing, until he shook himself.

"Shower, food, and bed," he said. "You shower first. I'll call the parliament and give everyone the requisite updates."

I pouted, wanting him to come shower with me, but he shook his head with a small smile.

"Get. There's a new showerhead. Go enjoy it. Then we'll eat and go to bed."

I did as he said, reluctantly leaving the Box of Ages on the dresser.

The bathroom had been retiled as well. The shower had kind of a sparkly moonlight-silver and pearl color mosaic with the same dark blue that'd accented the main spaces running in a line at hip height. All of my usual hair and skincare products were either on the shower shelf or on the bathroom counter, alongside Troy's, as close as possible to how they were arranged at home. Fluffy new towels and washcloths waited on the rack.

I stripped and chucked my clothes in the rattan hamper, suddenly feeling days' worth of grime clinging to me. We had showers at the camp, but they were small and cold. Basic hygiene, not luxury.

The new shower was definitely luxury, and I groaned as the hot water hit me in a massaging wave. I didn't pay much attention to creature comforts for myself, but damn, did I appreciate that Troy did. The man would live the bare life of a soldier without complaint if the situation called for it, but left to his own devices, it was comfort, luxury, and sensuous delight all the way.

I just hoped it would be enough to anchor me in the here and now, rather than what I'd seen in the Duat.

Chapter 29

After wrestling with my hair, scrubbing myself head to toe, and cleaning the dirt from under my nails, I reluctantly turned off the water and got out.

Troy was leaning in the doorway, still on the phone. His gaze ran down my body, hot with appreciation, even as he continued his conversation. "I know, Maria. But I won't risk Arden or the Triangle rushing this. The mundanes nearly caught us. We—"

He cut off, lips pressing together in frustration as she raised her voice to reply.

Wincing, I squeezed the water from my hair then wrapped myself in a towel before extending my hand. *Your turn.*

Thank you. He handed over the phone and started undressing, hanging the longknife in its sheath from a hook next to the shower where presumably he'd be able to grab it quickly if he was attacked in the shower. Of course he'd think of that.

Shaking my head, I focused on Maria.

"Are you even listening to me, Troy?"

"Hi, Maria," I said.

"Oh good, Queen Poppet herself. What is taking so damn long?"

Queen Poppet? "I'm gonna let that one slide on account of it being a real difficult time right now."

She hissed then spoke in a tone that sounded like it was coming through gritted teeth. "Of course, Arbiter."

Despite being tempted to rub it in with a "that's better," I simply answered her question. "What's taking so long is that

I've spent the last few days Dreamwalking through my worst nightmares collecting what's needed to restore magic."

"Dreamwalkers are myths," she said sharply.

"I've heard the same said about primordials. You wanna check your library for me?"

A long pause told me she was trying to think of the angles. "I could do that. Gratis, even, given how generous you've been in allowing your elves to visit my establishments."

Rather than giving into the reflex to decline the free service, I let warmth suffuse my voice. "I appreciate that, Maria. Oh, and you should know Cade and Lya are back in town. Staying in my end of the woods, or they were until recently."

"How very interesting." Her tone shifted, becoming less Mistress of Raleigh, more scared friend as she lowered her voice. "Arden, please tell me you can do this."

I swallowed hard, forcing the lump of my own doubt back down my throat. "I can do this."

"You even sound like you mean it."

"Put it this way: I've seen what happens if I, or Troy for that matter, fail. I won't let that happen. I can't, and I refuse. So please, for all our sakes, keep the Modernists or whoever is giving you hell in check for another day or two."

She sighed and didn't answer.

"Listen. Friend to friend, Troy wasn't just being protective. If I push right now, it might mean a hole in reality. Those quakes locally? The storms? That was me handling the aftermath of Dreamwalking. As much as I want to push, I can't. I cannot, Maria."

"Fuck." Even that one word carried a heaviness that told me she understood. "Then, friend to friend, know that I have your back. It'll cost me with the Modernists, maybe even some of my loyalists, but I'd rather have you as Arbiter than any of the alternatives."

"Thank you. If you happened to find a way to bring that up in any meetings you're about to run off and have, I'd appreciate it."

"I'll do that, poppet. Take care of yourself." She ended the call before I could tell her to do the same.

Troy was taking his time in the shower, as I had, so I set his phone on the counter and ran through my bedtime routine, with the additional step of blow-drying my hair on low, cool heat so I could go straight to bed. Then I dug a microwave meal out of the freezer, heated it, and ate. It was nowhere near as satisfying as one of Troy's, but it was food.

I was in bed by the time Troy finished in the bathroom, blackout curtains tightly closed against the daylight, on the verge of waking and sleeping but too apprehensive to let myself slip all the way under, no matter how comfortable the high-thread-count sheets were and how much I needed the sleep.

Troy climbed under the duvet and dragged me closer to him. "I know you're not sleeping."

"I'm scared." I hadn't meant to say the whispered words aloud, but he could read the bond. He knew.

"Your parliament is as prepared as they can be, as are the other faction heads I could reach in the Carolinas, Dominion, Atlanta, and New York. All of our people made it to safehouses, including Duke and Iaret. The feds pulled up to your house, but the last quake pulled them off before the pride were threatened." He kissed the spot behind my ear where an elf's scent patch would be then leaned close to inhale. "Everything is as secure as we can make it, cariñamí. The best thing for everyone now is for you to sleep."

I gripped his arm as he curled it around me and tucked myself as close against him as I could.

"What if I make another quake? Or a storm?" We were in a populated area now. I might bring down a building.

"You won't. And if you do, I'm here. I will bring you back."

I tried, but the idea of just closing my eyes and letting go terrified me. Almost every night for the last few days, that'd meant going into a nightmare.

"On your stomach," Troy said.

Frowning as much as the odd command as the snap of an order in his tone, I did as he said, only to groan as he straddled me and dug his fingers into my shoulders in a deep massaging touch. The scent of burnt marshmallow flared as Aether curled through me, light and teasing rather than forceful, and Troy's murmured elvish kept my mind focused on figuring out what he was saying rather than on my nightmares.

A word and a press at a time, he beguiled me into sleep.

I could have sworn I was only out for a minute, but when I opened my eyes at the trilling of my phone on the nightstand, late morning light slanted through a crack in the curtains.

"You going to get that?" Troy mumbled against my neck. He was sprawled across me, like he'd fallen asleep determined to protect my body with his.

I reached in the direction of the sound, snagged my phone, and answered without looking at it. "Finch."

"You have the damnedest luck," Cyrus said.

I stiffened, coming awake so fast that Troy sat up in alarm. "What do you want, Cyrus?"

"You cut a deal with Usir."

"It's not my fault if the gods choose to offer me things," I said.

"Maybe not your fault, but it will be your problem. We need to meet, and you need to bring the Box of Ages. All the keys as well."

An uncomfortable prickling feeling crawled over me. "Why do you know about that?"

"My patron has an interest. And if that's not enough..." A scream rang out in the background. "I found your little troublemaker. Do as I say, or the death of a celestial will be on your head. They don't tend to take that very lightly."

"That sounded like Harqil," Troy muttered.

"Is my boy there?" Cyrus snarled. "Of course he is. Good. Bring him too. *Before* you open the box, or I'll frame you for celestial murder, kill you myself, and throw your corpse in front of the gods in exchange for saving my son's life, just in case he's right about this bond bullshit."

My heart thundered.

"Quickly, Arbiter. I'm feeling generous, so I'll even let you choose the time and place."

I was tempted to twist in the bed and look at Troy. To ask him what I should do. But I couldn't do that. I was the Arbiter. I was the High Queen. Those were the roles I'd claimed. Eternal Huntress and Dreamwalker were roles I'd grown into. If I wanted to claim the Nightmare Court and the entire fucking Eastern Seaboard, I had to stand up and make this decision alone.

I rattled off a string of coordinates I unfortunately knew very well. "See you at noon, Cyrus."

"At least you have a flair for the dramatic. Come with Troy alone, or I kill everyone else with you."

I ended the call, gave myself a half breath to feel like shit, then propelled myself out of bed.

Troy's hand closed around my wrist. "Hang on a minute. What was that?"

"What was what?" I snapped, trying and failing to pull free.

"That unilateral decision to—"

"You can't own this one for me, Troy. Your dad is here because of me. Harqil's in trouble because of me. We face the threat now, before Cyrus can kill any more queens and drag either of us deeper into this mess. I'm the Arbiter. I hold the Box of Ages. I'll sort this out."

He was fixing to reply, anger making the gold flecks in his eyes spark, until I mentioned killing queens. Then he dropped his gaze—odd, for him. At least with me. Was that part of his secret past? Had he killed a queen?

Now wasn't the time for it. Whether he had or he hadn't, he wouldn't kill me. And if I was wrong, then so be it. I refused to add doubting Troy to my list of problems for today.

"Arbiter or not, I need you with me," I said in a softer tone. "My dad—Quinlan said that I could do this all alone but that I needed you because I shouldn't have to. He said the longknife would obey you and only you as long as you love me. That weapon and you wielding it have kept me safe up to now. Can we do this? Together?"

Something in there restored his confidence because he met my gaze again with fire in his. "You can *always* count on me, Arden."

"Then let's get going."

△▽△▽

Noon found us at the lich's lair. Or what remained of it anyway. A slight depression in the earth that still hadn't grown new plants, regardless of what the witches had done to cleanse the place. Salt had probably been involved, come to think of it. Hopefully it was that and not some lingering corruption.

Troy and I had barely reached the center of the clearing when reality twisted. Both of us went on guard as Harqil was shoved through a portal, crashing to the ground and staying there in a heap that reeked of blood and stone and burnt feathers. The latter smell was coming from a set of four wings, broken and seared.

My stomach twisted. Apparently, they hadn't been exaggerating about the angel thing. I gritted my teeth to stop myself from calling out to them. At my side, Troy drew his longknife, feeling grim in the bond.

"A dramatic entrance," Cyrus said, stepping through the portal and stopping a short distance from us, "but at least you know I'm serious."

Something was off about the way he moved, and it wasn't just the lack of a cane. I'd seen that motion before, a smoothness and contained violence that surpassed even Troy's, but couldn't place it until I looked into his eyes. The strangeness I thought I'd seen was gone as quickly as I noticed it. I blinked and looked again, taking the risk of unfocusing my vision to try and see the magic I could sense crackling over him.

"Dad, this has to stop," Troy said. "I don't know what the hell is going to happen at the eclipse, but you're not getting it."

"I think you'll find that I will." He prodded Harqil with a toe. "Angels are damn near irreplaceable these days. Their loss tends to be taken very seriously, so unless you want to take the fall for this one, give me the Box of Ages. Now." His grin showed the sharp teeth. "If you're a good boy, I might even let your queen live. Severed, but she'll live."

I was too distracted by the flat-out weirdness I was sensing to worry about the threat. There was something off about Cyrus's voice as well, not just his movement. I frowned, trying to match my memory of how the air felt when he spoke in my house with now, but the breeze whispering through the trees was off. Everything about this was off.

"You can't defeat Arden." Troy edged ever so slightly in front of me. "And before you try her, you'll have to go through me."

I gasped, unable to help myself, as I reached through Janae's ring and finally saw the unseen.

"Does Cyrus know what you did to his son?" I blurted.

"Arden, what—"

I snapped Chaos at Troy to get him to shut up. *That's not Cyrus.*

Sutekh looked at me through Cyrus's eyes. The overlay I'd seen before was back. And not only that. Now it was the god's eclipse-like gaze, fire ringing black, that met mine in a haze over Cyrus's natural grey eyes. "I am Cyrus. Of course I know what you've done to my son."

I shook my head. "Stop it, Sutekh. Let Cyrus go."

The god looked at Troy. "You see, son? I told you. Primordial energy is too much for a mortal to control. They all go mad sooner or later. Even your queen. She lost control of her power, didn't she?"

Troy glanced between the two of us. "What's going on?"

"That's not Cyrus." I pulled on the elements, drawing all four to me, even if fighting a god like this would warp reality. "It's *Sutekh!*"

"And now she's blaming a god for something she's done," Sutekh continued in Cyrus's mocking tones. "Just like I told you she would. Is it really the gods she sees when she speaks to nothing, or is it a figment of her imagination that she convinces you is real?"

"I'm not crazy!" I screamed. Sounding utterly out of my mind, of course. Especially when lightning crackled in a clear sky as I clenched my fists.

Troy didn't answer beyond sending a tendril of Aether to me.

I dropped my walls and let him in. *I'm telling the truth. That's not Cyrus. Can't you see Sutekh riding him?*

No.

I closed my eyes and shuddered. "No. I'm not crazy."

A squeeze on my foot startled me into looking down. I'd been so fixated on Cyrus/Sutekh that I'd missed Harqil crawling toward me.

"Now," they rasped.

Troy sprang forward. He hadn't missed anything, and he was taking me and what I said I was seeing on faith.

"Troy!" I screamed. No, no no no, I couldn't watch him die again. I drew deeper on the elements, pulling together what I needed for a primordial ball. I'd destroy everything in this clearing and tear a hole in reality before allowing Sutekh to hurt Troy again.

"Wait," Harqil said, gasping.

I looked down at them again.

"Come down here. Rude to be that tall."

When I knelt, they pressed a hand to my temple.

Another scream ripped from me as the knowledge of existence and nonexistence took on new meaning.

"Like that," Harqil said.

I rose to find Troy fighting Sutekh, one elf wielding a longknife that roared with magic racing blue down the length of the blade, the other spinning a *was* staff that could unmake Troy in a heartbeat if it landed.

I wouldn't let that happen, even as I understood now why Troy had only been mortally wounded before rather than unmade. Mami Wata had been right about the trap.

"Troy, down!" I hollered, weaving the elements into a chord.

Without question, he dropped.

Sutekh's spear passed over his head.

I added Chaos to my chord. Twisted it as the sound of shattering glass rang through the clearing. Hauled off and threw it at Sutekh.

The god raised his spear to impale Troy a second time, grinning at the knowledge that I wouldn't be able to save my bondmate in the real. He looked up just in time to see my ball of energy speeding toward him.

"No!" Sutekh howled.

It hit him, throwing him backward. Time slowed nearly to stopping as gold and black tendrils, the colors of my magic when a god was present, wrapped Sutekh. An endless howl, like a storm in a desert canyon, gripped me, forcing me to my knees as I covered my ears. Pressure dropped in the clearing, shifting the weather pattern from sun to tearing wind as clouds rolled in.

Then, with a subsonic boom that flattened me and the first ring of trees around the clearing, Cyrus's body dropped to the ground as my second sight showed Sutekh thrown back across the planes.

The portal closed behind him.

Troy scrambled over to where I lay dazed by the backlash of power. Two of him looked down at me, and his voice echoed as he said, "Arden?"

"Fine. I'm fine." I pulled my wits together, forcing myself to roll to my side. Harqil lay a short distance away, still looking like shit. "Harqil?"

"Anansi did say to serve you better than I had to date," they said. Then they slumped against the grass, going completely still as their broken wings drooped.

"Harqil!" I shouted.

Troy twisted to lay fingers alongside their throat. "Not dead. Not yet anyway. But I have no idea how to heal a celestial." He looked up then, paling to find his father lying in the dirt a short distance away. "Fuck. Dad."

"Go," I said. "Sutekh should be gone now."

I waited long enough to see that it really was Cyrus left in the grass with no godly influence, then dropped to lay flat on my back.

So much for getting some rest. This day had already been exhausting, and I hadn't even gotten around to restoring magic yet.

As soon as I caught my breath, it was time to set things right.

Chapter 30

We loaded Harqil into the backseat of Troy's car as gently as we could, laying him across the second row of back seats. Troy might not like the celestial's habit of sneaking up on him, but he didn't say a word against them. We dragged Cyrus in as well, both of us far more reluctant about it than we had been about Harqil but not wanting to leave prisoners for the mundanes if they found this spot.

"Better to have him under guard," Troy muttered as he fastened the seatbelt around his father. As he slid into the driver's seat and I hopped into the passenger's, he asked, "How did you know?"

"That Sutekh was riding him?"

"Yes."

"No cane. And he moved like Sutekh did right before he—" I cut off, unable to voice aloud what'd happened to Troy, then cleared my throat. "His voice and the eyes too."

"What? They just looked like their usual grey to me."

"No. They were eclipse-colored."

Troy's eyebrows shot up, but he didn't question me. For a man who needed solid evidence of a lot of things, he was definitely taking a lot on faith. "Home?"

"Yeah." I swallowed hard as I choked up, realizing all over again that he really had chosen me. Not just chosen but was growing alongside me. "I don't know what restoring magic entails, but I have a feeling I'm gonna need the grounding of my own land."

He pulled onto the main road and dialed Etain.

"Sir?" she answered.

"Get a detachment of the Guard to Arden's and sweep the area. Include Thana, Pascale, Haroun, Felip, Lachlan, and yourself," Troy said. "If Allegra and Darius have wandered, get them there as well."

All of those who were the utmost loyal to me.

"Understood, sir. Anything else?"

"Yeah," I said. "See if you can reach Cade, Lya, Mami Wata, and Mason. I want them there too. I'll get Duke and Iaret. And give the elementals and other factions a heads-up."

"Right," Troy said. "I'll call ahead to the weres and explain."

"Thank you, ma'am, sir. Out."

As soon as the call ended, he was calling Terrence. I touched his arm to indicate I'd take this one.

"Solari?" the wereleopard obong said.

"Hey, Terrence." I couldn't help my smile, and I hoped he heard it through the phone. He was okay. I was worried, given that the feds had been to my house. "Me and Troy are on our way home."

"So, we're gonna need to pack up and get ready to go." His tones were clipped and military. A man preparing for the need to make big moves. "I hope that's a good thing?"

"Packing up would be appreciated, but I want you to stick around," I said. "I'm going to open the Box of Ages, which should restore magic to Otherside. I'd like you and yours there."

"It'd be an honor, Miss Arden. We'll be ready." Terrence's pride shone through in his voice.

"Good. See you in an hour or less."

"Yes, ma'am."

The call ended, and I let out a shuddery breath. "It's finally time."

"Finally." Troy muttered a spell then pressed his foot down on the gas. "What do you want to bet I can make it there in thirty without getting caught?"

I laughed as I swiped out texts to the squad that'd helped me get the keys plus Duke and Iaret, then the elementals. "No bet, asshole."

He grinned and drove faster still.

△▽△▽

Ximena was waiting at the gate when we pulled up. She nodded, looking serious as hell as she opened the gate then shut it behind us.

I rolled down the window and leaned out. "You want a ride up?"

"I surely do." She opened the door behind me, eyebrows shooting up to find Cyrus and Harqil still unconscious. "Do I want to know where you found a beat-up angel?" She sniffed. "And why an elf that smells like Troy's family is bloody, unconscious, and reeks of the gods?"

"Probably not," Troy said.

"Okay then." She climbed in and closed the door.

As it had when I returned from Virginia, my land welcomed me. Magic might have been lost to Otherside, but the plants and earth had a magic of their own that nobody could take away. Mami Wata had been right about that when she'd drawn the bath for me. All that was needed was essence and, for a spark, me.

Troy shivered.

"Can you feel it too?" I asked as I reached for it, pouring my delight and gratitude into it, promising blood and magic to feed it.

"It feels...wild," he said. "Hungry. Untamed."

Ximena snorted. "If you're talking about the land, it's probably picking up some attitude from all the cats roaming here this past week. We've been closer to the edge than usual. Much closer. It's been a blessing having access to this property, Miss

Arden. I'm certain some of our pride would have been picked up for disorderly conduct at the very least if their cats hadn't had freedom to roam and hunt here."

"I'm blessed to have such dedicated custodians," I said. "Part of why I asked you to stay. I'll explain when we get to the house."

Terrence and a dozen leopards and jaguars—some in human shape, some in cat—waited in front of the steps up to my porch. He grinned his shit-eating cat grin as Troy parked, all lazy satisfaction.

"So, you managed not to die, Solari," he called as Troy got out of the car. A cat's mischievous grin curled his lips. "That's good. For your woman, at least."

"It was a damn near thing," Troy said seriously as he headed directly for the house, trusting Ximena to cover me while he satisfied his need to inspect the house. High praise for Ximena, to be sure, and high praise for Terrence not to be called out for referring to me as Troy's woman.

I let it go, knowing the tone of the friendship between Troy and the pride and Terrence in particular. Besides, the arch look Ximena was shooting her mate said she'd deal with him later on everyone's behalf.

The wereleopard pretended he didn't see it, tilting his head as he focused on Troy. "Oh?"

"I'm going to need a drink to talk about it." Troy embraced the smaller man with a friendly growl, and Terrence returned it with a clap on the back before pulling away to look at him.

"That you are," the leopard said softly. "Well then. I'm sure you'll want to inspect the place for yourself, but I think you'll be satisfied."

Troy squeezed his shoulder and leaped to the top of the three stairs up my porch in a single bound before disappearing into the house.

"Single-minded, isn't he?" Ximena said.

"You have no idea," I replied, shouldering my leather backpack, now full with the Box of Ages, even as my pockets bulged with the keys we'd recovered. Frankly, I was just glad at the prospect that Troy might open up to Terrence. I was still shaky about what'd happened and certain it would give me nightmares for the rest of my life. "Although it has its perks. Give me a hand with these two?"

We had Cyrus and Harqil laid out on the grass—the former cuffed, the latter on their belly to spare their wings from further hurt—by the time the Ebon Guards Troy had requested arrived, along with my squad with Duke and Iaret. After some negotiation, a mixed crew of Terrence's temporary second Malik, Pascale, Thana, and Ximena's second Joachim were chosen to stand guard while the rest accompanied me to the river.

Apprehension gripped me as we took the rocky trail down to the Eno. Troy walked at my side, the two of us heads of an energetically charged procession even as elves, half-elves, werecats, and gytrash ranged through the woods on guard.

This was it. This was my moment to prove myself. Not just to everyone else but to myself. I was still kicking myself for falling apart so bad on that last trial. I needed it to be worth something.

That and I needed it for my own damn self. People might scoff at my so-called empire building or call me power-mad, but for the love of Ishtar, I was going to do what it took to create and keep a space for myself. A space where I and the people sworn to me had the strength and motivation to hold our borders, secure our rights, and ensure we could thrive.

Because that was what growing House Solari came down to, I realized.

Thriving. Not hiding or surviving or getting by but thriving in community. I might be Arbiter and High Queen and Troy might be King, but the greater good was what had brought us together. It was how we'd build the true foundation of the future now. Not just us and our heirs but our people.

All I had to do was step up and use the gifts I'd been given. Harqil had been right to scold me. I was demeaning myself and all I had every time I said that I hadn't asked for this. It didn't matter if I'd asked for it; truth be told, I'd been blessed with it, and it behooved me to stand in the fullness of my lot in life.

That meant claiming the power that was mine by birth, by conquest, and by Fate.

Troy was eyeing me sideways. *All good?*

Yes. I let him read my savage pride in myself and in him.

He didn't respond, but his mood rose to meet mine, sending goosebumps prickling over my arms.

Yeah. I *could* do this alone. But like my father had said, I shouldn't have to. And with Troy, I wouldn't. With the people behind me and ranging through the woods, with my parliament and the alliances we were building, I wouldn't.

Together, we'd be more.

"Somebody should record this," Ximena said as we reached my practice area at the river's edge. "So there's no doubt what happened or who's responsible. It would go a long way toward cementing ties with the jaguar, leopard, bear, and fox clans in the Southwest Desert and Northwest Mountain realms."

"Got it covered," Lya said brightly somewhere behind us.

I'd never heard her sound quite so cheery, but that was the general mood of the people with us. Anticipatory. Excited. Hopeful.

Goddess, I hoped I didn't let them down.

You won't, Troy sent.

Everyone fanned out into a circle facing outward with the exception of Lya, who stood facing me and Troy with her phone at the ready.

I relaxed, both because we were under guard and because they weren't all going to watch me like I was some kind of spectacle.

Slinging my backpack in front of me, I carefully withdrew the box—only to gasp to find it ornately carved now, in a way it hadn't been before.

What's wrong? Troy asked.

The box is different.

"It's revealed itself," Harqil's voice called.

I spun to find them making their way down the slope toward us, stumbling like they were intoxicated.

"Harqil!" I said. "Shouldn't you be—"

"Yes, I should be resting, and no, I'm not going to have a lie down now." The angel sounded grumpy as hell and was limping badly with what remained of their wings dragging in the dirt but made it to me and Troy without falling. *You need to understand something.*

My eyes widened, and Troy's secondary teeth snapped down in a snarl as the celestial spoke to us mind-to-mind.

Oh please. You had to suspect I could do this, since I can hear you both, Harqil sent.

This wasn't the time or place to question it. *What do we need to understand?*

The box works by both order—which drawer you open first—and disorder—the chance proximity of those around you, they replied. *More than that is up to you to decipher.* They collapsed onto one of the logs I used as a bench, leaning over their knees and breathing hard in a way that seemed unnatural. *Fuck corporealness. Breathing? Hunger? Excretion? You lot do this all the time? Fuckedly unbearable.*

Another thing to ask about later.

I hefted the box, studying the new carvings. It seemed there were four bands now. The bottom one was carved with plants. The next one up with curling waves. Above that, swirls of wind. The top layer was dancing flames bracketing the phases of the Moon. All of them seemed to move as I looked at them.

"Arden?"

I inhaled sharply at Troy's verbal nudge, clawing for words. "Sorry. It's just so beautiful."

Concern tinged the bond, making me suspect he wasn't seeing what I was seeing. Okay. The drawer I opened first mattered. The werecats here were in the most danger, especially the newly turned Darnell. So...the one with the moon? And then the fire would be who?

The djinn. Their natural forms always involved fire of some kind.

Okay. That could work. The weres needed it, and I needed the djinn to see I wouldn't put the elves first by default.

Now, which key?

I sat cross-legged at the edge of the river and sank into the elements as I held the keys cupped in my hand.

"Guide me," I whispered, reaching for the afternoon sun.

That wasn't enough, so I snapped a lash of Fire at the pit. A few people cried out in surprise as a flame burst to life and were shushed by others.

Still not enough.

I held out a hand to Troy without taking my focus from the keys. *Need to bleed on them. Symbolic sacrifice.*

He drew his punchblade and made the smallest prick in my palm before licking the knife clean and tucking it away.

With blood welling and a fire burning behind me, one of the keys heated. I set the others on my thigh and focused on that one. "By the flame of my mother," I whispered, finding a whole new reason to choose this one first, "bless me and mine with magic rightfully stolen."

I closed my eyes and let my magical senses guide the small key to the hidden keyhole. Inserted it. Held my breath. Twisted. A small click sounded as loud as a gunshot, and I used the leverage of the key to pull the drawer open.

The key melted away as the drawer fully extended.

Yellow sparks flew outward, a seemingly endless number of them. A handful stabbed into the weres present, along with Duke and Iaret.

All of them shouted in alarm—only for that alarm to turn to joy. Hollering and roaring shook the clearing as human forms became cat and vice versa. Ululating cries rose to the sky as Duke and Iaret shifted to their fiery forms then to half a dozen others before settling back on their natural shapes.

"She did it! She did it!" Iaret sang. "I always knew she could!"

Tears ran down my face. After everything I'd done, everything I'd been through, I'd succeeded with at least two factions.

Tension rose in the clearing as the elves and half-elves watched others celebrating.

If the weres were the moon and the djinn were fire, the elves must be...the wind? They didn't feel like plants. They didn't feel like water. Individuals might, but when I thought of elves, I thought of Troy's power signature or even, Goddess damn her, Keithia. A slashing, icy gale.

The key of air, I whispered to the remaining ones as I pulled on that element.

The key from the first trial became chilly on my thigh. Scarcely daring to hope, I picked it up and inserted it in the keyhole that'd become available on the drawer carved with zephyrs.

"By the wind of my birth, bless me and mine with magic rightfully stolen," I said, more confidently this time.

The drawer opened. Millions of red sparks swirled forth, stabbing toward every elf and half-elf in the vicinity with the remainder racing for the sky like they were chasing the first set. My sense of the vitality of the world grew along with the celebrations of the elf-blooded around me. Power crackled in the clearing as my people filled themselves to bursting with Aether and tested their recovered magic.

Vampires and fae next, given that my sense of Cade and Mami Wata were now practically vibrating with their hunger for their magic to be returned.

That would be...water? Glamour and illusion felt like reflections on the water's surface, real and yet not. Torsten's power signature had felt like the throb of a heartbeat. Blood—the waters of the body—moving onward in life and undeath.

The key of water.

The doubled key chilled, and I split it to find one half colder than the other. "By the water I was reborn from, bless me and mine with magic rightfully stolen."

Another twist and pull and leaping of blue sparks.

Cade dropped to a knee. Tears of blood ran down his cheeks, which grew more youthful even as I watched.

Mami Wata laughed and roared her triumph, shifting to her massive python form before crashing into the Eno to roil the waters with joyful thrashing.

In the distance, the gytrash howled.

One more key, the second half of the last one.

"By the earth that nourishes and protects me, bless me and mine with magic rightfully stolen."

There were no witches or human sensitives present, but as even more green sparks than before raced free of the box, I had to hope they had their magic back too or would soon.

I leaned forward over my knees, no keys remaining, clutching an empty box. On an impulse, I smeared a little of my blood on it then used Earth to open a shallow hole, placed the Box of Ages inside it, and covered it over. "By the elements I bear, bless and protect me and mine with magic rightfully stolen."

The ground shivered in response. Thunder rolled in a clear sky overhead, and the plants lashed and danced in an unseen wind. The river sparked, sending droplets into the air like a reverse rainfall. Behind me, the fire flared with a roar before settling.

It was done.

I pressed my hands over the spot as Troy knelt beside me and gathered me into a hug. "You did it," he whispered. "Everyone here has their magic back."

My phone was buzzing nonstop, which made me hope that others more distant were getting theirs back too.

Lya knelt in front of us, her phone held sideways. "Any words for Otherside, Arbiter Arden Finch Solari?"

I looked up, straight into the camera lens, and said the first thing that came to mind whether it was good politics or not. "Magic was mine to give or withhold. I chose to give because giving begets giving. Kindness begets kindness. It isn't weak to say so. It's strong. Because now all of us have a chance to save or damn ourselves all over again." I paused, looking around my clearing and remembering what I'd done to kill the land at Jordan Lake. "The world is out of balance, which is why magic was taken from us. I call on all Othersiders to join with me and my parliament and allies in the Carolinas and Dominion demesnes and beyond, to seize this opportunity. Change is coming. Death is coming, if we don't unite to face it. Set aside your grievances. Set aside your feuds. And let us all come together as Othersiders to claim our place in the world, rebalance it for the good of all, and keep moving forward."

Silence hung in the clearing for all of a heartbeat before raucous applause and cheering broke out.

At my side, Troy said in a loud, firm voice, "I, Troy reg'no dom Solari naskit' princ' dom Monteague, claimed, oathed, and bonded king to Arden Finch Solari, stand with this Arbiter and ally all affiliated elven Houses and territories with her."

As I tried to keep my face straight at Troy's using his full elvish name, a soft crunch of gravel behind me preceded Terrence and Ximena stepping up and speaking similar words as Lya panned the camera up to see them. Then to Duke and Iaret, declaring for the djinn. Then to Mami Wata, who shifted smoothly back to her human shape and declared for the fae of the Eastern Carolinas territory, Mason for the wolves, and Cade as a vampire vagabond.

"Fuck it," Harqil called. "There's a celestial on board as well, if twice-fallen angels count."

With a chuckle, Lya brought the camera back to me.

I closed my eyes, seeking the proper words, the gravitas, and the presence for this. "I may have faced the trickster gods to restore magic, but as you can see, I didn't do this alone. Troy Solari, the vampire Cade, his half-elven solidaire and partner Lya Desmarais, the werewolf Mason of the Blood Moon clan, and the fae Mami Wata all joined me in Dreamwalking to face the trickster gods at great danger to themselves. The elves and half-elves of the Ebon Guard and the Eastern Darkwatch shielded me. The djinn commonly called Duke and Iaret crafted items that saved my life. Harqil the angel put themself at mortal risk to guide me. A pair of gytrash and the Jade Tooth jaguars and Acacia Thorn leopards circled and guarded me and what's mine so that I could give everything for this. And all the while, the mundane Bureau for Supernatural Investigation hunted me. Everyone here faced death or worse for the greater good of us all."

I paused, staring straight into the lens.

"I say this both to recognize the offerings and allyship of so many different factions and to illustrate what's possible when we come together. I call upon all of Otherside to model themselves after those whose bravery made the return of magic possible. And hear me when I say this: unfounded and bloodthirsty attacks on the mundanes are not the answer. But that doesn't mean I will leave the recent oversteps and attacks unanswered. It doesn't mean that I'll let these laws they're pushing through stand. Otherside will have balance, and I will ensure it—with your support. Hear me, Otherside. You are with me, Arbiter Arden Finch, High Queen of House Solari, Eternal Huntress, and primordial elemental, or you are against me. There is no time and no space for games. Decide."

With a dramatic flourish, Lya stopped the video. "Fuck me but you have a way about you."

"I'd fuck you in a heartbeat," Cade growled to her under his breath. "One of yours, not mine."

As ribald teasing broke out around me, Etain, Darius, and Allegra stepped close and knelt, all of them grinning uncontrollably and brimming with as much Aether as they could hold to spice the air with the scent of burnt marshmallow and smoky herbs.

"Orders?" Etain asked.

Troy glanced at me. *I think a celebration is well deserved.*

I pushed past my usual reticence to have people on my property. "Invite everyone local here. My land is open for one night only, to everyone who agrees to behave in line with the Détente, for celebration and prayer. Some folks will need to stand guard though. This is too big an opportunity for the mundanes to wipe us out with a bomb or some bullshit, and we already know the feds are in town. We have magic back. Let's keep them busy."

Etain's expression turned savage. "The Guard will be happy to keep them busy. They're pissed about being forced to leave Jordan Lake."

"Perfect," I said. "Then the Guard get their own celebration here tomorrow night."

"That'll work, my queen," she said. "That'll definitely work."

Allegra whooped, already digging out her phone. "Maria will be here."

I fished in my bag for mine. "I'll see if Zanna can arrange some refreshments."

I might wish that I could take the night off, but I'd worked too hard and gone through too much not to celebrate with everyone who'd taken my side in the last few years. The Bureau for Supernatural Investigation would be looking for me, but they always would be. Acting Director Lara fucking Sinclaire was probably still looking for an update from me, but fuck her and her ambitions of a tame elemental superhero.

Besides. I could always kick mundane ass tomorrow.

Somehow, I had a feeling I'd have to.

Chapter 31

Arbiter or not, and maenad or not, I got sloppy drunk over the course of the evening. After the tension and death and fear and all-around fuckery of the last few days, I needed to let loose. There were enough people here to disperse the maenad magic into a euphoric good feeling rather than a murder. Hell, when I warned them, cheers rang out as Maria topped up my wine glass with a grin wide enough to show fangs.

Everyone was dancing under the waning crescent moon. Fires burned. Booze flowed. The people around me were in even worse shape, except for the Ebon Guard, who stood watch at the borders of my property with a delightedly fierce mien as they both watched for mundane spies and kept the various Othersider celebrants within the safe bounds of my property.

It was probably incredibly stupid, but I think we were all feeling cocky after a week of vulnerability and fear without magic.

Fortunately for me, my people took my inebriation as a sign that I was relatable and approachable rather than weak. I was still a level or ten above them, power-wise, and I was scary as fuck, as evidenced by my demonstrating some primordial magic, but I would use it in service, not in terror. Coming to celebrate with them was endearing in a way Callista could never have accomplished, and that realization made me a lot looser than I might otherwise have been.

Which meant there were consequences as the night went on and the wine hit my system hard.

"Hey," I slurred in Troy's ear as he led me in a dance in the backyard. "Need you."

A low purr rippled from him as he clasped the back of my neck and squeezed hard enough that I shuddered. "Is that so?"

"Fuck, Troy. Please?" Usually, it took me much longer to play his bedroom games, but I was going to explode. We hadn't fucked since the pull-off in the car at Jordan Lake days ago, and as good as that had been, I needed more of him. Blood maybe, as odd as that still was to me as an elemental and not something more predatory.

The scent of rosemary and sage and *him* spiked with his pleasure. "What will you do if I say no?"

I quivered, and my breath caught. It wasn't that I assumed or took for granted that he'd say yes. It was that I knew he was the only one who could survive me at my worst.

Pressing myself tighter against him, I snaked an arm over his shoulder and around his neck as I leaned to whisper in his ear. "Please say yes. I know I've asked a lot of you lately. But please say yes."

"Mmm. That's right, you have asked a lot."

Damn the man for toying with me. "Blood for blood?"

"I want assurances."

That could be taken at surface level, elven king to Arbiter.

I could also read the painful vulnerability under it. "You have them."

"We'll see. Shall we go negotiate?"

If it wasn't for the need to keep up appearances, I think he would have thrown me over his shoulder and carried me inside. As it was, he provided a gentlemanly arm for me to lean on while I tried my damnedest to look serious and professional as I made the rounds and said good night—or more accurately, good morning, given the lightened sky of false dawn—to everyone still up and celebrating.

Professionalism lasted until we made it inside. Someone was using the bathroom, but two of the Ebon Guard were present, one leaning against the half wall separating the front entry from the dining area and one squarely in front of my bedroom door.

That was good. I hated people being in my bedroom. Bless the Ebon Guard.

"Majesties," the latter said.

I didn't recognize her, so I nodded in as queenly a manner as I could. "Thank you for your service this evening."

"Of course, ma'am." A grin flickered and was buried. "Especially given that I hear it's our turn to celebrate tomorrow."

I laughed over Troy's warning growl. "It definitely is. Carry on. A little farther away from this particular room, please."

"Ma'am." The guard opened my bedroom door and stepped aside then pulled it closed behind me and Troy.

Tension stretched between me and my bondmate in the dark as I yanked my shoes off and threw them to the side, then my socks, then my shirt and bra. His scent slowly filled the enclosed space, dizzying me with need. I shuddered from the effort of holding myself back.

"You poor thing," he murmured, viciously gentle as he traced a single finger along my jaw before using it to tip my chin up. "All that hunger for me?"

"*Yes,*" I groaned. "And you know it, you bastard."

All of a sudden, the finger was gone. Shifting air molecules was the only sense I got that he'd moved until his voice came from behind me. "Then take what you need."

I whirled, reaching for where he'd been only to find he'd already moved away. My bare toes encountered a shirt too close and too warm to be mine.

Goddess, he was stripping.

"When I catch you—"

He chuckled, somewhere off to the side. "I think that's an 'if' in your current state."

Fuck that. I pulled on Air as I read the shifting molecules. He was dancing around me on silent elven feet, but even Troy had to breathe.

I stripped out of my jeans and panties then snatched him with Air and threw him on the bed, hesitating as I worried if that was too much.

His growl made me shiver. "You're never too much for me."

When I pounced on the bed and him, my knees found his bare hips. I must have been drunk if he'd managed to strip naked in the dark while I was still trying to figure out where he was.

Troy's hand gripped mine and pressed something hard into it. A knife hilt.

"Take your blood, little maenad," he said.

All the teasing in his voice was gone, replaced by the heavy breathing of need.

His surrender thrilled me. Everyone made everything so difficult, but with Troy, it was so fucking easy. Or if not easy, then at least not difficult where it didn't need to be.

"I love you," I whispered as I traced my hands over his body to find the scar over his heart.

As I dragged the tip of the knife he'd given me in a line above the scar, he groaned, hips arching up against me. "I love you too."

I sucked his blood from the knife before setting it on the nightstand and leaning over to pull from him. Rosemary and sage spiked with iron hit my tongue, and the maenad, now fully freed, roared forward. I spiraled into the blood, his pleasure in the bond, the need of both our bodies for each other.

With one hand, he held me to his chest, cradling the back of my head. The other slid between us and guided his cock into me before gripping my hip as he thrust upward.

I couldn't help a muffled cry.

"That's right," Troy said, a growl underlying the words. "You're mine. Never forget it."

As if I could. He was fucking me as I drank from him, and for all I had initiated all of this, I was under his power. The maenad in me faded, completely sated by blood and sex and the magic both in this room and in the night around us.

I pulled away, arching back and shifting my hips to ride him.

"No," he snarled. "You're *mine.*"

Before I could react, he'd flipped us.

"Prove it," I panted. "Bite me."

"I will. When I'm ready." His hand closed around my throat, and he growled again, with more threat in it this time. "I've had to share you too much lately, Arden. I didn't like it."

"Greater good," I gasped, hoping he'd push anyway.

"Fuck the greater good." He paused in his movement, like he'd shocked himself with the declaration, then redoubled it, pressing me into the bed as he leaned to whisper in my ear. "You are all that matters. You are all that has *ever* mattered."

I spiraled into a climax, and he pressed a hand over my mouth as I groaned.

"Shh. Unless you want everyone outside to hear how well I fuck you."

Oh Goddess. I didn't want people to hear, but at the same time the idea was so taboo that I did.

"Tell me what you want," he taunted.

"You," I gasped. "All of you. Bite me. Please."

"Since you asked nicely on the first try..."

Aether sliced through me, dragging another orgasm to the surface on the heels of the one that'd just wracked me. As I gave myself over to it and arched against Troy, he bit me.

Even with his hand over my mouth, someone probably heard my muffled scream.

He came in hard, tight thrusts against me even as he pulled on my blood. A wildness danced between us both alongside our pleasure.

Consciousness fled. There was only Troy and blood and pleasure and love.

△▽△▽

Troy's space on the bed was empty and cooling fast when I woke. That couldn't be good. He liked watching me sleep. I thought it was equal parts adoration and prey drive—his love for me tangled up with the intense satisfaction he got from hunting me, especially after he'd taken my blood.

His raised voice in the other room confirmed that somebody was having or about to have a bad fucking day.

"I don't care," he said harshly. "I was within my rights."

I went cold. What the hell was this about?

"No. I don't know how many ways I can say it. I don't want them here. They sent someone after Arden. You were there. You know why I'm saying no."

I got out of bed and dragged on a robe in the pause as he listened to the response.

He looked up as I pulled the bedroom door open. Anger and something else in his gaze, something raw and pained, stopped me in my tracks. "Alli. Allegra! I will talk to Arden and call you back. Do not move on this until I do, or so help me you will regret it."

I waited until he ended the call to approach. "What's wrong?"

"Lestari." The growled word held frustration, and the bond roiled with a complex blend of emotions I couldn't begin to tease apart. "Naming Cade and Lya last night exposed them as collaborators. Or rather, betrayers, since they took the House's money and then helped you instead of killing you."

"Oh, for Ishtar's sake." I closed my eyes. "Lya had the camera, and I didn't even think to keep her behind it. Fuck."

"She was the one who volunteered. For what it's worth, we can pay off their debt. They've earned it for their service, and I think it was more important to make the point that restoring magic was a mixed-faction effort."

"So it looks less like a power grab on my part?"

Troy nodded. "That and to prove you can move politically. You persuaded assassins to join you. Which leads me to our problem. They want to send their prince, Rio, and an entourage. As observers. Likely also to come for Cade and Lya but mostly as observers."

"Okay? I don't like it, but we already allowed the Lyon Houses to come."

"Arden…" He sighed, crossed his arms, and looked at the floor. "I have history with that House."

"I guessed that." I tried to figure out how to get to the bottom of all this, all of his secretiveness the last few days, without prying too deeply into his past. I tried to keep my voice light as I asked, "Anything you want to tell me?"

His gaze flicked up to mine and back down. "Seattle."

"You've mentioned it before. Once."

"My Darkwatch initiation mission was to assassinate the High Queen. Rio's mother. Alone. While he was away on a mission of his own."

Oh. Damn. Knowing Troy was an assassin was different to hearing about a hit—or having a loose end want to pay us a visit.

"His sister was delighted when I succeeded. Despite catching me with the body immediately after. She asked Keithia if she could keep me."

Heat flared in me, an unusual flash of jealousy that I tried to push away. He was mine now, and he wanted to be here.

His voice deadened further. "She wanted me to breed her. I refused. I didn't want to give any queen a child of my body to abuse. Like I had been. So, she had me fight six on one in every Darkwatch training session. She ordered me to kill people, just to see me agonize over it. For *years*, Arden." He snorted. "Training. More like gladiator events. Vina said it would stop if I bedded her." He paused. "That's not even all of it. Suffice to say, it was a relief when Keithia wanted me recalled to Chapel Hill to deal with the Redcaps. Vina refused. Keithia ordered her killed for the offense."

I shook, full-body trembles that I couldn't tell if they were rage or pain.

"So, I followed orders," Troy said. "I killed both queens. Although, officially, they killed themselves. And I regret neither. Not after what they put me through." He hesitated then plowed forward in a rush. "I don't regret killing the House Guard captain they sent to assassinate you last June either."

"What?" I went cold.

I'd known there'd been threats, but this was the first I had heard that not only had there been an attempt prior to Cade and Lya but that they had gotten close enough that Troy had dealt with them personally. Last June had been a weird time, and I'd always assumed it was because Troy was still settling into being a live-in consort while wrestling with his hormonal readjustment and trying to run the elven part of our territory all at the same time.

Apparently, it'd been more than that.

His expression was the locked-down Darkwatch agent as he settled into parade rest. "They tried to claim blood for blood. My life and yours for the two queens I took. I denied it and made the assassin kill himself. At the boathouse."

I stared at him, stomach falling as I waited for an explanation or justification that didn't come. Part of my shock was his method. I'd seen him fight, and kill, before. He was brutally effective. But multiple assassinations by staged suicide? Probably magically induced? No wonder he found me to be completely unsubtle. I'd known he was dangerous, but this took it to a whole new level. Especially given that he'd dealt with this assassin while bonded to me and I'd had no fucking clue.

That and the fact that his father had the same MO. Would that cast suspicion on Troy?

The other part was that blood for blood was Otherside justice. We should have had to fight for our lives, at the very least. Troy lived and died by the law, or at least he had. But I knew—had known for some time—that my life and safety came ahead of literally everything else on Troy's list, even if it'd been a surprise to him to say it out loud last night.

I also knew that he'd have done it knowing I'd be upset, maybe even fearing I would send him away for undermining me or breaking the Détente. Or for hiding all of this from me. I could read it in the twitch of the muscle in his left cheek and the tightness of the skin around his eyes, even if the crack in the walls he'd pulled up in the bond wasn't roiling with suppressed fear.

Insight flashed, and I closed my eyes.

This was why he was so caught up in whether he was a monster. Why his father's assassinations of elven queens by making it look like a suicide had been so problematic. Why he was so insistent that I make certain moves to secure the territory.

Because he'd actively been dealing with threats that he didn't think he could tell me about.

And that was on me.

I opened my eyes, went to him, and pressed up on my toes to kiss his cheek. "I'm so sorry."

Confusion shattered both his physical and Aetheric facades as he jerked away. "What?"

"I keep forcing you to give everything you are. But I haven't made it safe for you to even tell me how much that is or what it costs you."

"You're not going to send me away?"

"No. Goddess, Troy, no. The queens you killed, I don't see how you had any other choice that wouldn't have ended in your death. Denying blood for blood might technically be against the Détente, but if anyone has a problem with it, they can step to me." I cupped his jaw and tried to get him to meet my eye. "I don't like using might-makes-right as a justification, but I also refuse to allow myself to be pulled into a squabble between two queens who've been dead for years. You're not the only one who has had to learn and grow this past year. This is on me too."

Finally, he met my gaze. The wall on his side of the bond came down another crack, and he nudged against mine. I let him in entirely, shivering as he sent a tendril of Aether twining through my mind.

"You're really not mad," he said, sounding confused as he searched my face. "You're not disgusted by me either."

"Is *that* why you've kept all this a secret?"

He withdrew from my mind. "Maybe. You see so much good in me. I didn't want to let you see the evil. What I did. What I'm capable of."

My heart clenched, and I kissed him. "Oh, Troy. You're not evil. You've carried out some evil orders from people who had the power to kill you without consequence if you didn't obey. You've acted to protect your bondmate. What's evil is the system that made all of that necessary or forced it on you in the first place."

"You really believe that."

"Yeah," I said, committing to that particular slippery slope. He was worth it. "And I'll say it publicly if anyone comes for you. You're mine. I'm yours. I still want to marry you. More than ever, now that you've finally shown me these secrets."

His arms came around me and squeezed. "I—" He exhaled heavily. "I was going to say I don't deserve you. But instead, I'm going to say that I'm grateful the person I pour so much of myself into pours back into me."

I hugged him back, hard, willing him to feel loved and glad that he was finally seeing the value he brought to our relationship rather than seeing it as something he was obliged to offer one-way. "That's how it should be. If you ever feel like this relationship is unbalanced, you tell me, okay?"

"Yes. And same."

We stayed like that for a minute, just breathing. Settling mentally and emotionally after the intense conversation.

When he'd stopped trembling, Troy pulled away and cleared his throat. "I need to call Alli back. You sure you're good with allowing observers?"

"I'm choosing to see it as an opportunity to plant seeds," I said. "The Eastern Seaboard is a good start, but I meant what I said about taking the whole country if I have to. Otherside has to change, and the mundanes along with us. It's time for a new chapter. I'm not going to elementally remake the world, but I can do something to change society." I pressed up on my toes to kiss him again. "Especially if that's what carves out space to feel safe. I want our family, Troy."

He reached for his phone, confidence back in the set of his shoulders and his sure movements. "Lestari first then. Sinclaire next. I want this threat from the feds handled."

Good. I was going to change the world and create space for us to thrive, and like my dad had said, I shouldn't have to do it alone.

Epilogue

I might have been ready for change, but the Bureau for Supernatural Investigation and the US Congress were not.

Iago had successfully stalled the execution of the subpoena, for now. Which meant Sinclaire was furious. Not that she told me. No, she didn't take my call or call me back. She just stood behind Senator Wright, looking darkly pleased as he announced legislation had passed the Senate and was on its way to the House of Representatives.

Troy's fist clenched on the table, and fury bounced between us both as the senator spoke.

"With this bill, we will secure American homes and families against the new supernatural threat. It has multiple parts. First, all supernaturals will be required to register themselves as such, including a full listing of their powers and abilities. Second, those determined to be dangerous to our society will be relocated to a secure location, for their safety and ours. Third, we will be expanding the powers of the Bureau for Supernatural Investigation, which will be tasked with finding and detaining any supernaturals who do not voluntarily come forward." Turning, Wright waved Sinclaire forward. "We are also confirming Acting Director Lara Sinclaire in her role as Director of the Bureau for Supernatural Investigation. Director Sinclaire?"

She stepped to the mic. "Thank you, Senator. My fellow Americans, I am humbled and honored to be here today and to accept this charge. While I can't discuss the full details of our upcoming work for security reasons, rest assured that dangerous supernaturals, like those operating out of Raleigh-Durham in North Carolina, will be dealt with to the fullest extent of the law. Thank you, and God bless these United States of America."

"She just called us out," I said as the newsreader switched to commentary and reactions, ignoring the part where she called us Raleigh-Durham. Only outsiders did that. "She just called us the fuck out."

"She'll regret that," Troy replied coldly. "If I have to make sure of it personally."

We'd known this was coming. The powerful operated the same, whether Othersider or mundane: if they couldn't control it, they would destroy it. Only this time, that meant us. Our effort to get ahead of accidental exposures with the Reveals was being repaid with this bullshit—efforts to control us, which if history was any indication, would swiftly become efforts to eradicate us.

We'd gotten magic back just in time. I'd made the right choice because I wouldn't have been able to live with myself if I'd hoarded magic and left everyone else to face this without their full strength.

"I need to get a comment prepped," I said. "Jo is probably going to call soon."

Even as I said it, my phone chirped, and her number came up on the caller ID.

"Take it," Troy prompted. "We can't let this run while we try to figure out the perfect thing to say."

I answered. "Finch."

"Hi, Ms. Finch. It's Jo. I guess you know why I'm calling?"

"Yeah, I guess I do."

"For the sake of clarity, would you comment on the announcement of Otherside legislation and expanded powers for the Supernatural Bureau, on the record? And I'd like to record, if that's okay."

"Go ahead." I gave myself a minute to organize my rage into something coherent. "While I would like to have legal experts review the exact text of this legislation and its ramifications, any efforts to treat Othersiders differently than mundane humans on account of features or abilities we were born with goes against the stated values of this country and its existing laws. We have always been here, living in integrated communities. The only thing that has changed is the awareness of non-Othersiders.

"The announcement today is reminiscent of actions we've seen taken against people in this country before, from the genocide and theft committed against the people of the Indigenous Nations, to the inhumane crimes against enslaved Africans and their descendants, to the Japanese internment camps and the keeping of migrant children in cages. All of these were and are ugly periods in our shared history, with ugly and ongoing ramifications today. I urge the American people to consider that, as well as the slippery slope it creates. They'll come for Othersiders today. If this legislation is allowed to pass, who's to say they won't come for you next?"

The clattering keyboard in the background said Jo was typing as well as recording. "Thank you, Ms. Finch. Anything to say about the Bureau for Supernatural Investigation?"

"Again, I need to consult with legal experts to understand the full ramifications of their powers. Although, I do find it telling that the party who is always railing against government overreach and budget bloat is taking action that would appear to add to exactly that. It seems like the federal government has all the money in the world for military action abroad and violating the rights of our own citizens at home, and yet there's none for worthy causes like universal healthcare, free higher education, a universal basic income, or upgrading the nation's aging infrastructure to make life better and more accessible for all." No way in hell was I going to mention my own subpoena.

"Again, thank you Ms. Finch. As always, I appreciate your candor."

"Thanks for the opportunity to have a balanced discussion, Jo."

I slumped when the call ended, exhausted by having to string together so many political words and causes in a sitting.

Troy took my hand and kissed my knuckles. "That was good."

"Thanks." I blew out a breath and let a zephyr swirl through the house. "I was really hoping the only drama to deal with today would be sorting out what to do with Cyrus and figuring out where to stash a twice-fallen angel who's adjusting to being corporeal."

"My dad's still out. Apparently, being ridden by a god is physically and auratically draining."

"He gonna be okay?"

Troy shrugged, trying for casual but still looking worried. "Felip says something's off with his aura. We're keeping him under observation at one of the safehouse field hospitals for now. Nothing to do until he wakes up. I just hope it was Sutekh and not him who made all those threats against you." He sighed, scrubbing a hand over his face. "As for Harqil, they can stay at the Solari mansion as a guest for the time being. There's enough privacy and security that they should have space to recover. Or adjust. Or whatever it is they're doing."

"Which just leaves securing the Eastern Seaboard and taking on the mundanes. Okay."

The gold flecks in Troy's gaze sparked as he gave me a sharp look. "When you say 'taking on the mundanes,' that means what exactly?"

"I mean, I will not allow this bill or any other like it to pass. We need to tackle this on multiple levels. Everything from sanctuary cities to protests to super PACs to covert ops. Local, state, and federal levels. We hit not only their politics but also their money." Agitated, I got up and paced. "Hell, if they think they're going to start kidnapping Othersiders and rounding us up, I'll even go up to and including authorizing war. I know Harqil advised us not to attack the mundanes, but we're not the ones striking first here. I'm not having this, Troy. Our people deserve to feel safe. We tried doing shit the 'right' way. We did the 'right' thing with legislation and negotiation the first time, and they're rolling it all back. Beyond back. We, or even I alone, have the power to secure our rights, even if that means that we burn everything down. So as long as we can strike in such a way that innocents aren't harmed and we don't lose what little popular support we have, let's fucking do it."

He smiled, looking dangerous. "I'm so glad we're on the same page."

I smiled back. "I'm so glad it won't be me against the world alone."

Push had come to shove, and I was tired of being shoved. By Othersiders, by the gods, by the mundanes. Every time I'd tried playing by someone else's rules, it turned out badly for me and the people I cared about. I'd thought that was just shit luck in how the world worked. I'd thought it was how I had to do things. But now I finally saw that those rules were never set up to allow me and mine to live in peace, let alone thrive.

So just like with the trickster gods and the Duat, it was time to write my own damn rules.

It was time for everyone else to play *my* game.

Acknowledgments

For this book, I wanted to try something different and take Arden even further outside her comfort zone than usual. My notes for it tell me to combine two of my favorite video games, Ancient Egyptian myths, and a heist, so if you enjoyed reading this wild ride as much as I enjoyed writing it, you have my gratitude!

Taking creative risks requires a strong team to find the holes, so a big thank you goes to each of my beta readers and to my editor Jeni Chappelle. Insightful questions and feedback made the story stronger while pushing characters to evolve, and I love where this book ended up as a result.

Last but not least, I'm forever grateful to my family and friends for helping me stay on top of everything else going on in my life, so that I can pour so much of myself into these books.

Also by Whitney Hill

The Shadows of Otherside series
Elemental
Eldritch Sparks
Ethereal Secrets
Ebon Rebellion
Eternal Huntress
Shadows and Honor
Tempered Illusions
Talion Rule
Temporal Gifts
Trickster Magic

The Otherside Heat series
Secrets and Truths
Curses and Faith
Menace and Memory

The Flesh and Blood series (as Remy Harmon)
Bluebloods

About the Author

Whitney Hill is an author and speaker. The bestselling first book in her Shadows of Otherside series, Elemental, was the grand prize winner of the 8th Annual Writer's Digest Self-Published E-Book Awards and a Finalist in the Next Generation Indie Book Awards. Her second book, Eldritch Sparks, was named one of the Top 100 Indie Books of 2021 by Kirkus Reviews.

When she's not writing, Whitney enjoys hiking in North Carolina's beautiful state parks and playing video games.

Learn more or get in touch: whitneyhillwrites.com
Get email updates: whwrites.com/newsletter
Twitter: twitter.com/write_wherever
Instagram: instagram.com/write_wherever

Get the *Shadows and Honor* novella direct from the author: whwrites.com/shadows-honor

www.ingramcontent.com/pod-product-compliance
Lightning Source LLC
Chambersburg PA
CBHW030141310726
48970CB00005B/1534